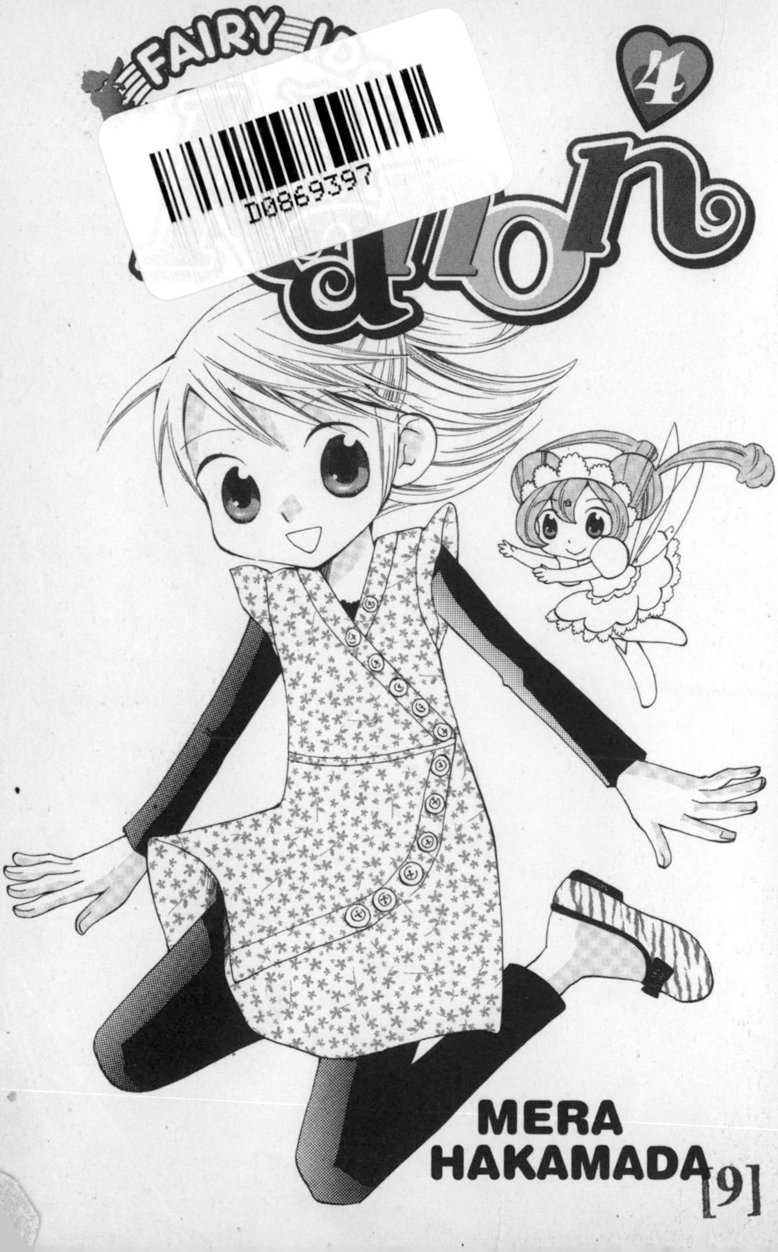
FAIRY
4

MERA
HAKAMADA

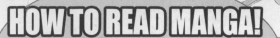

HOW TO READ MANGA!

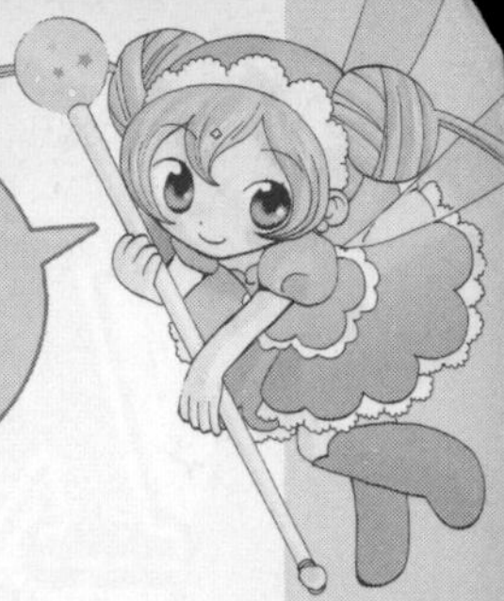

Hello there! My name is **Alto,** and this the latest chapter of **Fairy Idol Kanon**! It is a comic book originally created in the country of **Japan,** where comics are called **manga.**

A manga book is read from **right-to-left,** which is **backwards** from the normal books you know. This means that you will find the first page where you expect to find the last page! It also means that each page begins in the top right corner.

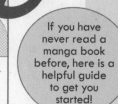

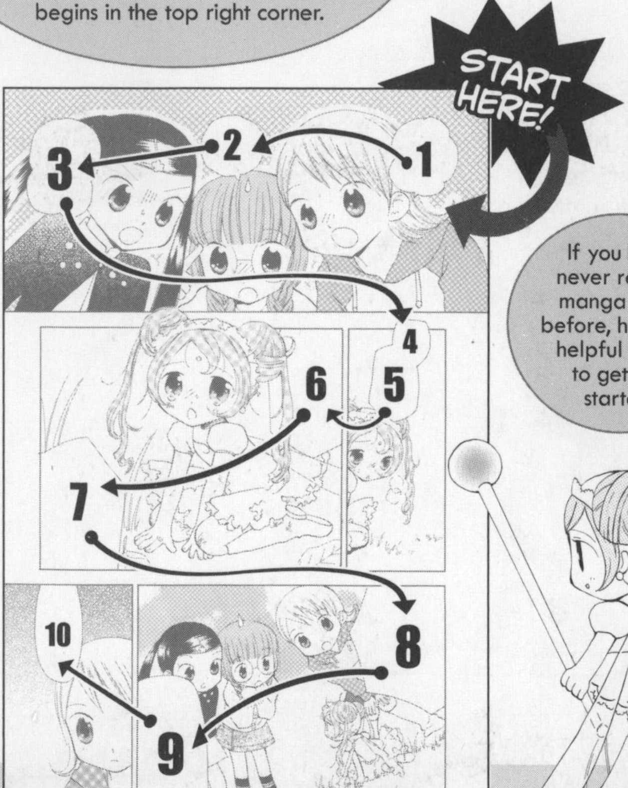
START HERE!
1
2
3
4
5
6
7
8
9
10

If you have never read a manga book before, here is a helpful guide to get you started!

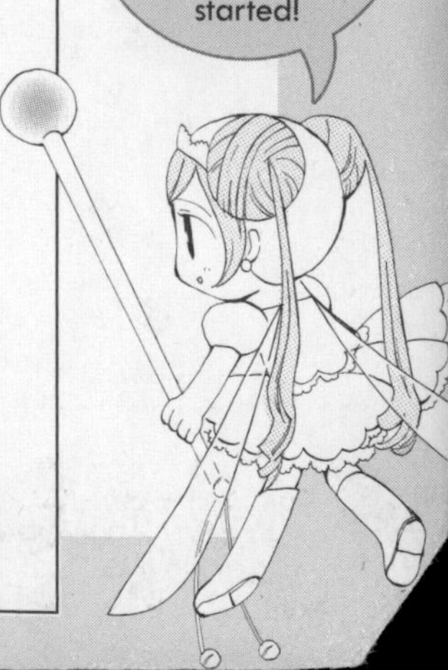

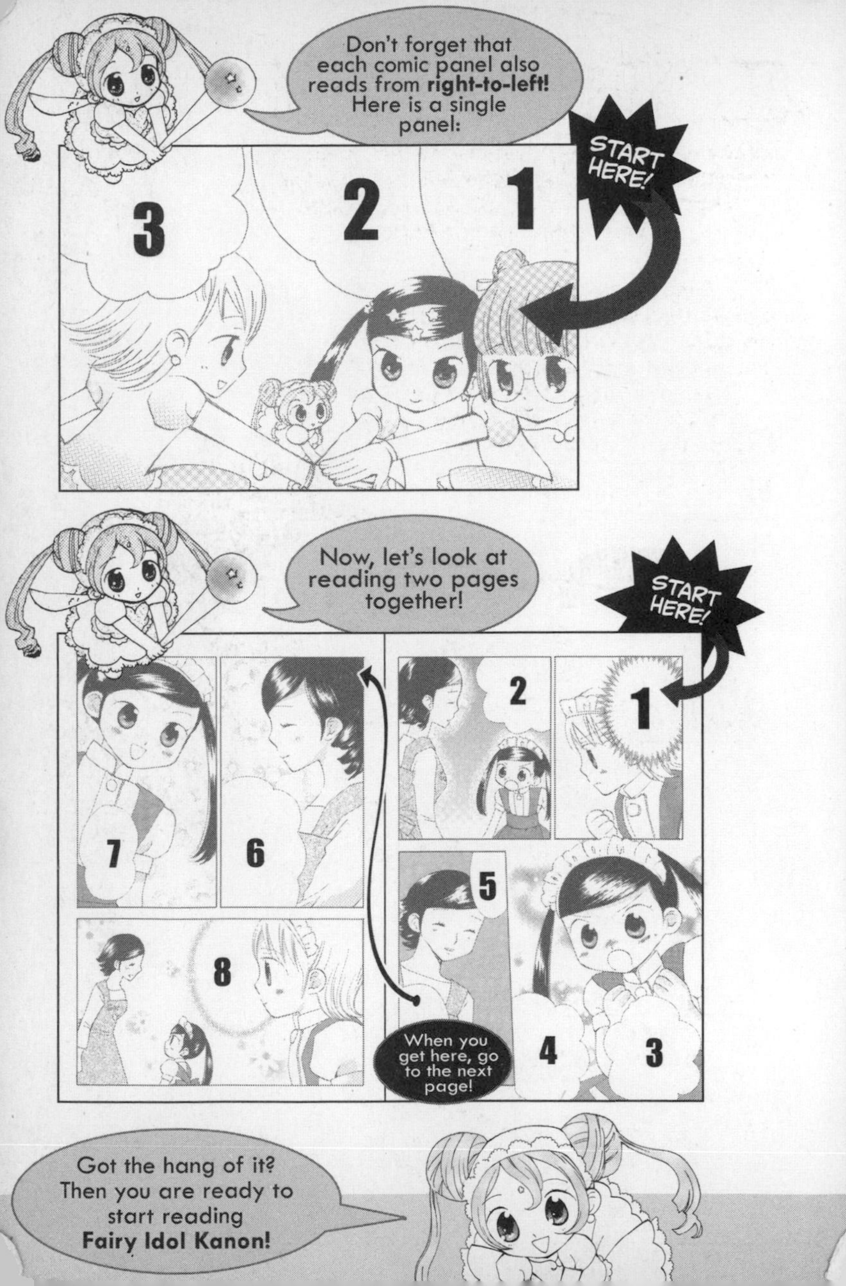
Don't forget that each comic panel also reads from **right-to-left!** Here is a single panel:
START HERE!
1
2
3
Now, let's look at reading two pages together!
START HERE!
1
2
3
4
5
When you get here, go to the next page!
6
7
8
Got the hang of it? Then you are ready to start reading **Fairy Idol Kanon!**

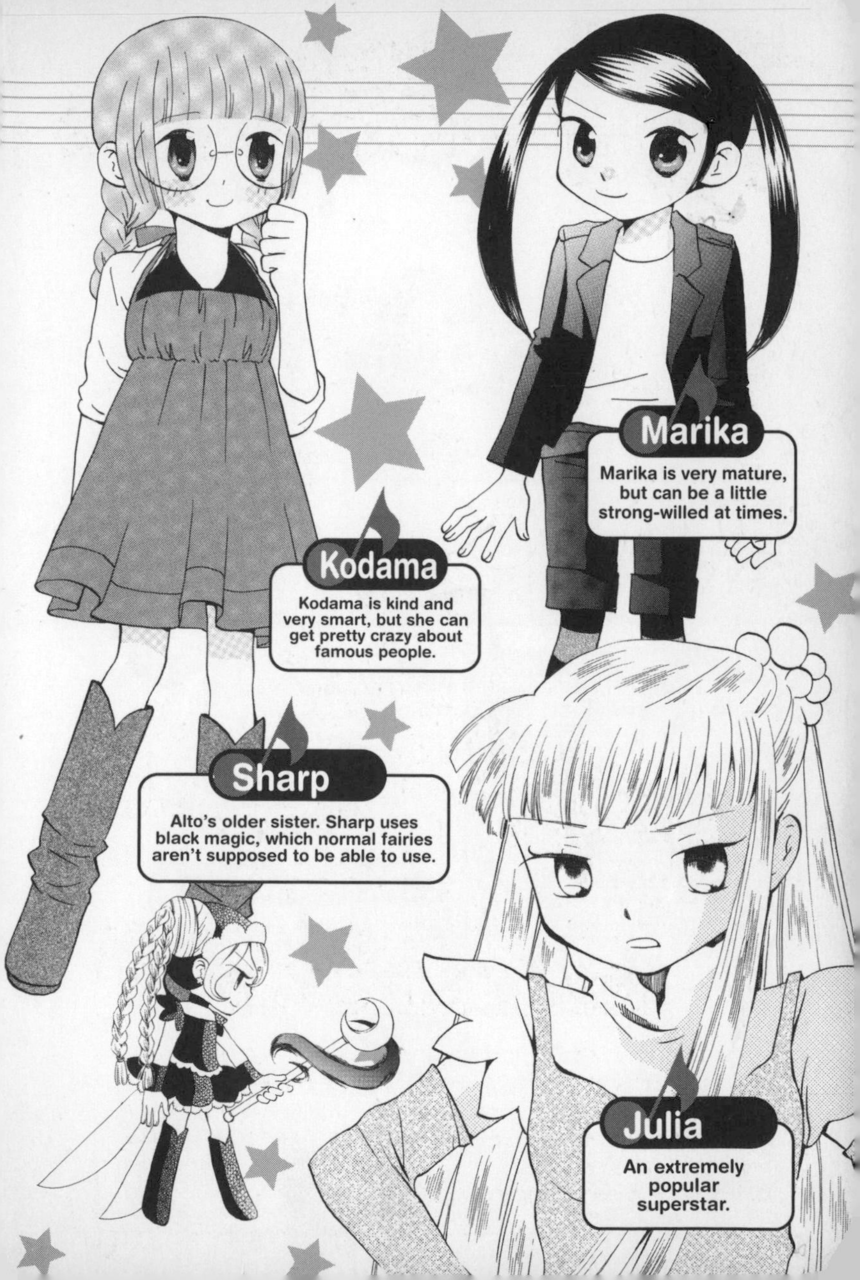
Marika
Marika is very mature, but can be a little strong-willed at times.
Kodama
Kodama is kind and very smart, but she can get pretty crazy about famous people.
Sharp
Alto's older sister. Sharp uses black magic, which normal fairies aren't supposed to be able to use.
Julia
An extremely popular superstar.

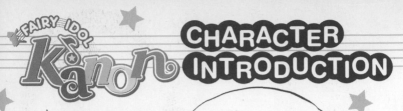

FAIRY IDOL Kanon CHARACTER INTRODUCTION

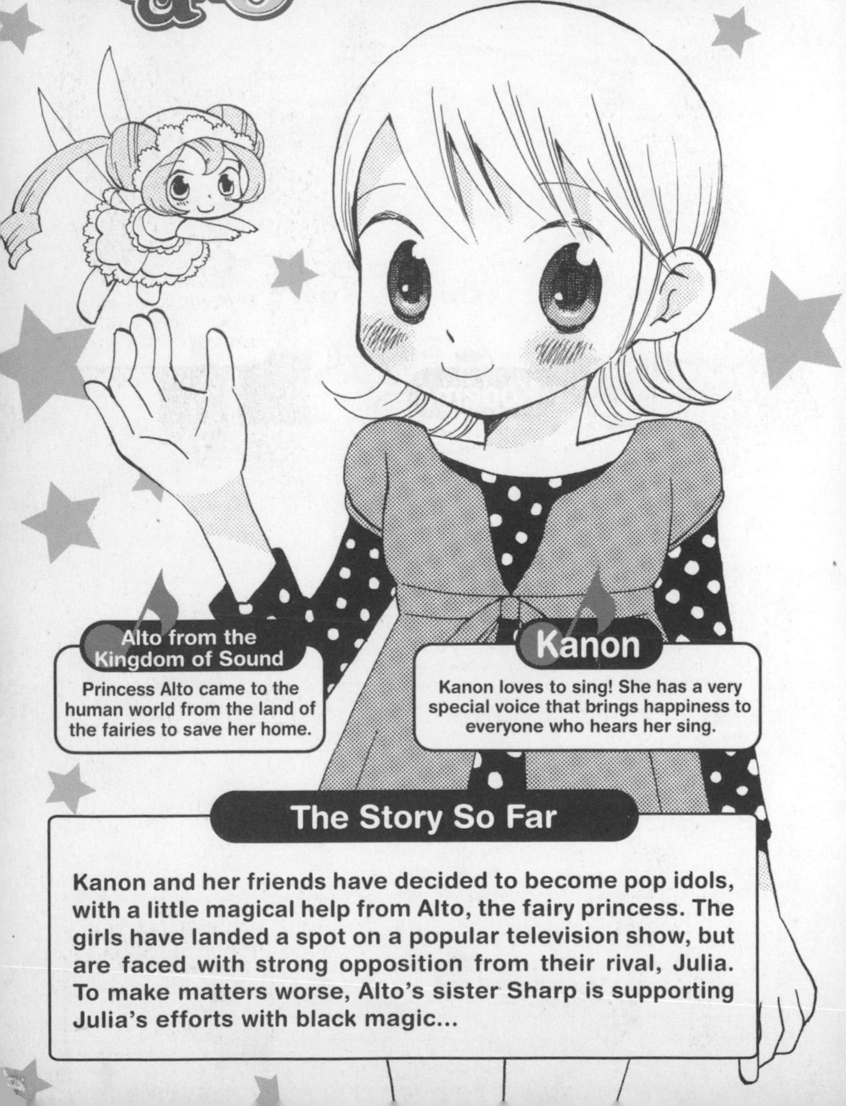

Alto from the Kingdom of Sound

Princess Alto came to the human world from the land of the fairies to save her home.

Kanon

Kanon loves to sing! She has a very special voice that brings happiness to everyone who hears her sing.

The Story So Far

Kanon and her friends have decided to become pop idols, with a little magical help from Alto, the fairy princess. The girls have landed a spot on a popular television show, but are faced with strong opposition from their rival, Julia. To make matters worse, Alto's sister Sharp is supporting Julia's efforts with black magic...

FAIRY IDOL Kanon 4

CONTENTS

Stage 21
You Can Do It! 5

Stage 22
On Stage 31

Stage 23
The Decision 59

Stage 24
Comeback 87

Stage 25
The Secret of the Black Orb 113

Stage 26
Risking Her Life 139

Stage 27
Always With You 165

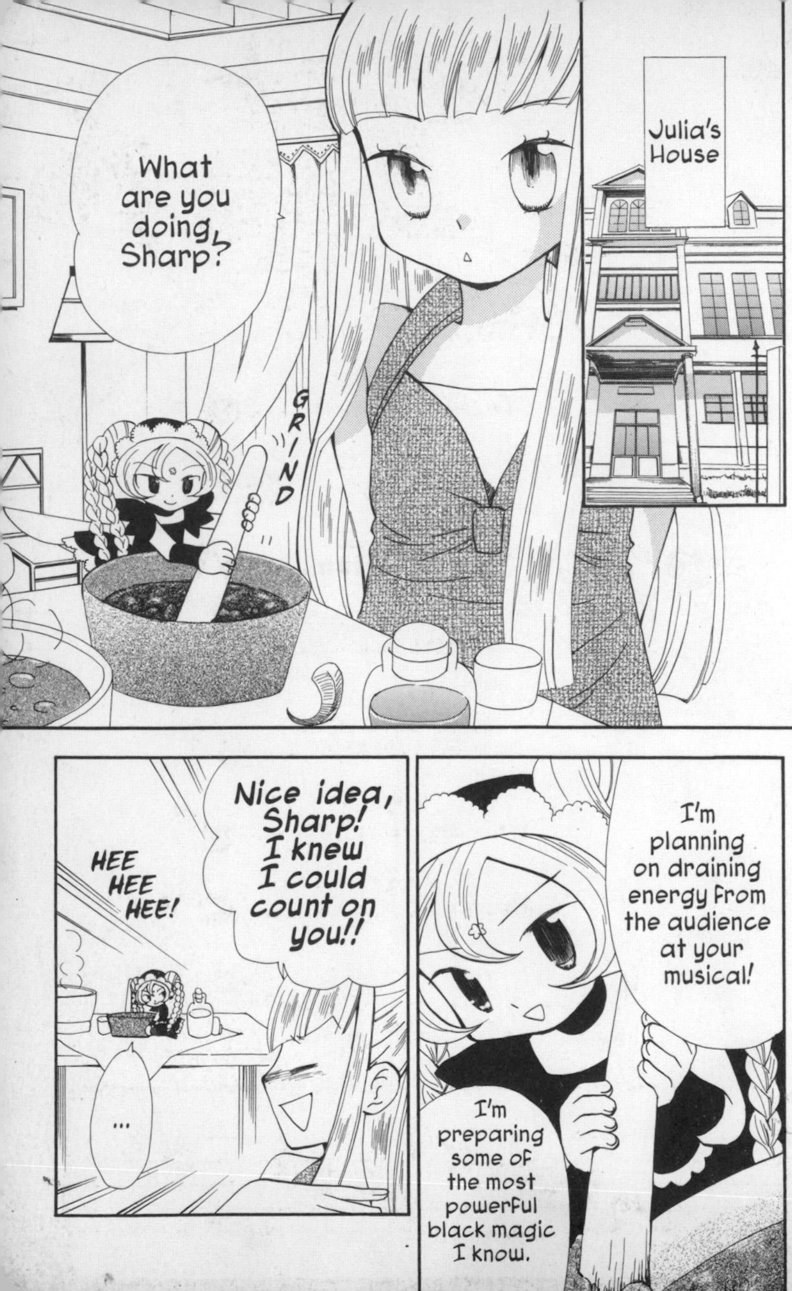
Julia's House
What are you doing, Sharp?
GRIND
I'm planning on draining energy from the audience at your musical!
I'm preparing some of the most powerful black magic I know.
Nice idea, Sharp! I knew I could count on you!!
HEE HEE HEE!
...

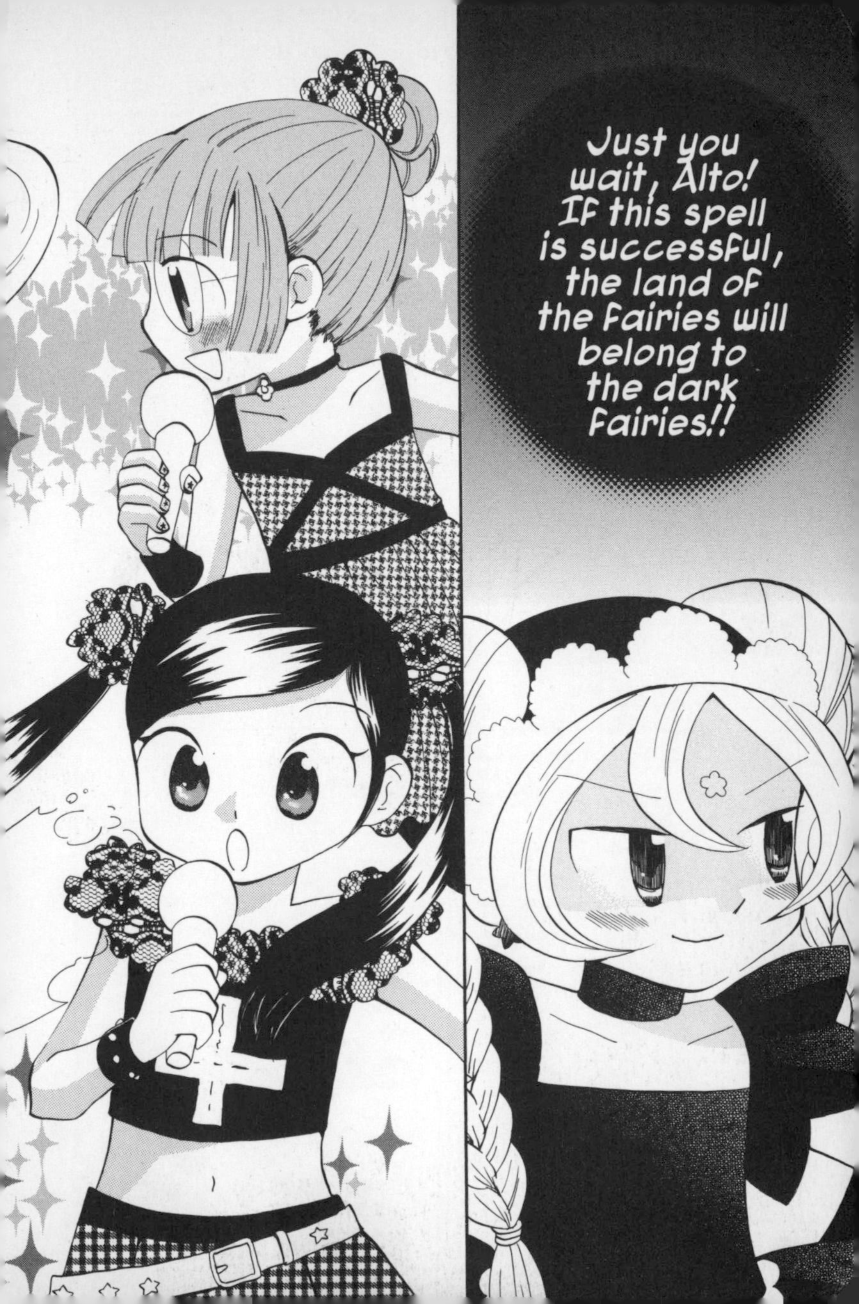
Just you wait, Alto! If this spell is successful, the land of the fairies will belong to the dark fairies!!

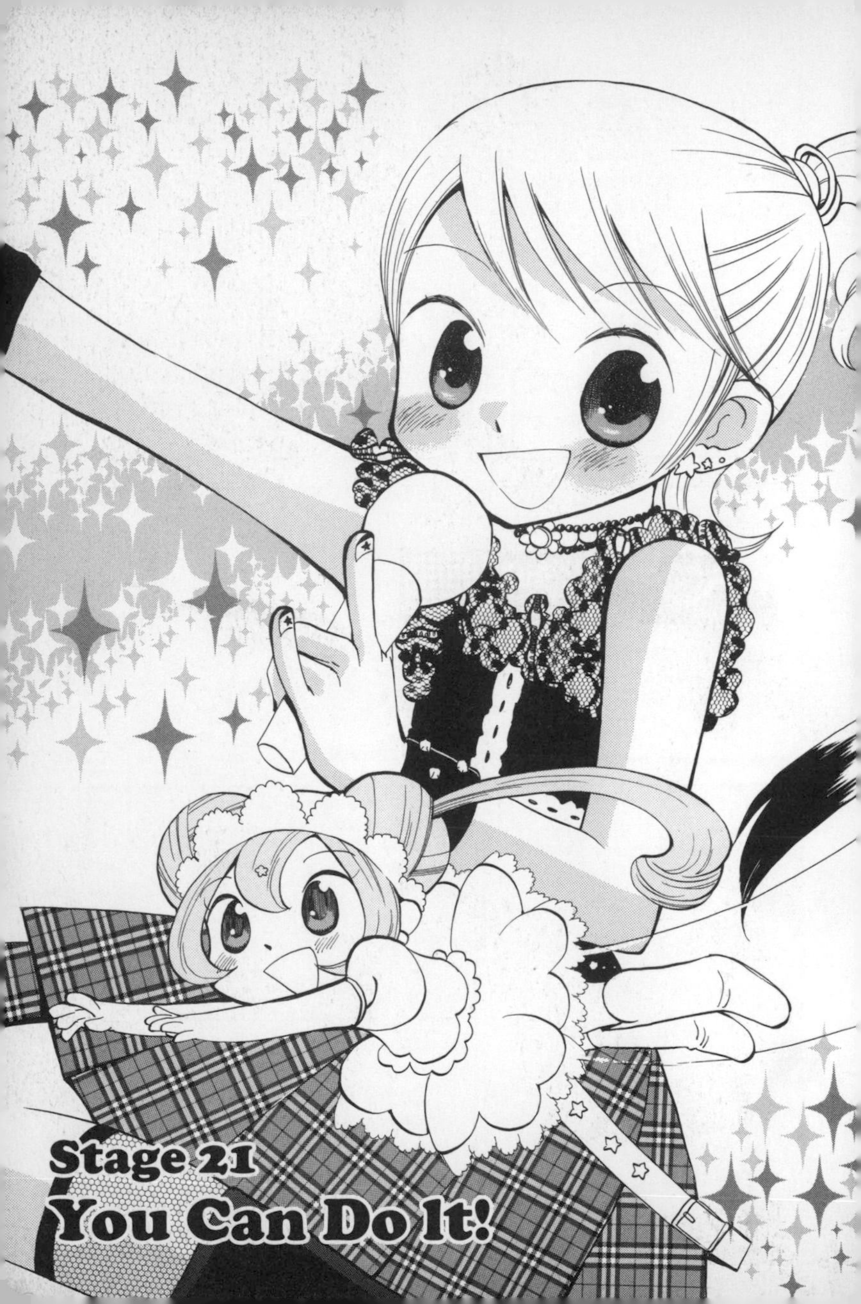
Stage 21
You Can Do It!

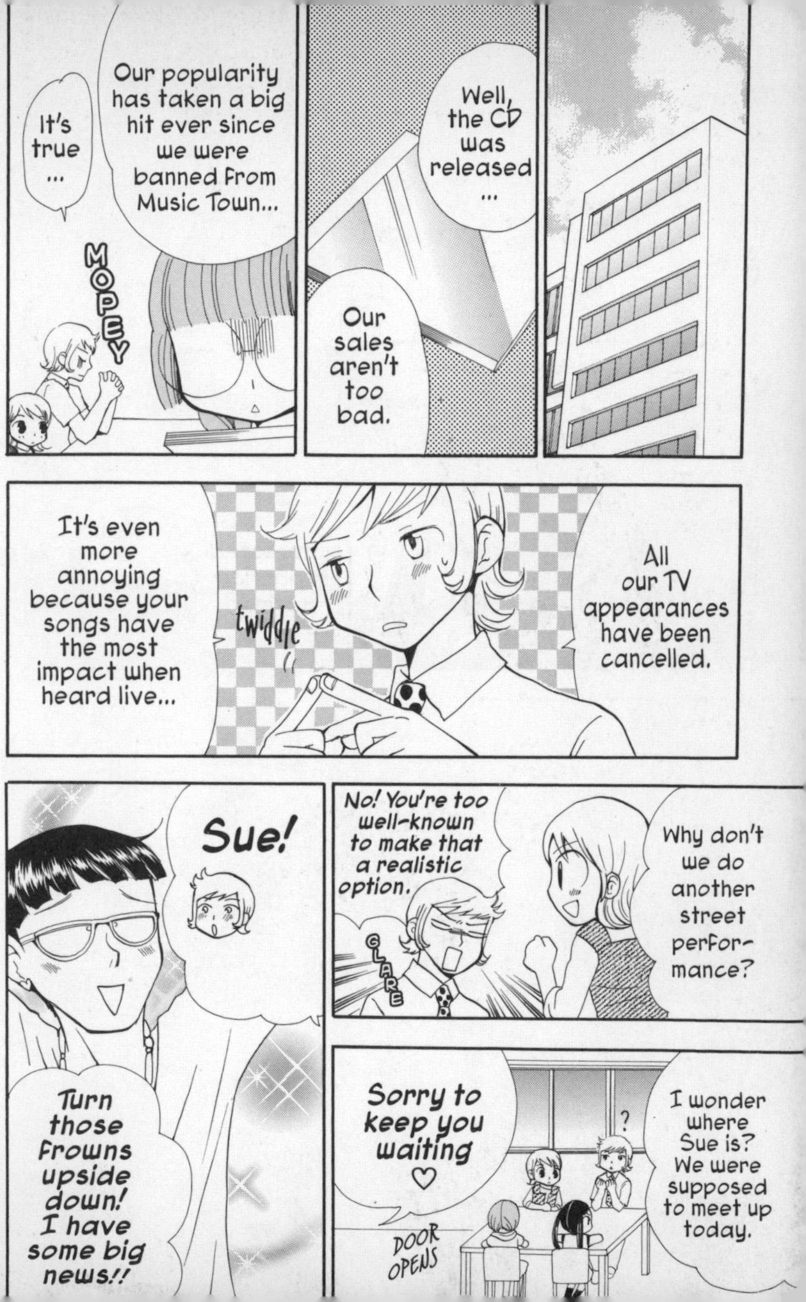

Well, the CD was released ...
Our sales aren't too bad.
Our popularity has taken a big hit ever since we were banned from Music Town...
It's true ...
MOPEY
All our TV appearances have been cancelled.
twiddle
It's even more annoying because your songs have the most impact when heard live...
Why don't we do another street performance?
No! You're too well-known to make that a realistic option.
GLARE
I wonder where Sue is? We were supposed to meet up today.
?
Sorry to keep you waiting ♡
DOOR OPENS
Sue!
Turn those frowns upside down! I have some big news!!

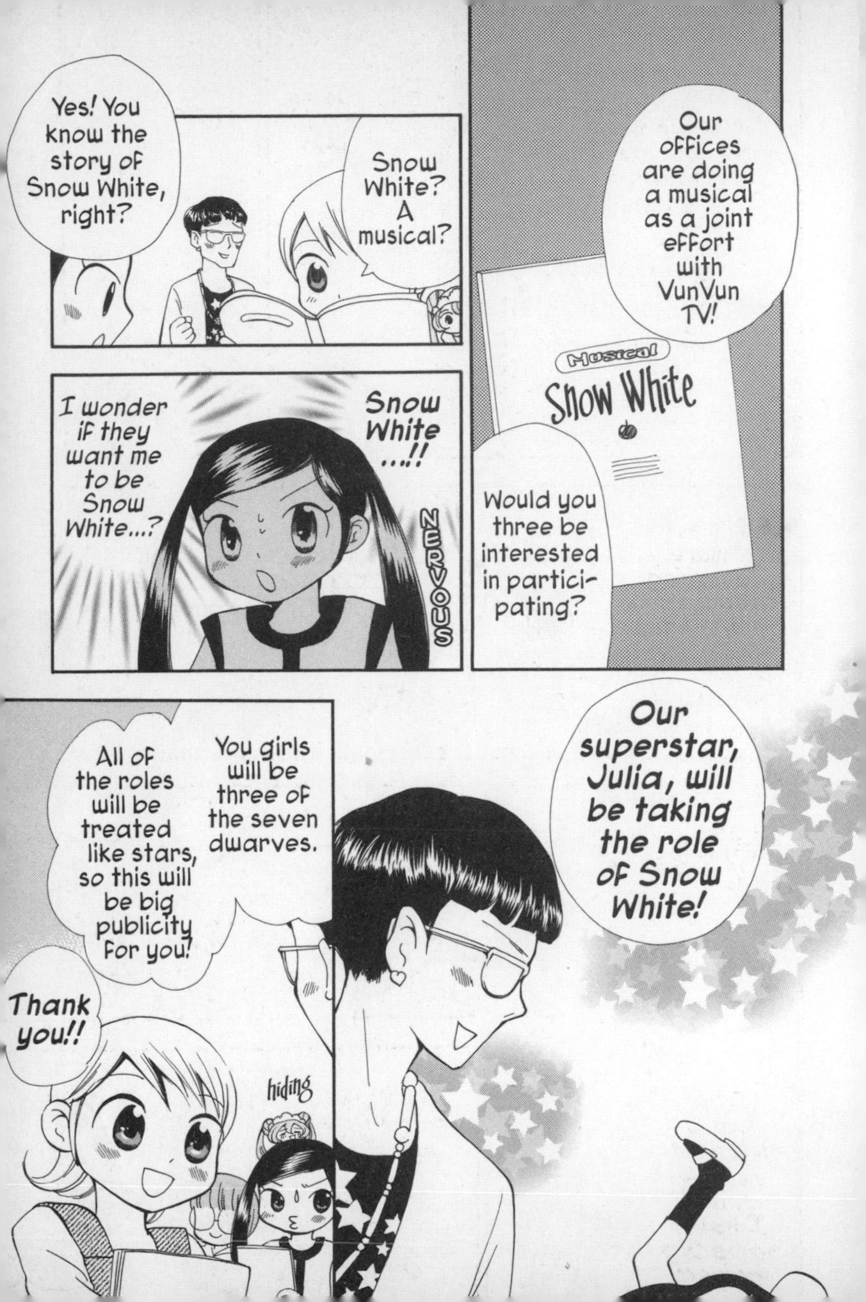
Our offices are doing a musical as a joint effort with VunVun TV!
Musical
Snow White
Would you three be interested in participating?
Snow White? A musical?
Yes! You know the story of Snow White, right?
Snow White ...!!
NERVOUS
I wonder if they want me to be Snow White...?
Our superstar, Julia, will be taking the role of Snow White!
You girls will be three of the seven dwarves.
All of the roles will be treated like stars, so this will be big publicity for you!
Thank you!!
hiding

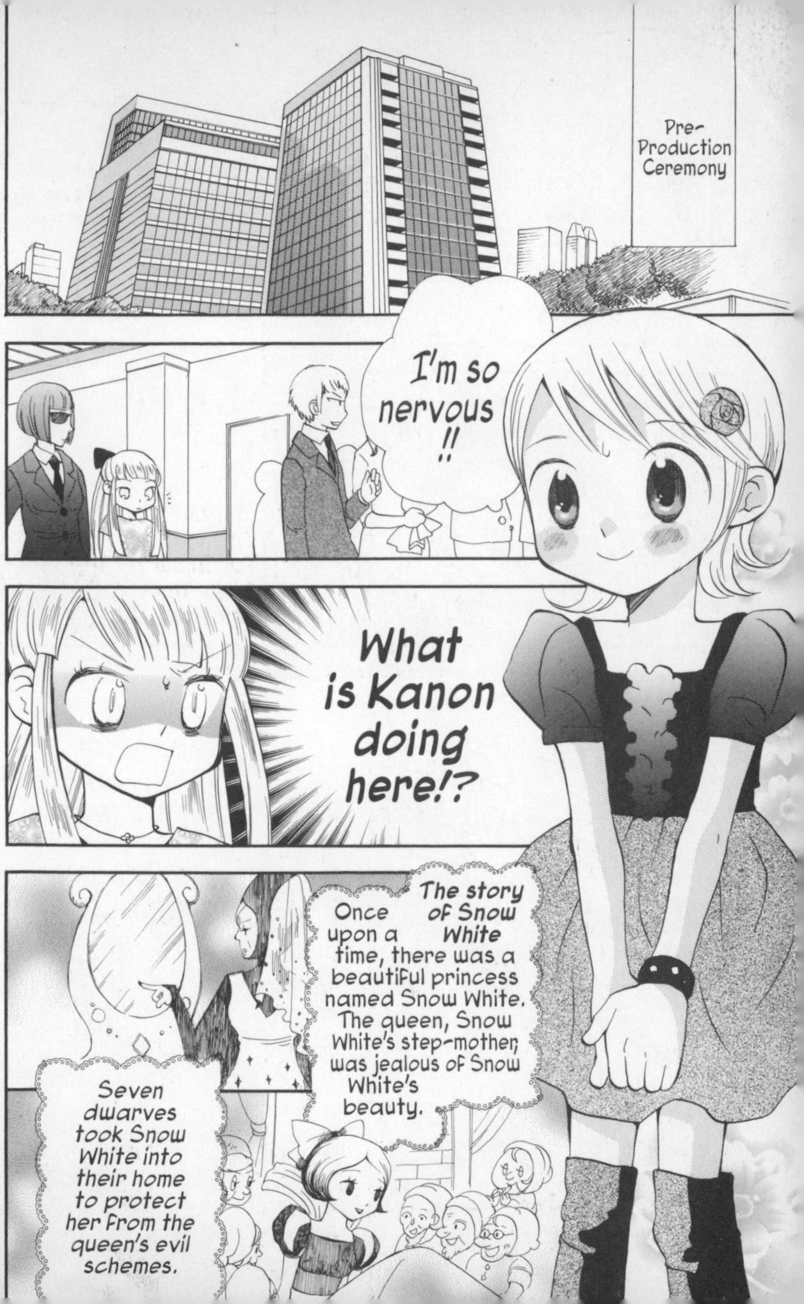
Pre-Production Ceremony
I'm so nervous!!
What is Kanon doing here!?
The story of Snow White
Once upon a time, there was a beautiful princess named Snow White. The queen, Snow White's step-mother, was jealous of Snow White's beauty.
Seven dwarves took Snow White into their home to protect her from the queen's evil schemes.

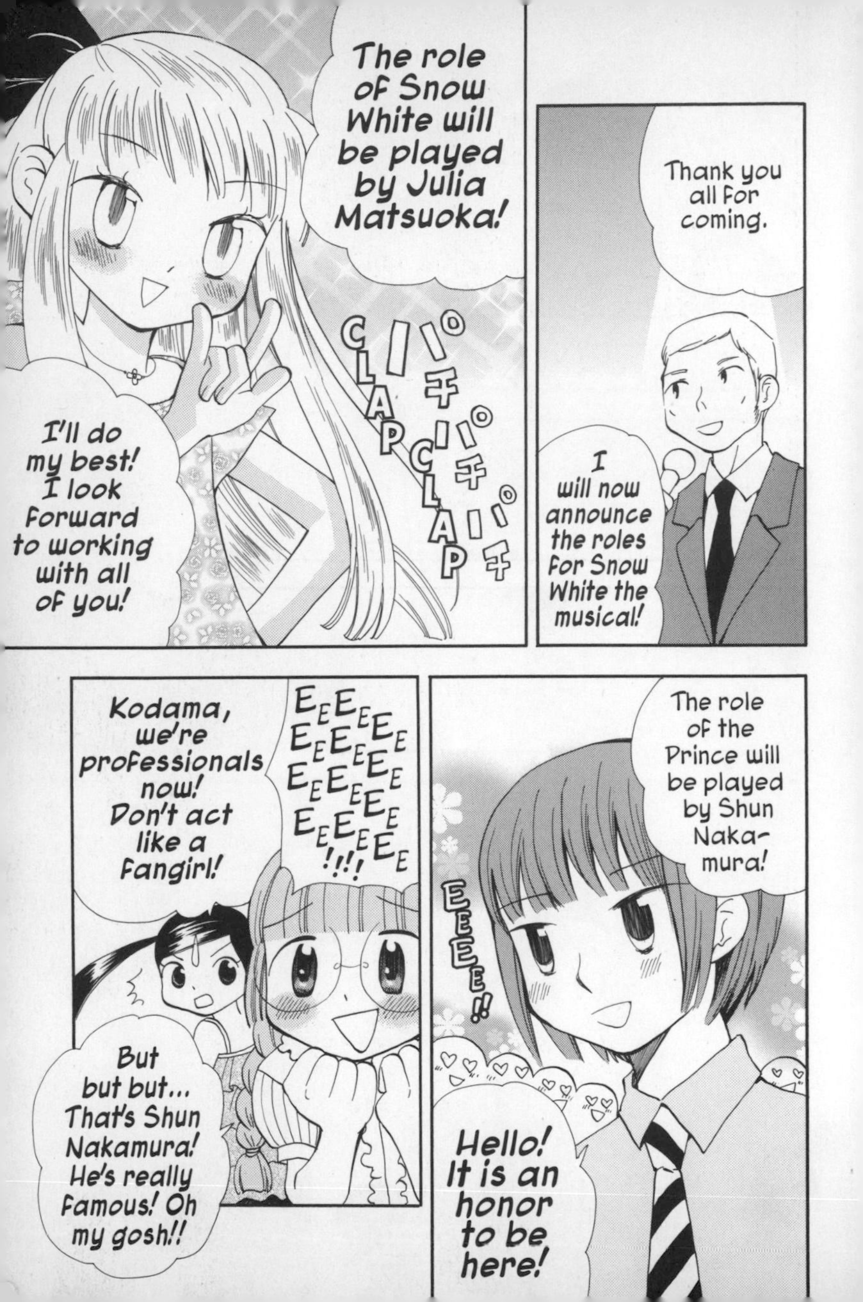
Thank you all for coming.
I will now announce the roles for Snow White the musical!
The role of Snow White will be played by Julia Matsuoka!
CLAP CLAP CLAP
I'll do my best! I look forward to working with all of you!
The role of the Prince will be played by Shun Nakamura!
EEEEE!!
Hello! It is an honor to be here!
EEEEEEEEEEEEEEEEEEEEEEEE!!!
Kodama, we're professionals now! Don't act like a fangirl!
But but but... That's Shun Nakamura! He's really famous! Oh my gosh!!

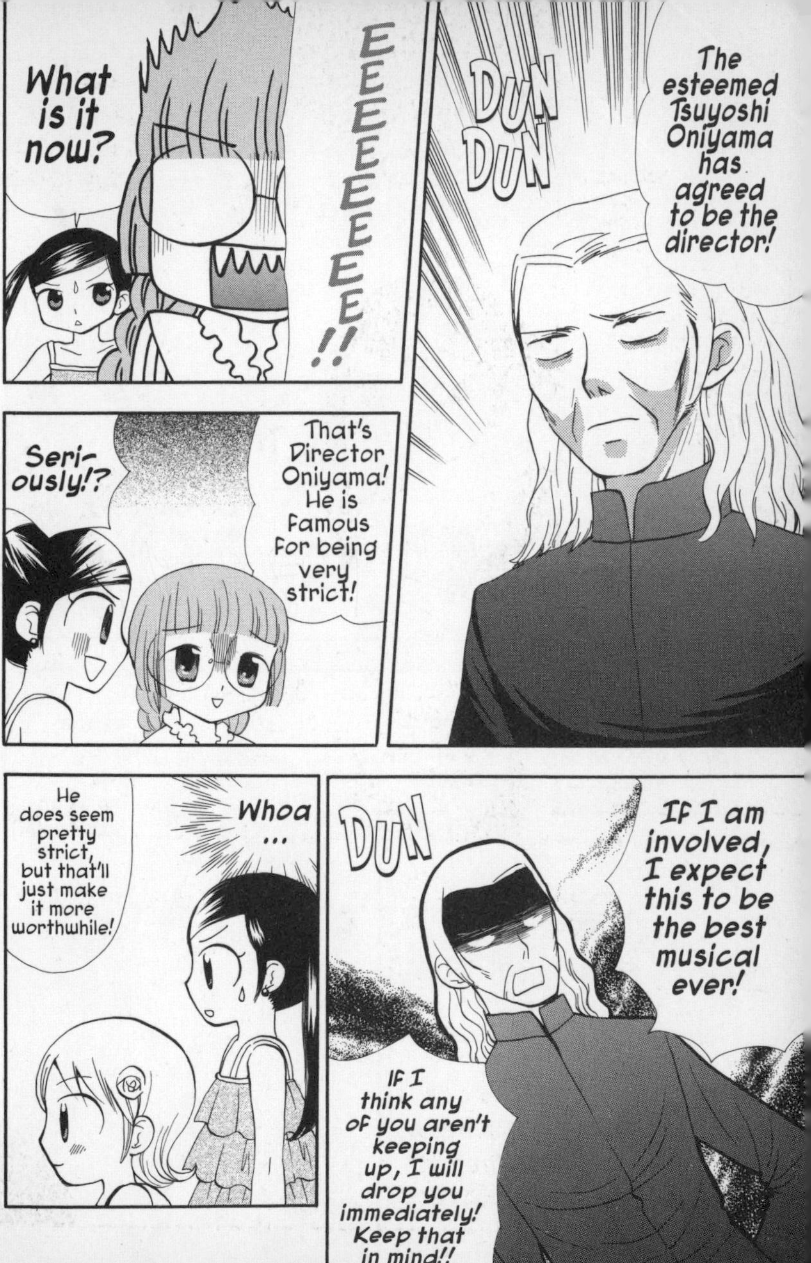
DUN DUN
The esteemed Tsuyoshi Oniyama has agreed to be the director!
EEEEEEEEEE!!
What is it now?
That's Director Oniyama! He is famous for being very strict!
Seri-ously!?
DUN
If I am involved, I expect this to be the best musical ever!
If I think any of you aren't keeping up, I will drop you immediately! Keep that in mind!!
Whoa ...
He does seem pretty strict, but that'll just make it more worthwhile!

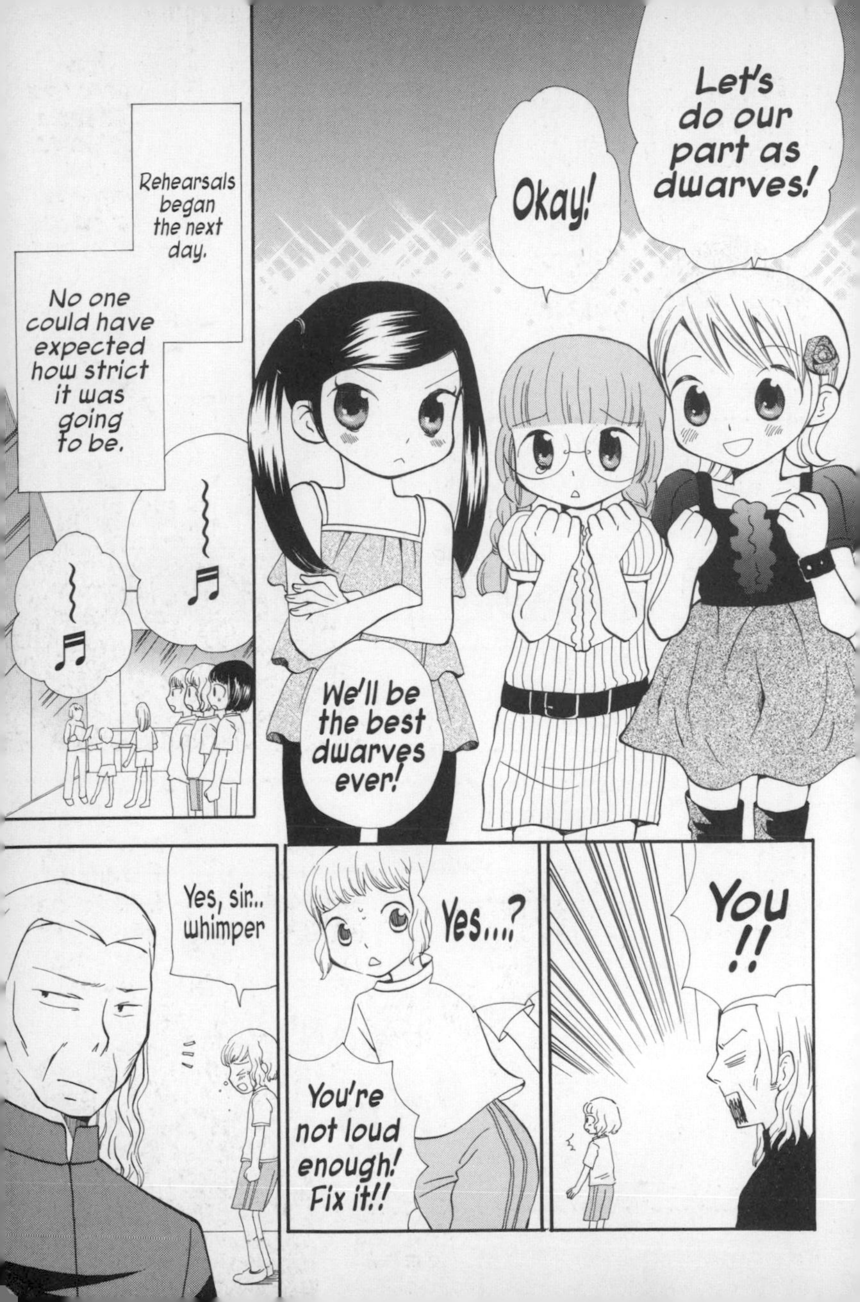
Let's do our part as dwarves!
Okay!
We'll be the best dwarves ever!
Rehearsals began the next day.
No one could have expected how strict it was going to be.
You!!
Yes...?
You're not loud enough! Fix it!!
Yes, sir... whimper

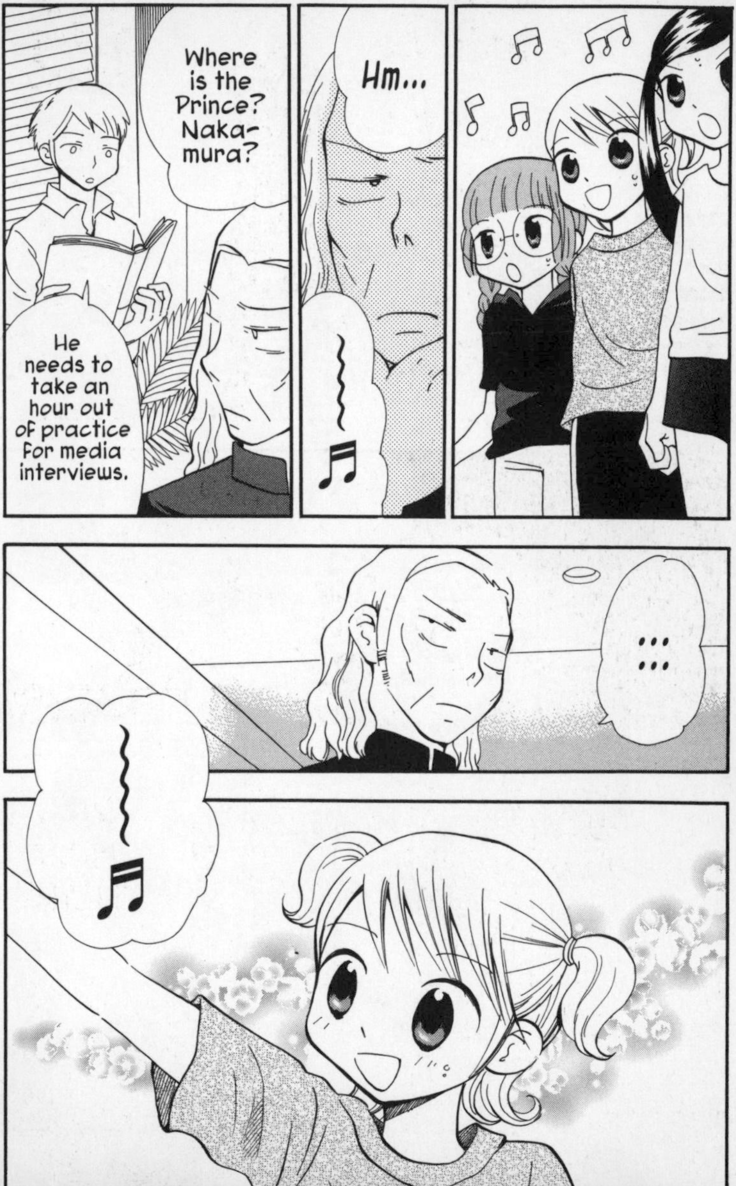
Hm...
Where is the Prince? Nakamura?
He needs to take an hour out of practice for media interviews.
......

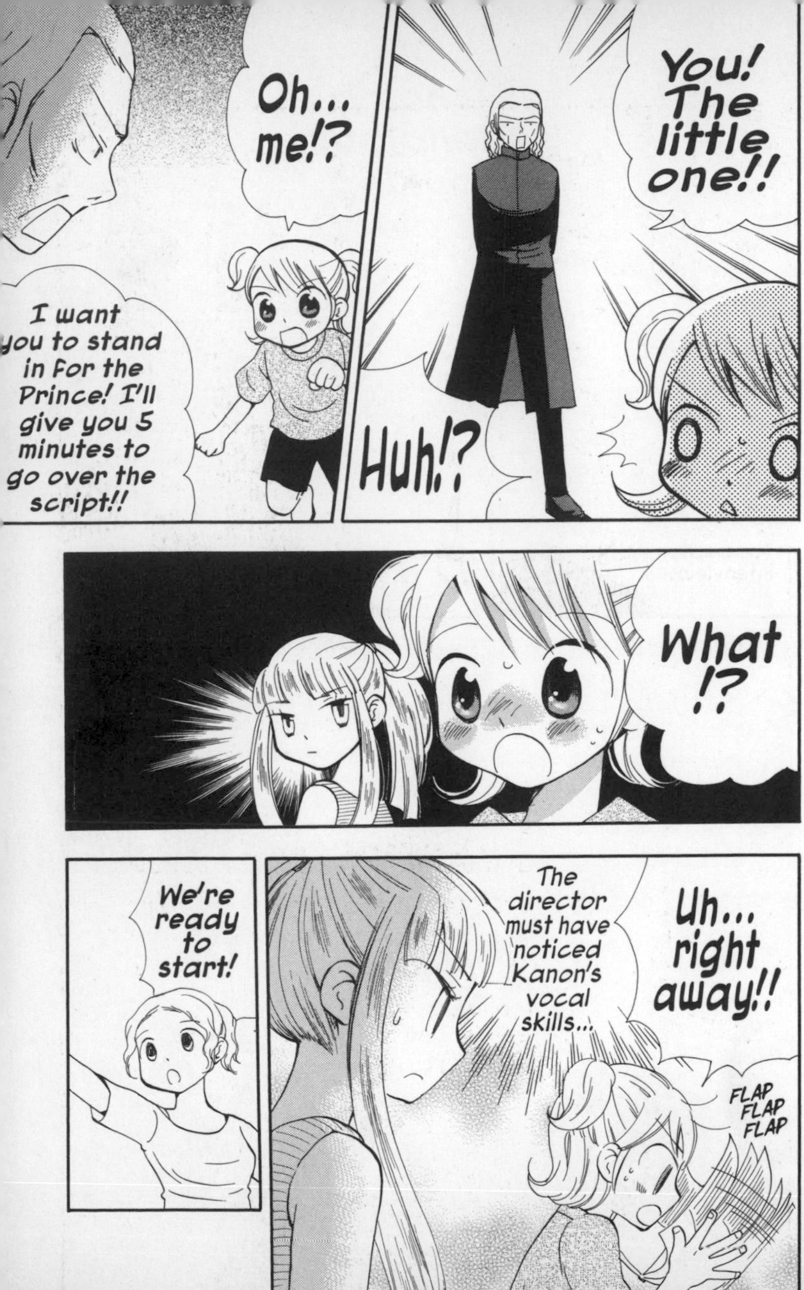
You! The little one!!
Huh!?
Oh... me!?
I want you to stand in for the Prince! I'll give you 5 minutes to go over the script!!
What!?
Uh... right away!!
The director must have noticed Kanon's vocal skills...
FLAP FLAP FLAP
We're ready to start!

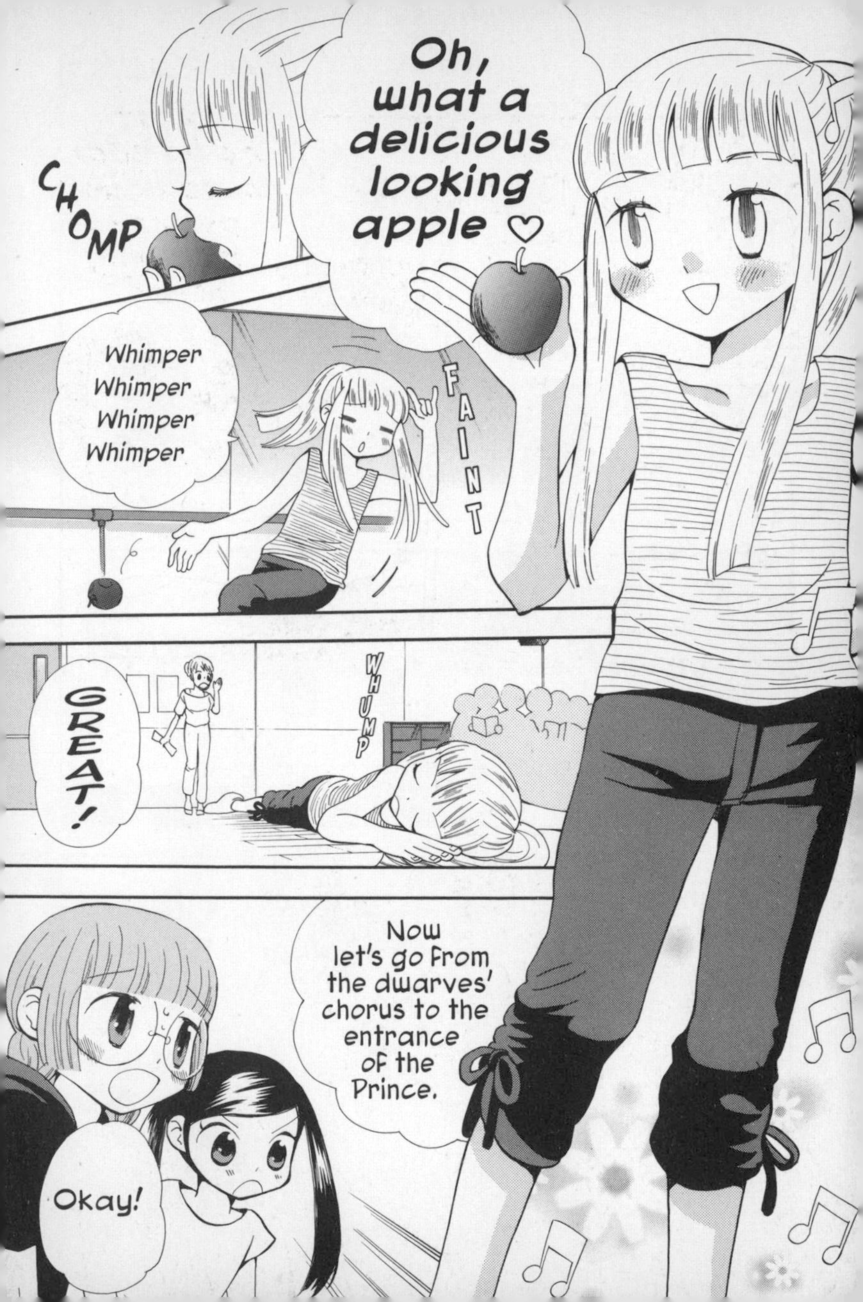

Oh, what a delicious looking apple ♡
CHOMP
FAINT
Whimper Whimper Whimper Whimper
WHUMP
GREAT!
Now let's go from the dwarves' chorus to the entrance of the Prince.
Okay!

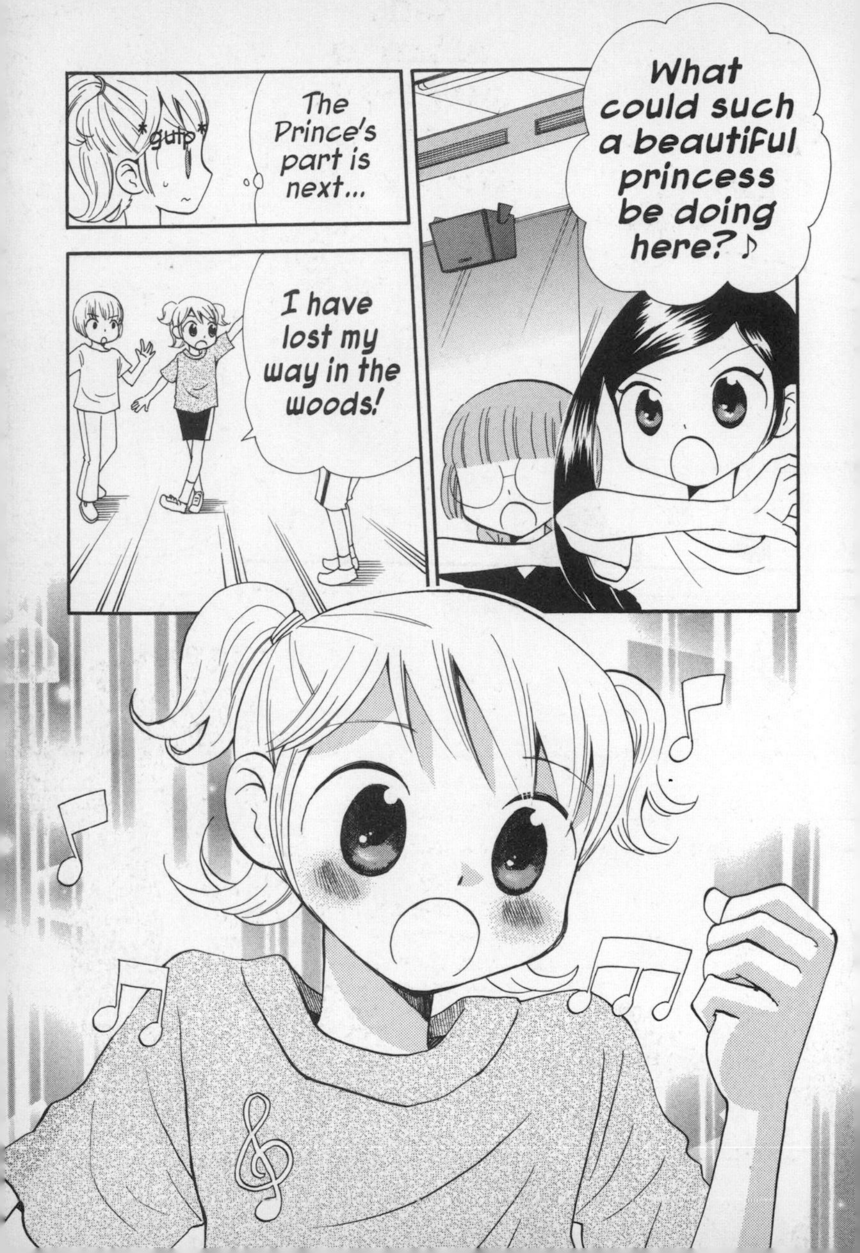
What could such a beautiful princess be doing here? ♪
gulp
The Prince's part is next...
I have lost my way in the woods!

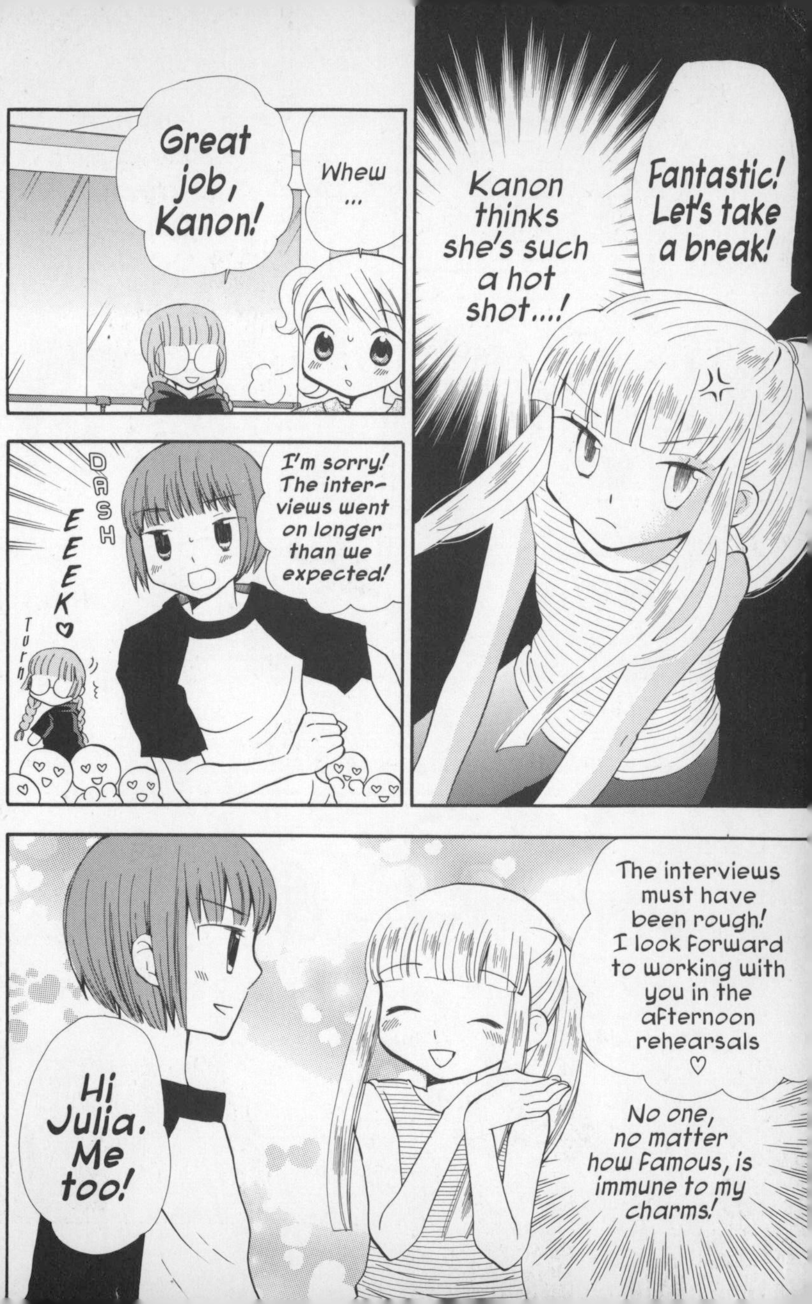
Fantastic! Let's take a break!
Kanon thinks she's such a hot shot...!
Great job, Kanon!
Whew ...
I'm sorry! The inter-views went on longer than we expected!
DASH
EEEEK♡
Turn
The interviews must have been rough! I look forward to working with you in the afternoon rehearsals ♡
No one, no matter how famous, is immune to my charms!
Hi Julia. Me too!

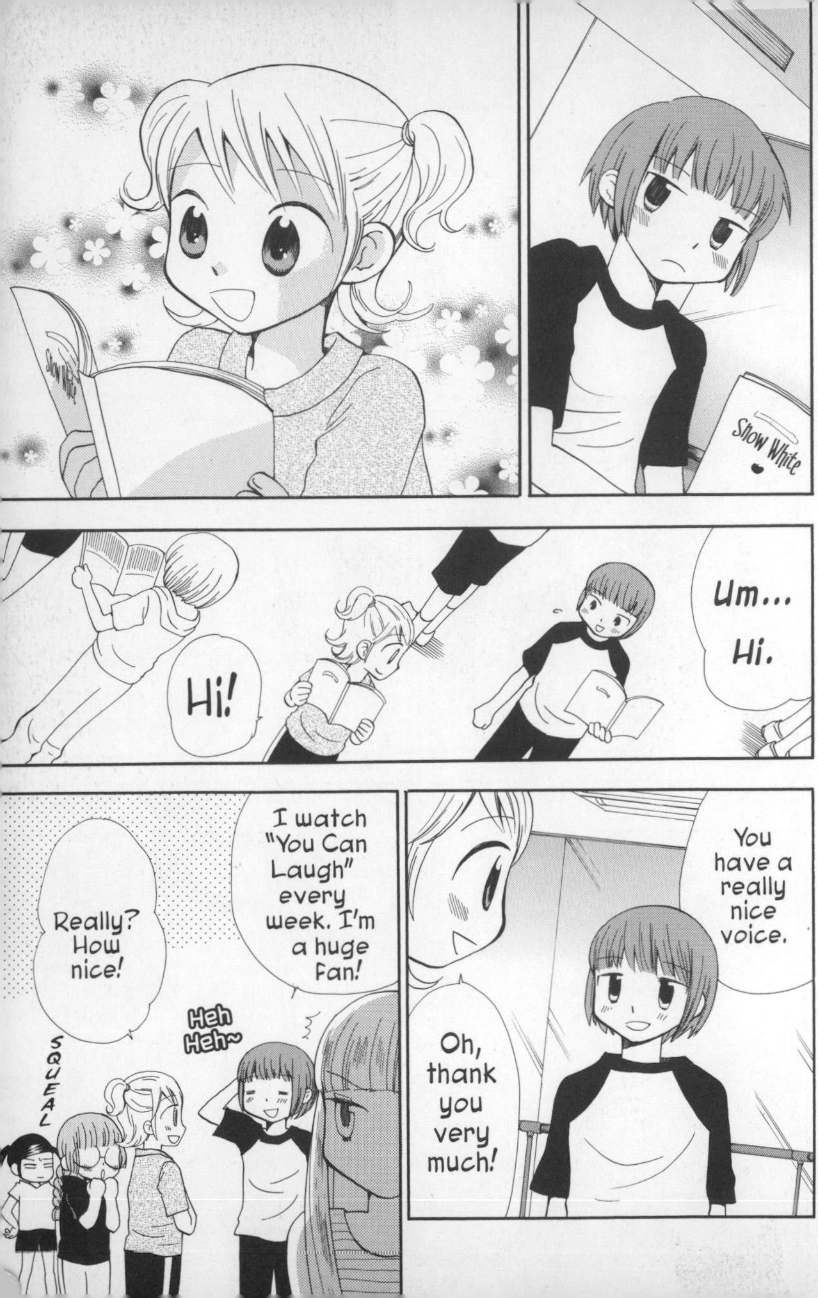

Snow White
Snow White
Um... Hi.
Hi!
You have a really nice voice.
Oh, thank you very much!
I watch "You Can Laugh" every week. I'm a huge fan!
Really? How nice!
Heh Heh~
SQUEAL

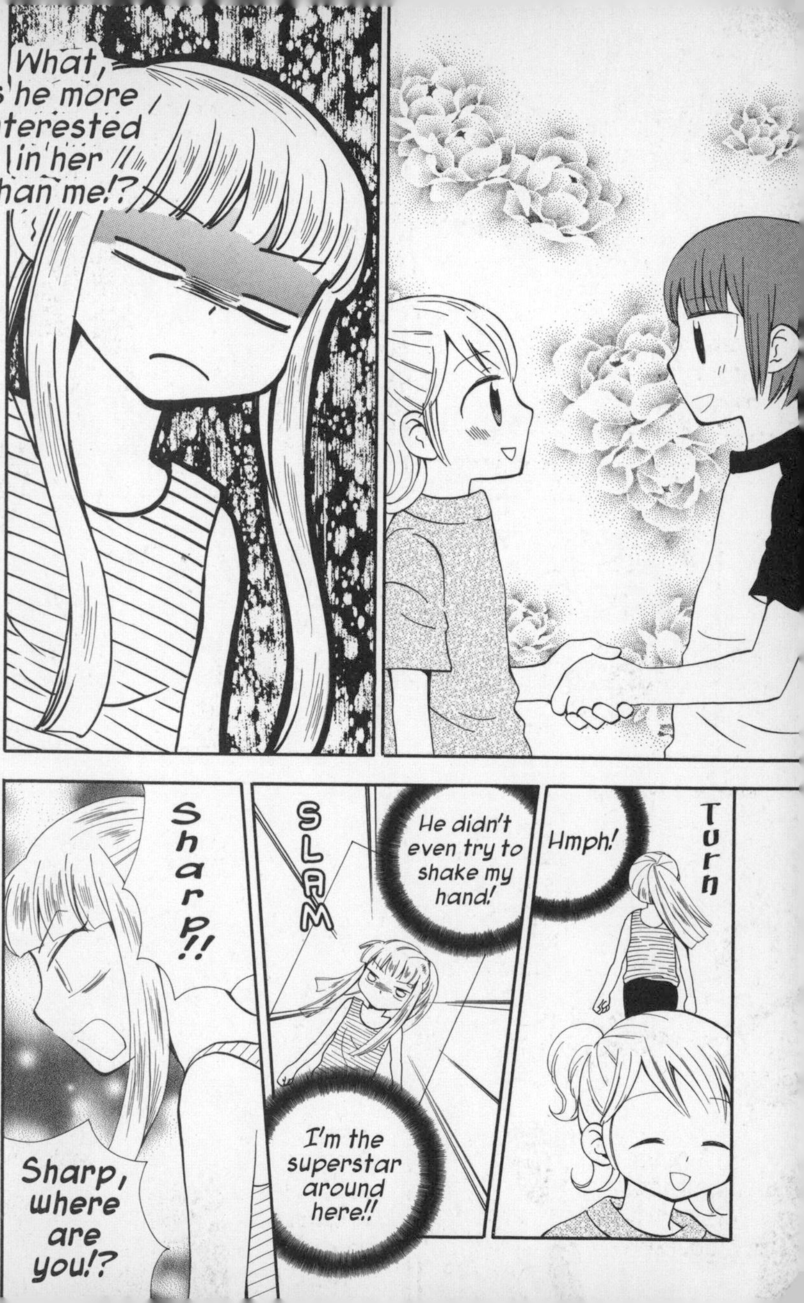
What, is he more interested in her than me!?
Turn
Hmph!
He didn't even try to shake my hand!
SLAM
I'm the superstar around here!!
Sharp!!
Sharp, where are you!?

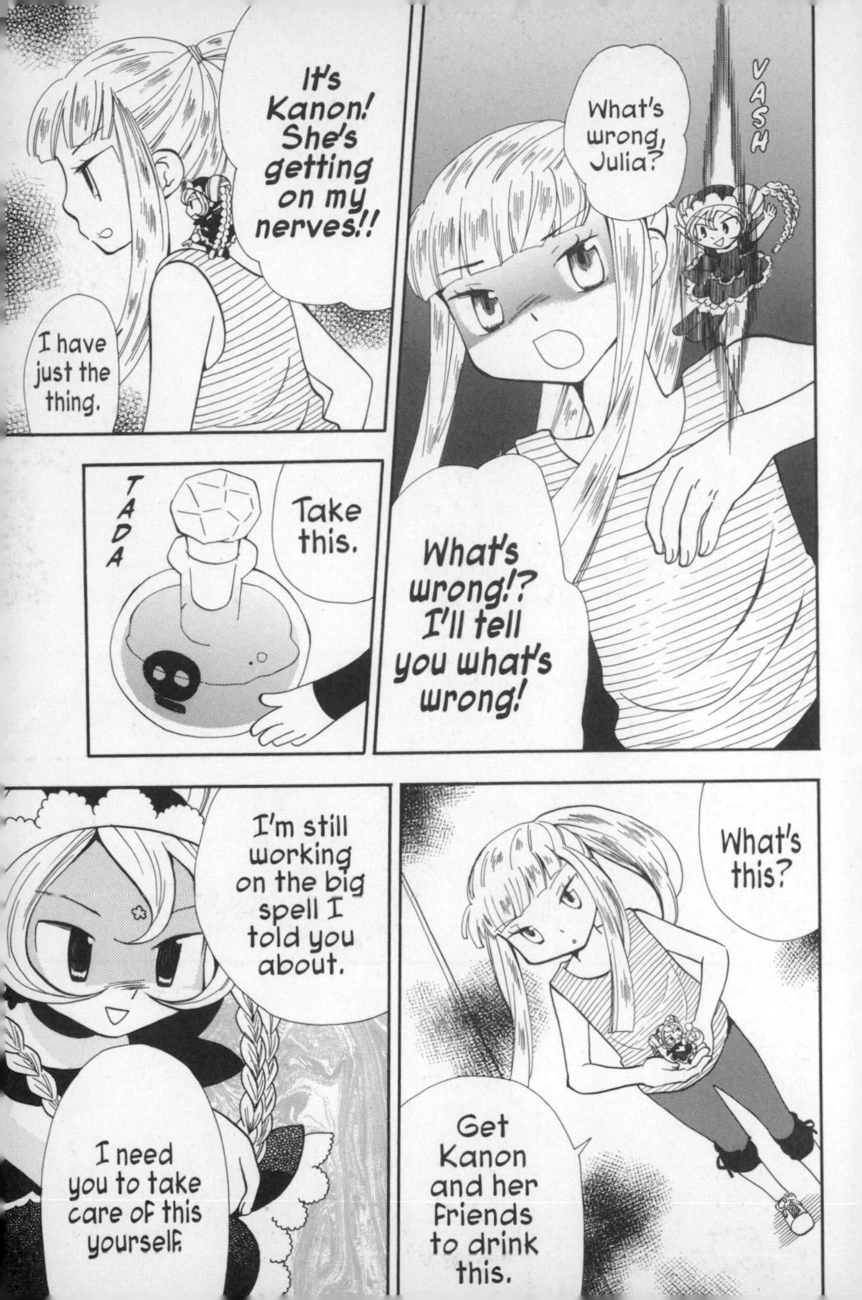
VASH
What's wrong, Julia?
What's wrong!? I'll tell you what's wrong!
It's Kanon! She's getting on my nerves!!
I have just the thing.
Take this.
TADA
What's this?
Get Kanon and her friends to drink this.
I'm still working on the big spell I told you about.
I need you to take care of this yourself.

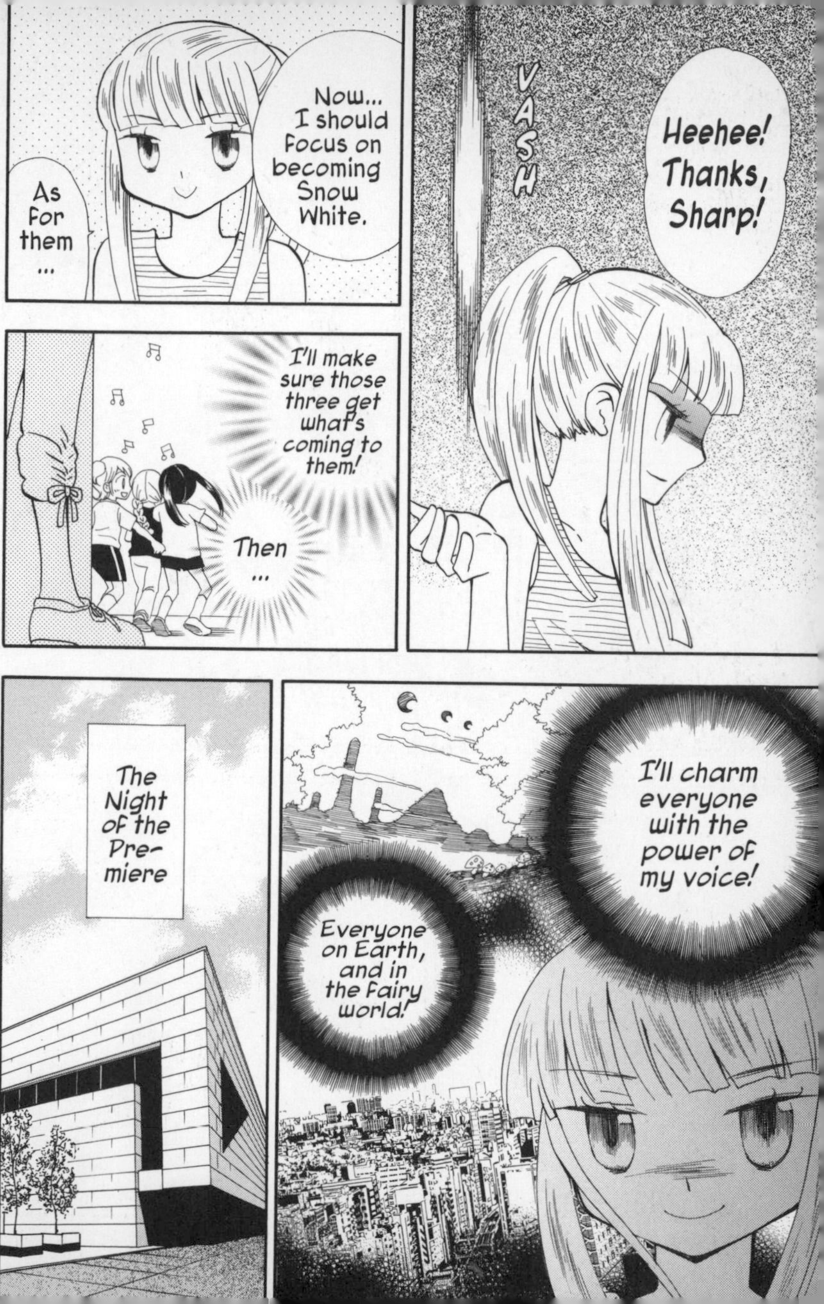

Heehee! Thanks, Sharp!
VASH
Now... I should focus on becoming Snow White.
As for them ...
I'll make sure those three get what's coming to them!
Then ...
I'll charm everyone with the power of my voice!
Everyone on Earth, and in the fairy world!
The Night of the Pre-miere

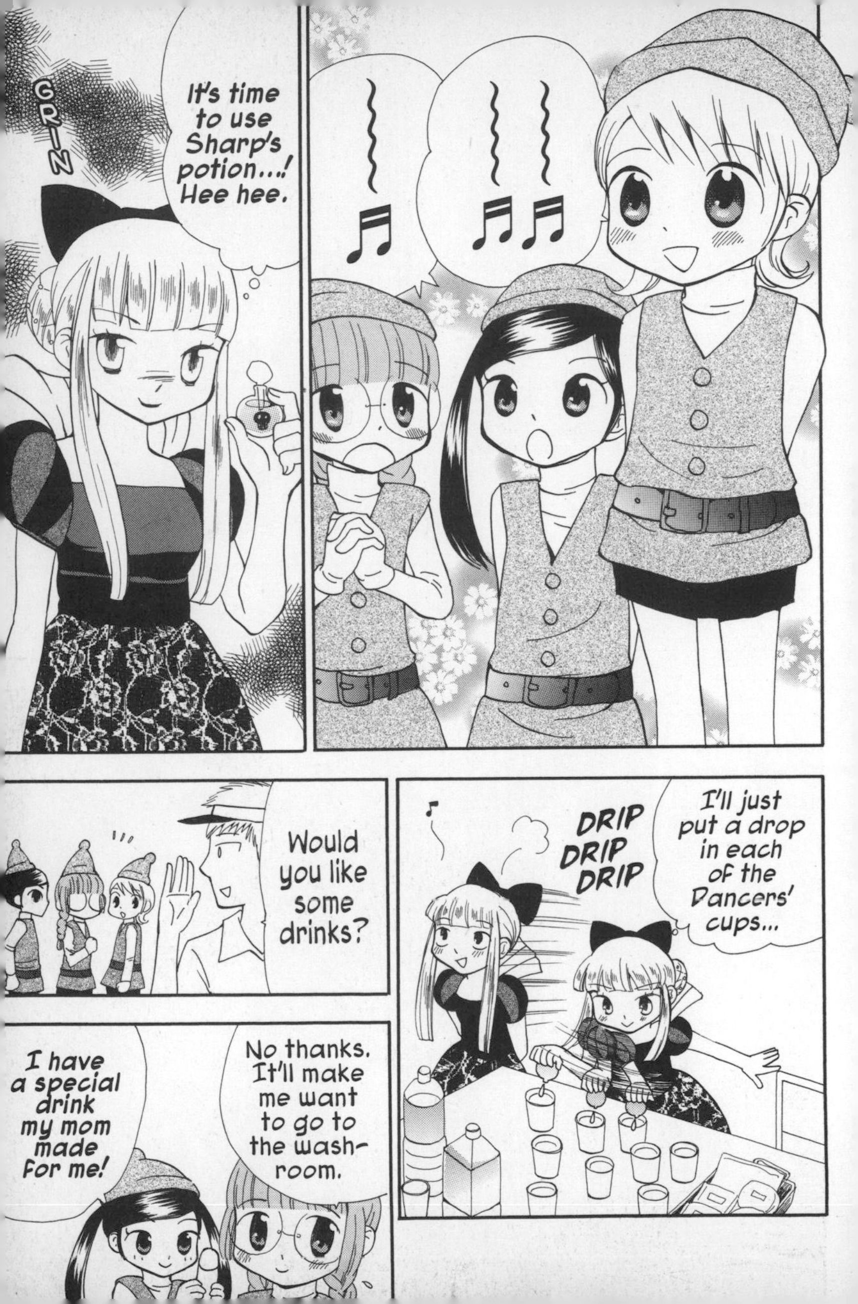
GRIN
It's time to use Sharp's potion...! Hee hee.
I'll just put a drop in each of the Dancers' cups...
DRIP DRIP DRIP
Would you like some drinks?
No thanks. It'll make me want to go to the wash-room.
I have a special drink my mom made for me!

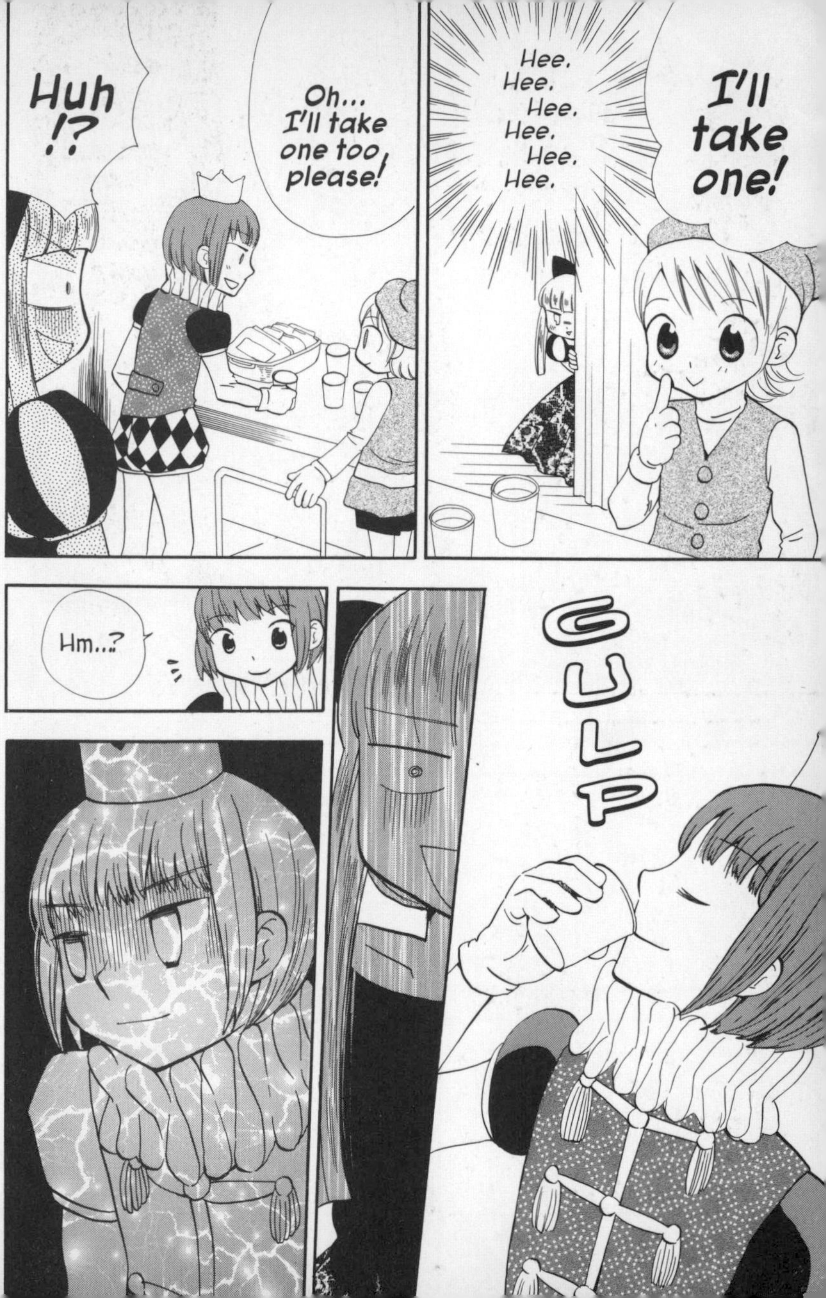
I'll take one!
Hee. Hee. Hee. Hee. Hee. Hee.
Oh... I'll take one too please!
Huh!?
GULP
Hm...?

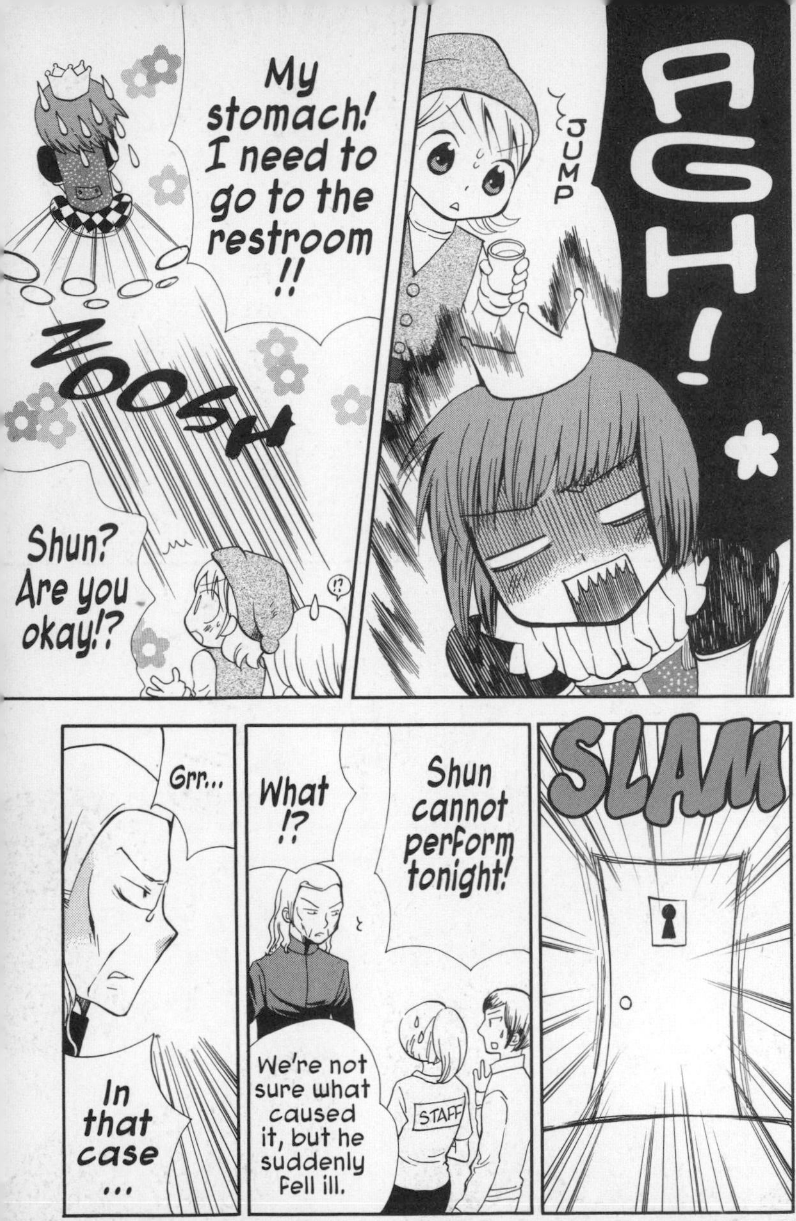
AGH!
JUMP
My stomach! I need to go to the restroom !!
ZOOSH
!?
Shun? Are you okay!?
SLAM
Shun cannot perform tonight!
What !?
We're not sure what caused it, but he suddenly fell ill.
Grr...
In that case ...

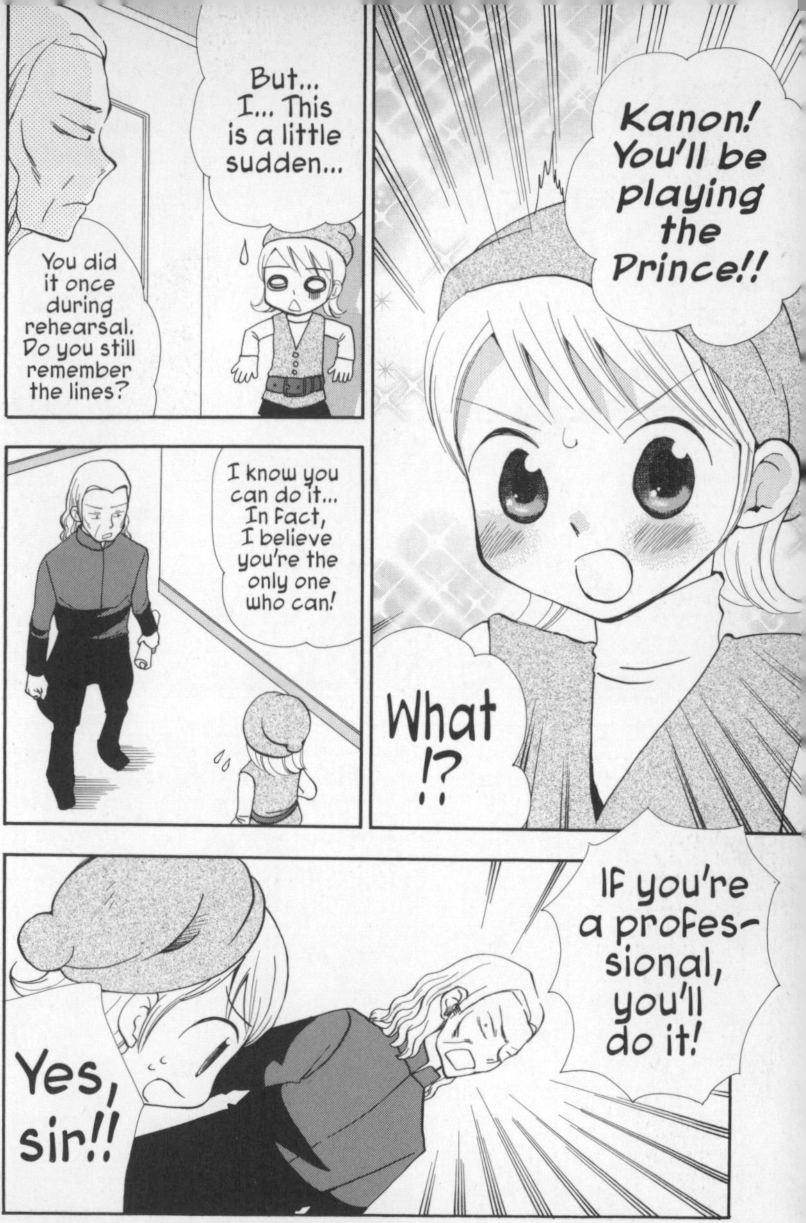
Kanon! You'll be playing the Prince!!
What!?
But... I... This is a little sudden...
You did it once during rehearsal. Do you still remember the lines?
I know you can do it... In fact, I believe you're the only one who can!
If you're a profes-sional, you'll do it!
Yes, sir!!

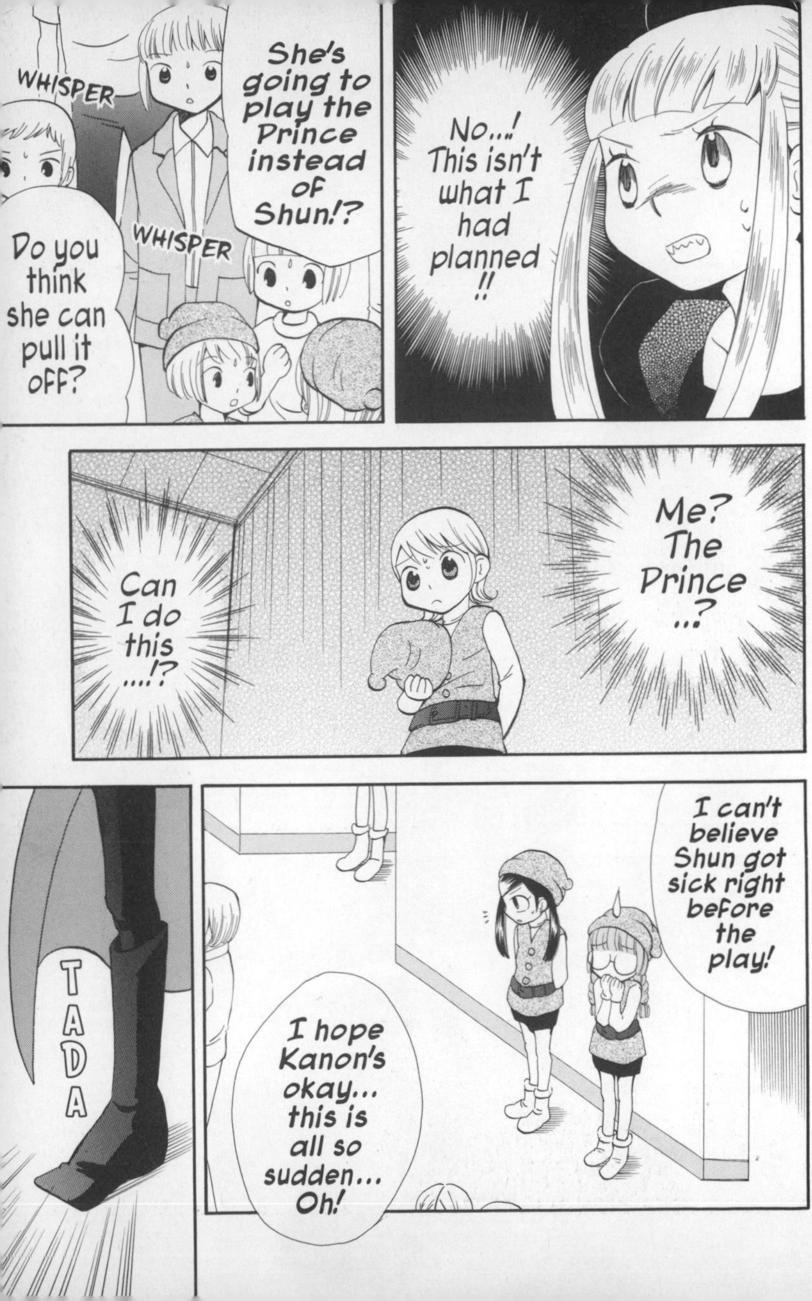
No...! This isn't what I had planned!!
She's going to play the Prince instead of Shun!?
WHISPER
WHISPER
Do you think she can pull it off?
Me? The Prince...?
Can I do this...!?
I can't believe Shun got sick right before the play!
I hope Kanon's okay... this is all so sudden... Oh!
TADA

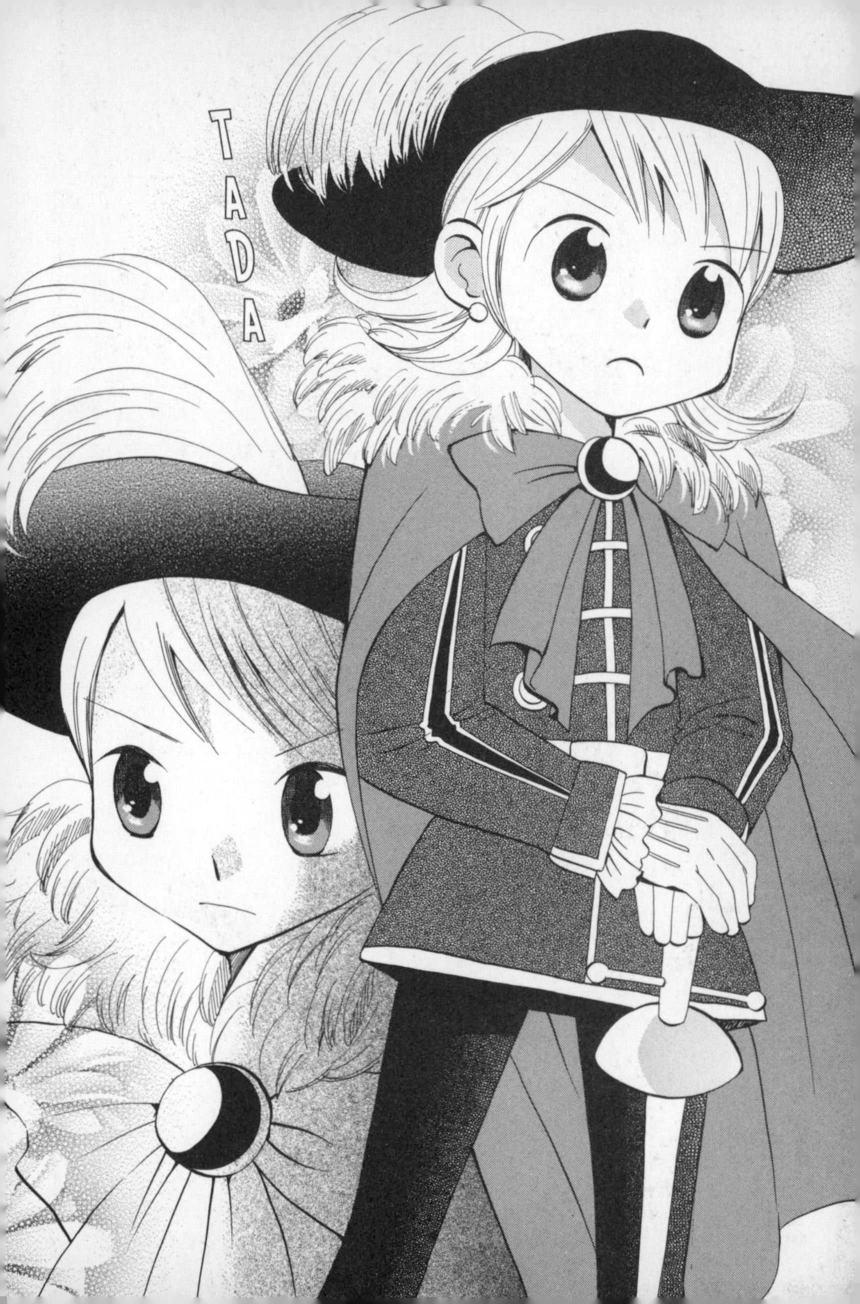
TADA

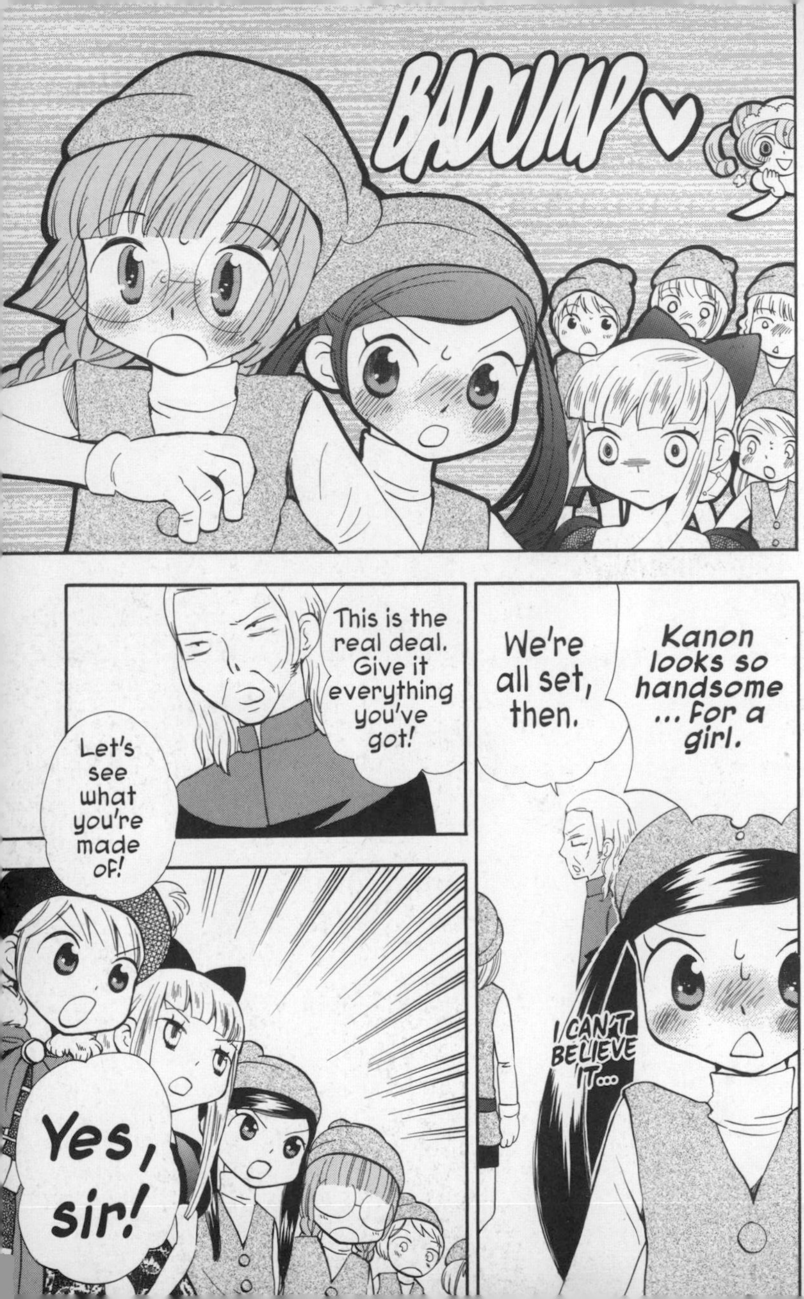
BADUMP ♥
Kanon looks so handsome ... for a girl.
We're all set, then.
I CAN'T BELIEVE IT...
This is the real deal. Give it everything you've got!
Let's see what you're made of!
Yes, sir!

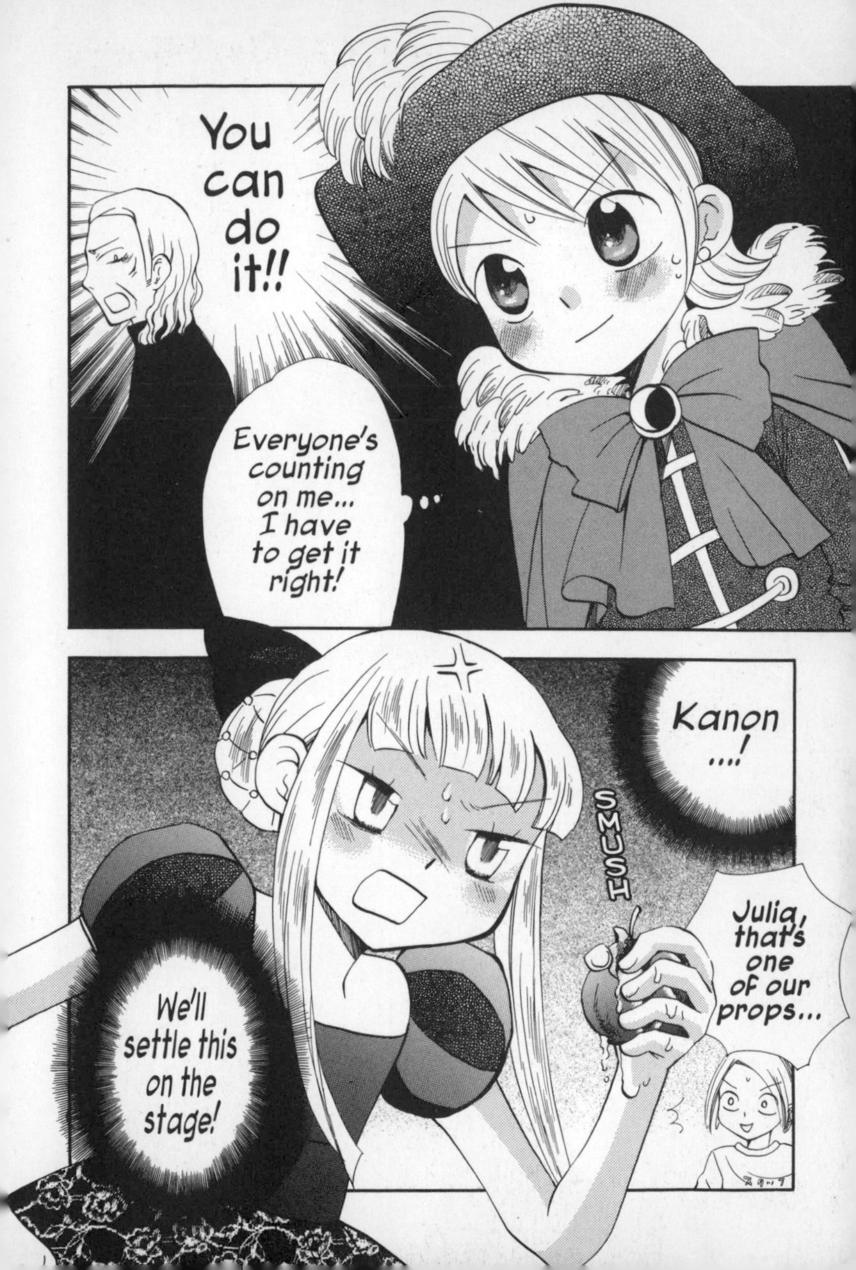
You can do it!!
Everyone's counting on me... I have to get it right!
Kanon ...!
SMUSH
Julia, that's one of our props...
We'll settle this on the stage!

Stage 22: On Stage

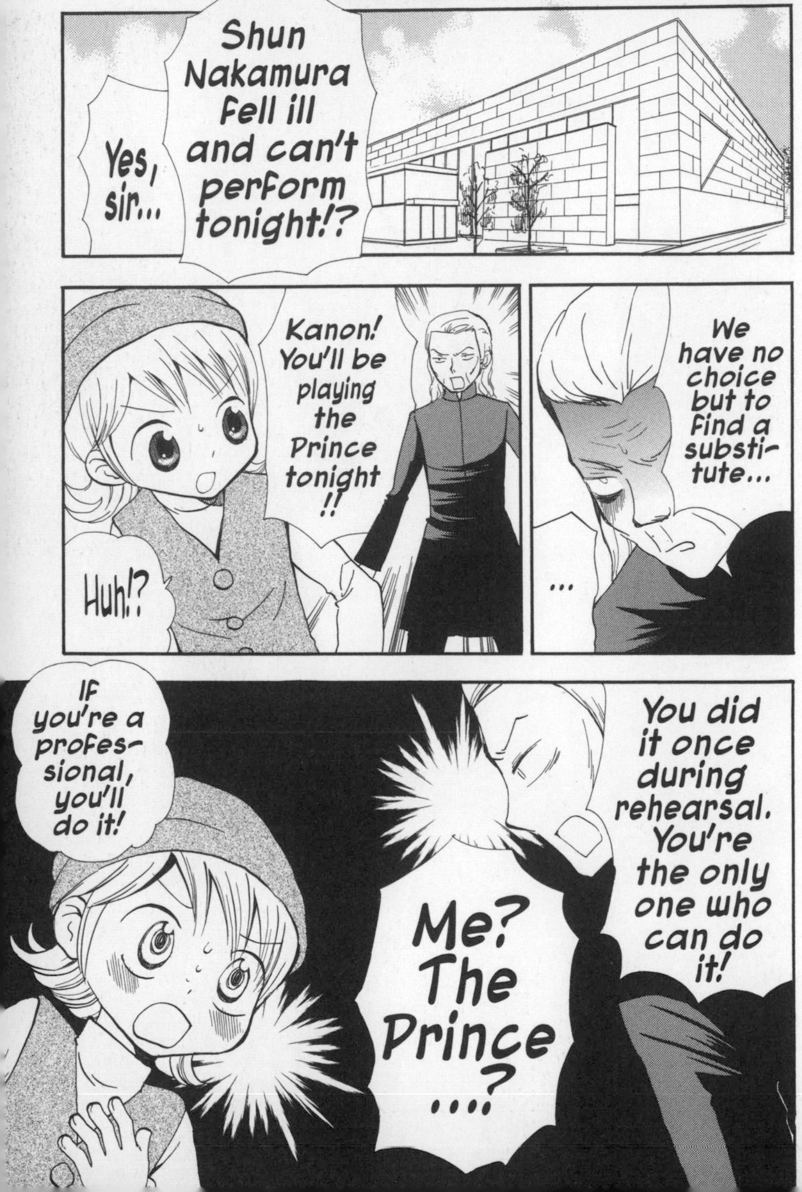
Shun Nakamura fell ill and can't perform tonight!?
Yes, sir...
We have no choice but to find a substitute...
...
Kanon! You'll be playing the Prince tonight!!
Huh!?
You did it once during rehearsal. You're the only one who can do it!
Me? The Prince...?
If you're a professional, you'll do it!

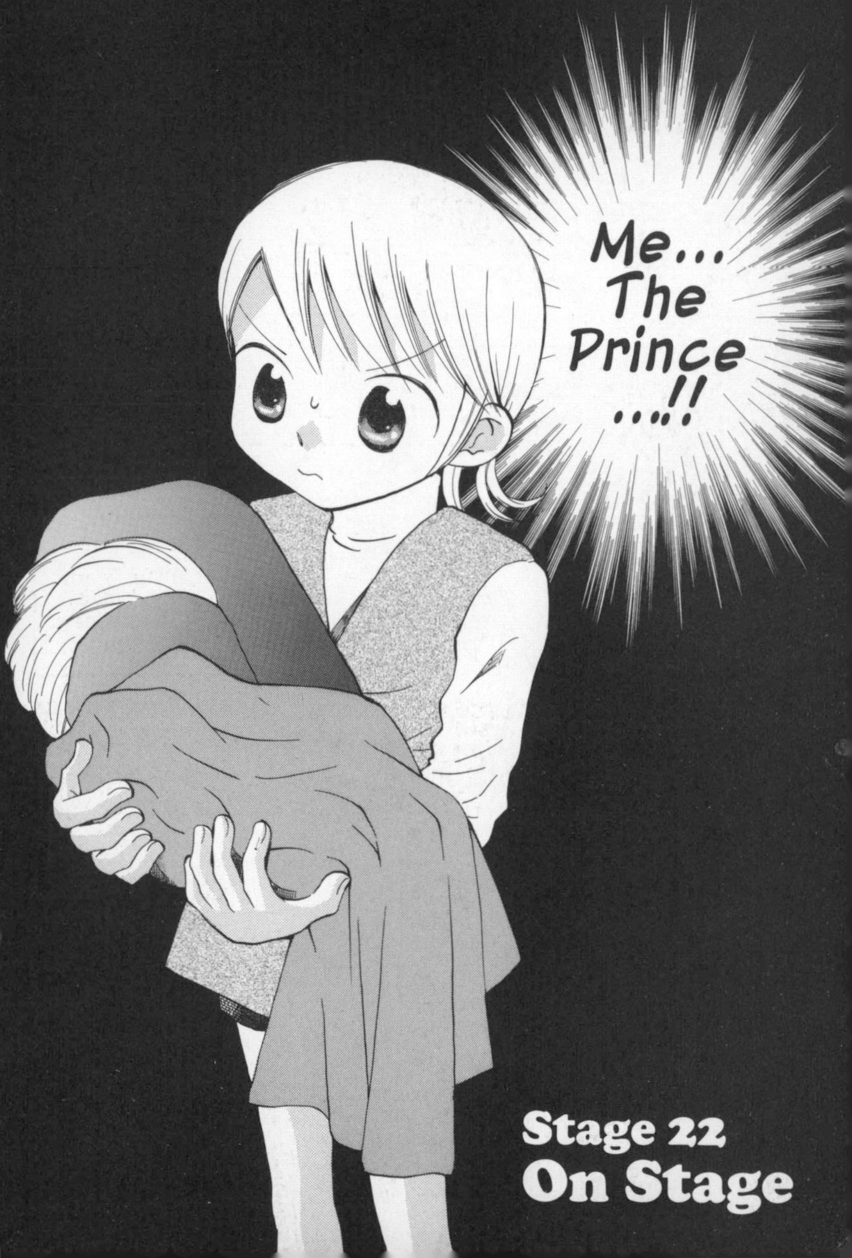
Me... The Prince ...!!

Stage 22
On Stage

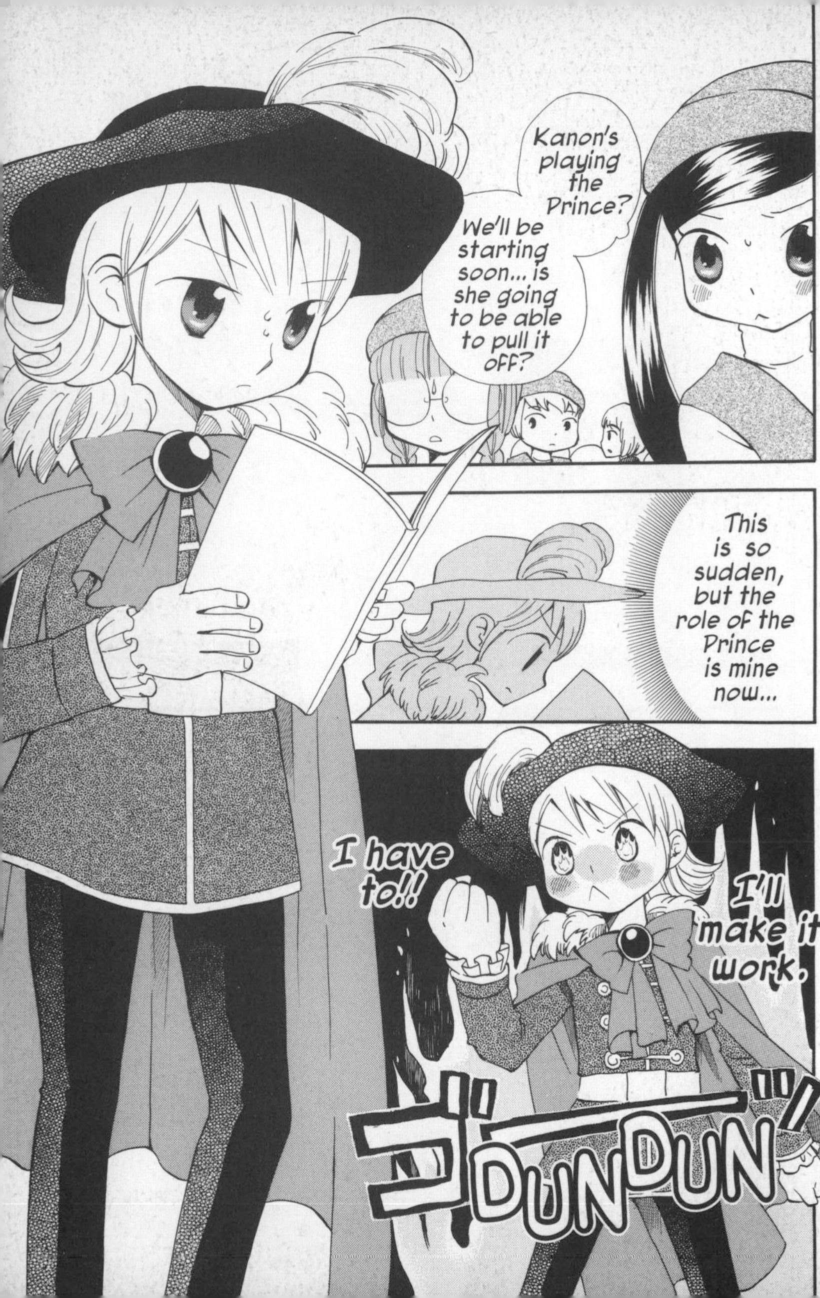
Kanon's playing the Prince?
We'll be starting soon... is she going to be able to pull it off?
This is so sudden, but the role of the Prince is mine now...
I'll make it work.
I have to!!
DUNDUN

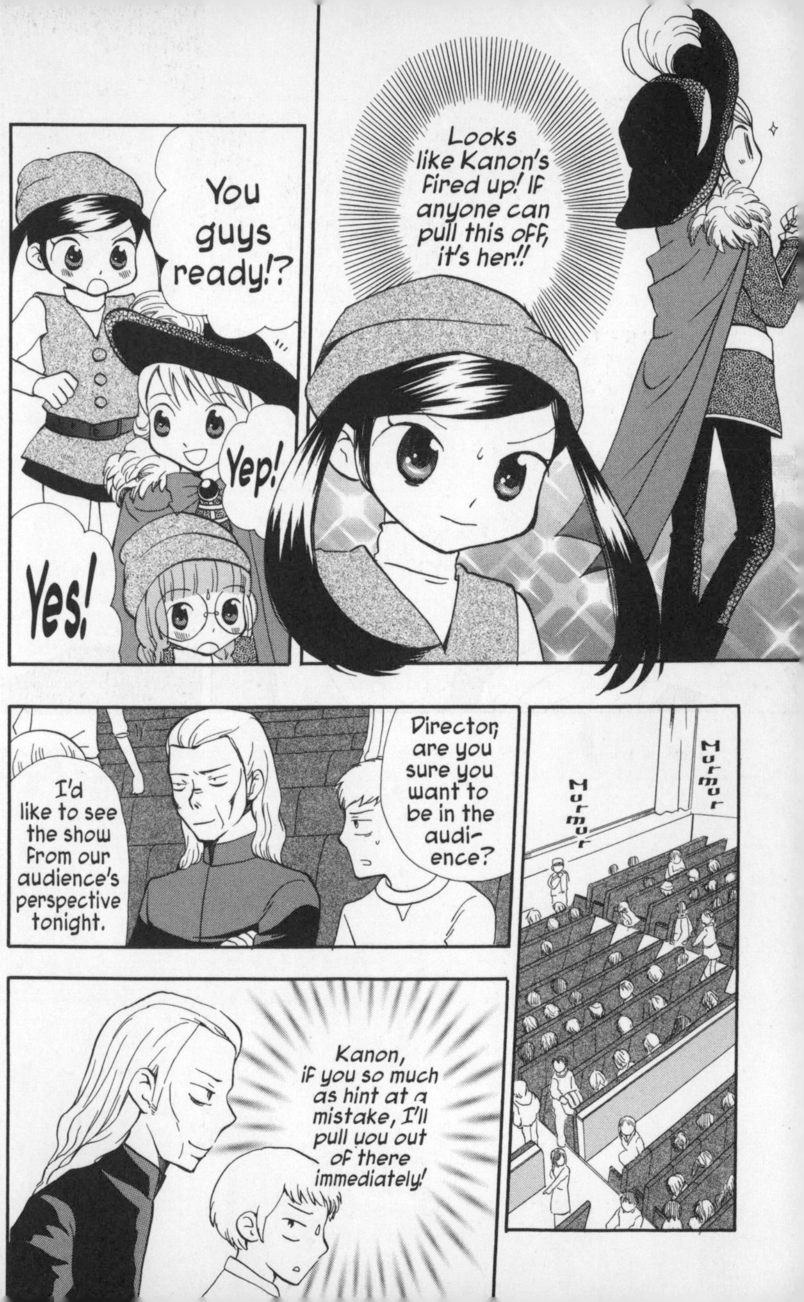
Looks like Kanon's fired up! If anyone can pull this off, it's her!!
You guys ready!?
Yep!
Yes!
Murmur
Murmur
Director, are you sure you want to be in the audi-ence?
I'd like to see the show from our audience's perspective tonight.
Kanon, if you so much as hint at a mistake, I'll pull you out of there immediately!

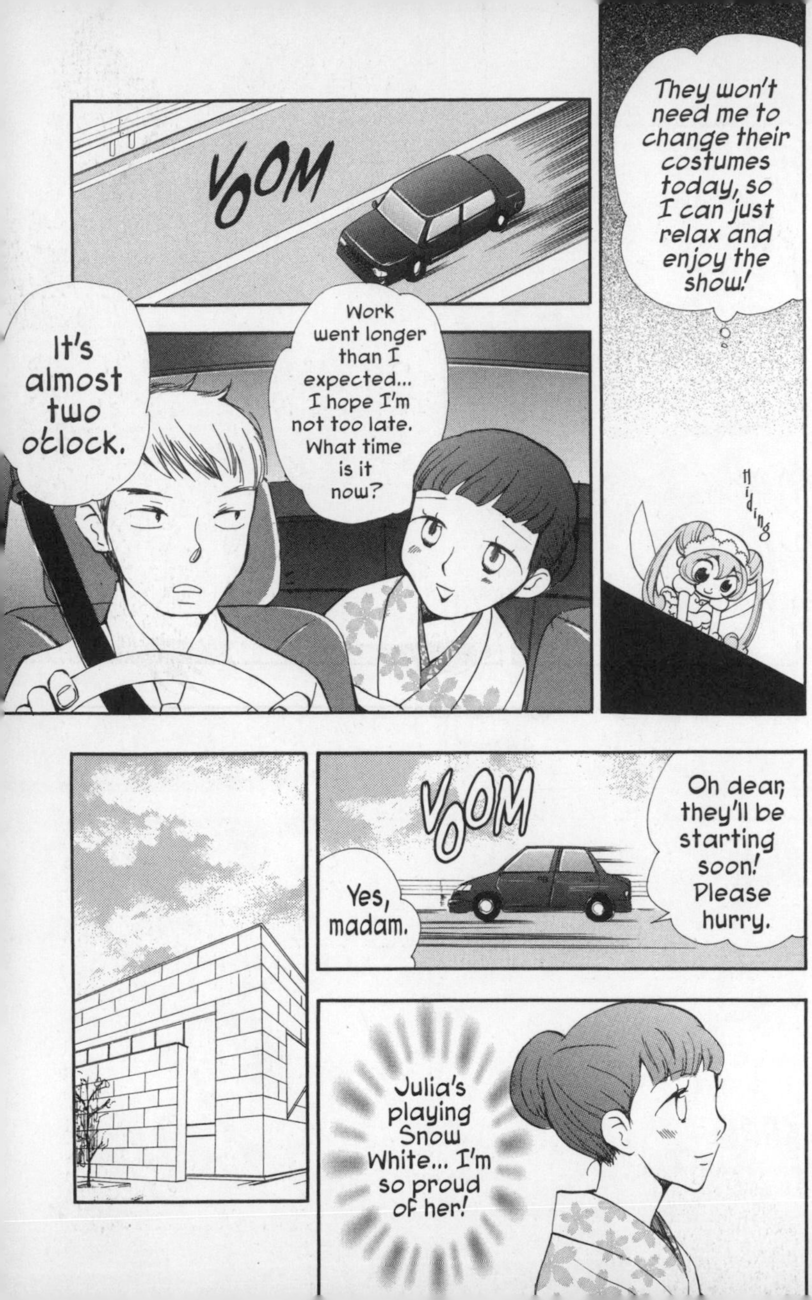
They won't need me to change their costumes today, so I can just relax and enjoy the show!
hiding
VOOM
Work went longer than I expected... I hope I'm not too late. What time is it now?
It's almost two o'clock.
Oh dear, they'll be starting soon! Please hurry.
VOOM
Yes, madam.
Julia's playing Snow White... I'm so proud of her!

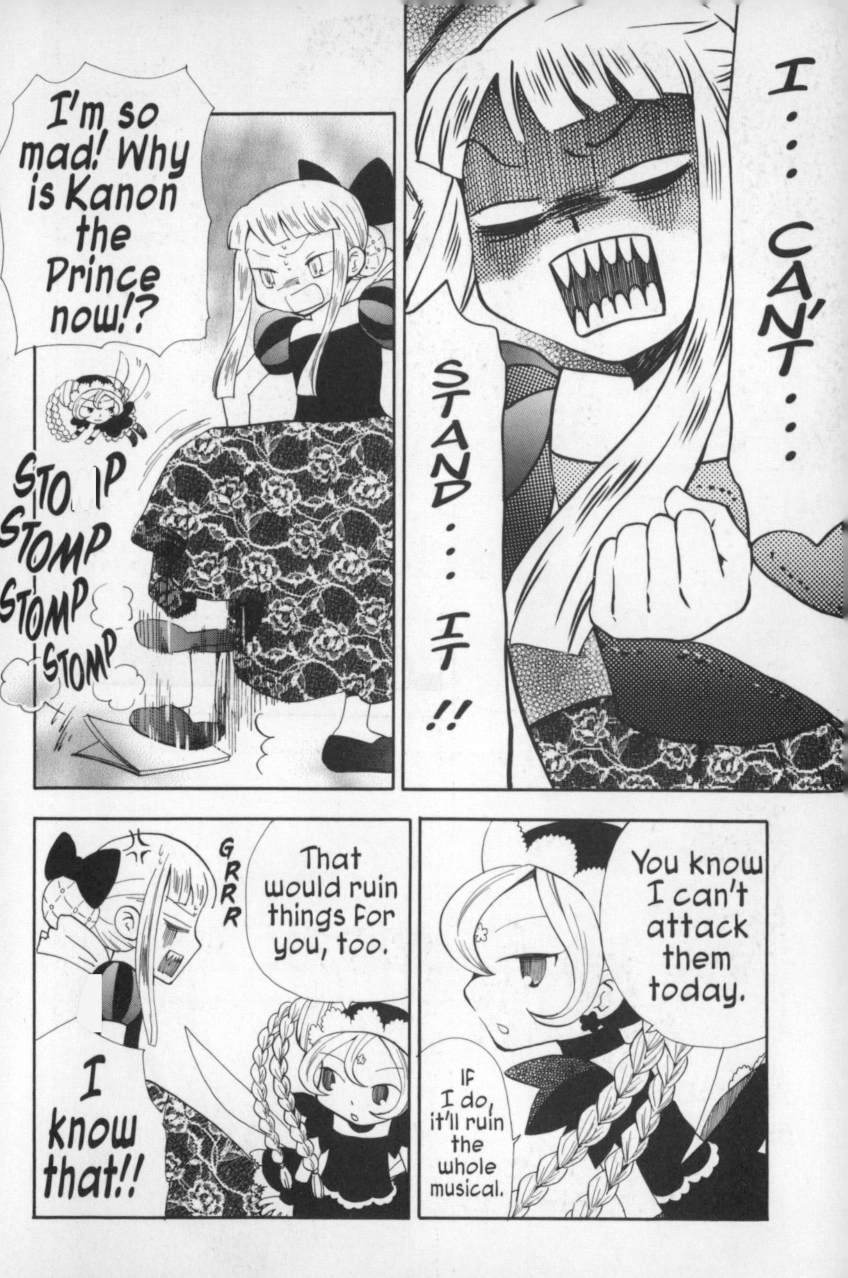
I... CAN'T STAND... IT!!
I'm so mad! Why is Kanon the Prince now!?
STOMP STOMP STOMP STOMP
You know I can't attack them today.
If I do, it'll ruin the whole musical.
That would ruin things for you, too.
GRRR
I know that!!

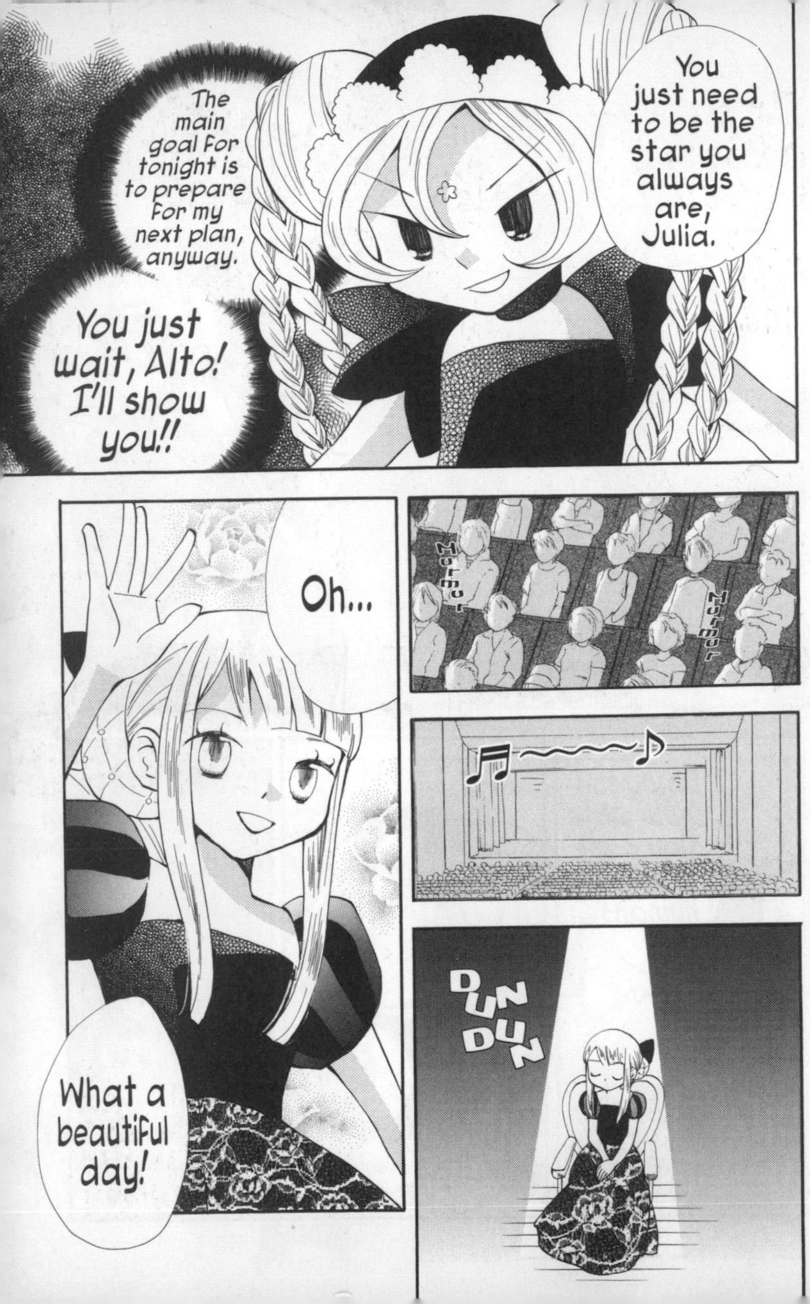

You just need to be the star you always are, Julia.
The main goal for tonight is to prepare for my next plan, anyway.
You just wait, Alto! I'll show you!!
Murmur
Murmur
DUN DUN
Oh...
What a beautiful day!

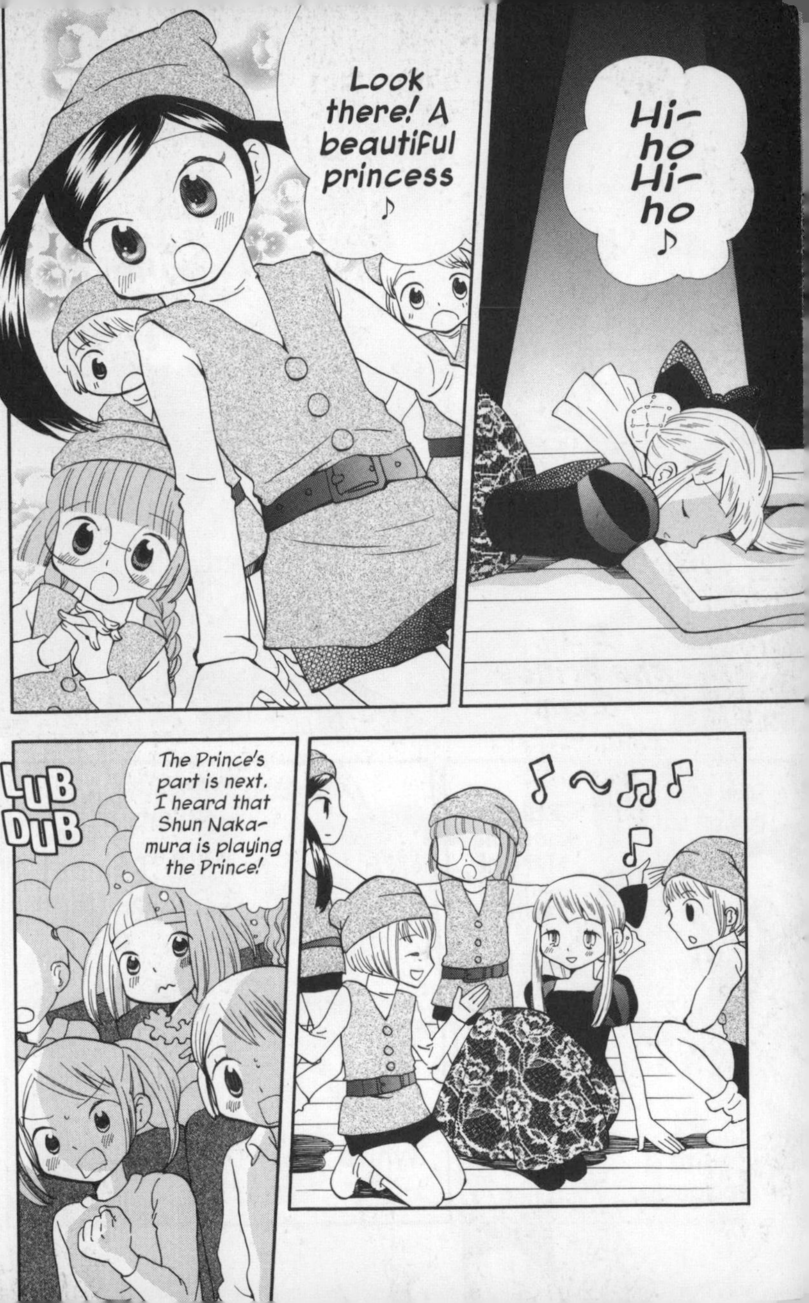
Hi-ho Hi-ho ♪
Look there! A beautiful princess ♪
♪ ~ ♫ ♪ ♪
LUB DUB
The Prince's part is next. I heard that Shun Nakamura is playing the Prince!

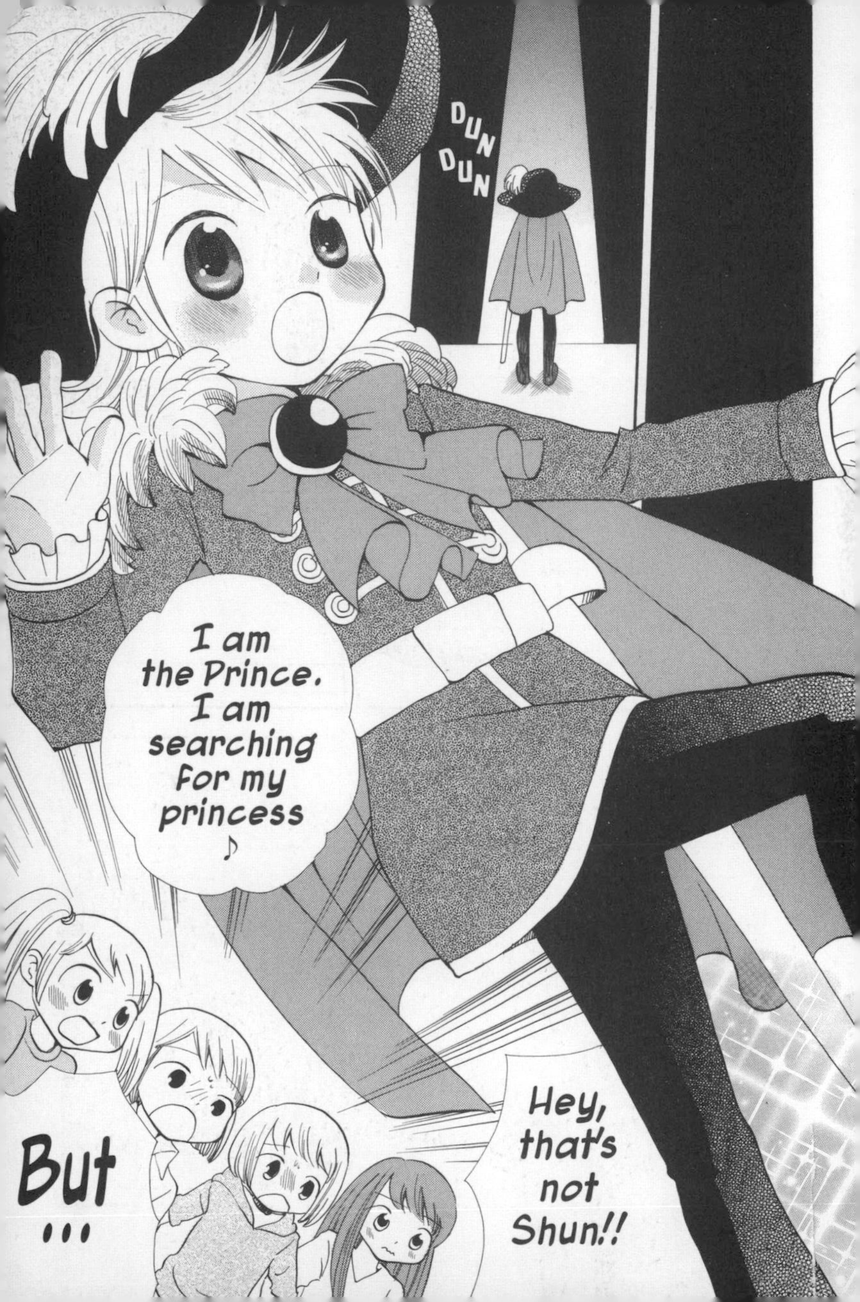
DUN DUN
I am the Prince. I am searching for my princess ♪
Hey, that's not Shun!!
But ...

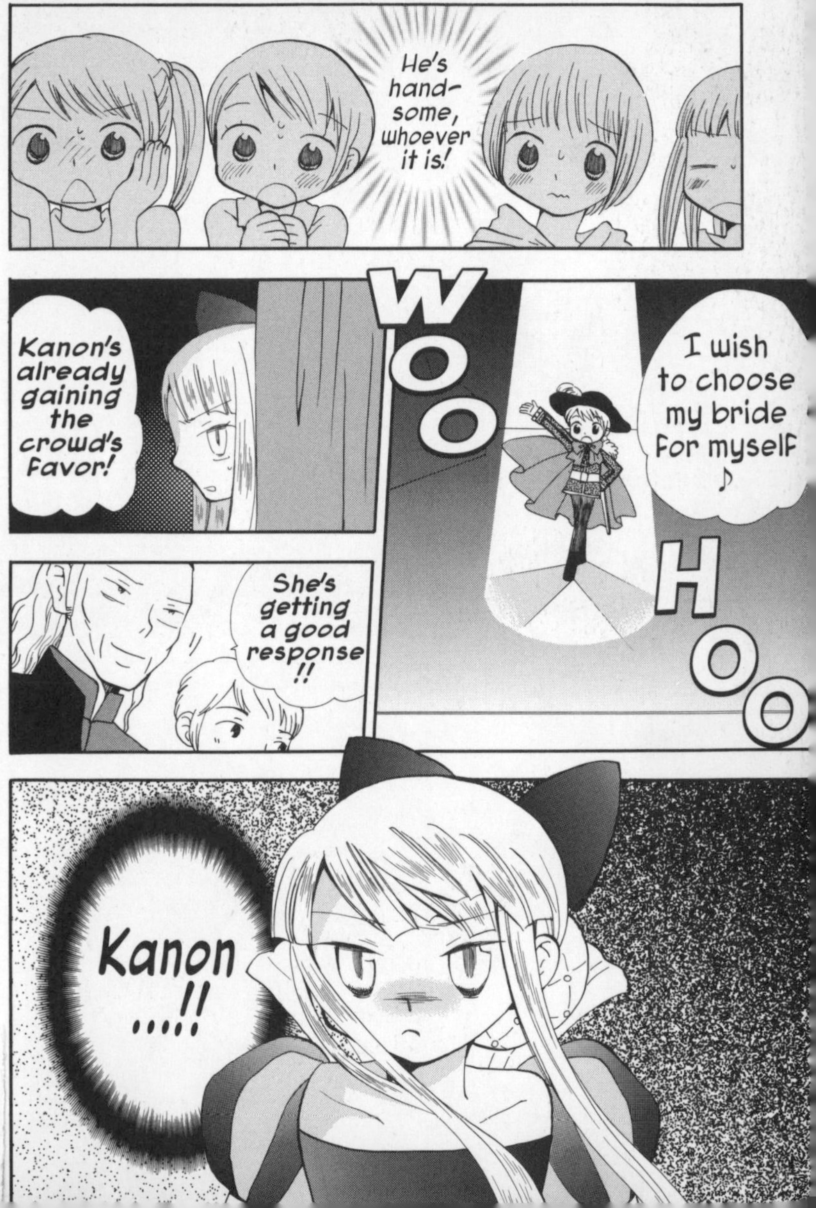
He's handsome, whoever it is!
WOO
HOO
I wish to choose my bride for myself ♪
Kanon's already gaining the crowd's favor!
She's getting a good response!!
Kanon .....!!

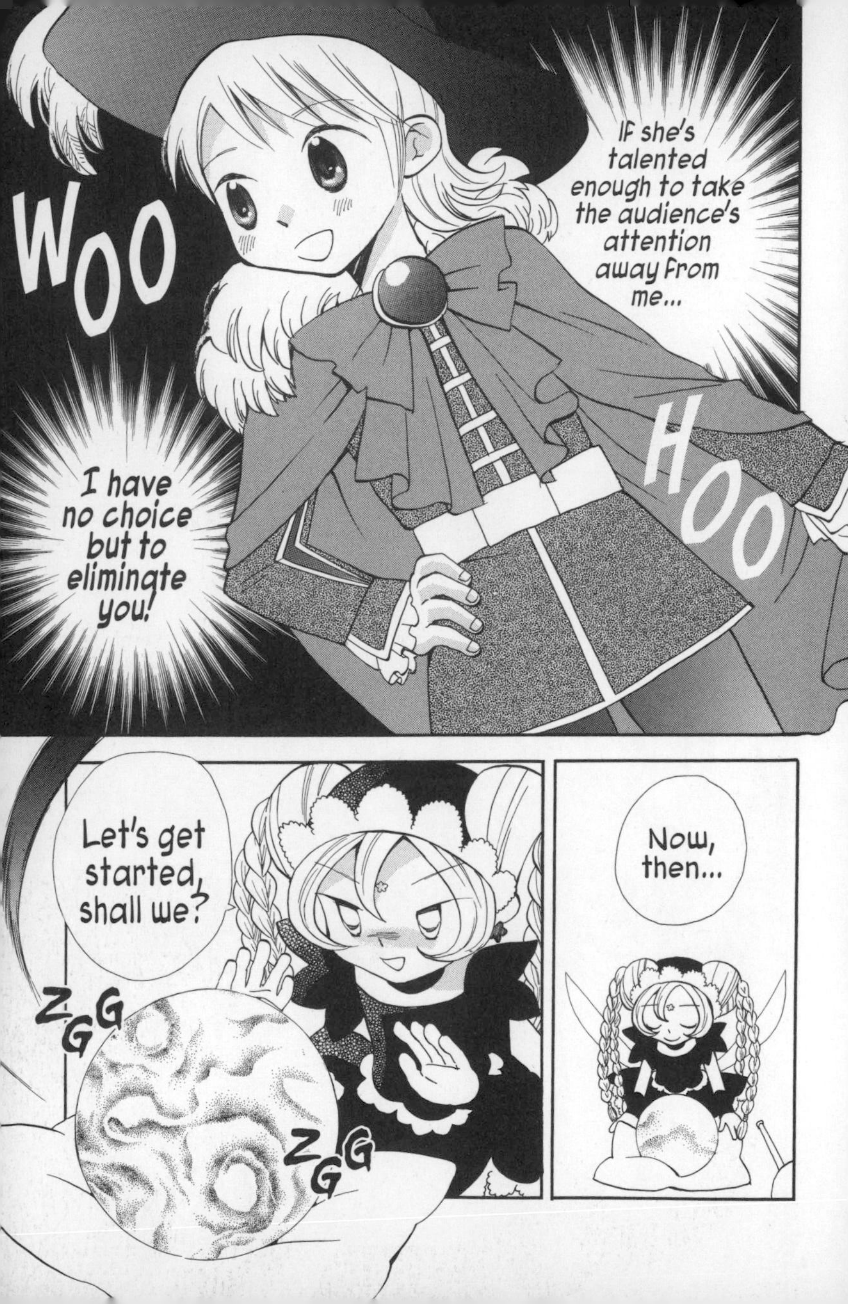
If she's talented enough to take the audience's attention away from me...
WOO
HOO
I have no choice but to eliminate you!
Now, then...
Let's get started, shall we?
ZGG
ZGG

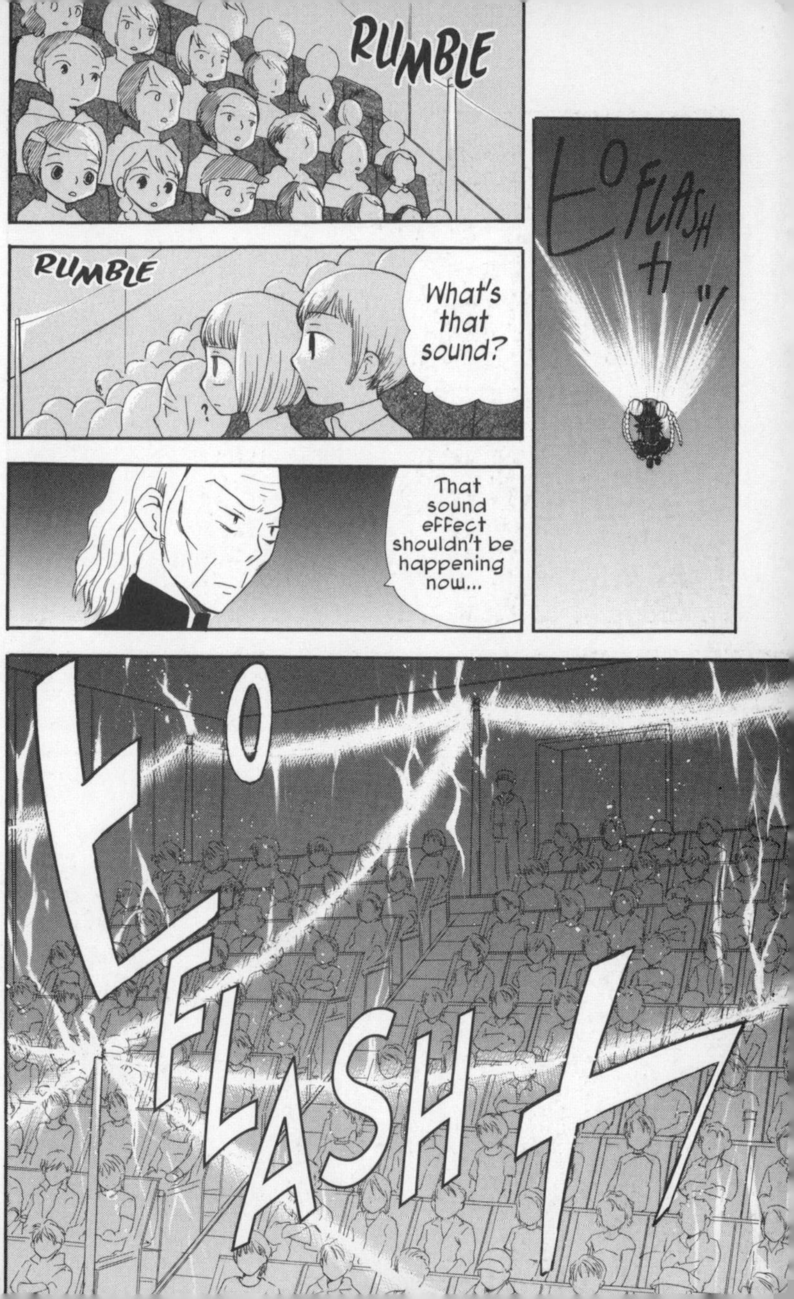
FLASH
RUMBLE
RUMBLE
What's that sound?
?
That sound effect shouldn't be happening now...
FLASH

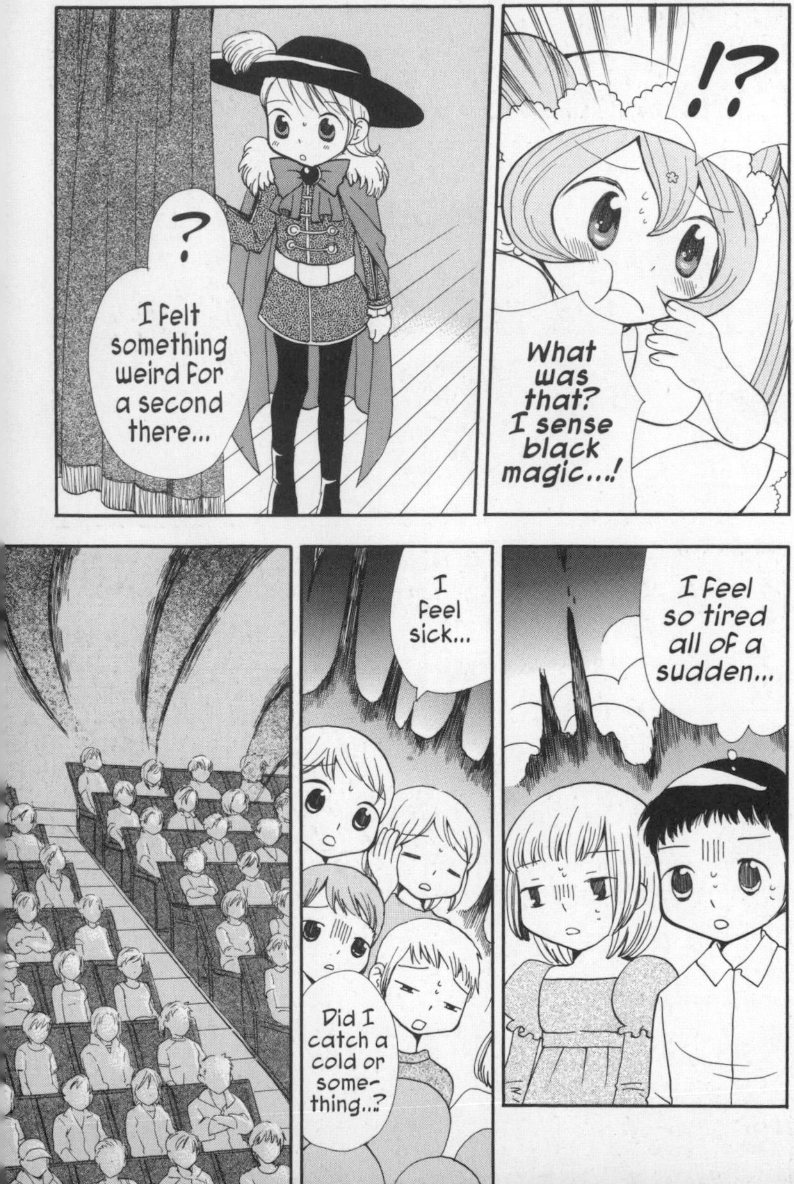
!?
What was that? I sense black magic...!
?
I felt something weird for a second there...
I feel so tired all of a sudden...
I feel sick...
Did I catch a cold or some-thing...?

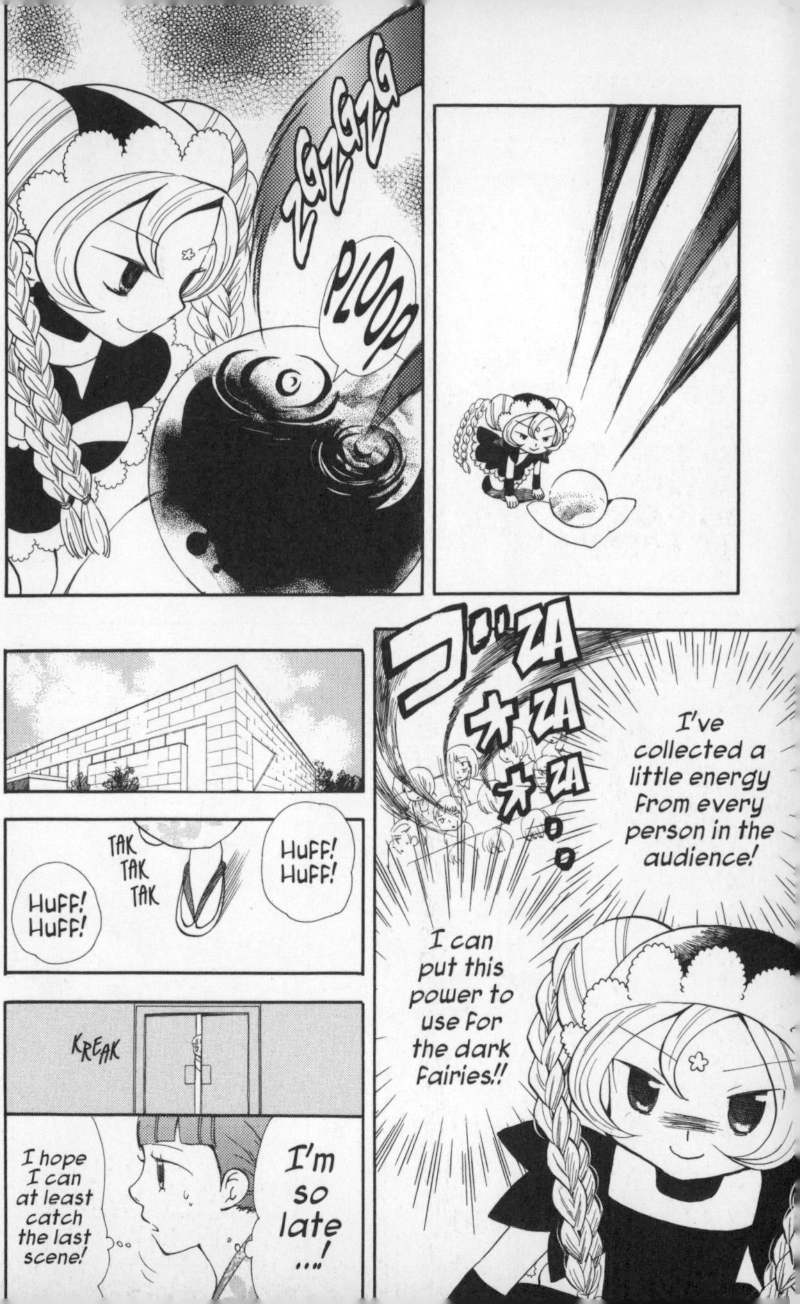
ZGZGZG
PLOOP
ZA
ZA
ZA
I've collected a little energy from every person in the audience!
I can put this power to use for the dark fairies!!
Huff! Huff!
TAK TAK TAK
Huff! Huff!
KREAK
I'm so late...!
I hope I can at least catch the last scene!

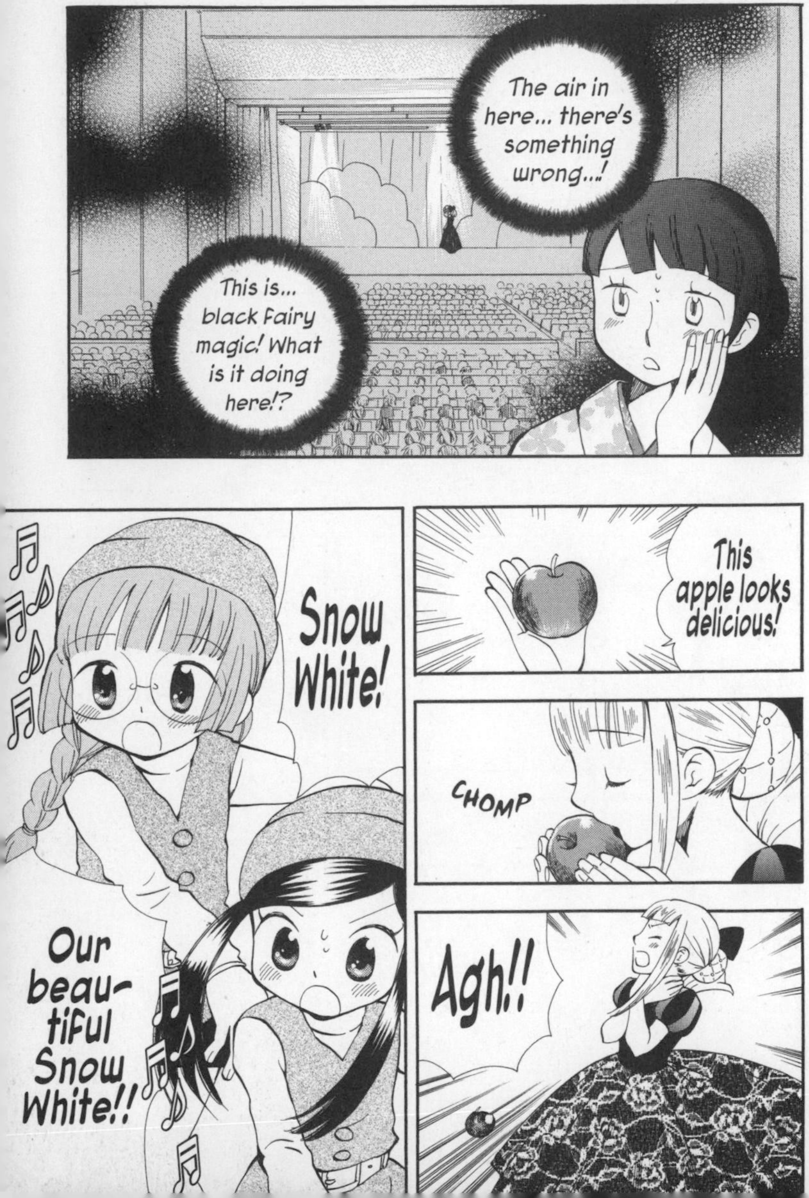
The air in here... there's something wrong...!
This is... black fairy magic! What is it doing here!?
This apple looks delicious!
CHOMP
Agh!!
Snow White!
Our beau-tiful Snow White!!

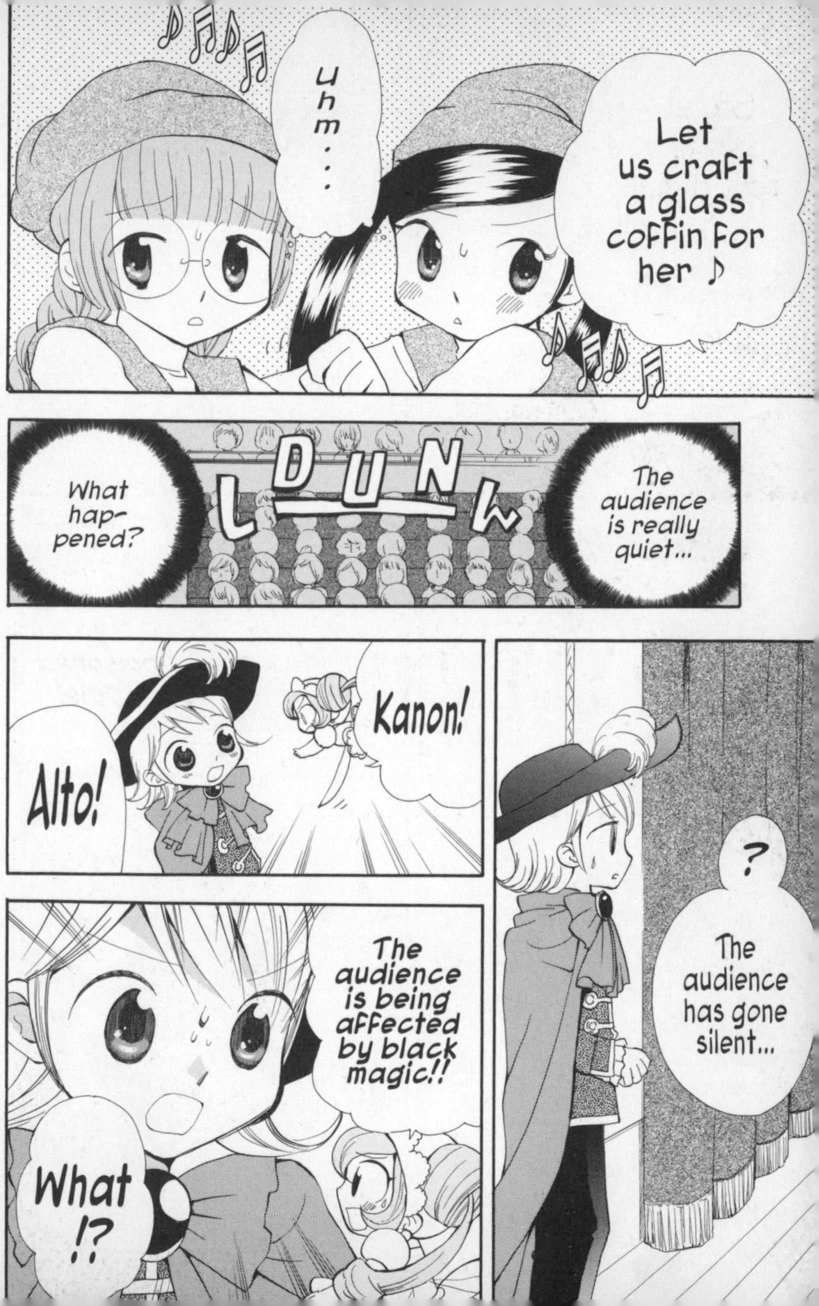

Let us craft a glass coffin for her ♪
Uhm...
The audience is really quiet...
What happened?
?
The audience has gone silent...
Kanon!
Alto!
The audience is being affected by black magic!!
What!?

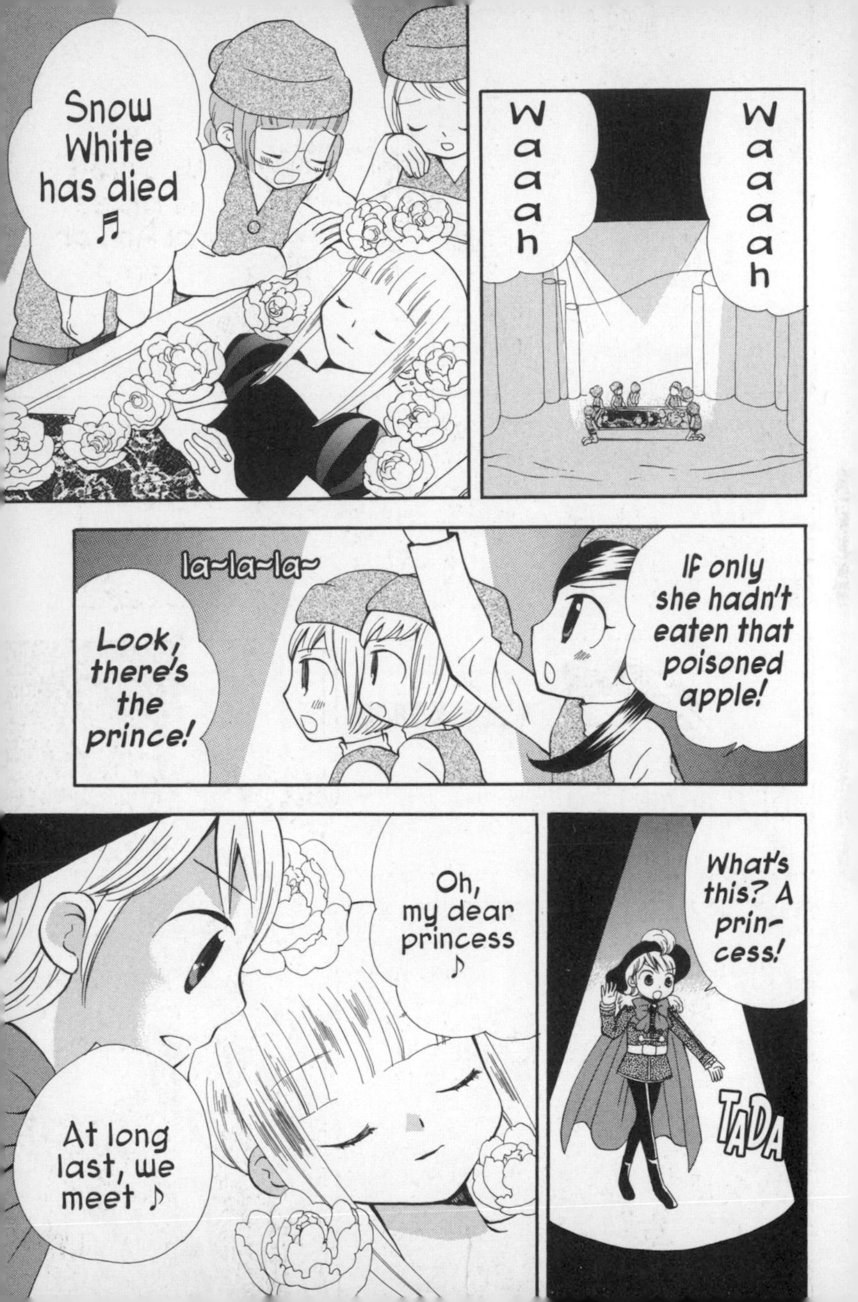
Waaaaah
Waaah
Snow White has died ♬
If only she hadn't eaten that poisoned apple!
la~la~la~
Look, there's the prince!
What's this? A prin-cess!
TADA
Oh, my dear princess ♪
At long last, we meet ♪

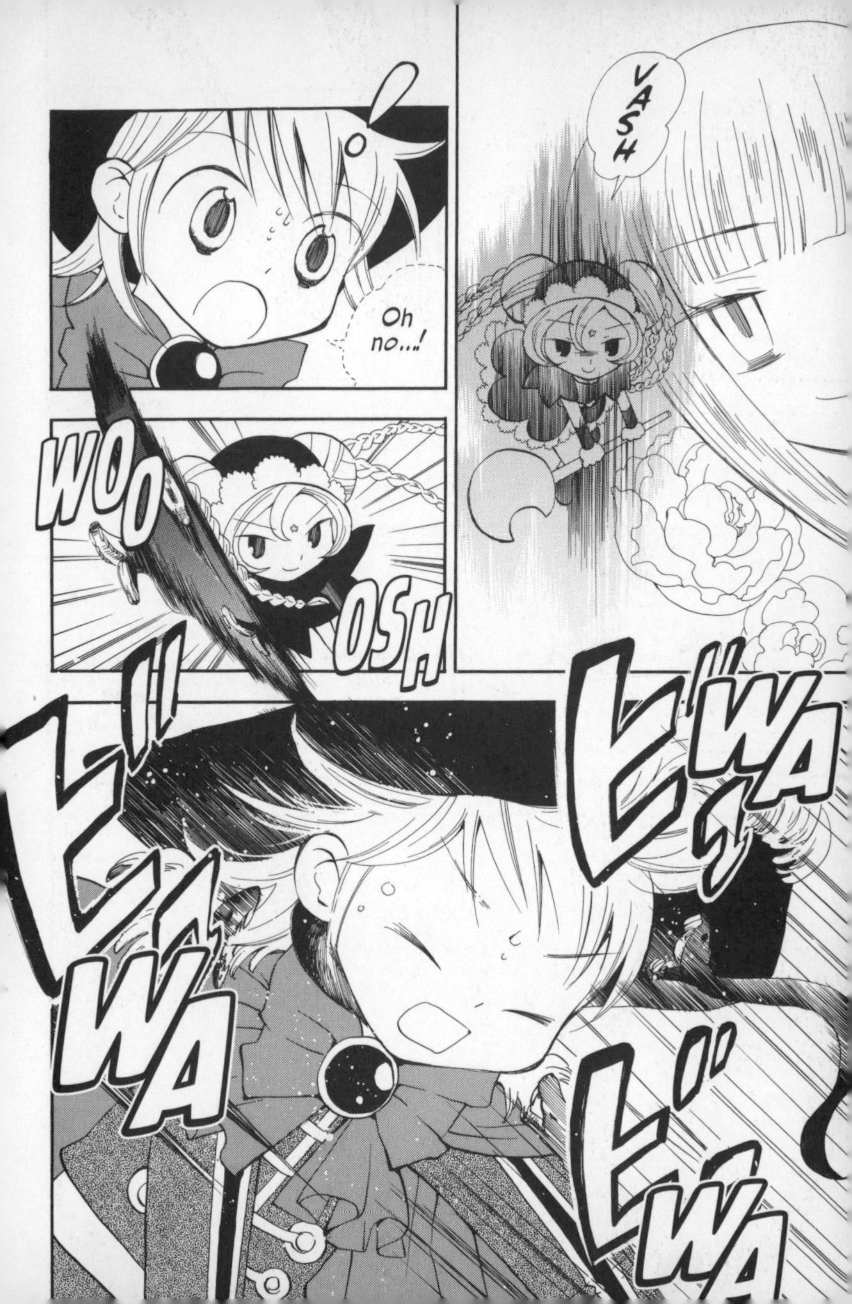
VASH
!
Oh no...!
WOOOSH
ZWA
ZWA
ZWAWA

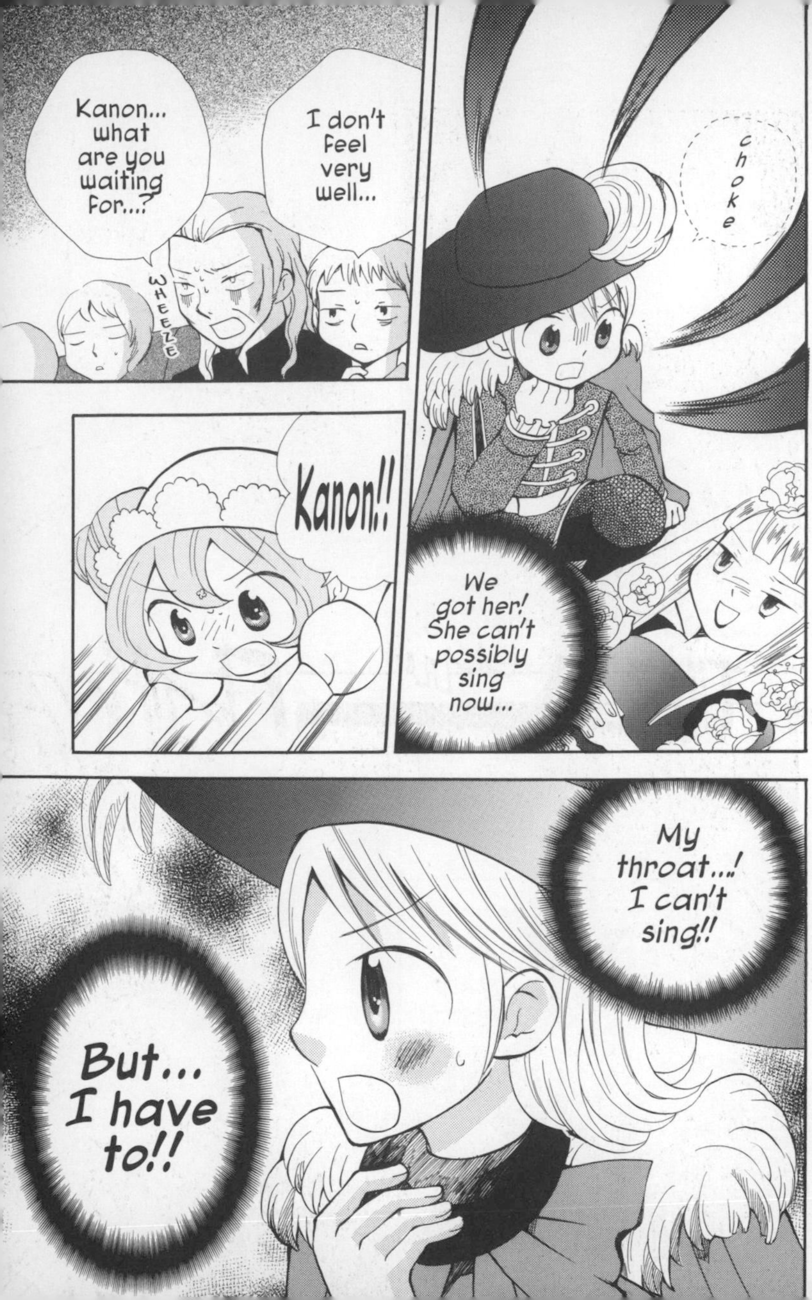
choke
We got her! She can't possibly sing now...
I don't feel very well...
Kanon... what are you waiting for...?
WHEEZE
Kanon!!
My throat...! I can't sing!!
But... I have to!!

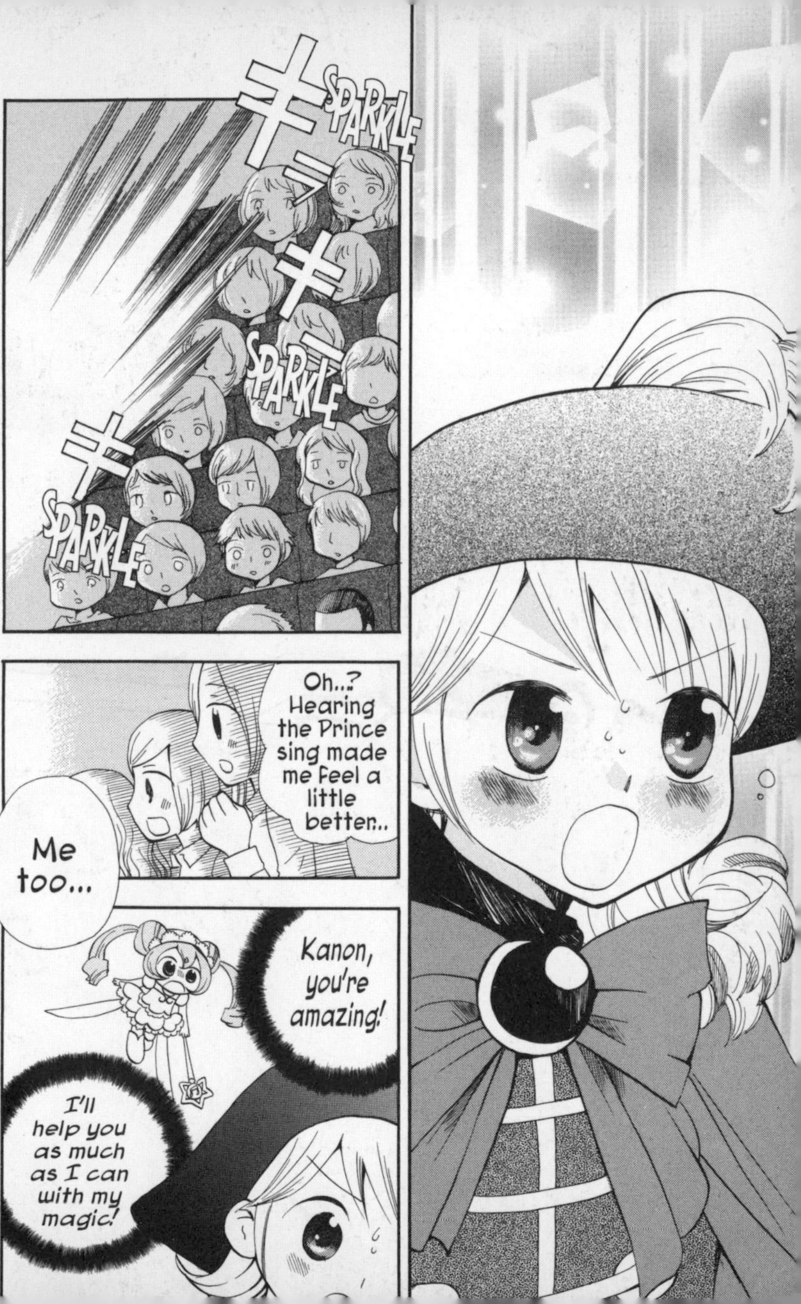
SPARKLE
SPARKLE
SPARKLE
Oh...? Hearing the Prince sing made me feel a little better...
Me too...
Kanon, you're amazing!
I'll help you as much as I can with my magic!

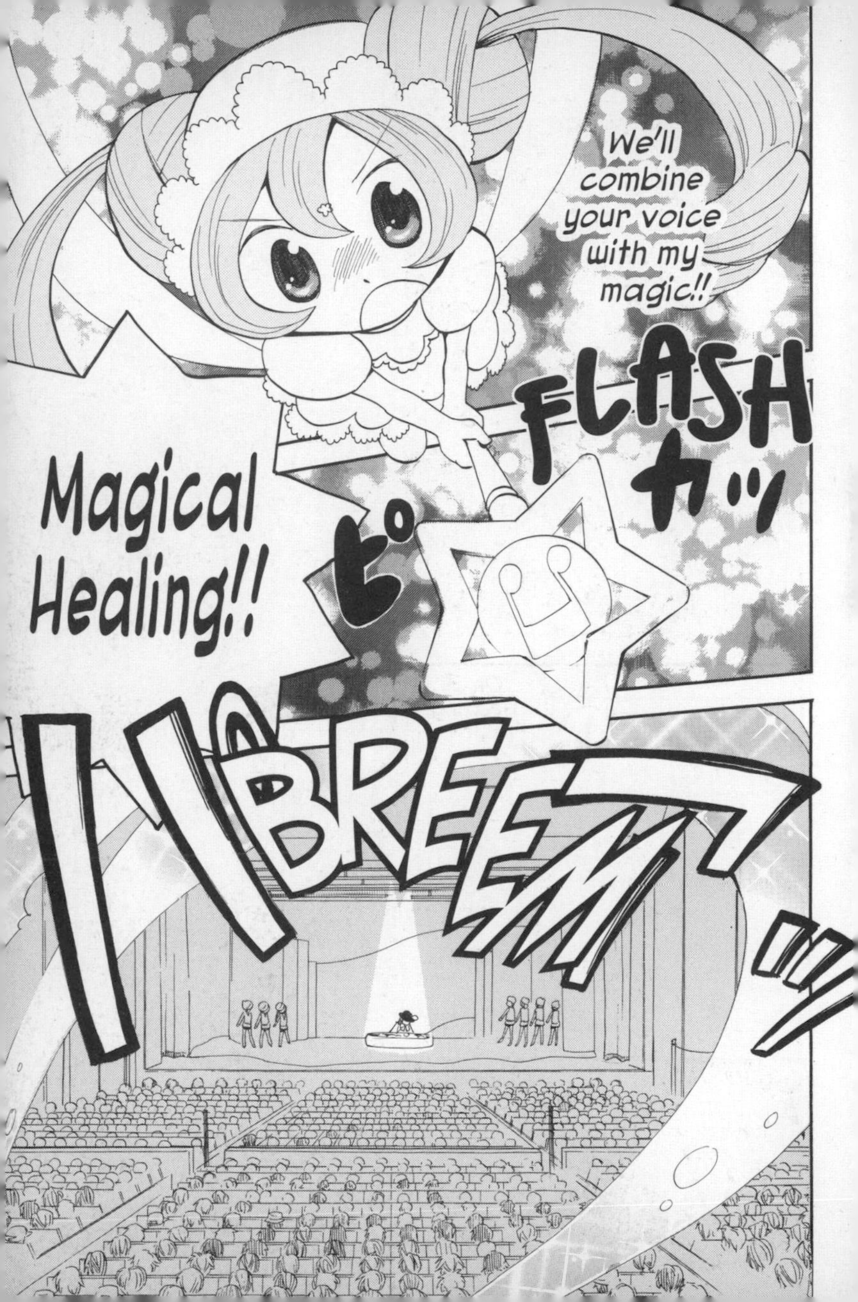
We'll combine your voice with my magic!!
FLASH
カッ
Magical Healing!!
BREEM

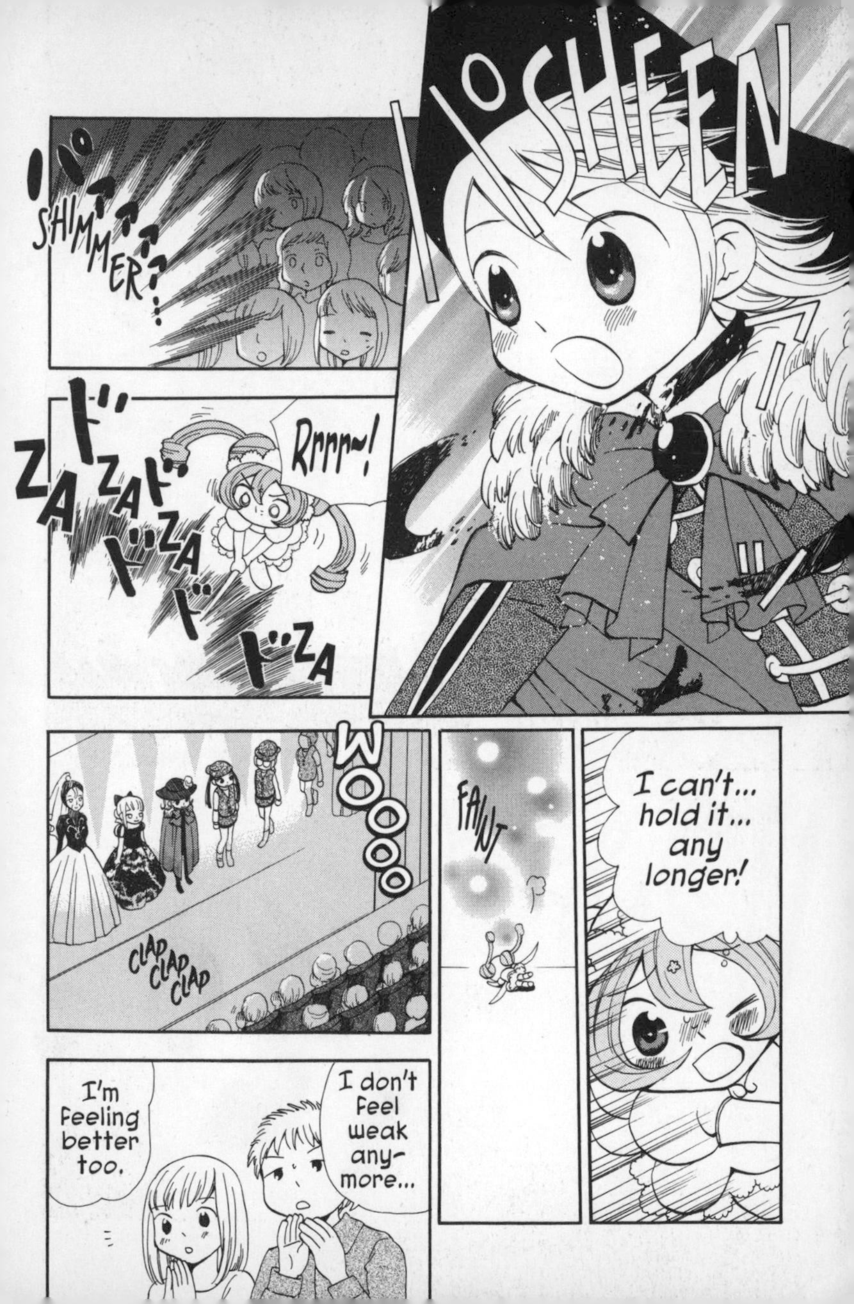
SHEEN
SHIMMER
ZA ZA ZA ZA ZA
Rrrr~!
I can't... hold it... any longer!
FAINT
WOOOO
CLAP CLAP CLAP
I don't feel weak any-more...
I'm feeling better too.

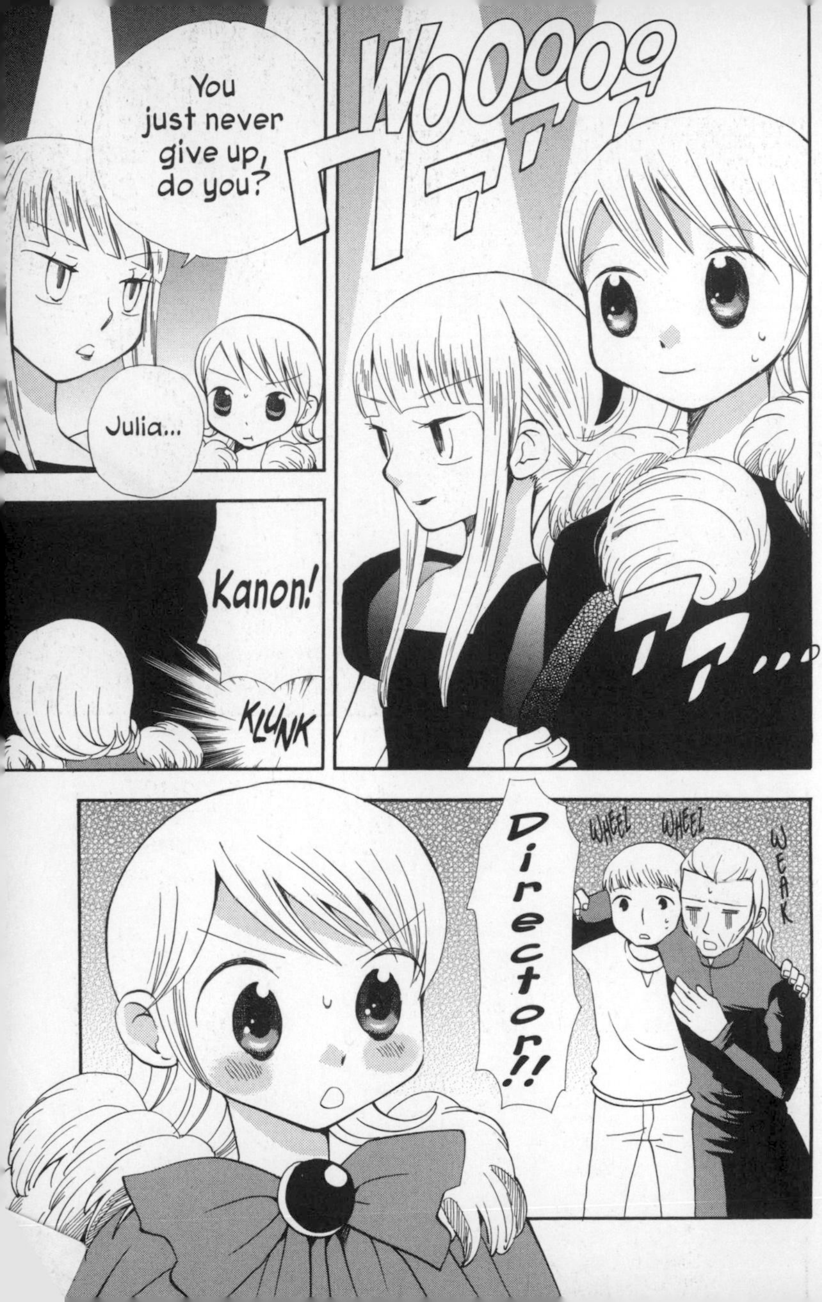
WOOOOO
You just never give up, do you?
Julia...
Kanon!
KLUNK
Director!!
WHEEZ
WHEEZ
WEAK

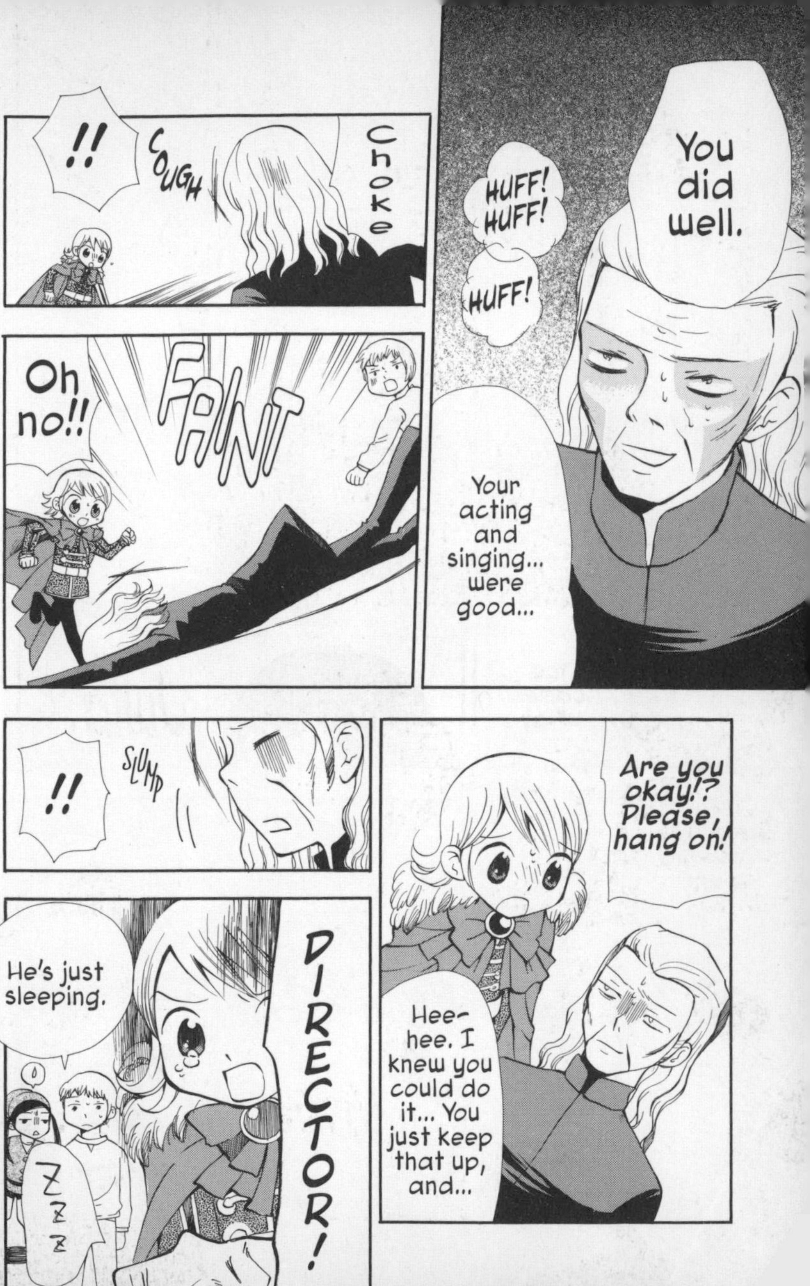

You did well.
HUFF! HUFF!
HUFF!
Your acting and singing... were good...
Choke
COUGH
!!
FAINT
Oh no!!
Are you okay!? Please, hang on!
Hee-hee. I knew you could do it... You just keep that up, and...
SLUMP
!!
DIRECTOR!
He's just sleeping.
Zzz

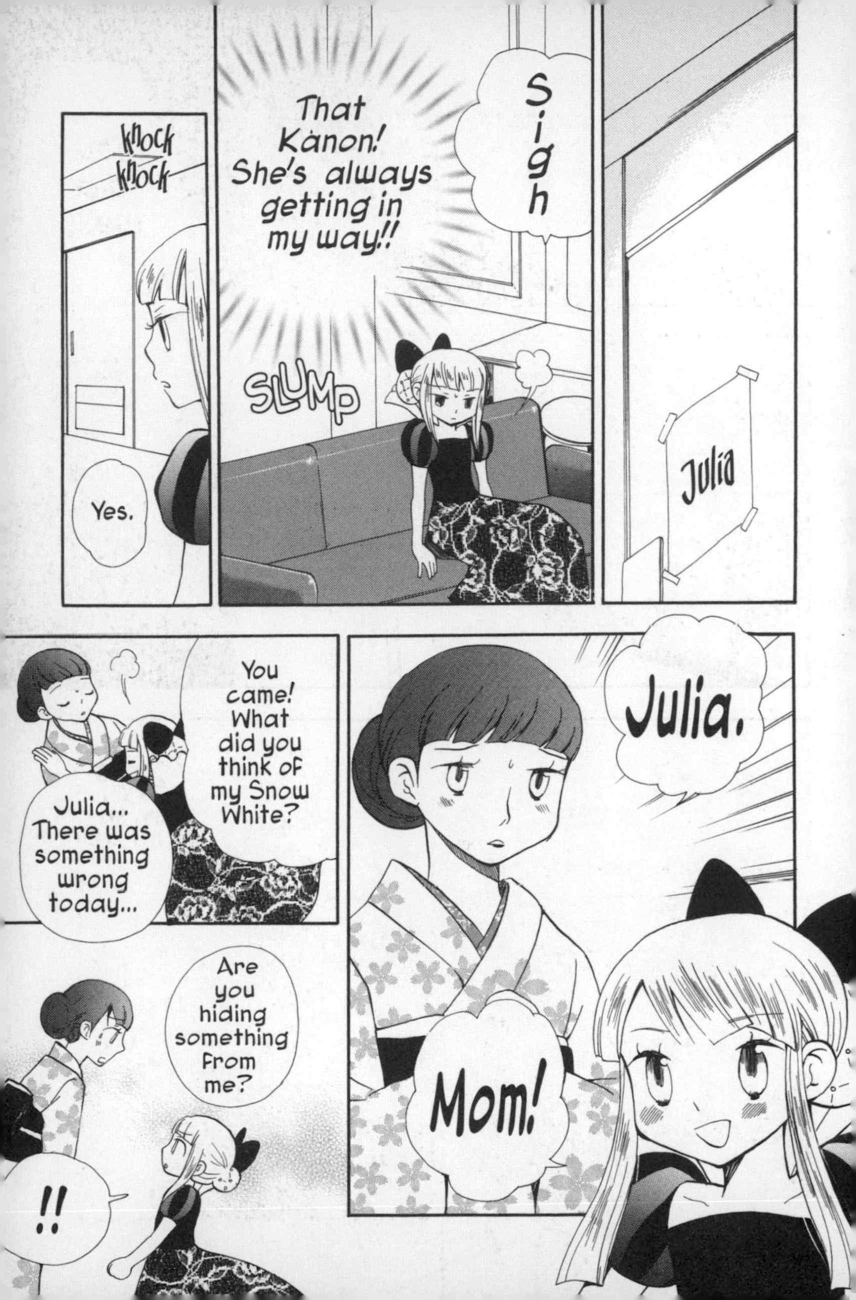
Julia
Sigh
That Kanon! She's always getting in my way!!
SLUMP
knock knock
Yes.
Julia.
Mom!
You came! What did you think of my Snow White?
Julia... There was something wrong today...
Are you hiding something from me?
!!

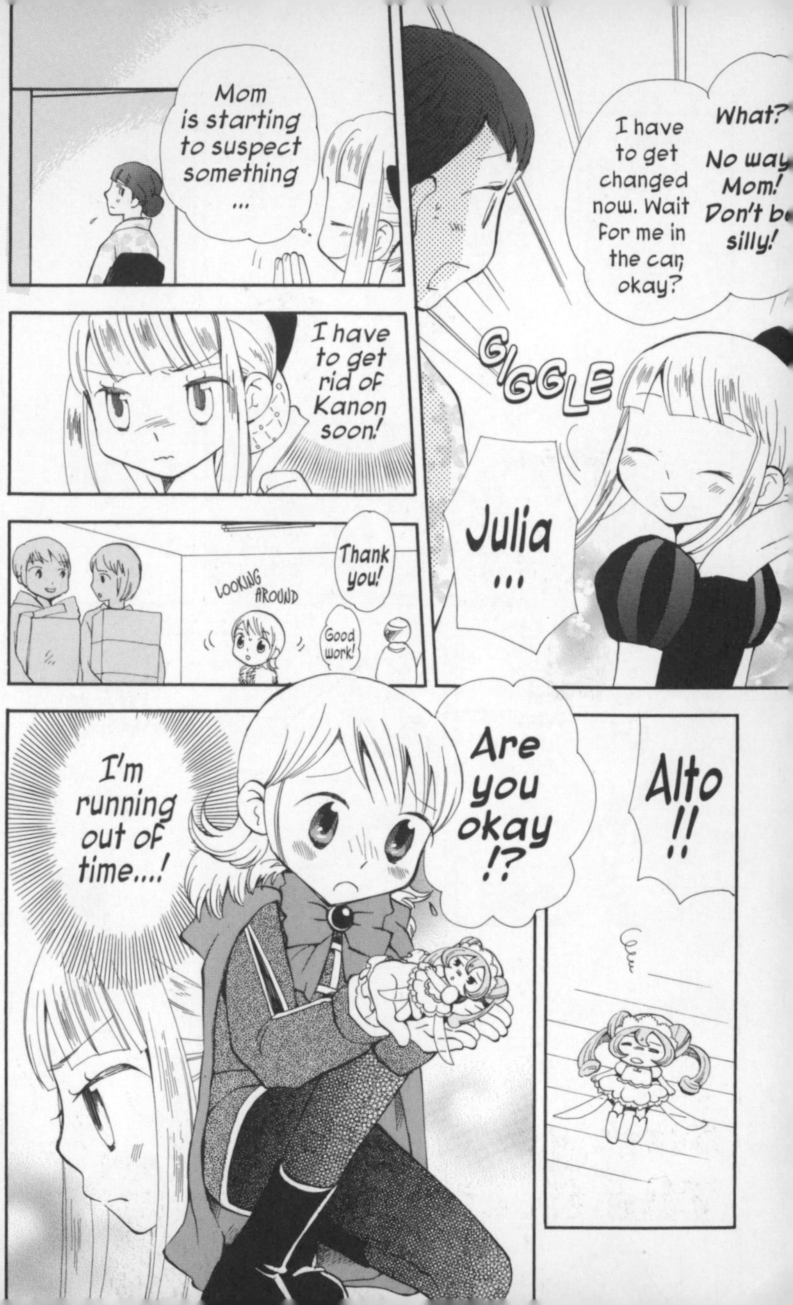
What? No way Mom! Don't be silly!
I have to get changed now. Wait for me in the car, okay?
GIGGLE
Julia ...
Mom is starting to suspect something ...
I have to get rid of Kanon soon!
Thank you!
LOOKING AROUND
Good work!
Alto !!
Are you okay !?
I'm running out of time...!

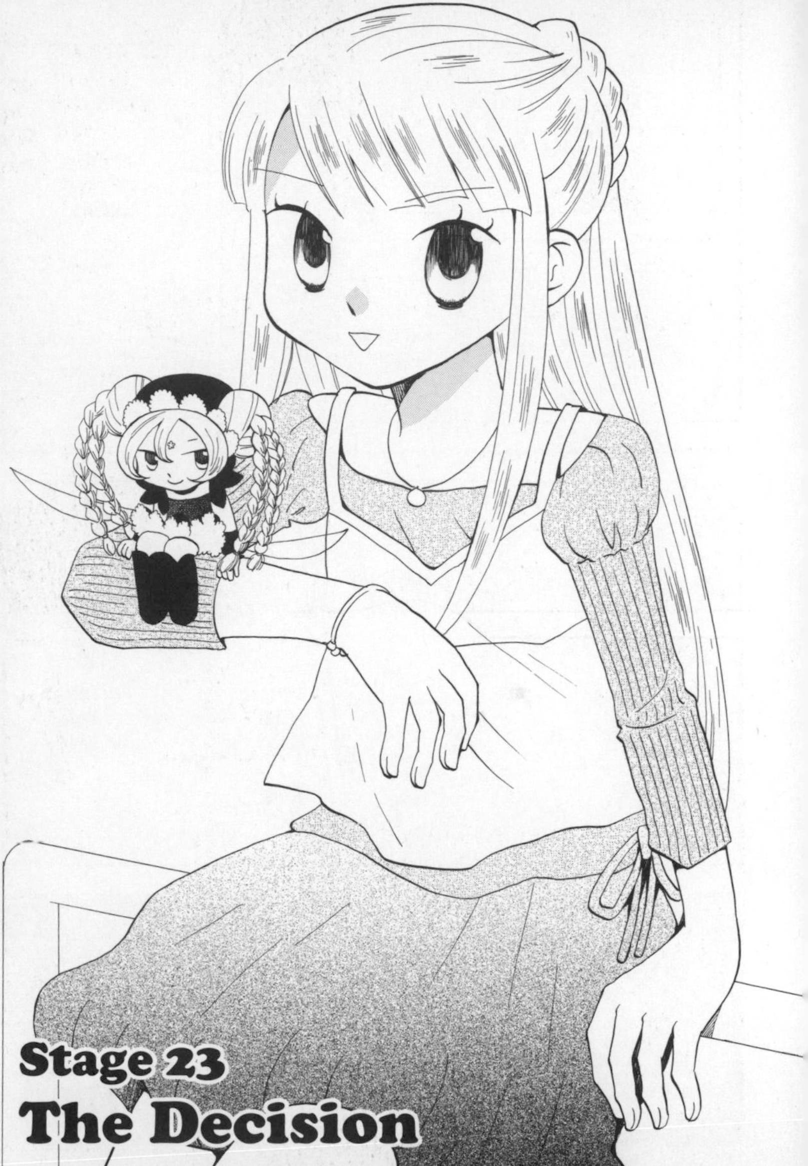
Stage 23
The Decision

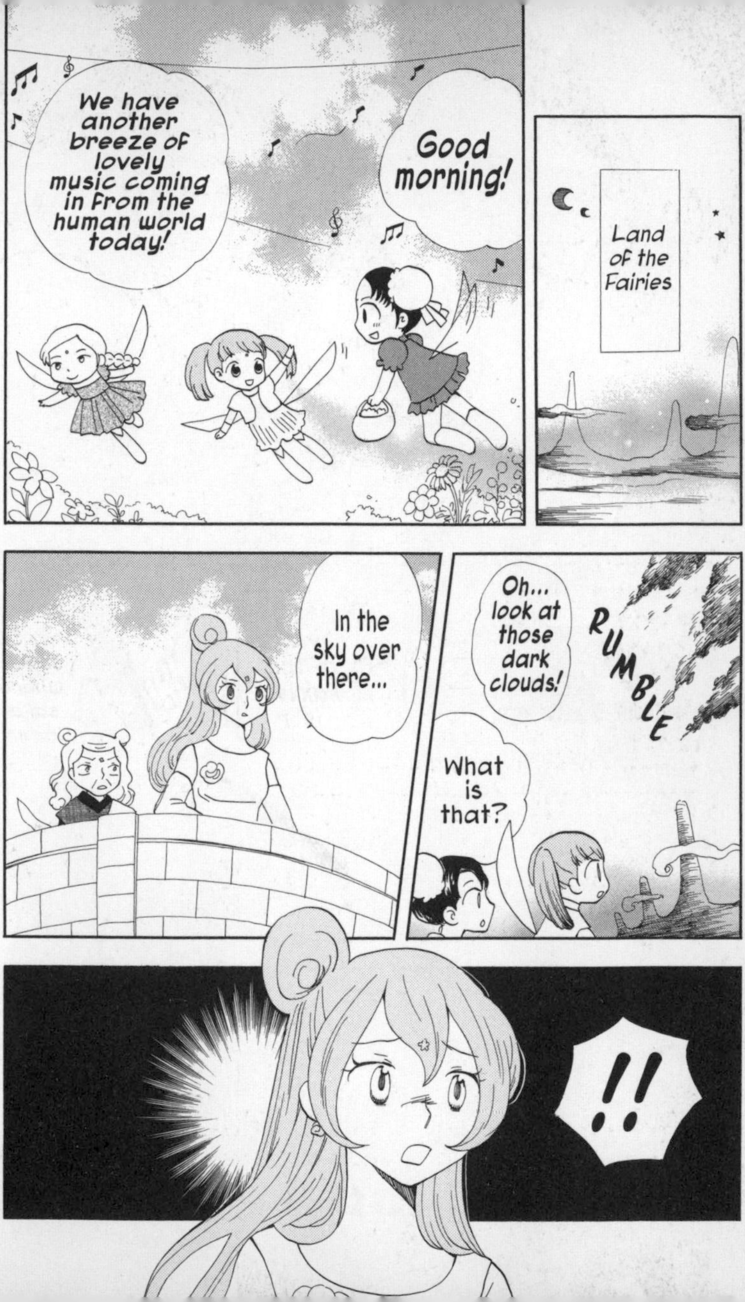
Land of the Fairies
Good morning!
We have another breeze of lovely music coming in from the human world today!
Oh... look at those dark clouds!
RUMBLE
What is that?
In the sky over there...
!!

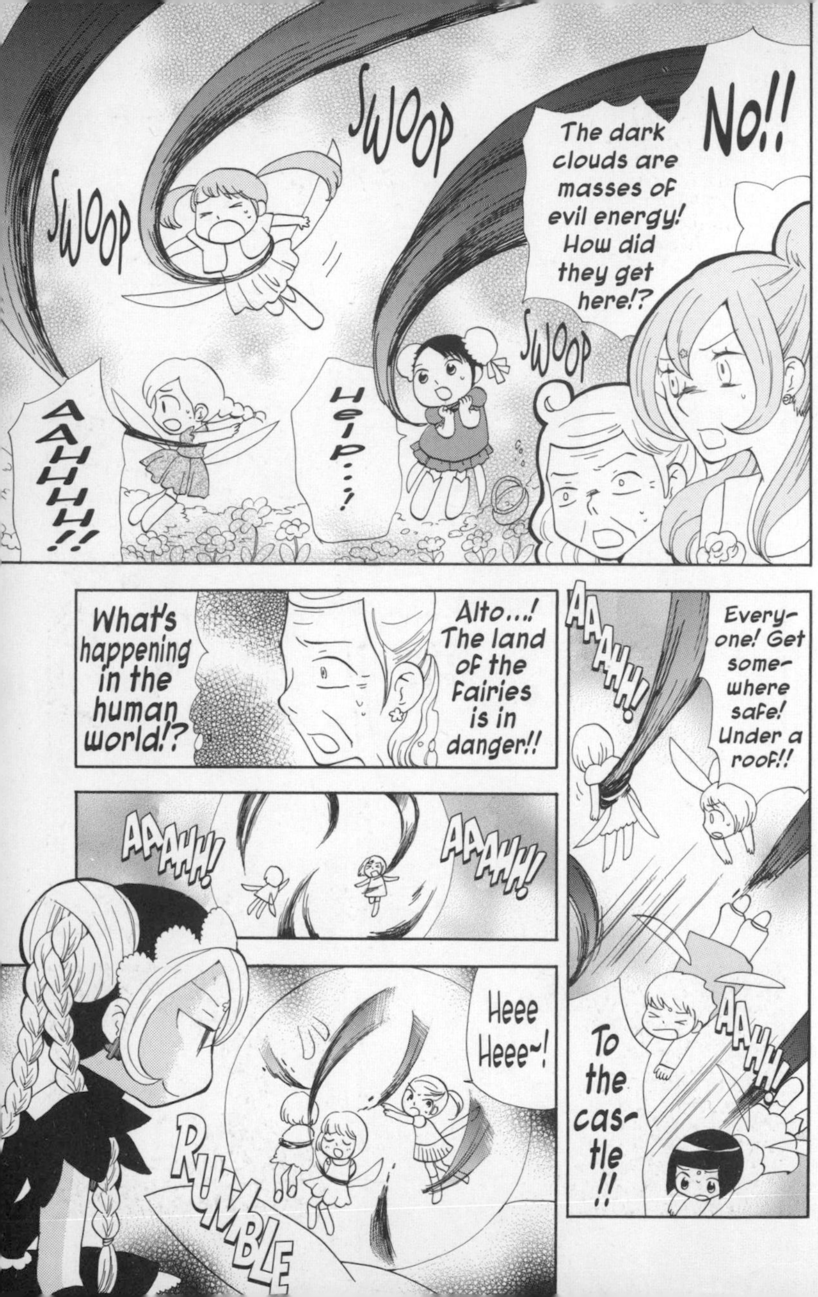

No!!
The dark clouds are masses of evil energy! How did they get here!?
SWOOP
SWOOP
Help...!
SWOOP
AAHHHH!!
Every-one! Get some-where safe! Under a roof!!
AAAHH!
AAHH!
To the cas-tle!!
Alto...! The land of the fairies is in danger!!
What's happening in the human world!?
AAAHH!
AAAHH!
Heee Heee~!
RUMBLE

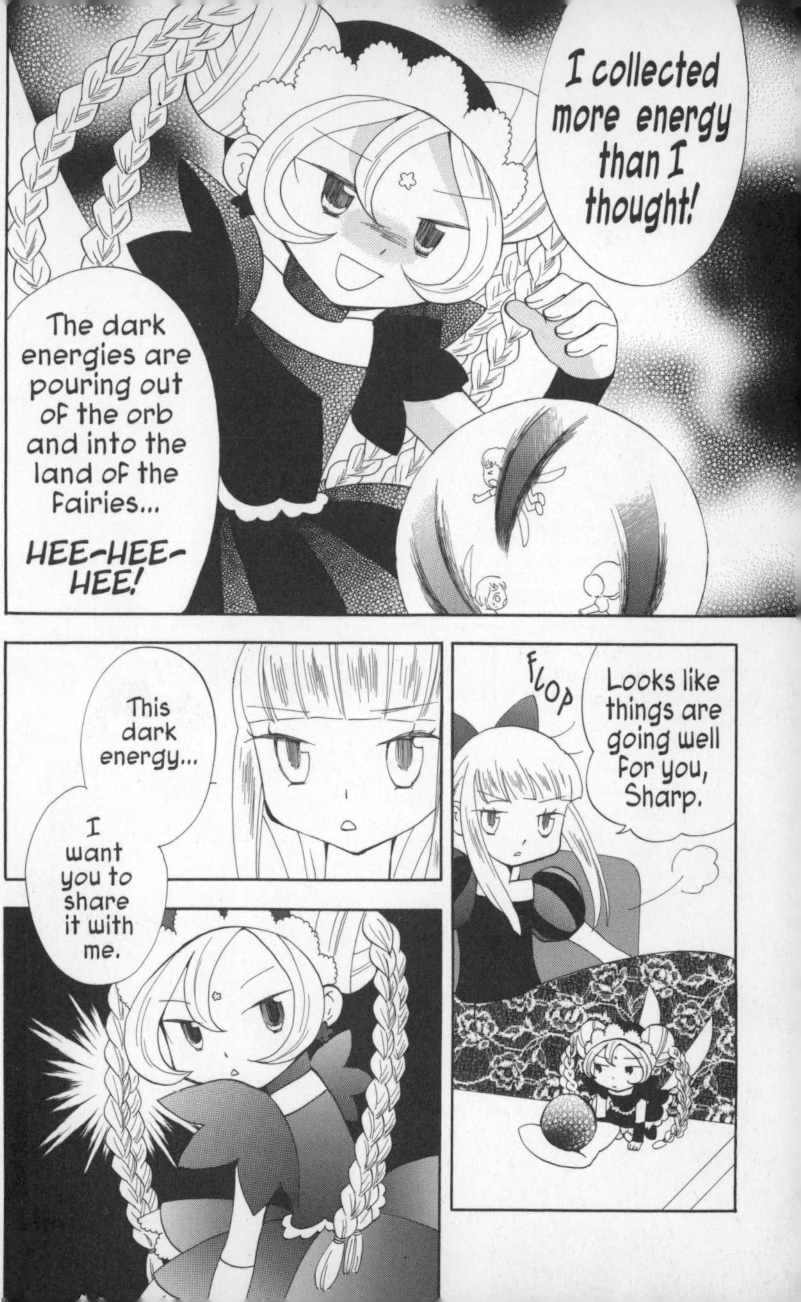
I collected more energy than I thought!
The dark energies are pouring out of the orb and into the land of the fairies...
HEE-HEE-HEE!
FLOP
Looks like things are going well for you, Sharp.
This dark energy...
I want you to share it with me.

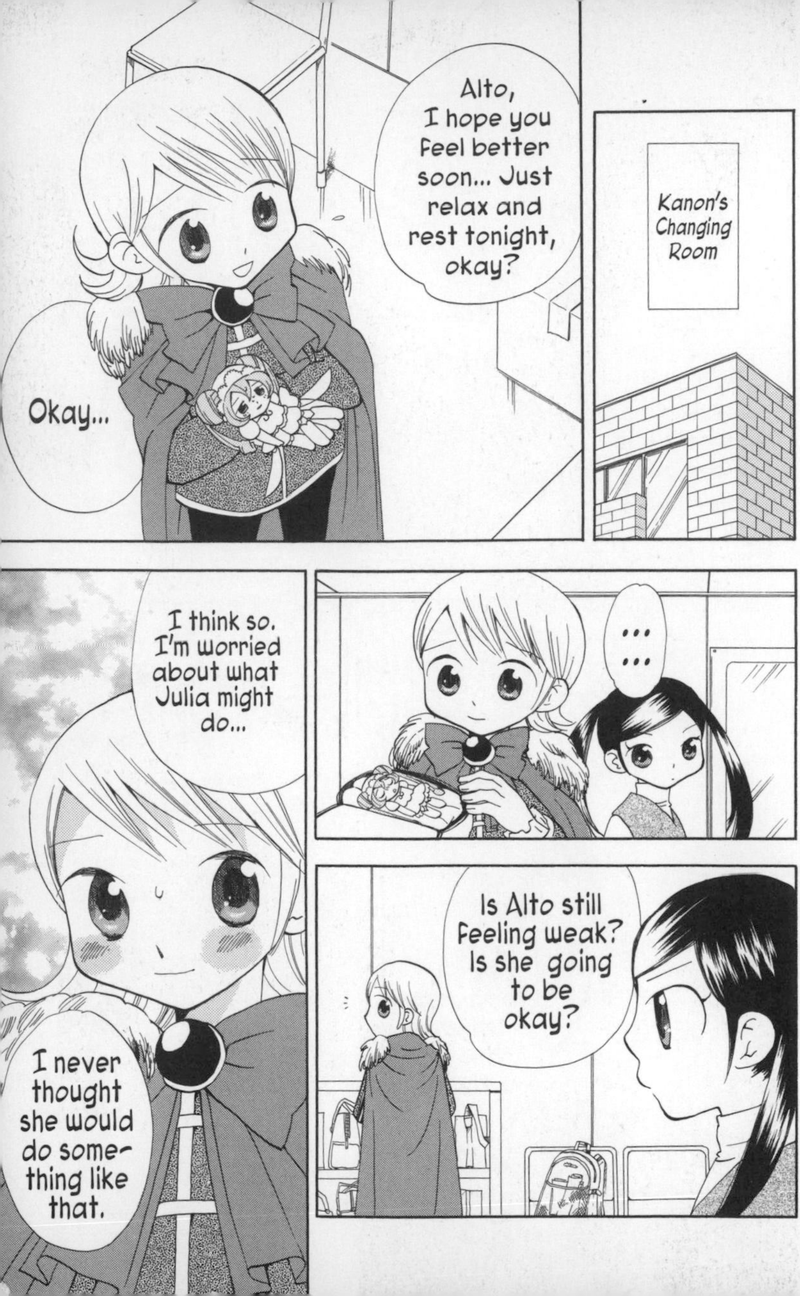
Kanon's Changing Room
Alto, I hope you feel better soon... Just relax and rest tonight, okay?
Okay...
... ...
Is Alto still feeling weak? Is she going to be okay?
I think so. I'm worried about what Julia might do...
I never thought she would do some-thing like that.

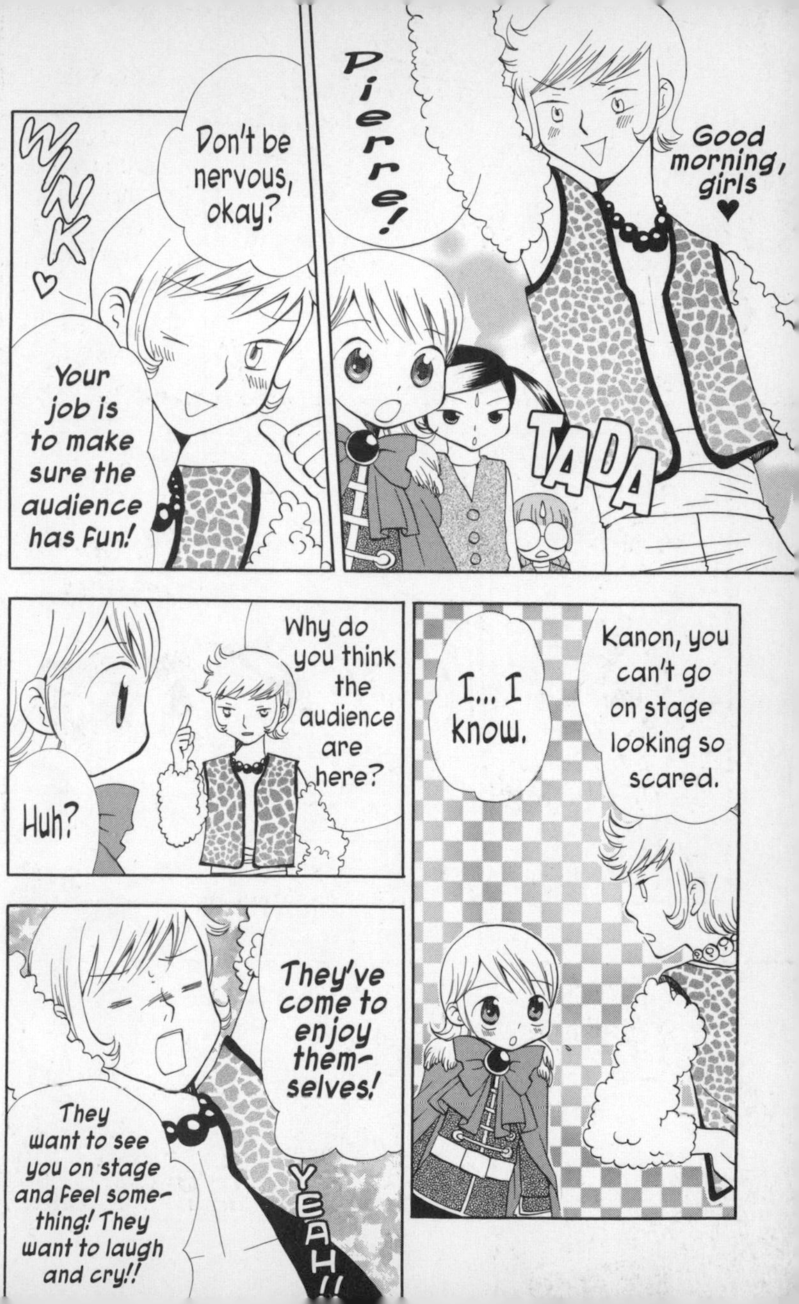
Good morning, girls ♥
TADA
Pierre!
Don't be nervous, okay?
WINK ♥
Your job is to make sure the audience has fun!
Kanon, you can't go on stage looking so scared.
I... I know.
Why do you think the audience are here?
Huh?
They've come to enjoy them-selves!
They want to see you on stage and feel some-thing! They want to laugh and cry!!
YEAH!!

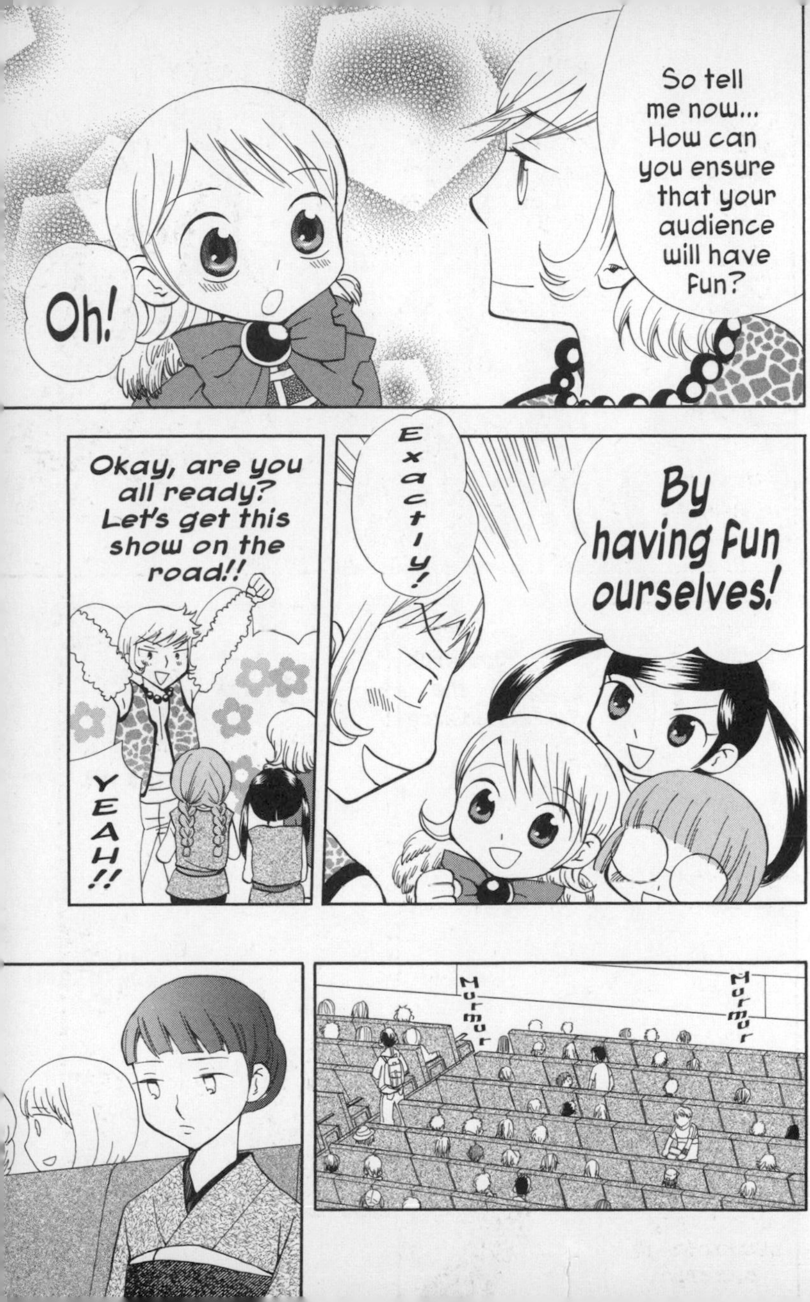
So tell me now... How can you ensure that your audience will have fun?
Oh!
By having fun ourselves!
Exactly!
Okay, are you all ready? Let's get this show on the road!!
YEAH!!
Murmur
Murmur

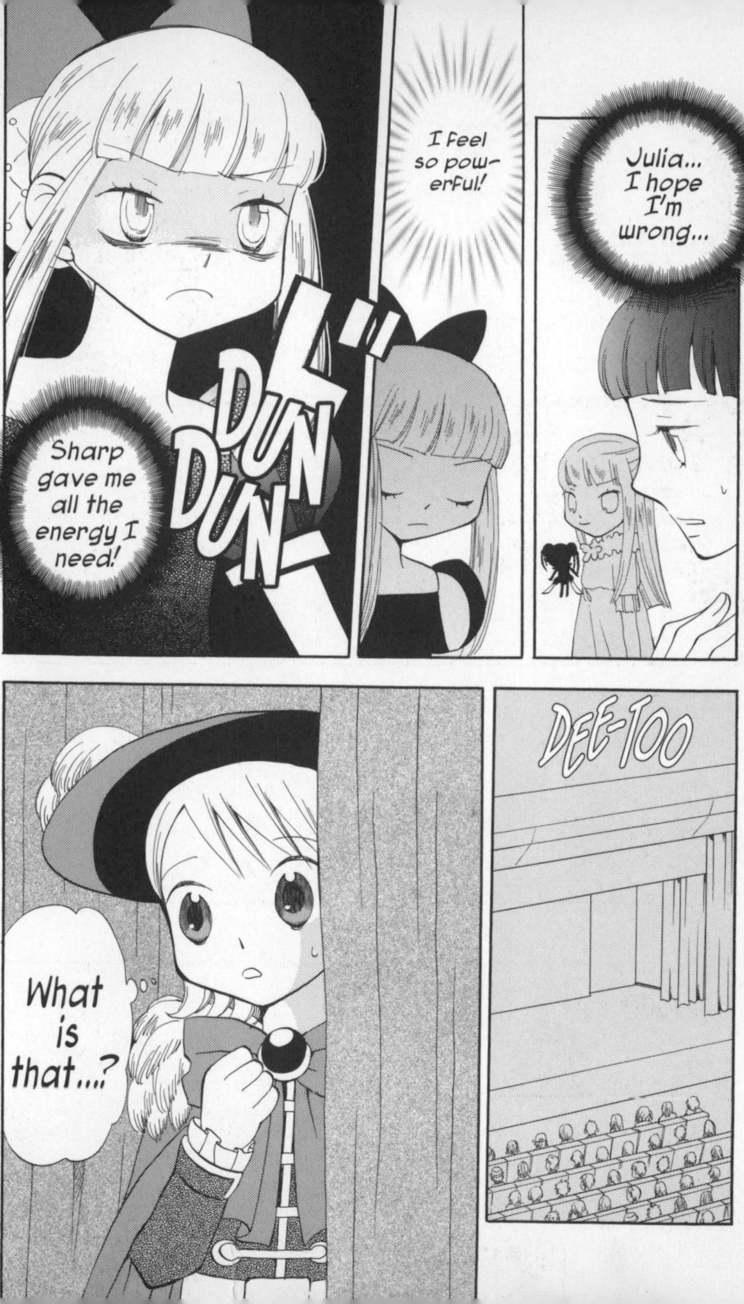
Julia... I hope I'm wrong...
I feel so pow-erful!
DUN DUN DUN DUN
Sharp gave me all the energy I need!
DEE-TOO
What is that...?

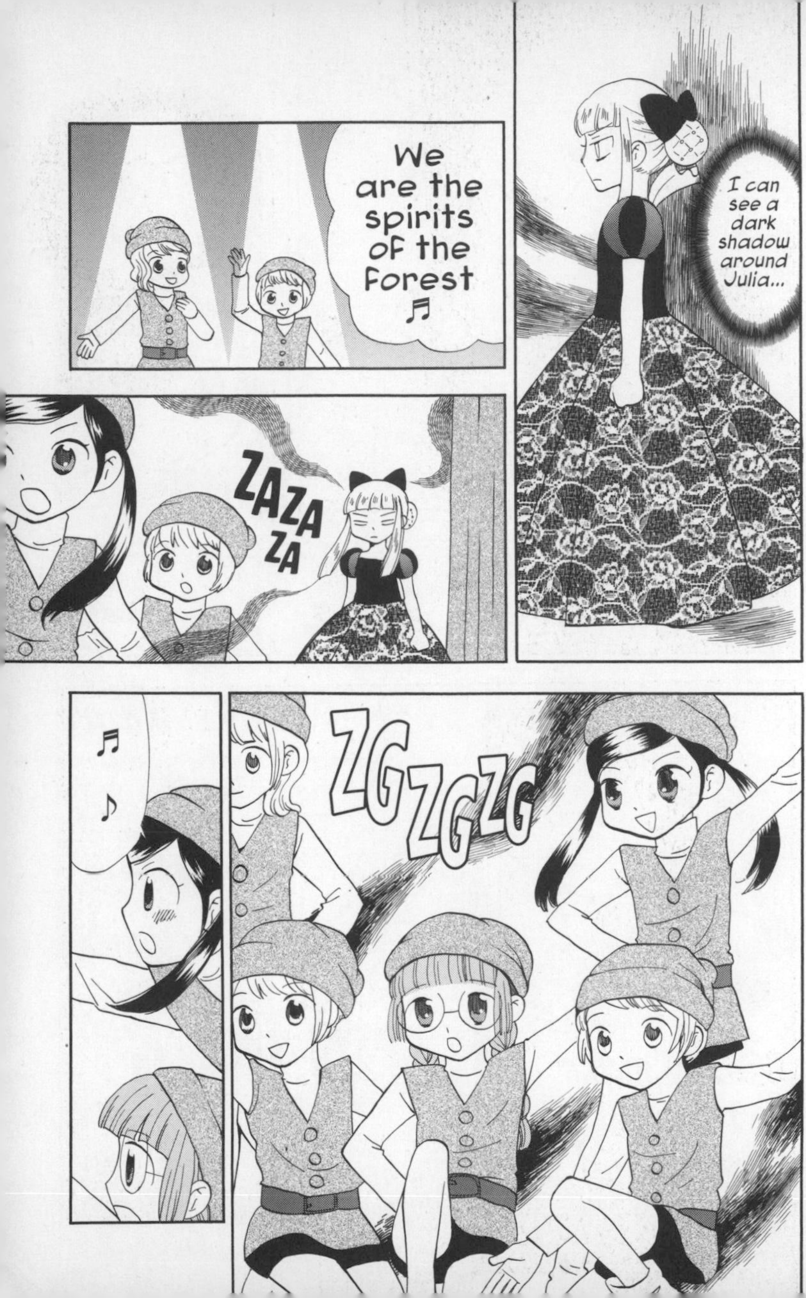

I can see a dark shadow around Julia...
We are the spirits of the forest ♬
ZAZAZA ZA
ZG ZG ZG
♬ ♪

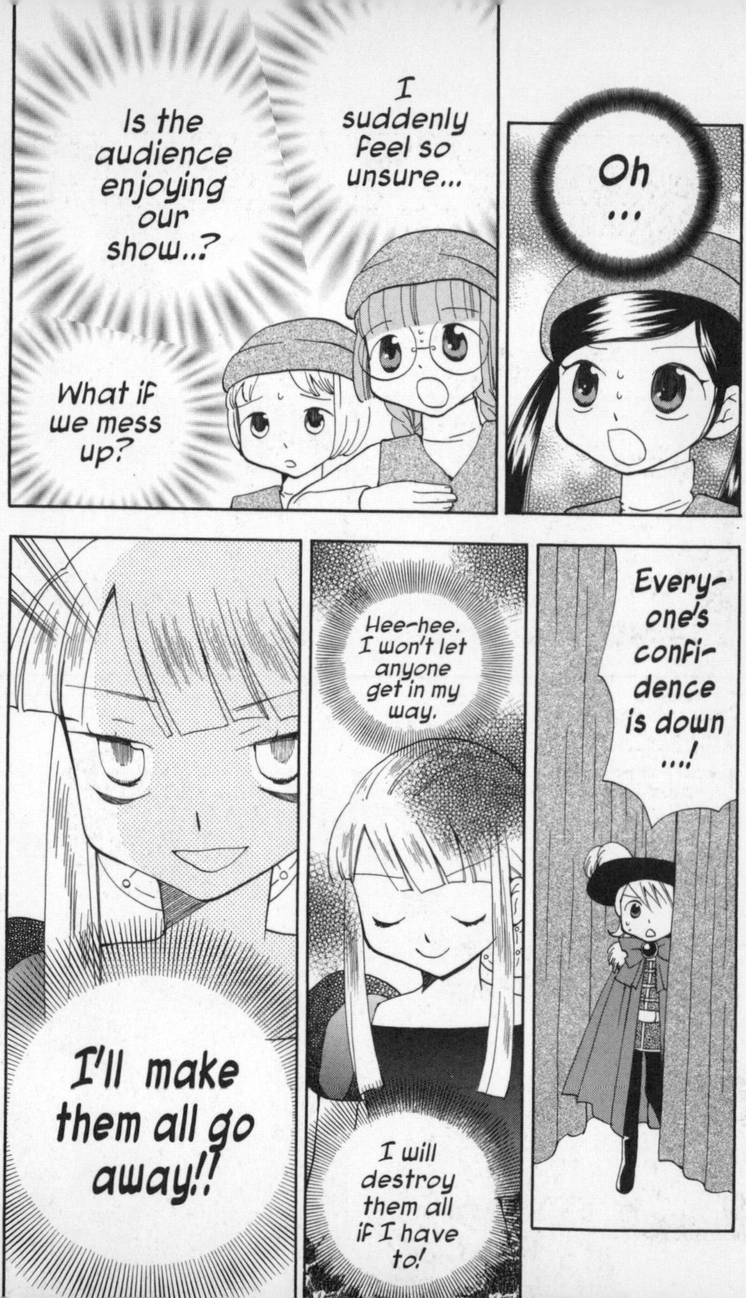
Oh ...
I suddenly feel so unsure...
Is the audience enjoying our show..?
What if we mess up?
Every-one's confi-dence is down ...!
Hee-hee. I won't let anyone get in my way.
I will destroy them all if I have to!
I'll make them all go away!!

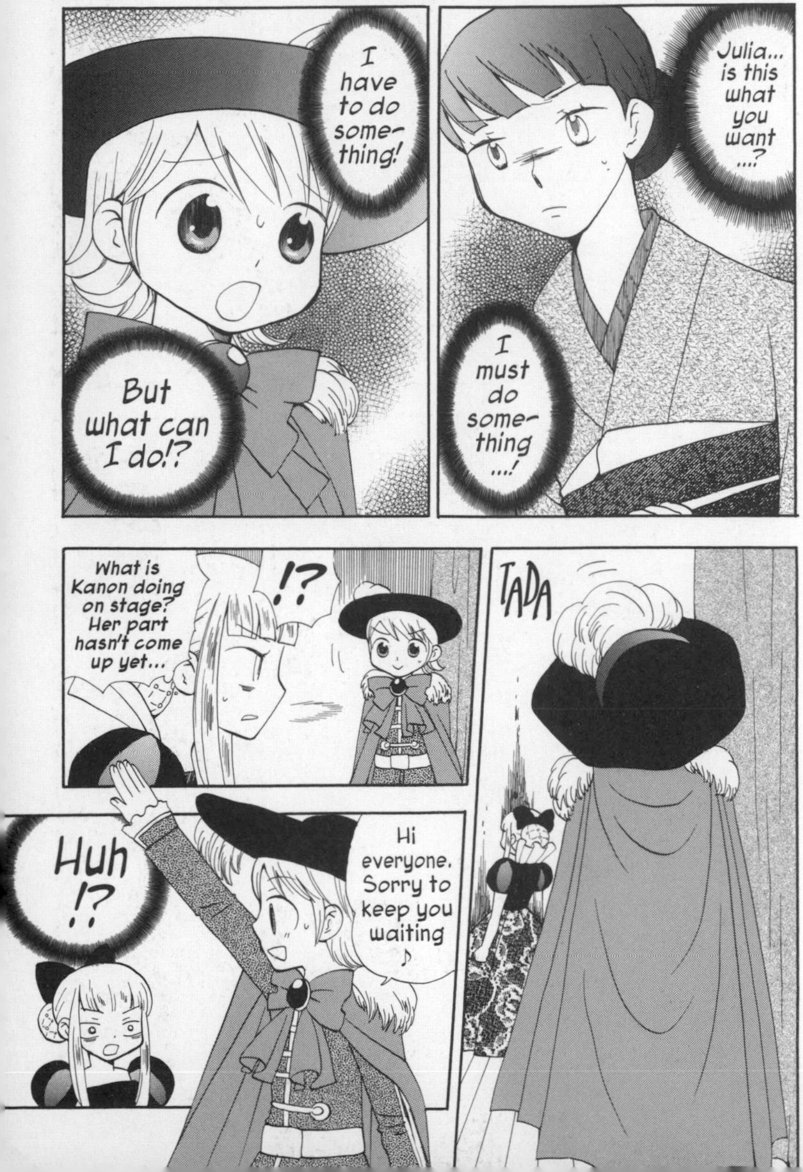
Julia... is this what you want ...?
I must do some-thing ...!
I have to do some-thing!
But what can I do!?
TADA
!?
What is Kanon doing on stage? Her part hasn't come up yet...
Hi everyone. Sorry to keep you waiting ♪
Huh !?

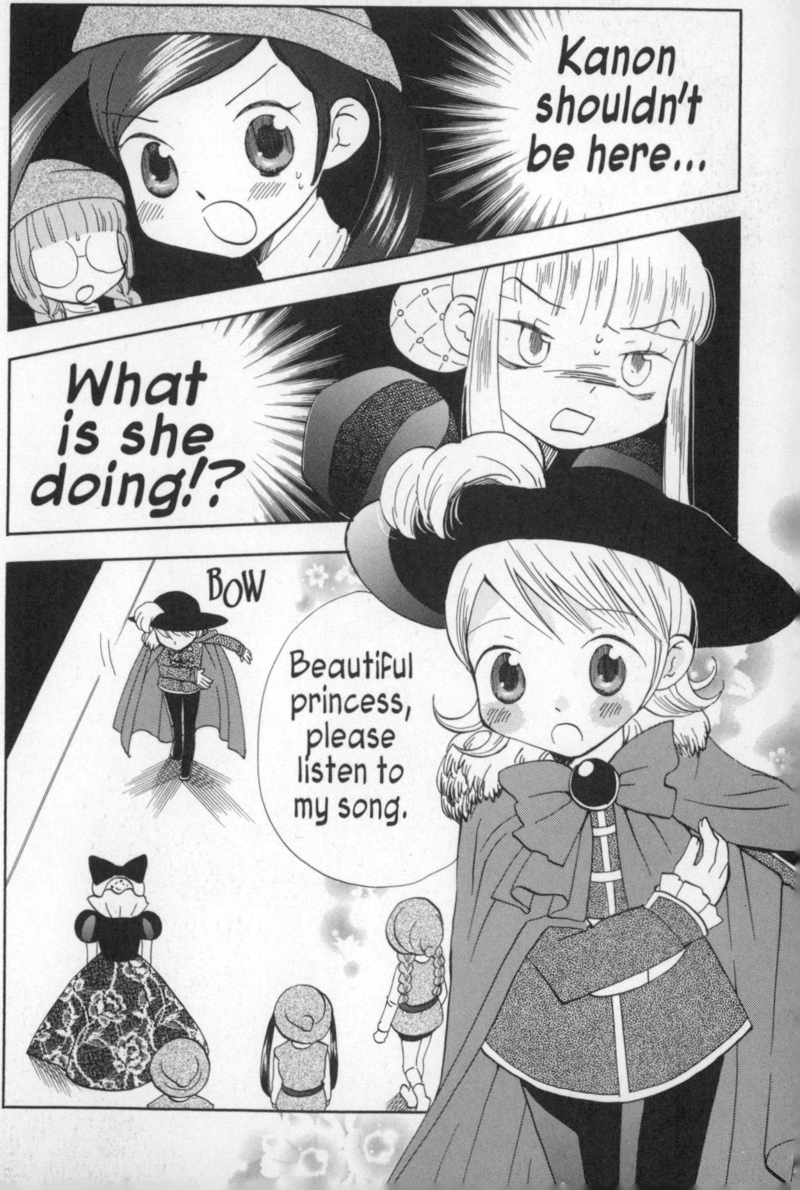
Kanon shouldn't be here...
What is she doing!?
Beautiful princess, please listen to my song.
BOW

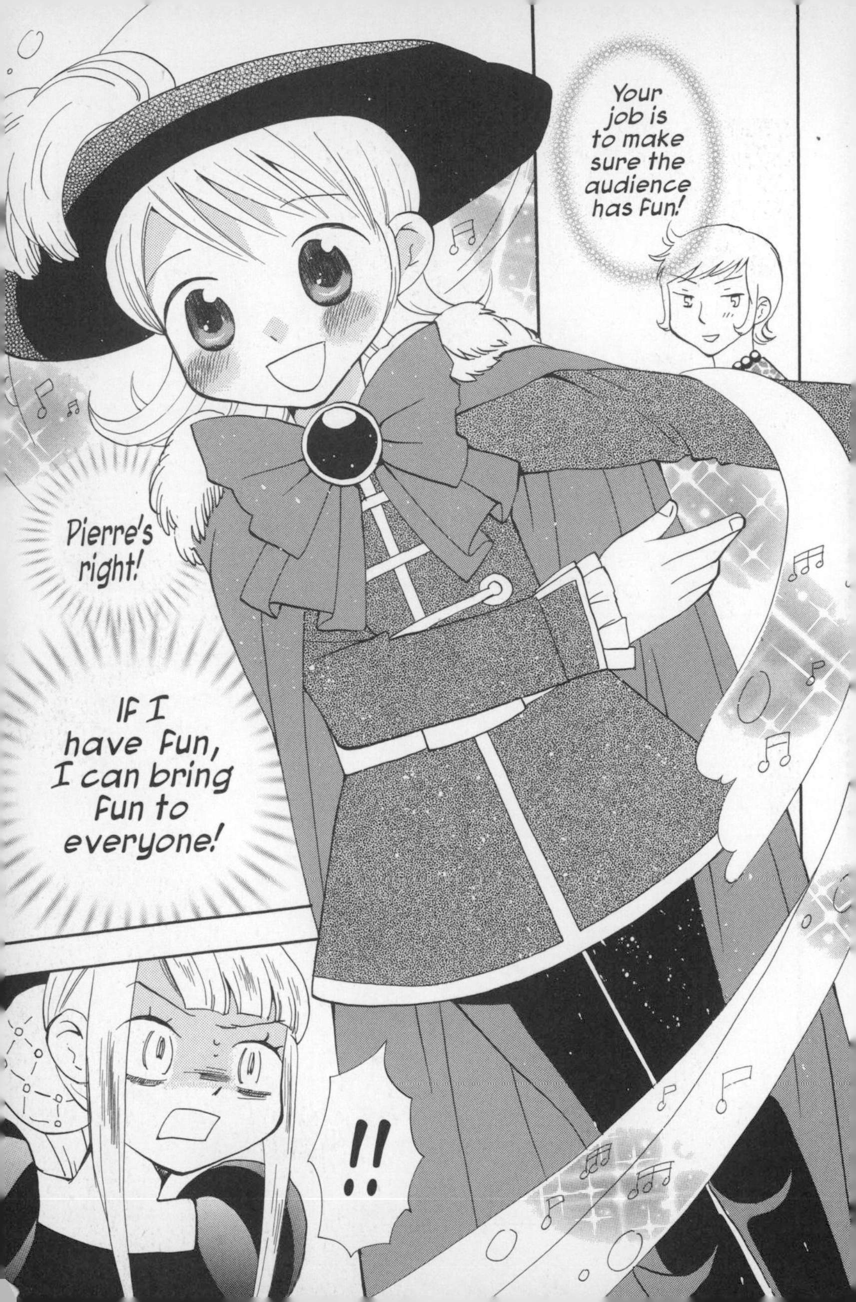
Your job is to make sure the audience has fun!
Pierre's right!
If I have fun, I can bring fun to everyone!
!!

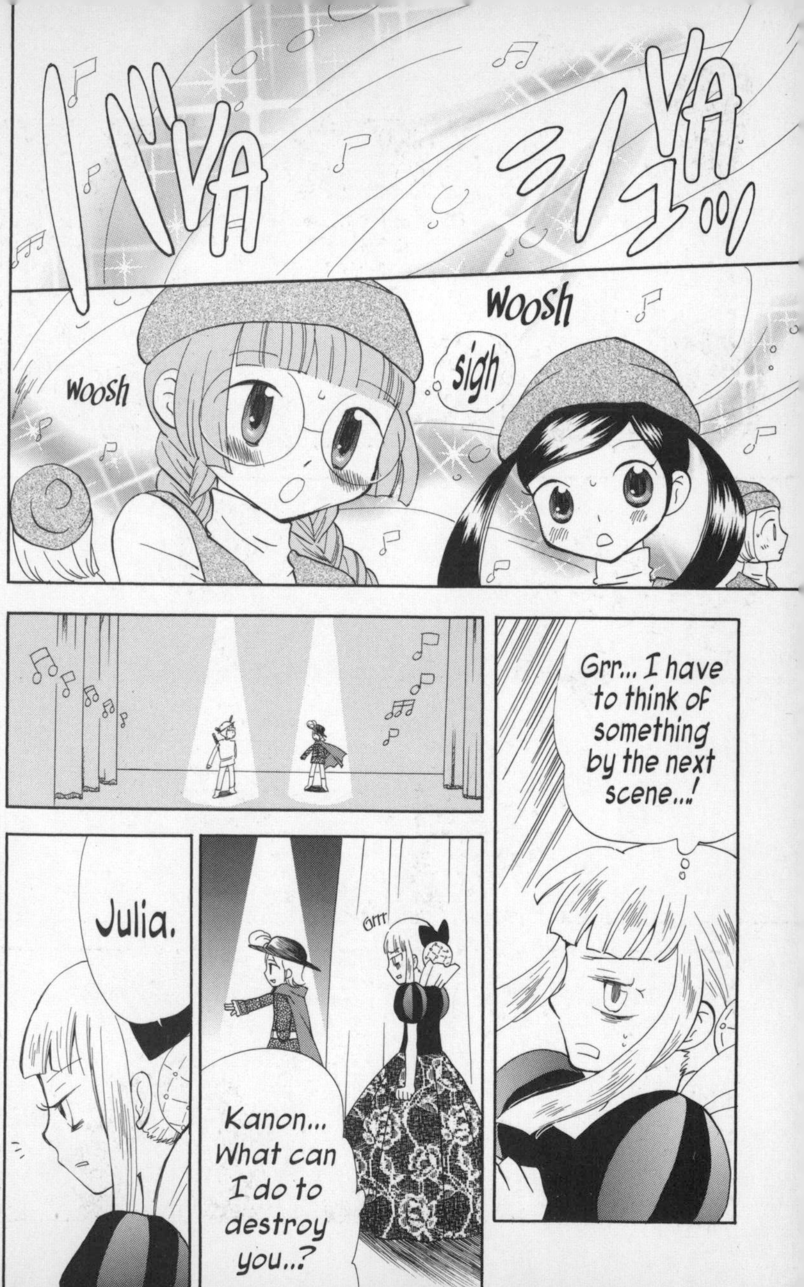
VA
VA
woosh
sigh
woosh
Grr... I have to think of something by the next scene...!
Grrr
Kanon... What can I do to destroy you...?
Julia.

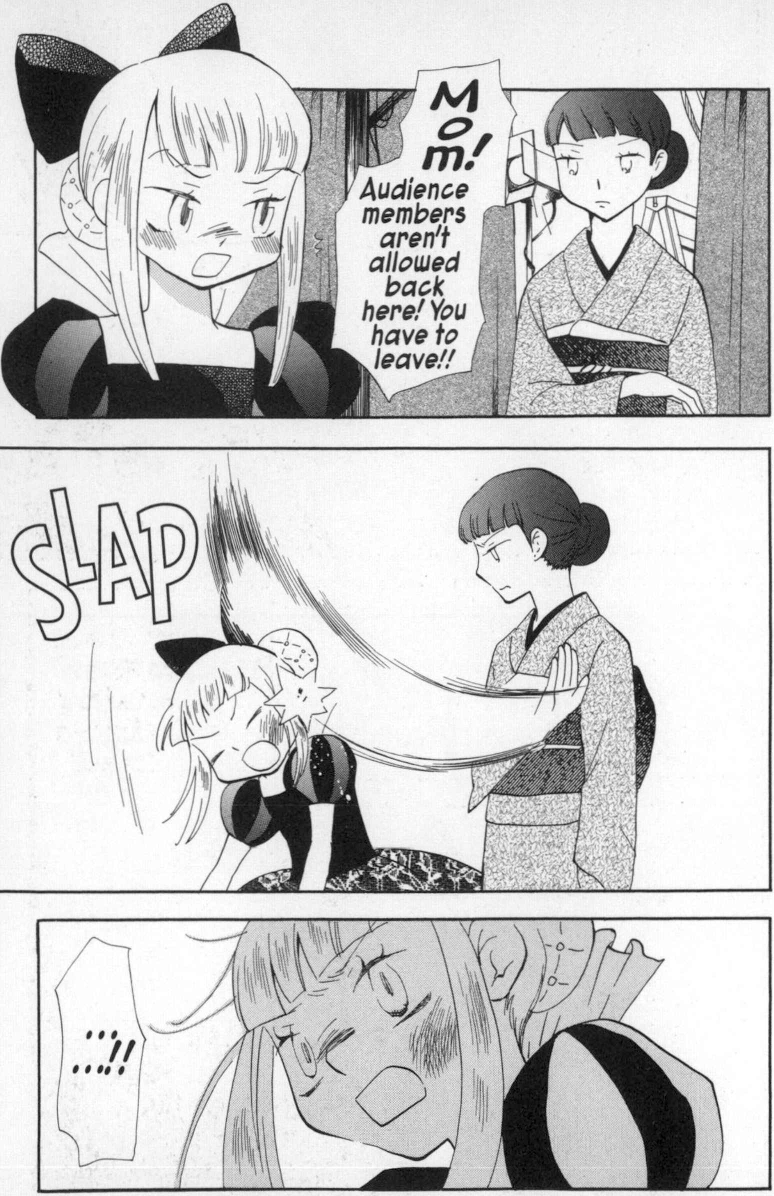
Mom!
Audience members aren't allowed back here! You have to leave!!
SLAP
......!!

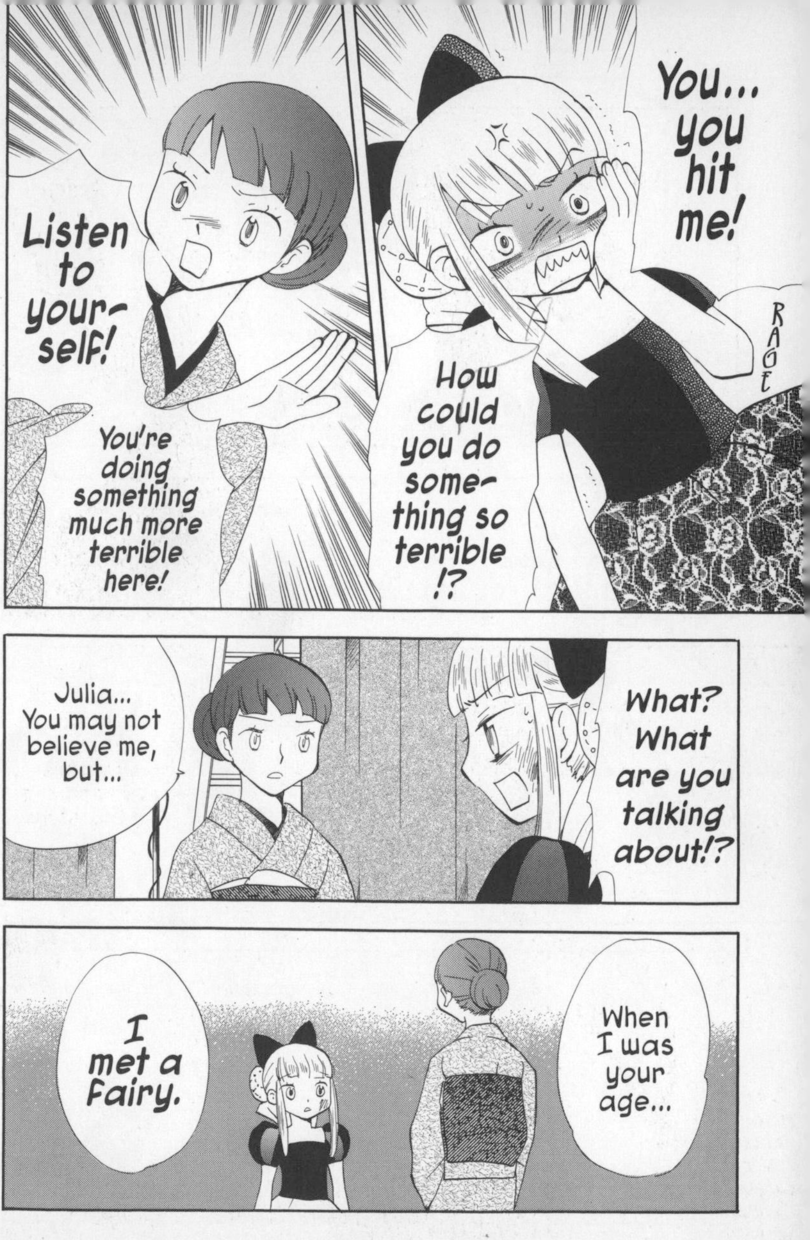
You... you hit me!
RAGE
How could you do something so terrible!?
Listen to yourself!
You're doing something much more terrible here!
What? What are you talking about!?
Julia... You may not believe me, but...
When I was your age...
I met a fairy.

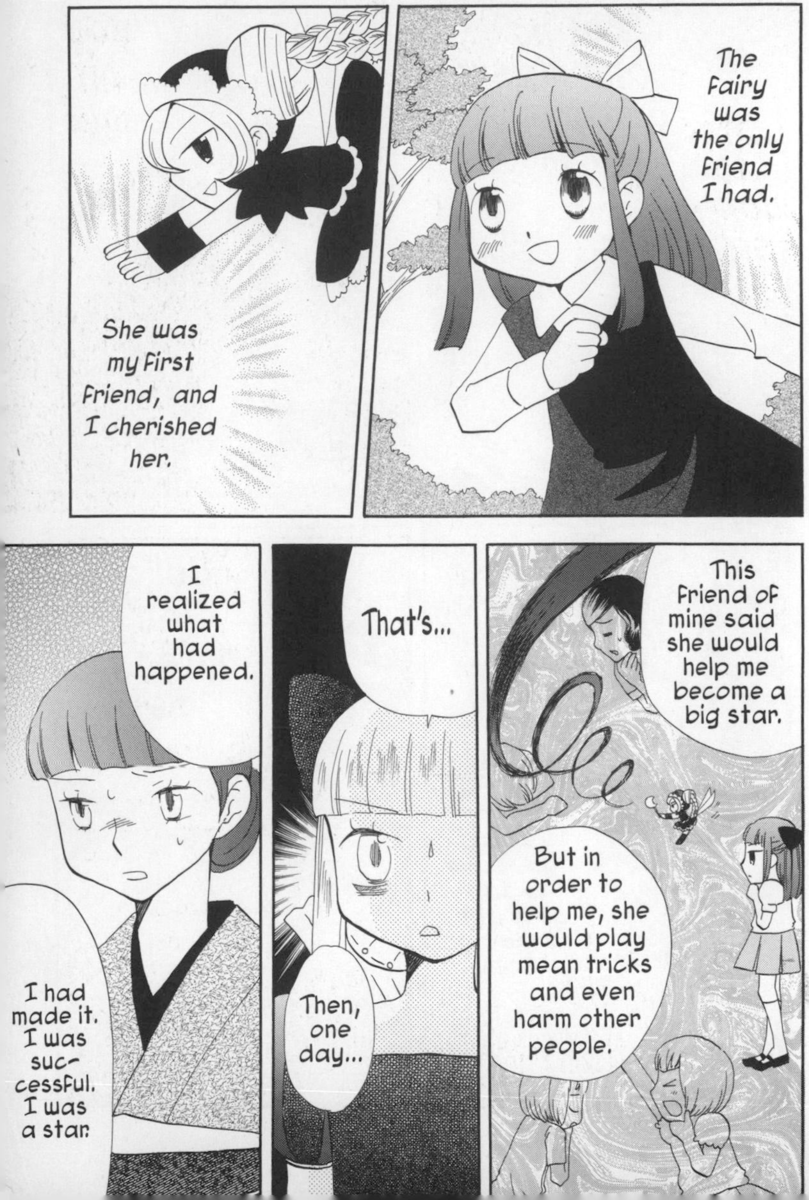
The fairy was the only friend I had.
She was my first friend, and I cherished her.
This friend of mine said she would help me become a big star.
But in order to help me, she would play mean tricks and even harm other people.
That's...
Then, one day...
I realized what had happened.
I had made it. I was suc-cessful. I was a star.

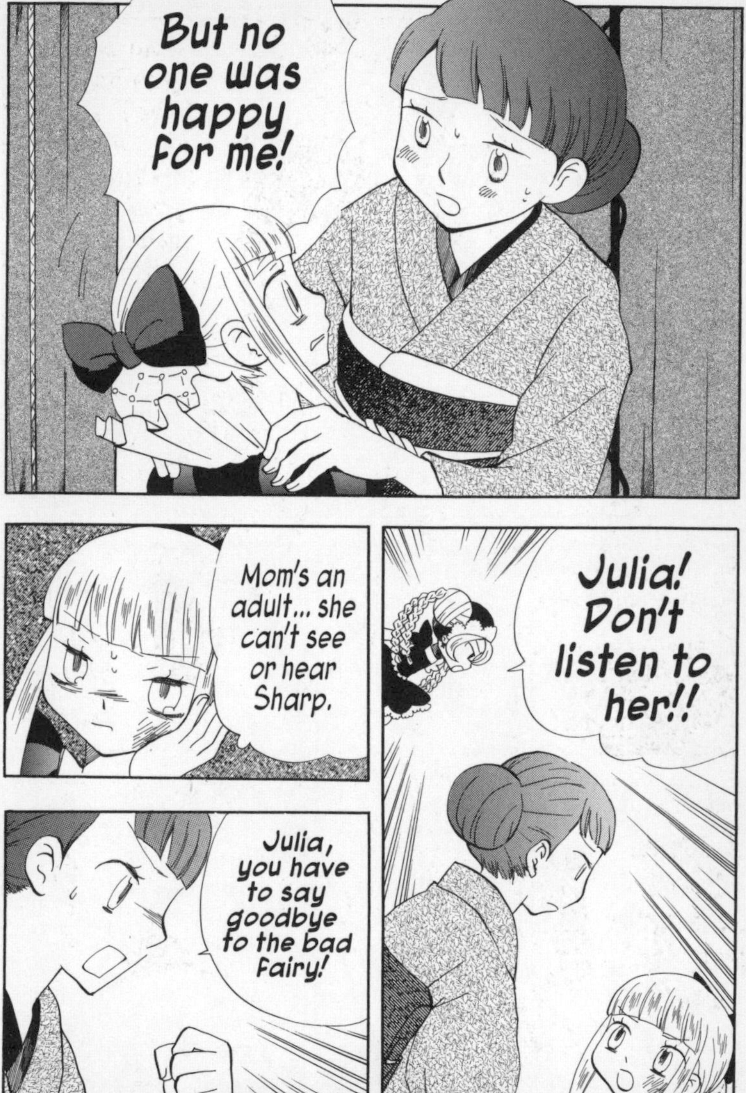
But no one was happy for me!
Julia! Don't listen to her!!
Mom's an adult... she can't see or hear Sharp.
Julia, you have to say goodbye to the bad fairy!

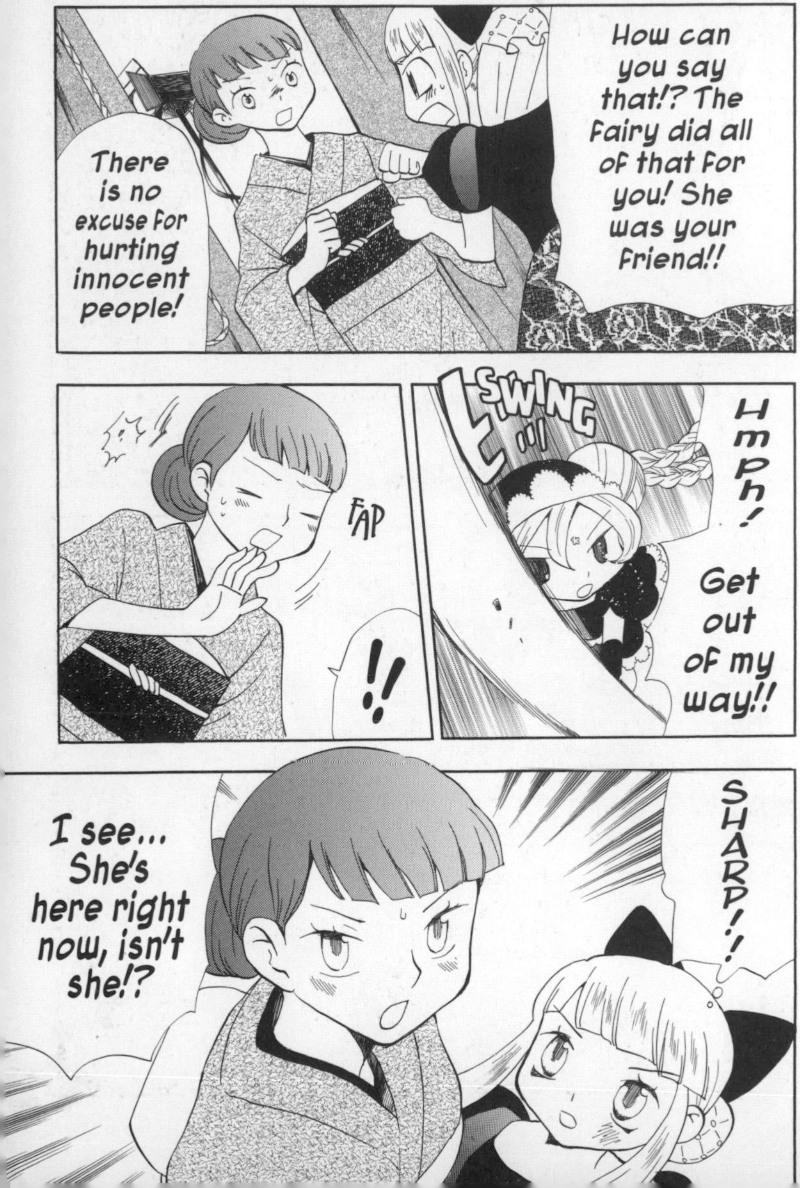

How can you say that!? The fairy did all of that for you! She was your friend!!
There is no excuse for hurting innocent people!
SWING
Hmph!
Get out of my way!!
FAP
!!
SHARP!!
I see... She's here right now, isn't she!?

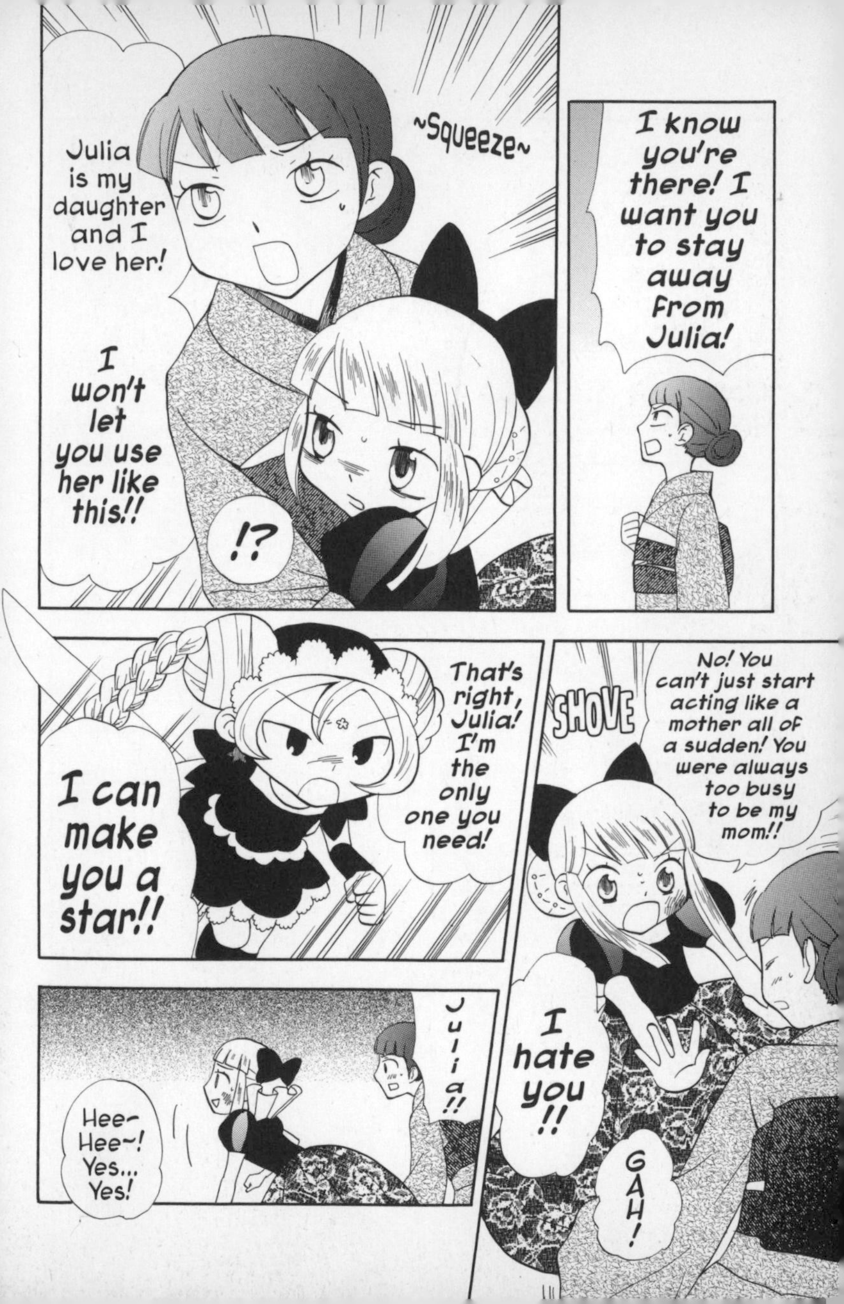
I know you're there! I want you to stay away from Julia!
~Squeeze~
Julia is my daughter and I love her!
I won't let you use her like this!!
!?
No! You can't just start acting like a mother all of a sudden! You were always too busy to be my mom!!
SHOVE
I hate you!!
GAH!
That's right, Julia! I'm the only one you need!
I can make you a star!!
Julia!!
Hee-Hee~! Yes... Yes!

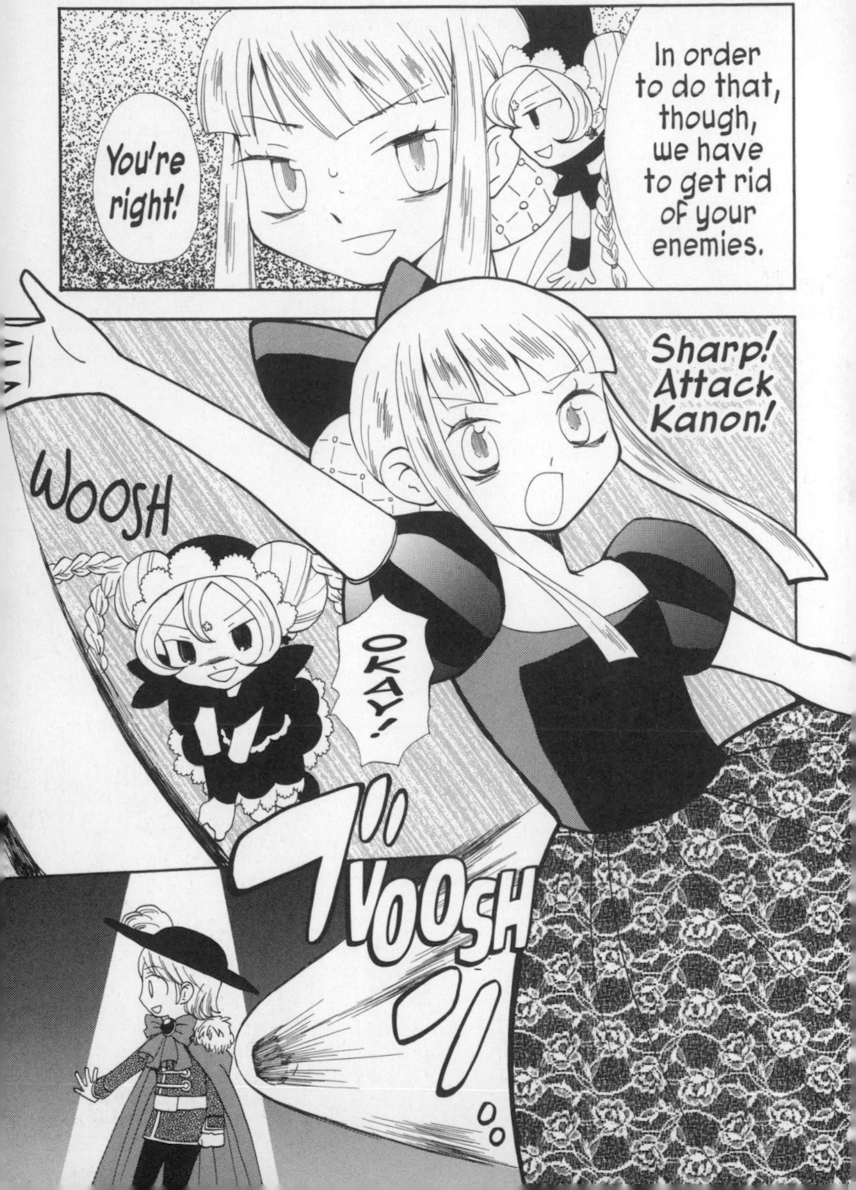
In order to do that, though, we have to get rid of your enemies.
You're right!
Sharp! Attack Kanon!
WOOSH
OKAY!
VOOSH

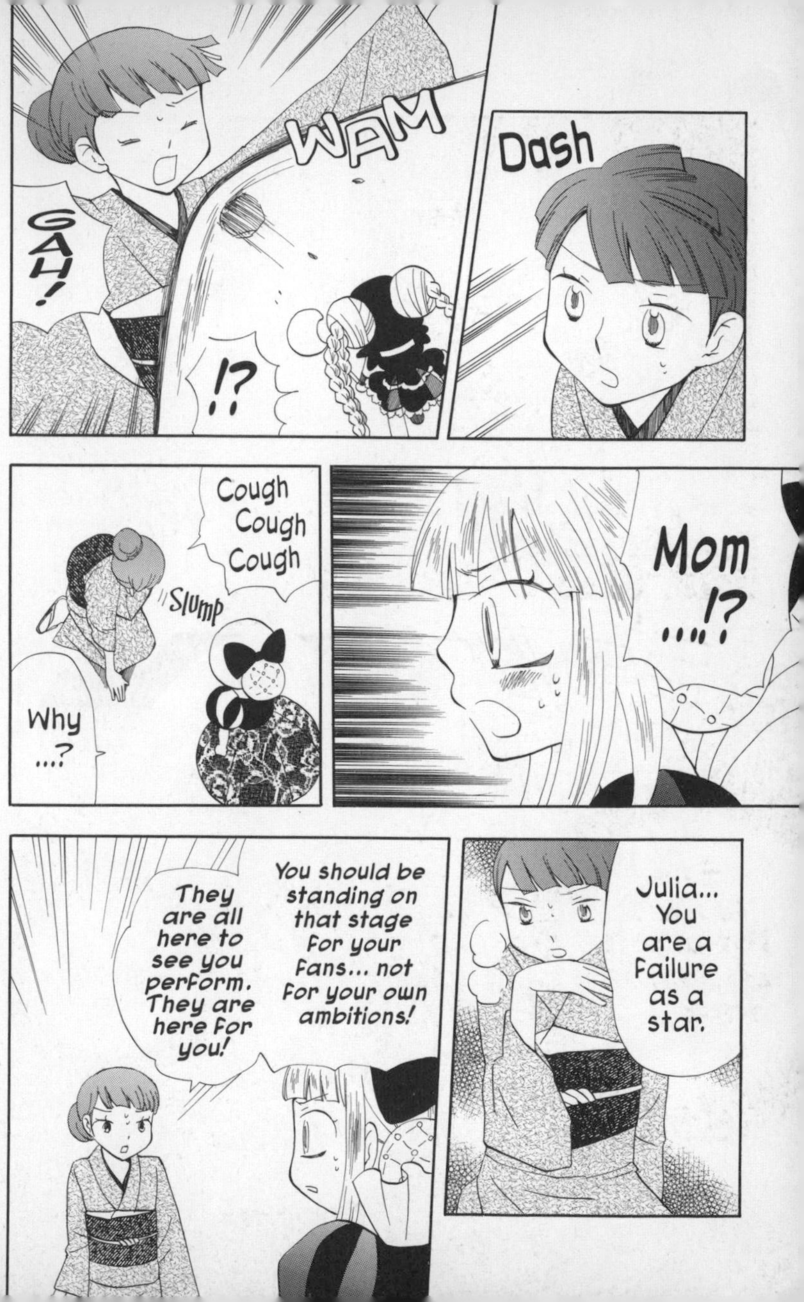
Dash
WAM
GAH!
!?
Mom ...!?
Cough Cough Cough
Slump
Why ...?
Julia... You are a failure as a star.
You should be standing on that stage for your fans... not for your own ambitions!
They are all here to see you perform. They are here for you!

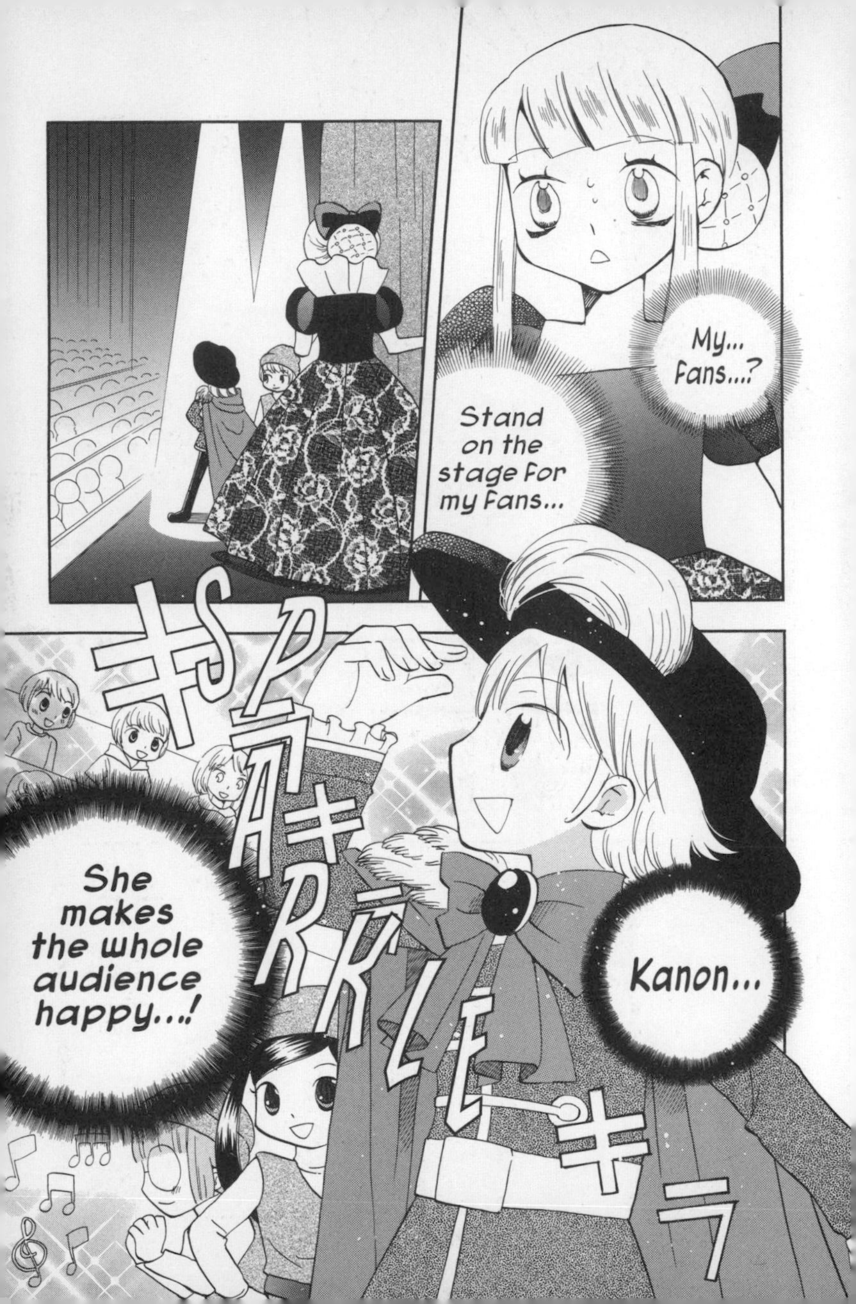
My... fans...?
Stand on the stage for my fans...
SPARKLE
キラキラ
Kanon...
She makes the whole audience happy...!

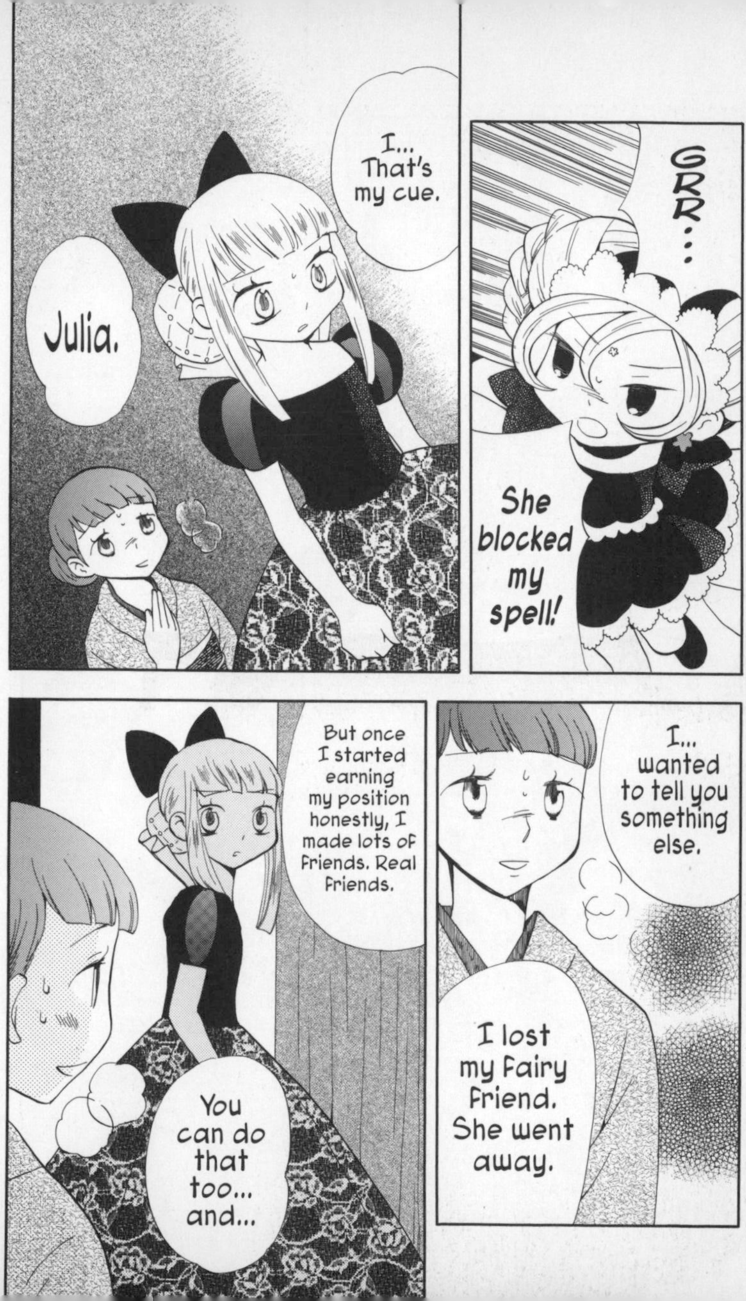
GRR...
She blocked my spell!
I... That's my cue.
Julia.
I... wanted to tell you something else.
I lost my fairy friend. She went away.
But once I started earning my position honestly, I made lots of friends. Real friends.
You can do that too... and...

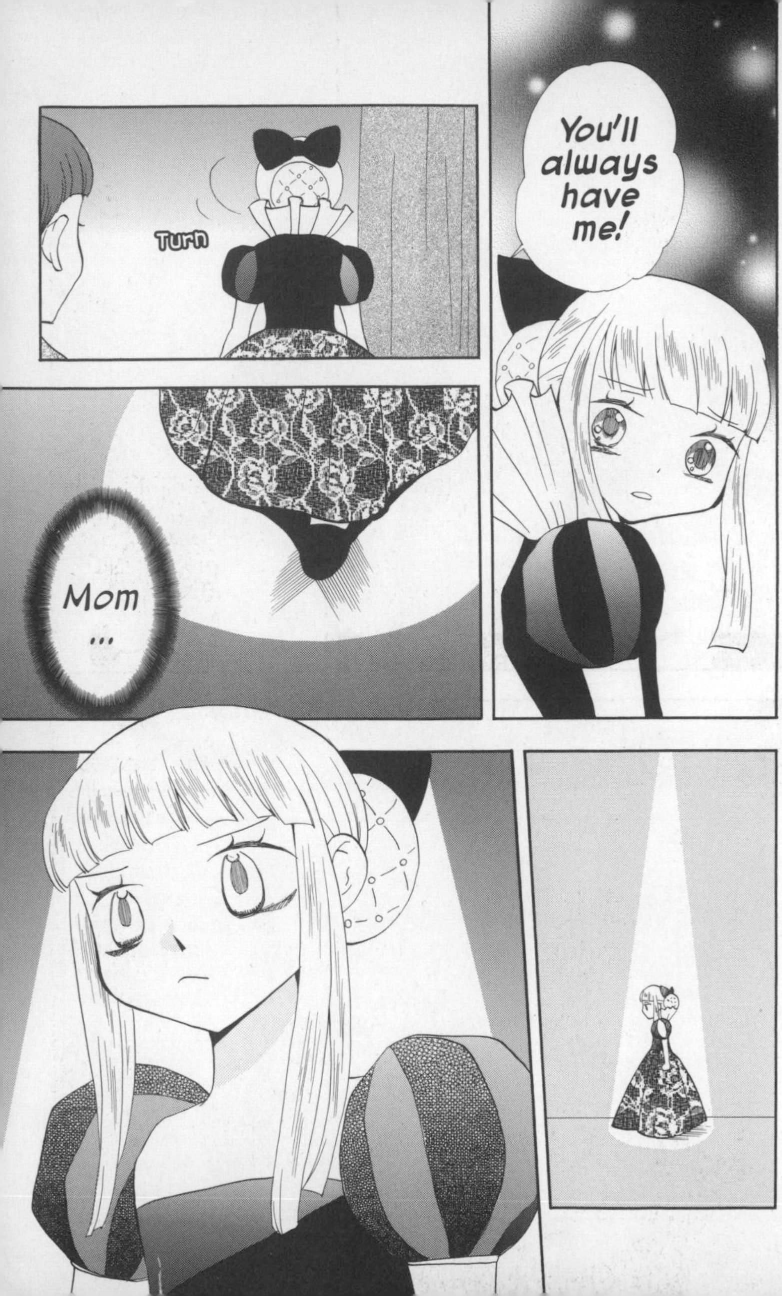
You'll always have me!
Turn
Mom ...

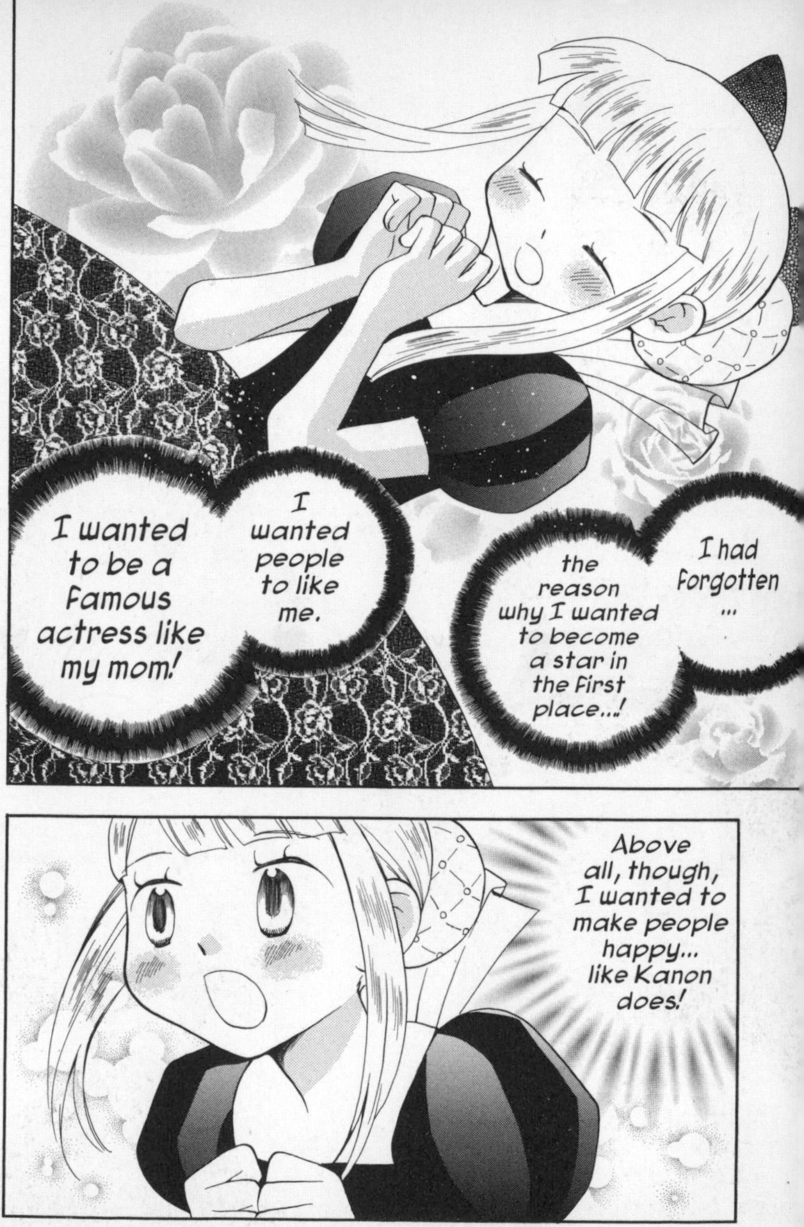

I had forgotten...
the reason why I wanted to become a star in the first place...!
I wanted people to like me.
I wanted to be a famous actress like my mom!
Above all, though, I wanted to make people happy... like Kanon does!

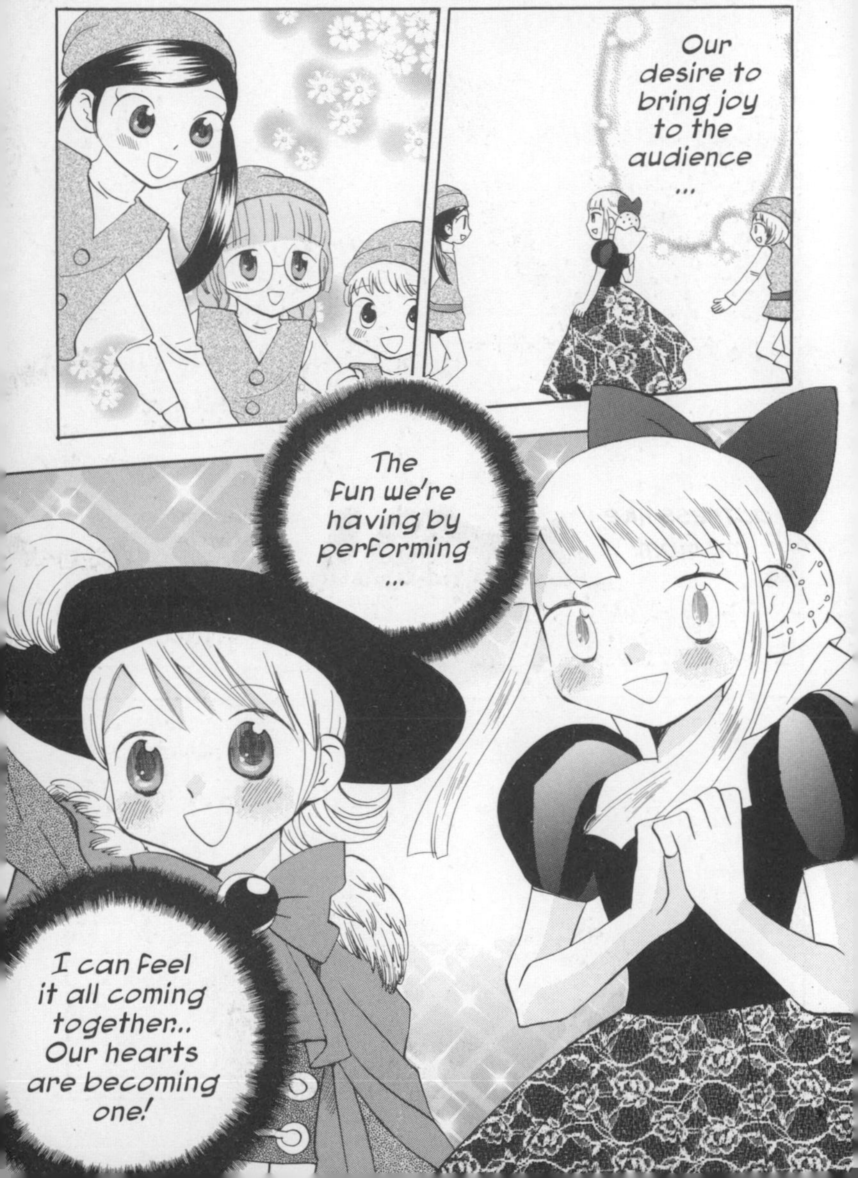
Our desire to bring joy to the audience ...
The fun we're having by performing ...
I can feel it all coming together... Our hearts are becoming one!

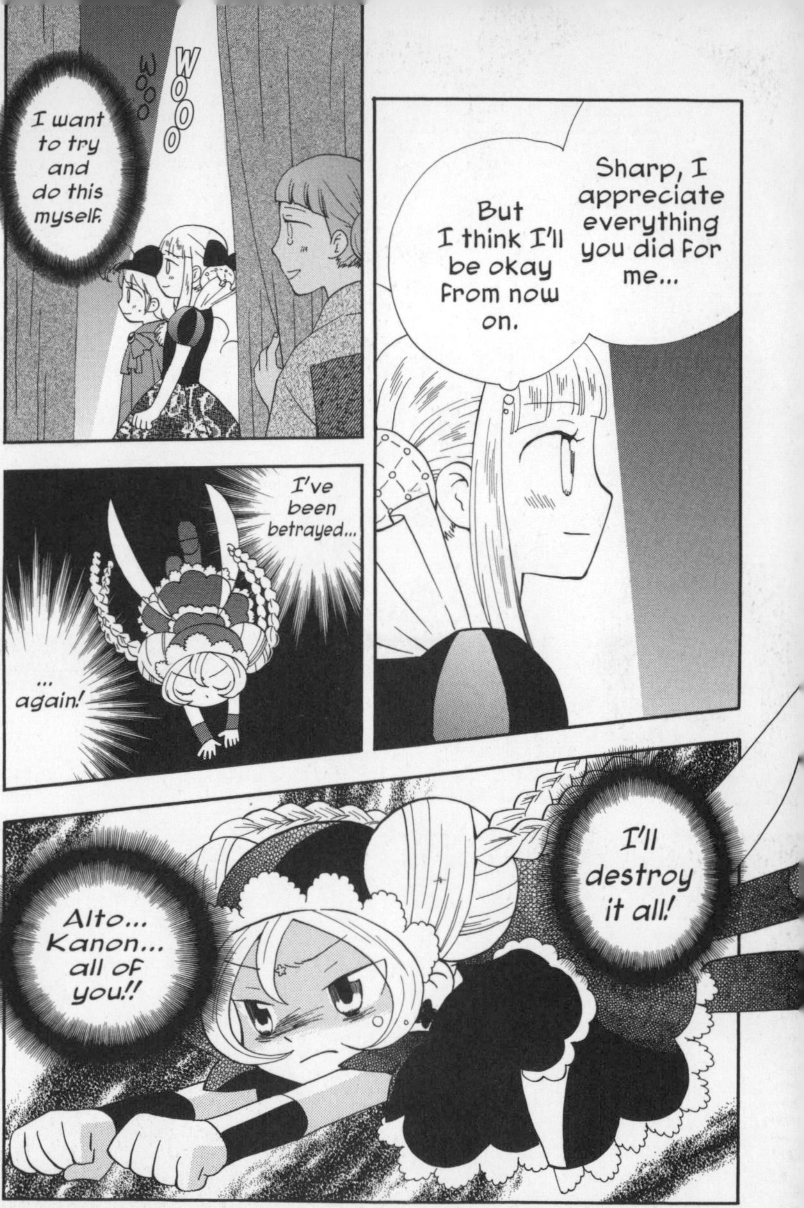
Sharp, I appreciate everything you did for me...
But I think I'll be okay from now on.
WOOO
WOOO
I want to try and do this myself.
I've been betrayed...
... again!
I'll destroy it all!
Alto... Kanon... all of you!!

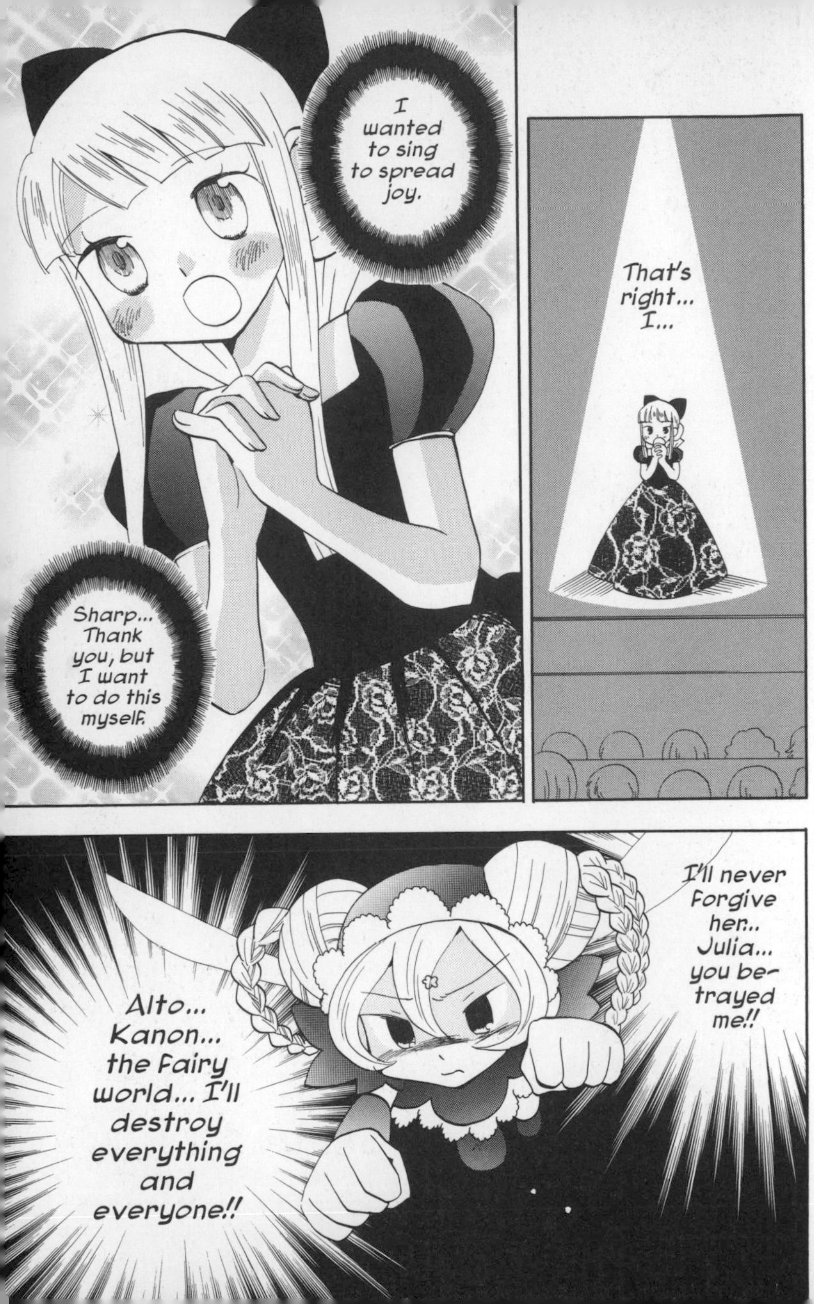
That's right... I...
I wanted to sing to spread joy.
Sharp... Thank you, but I want to do this myself.
I'll never forgive her.. Julia... you betrayed me!!
Alto... Kanon... the fairy world... I'll destroy everything and everyone!!

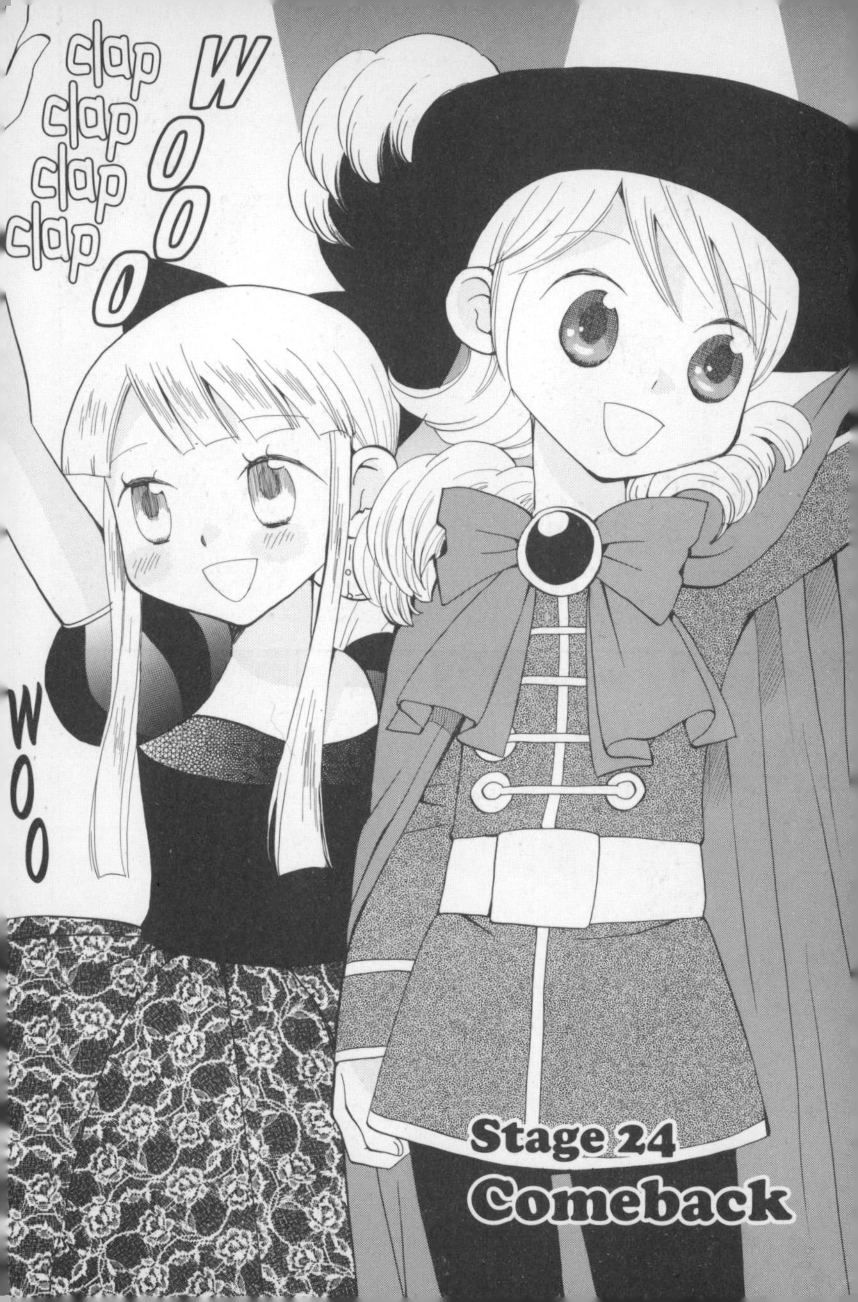
clap clap clap clap
WOOO
WOO
Stage 24
Comeback

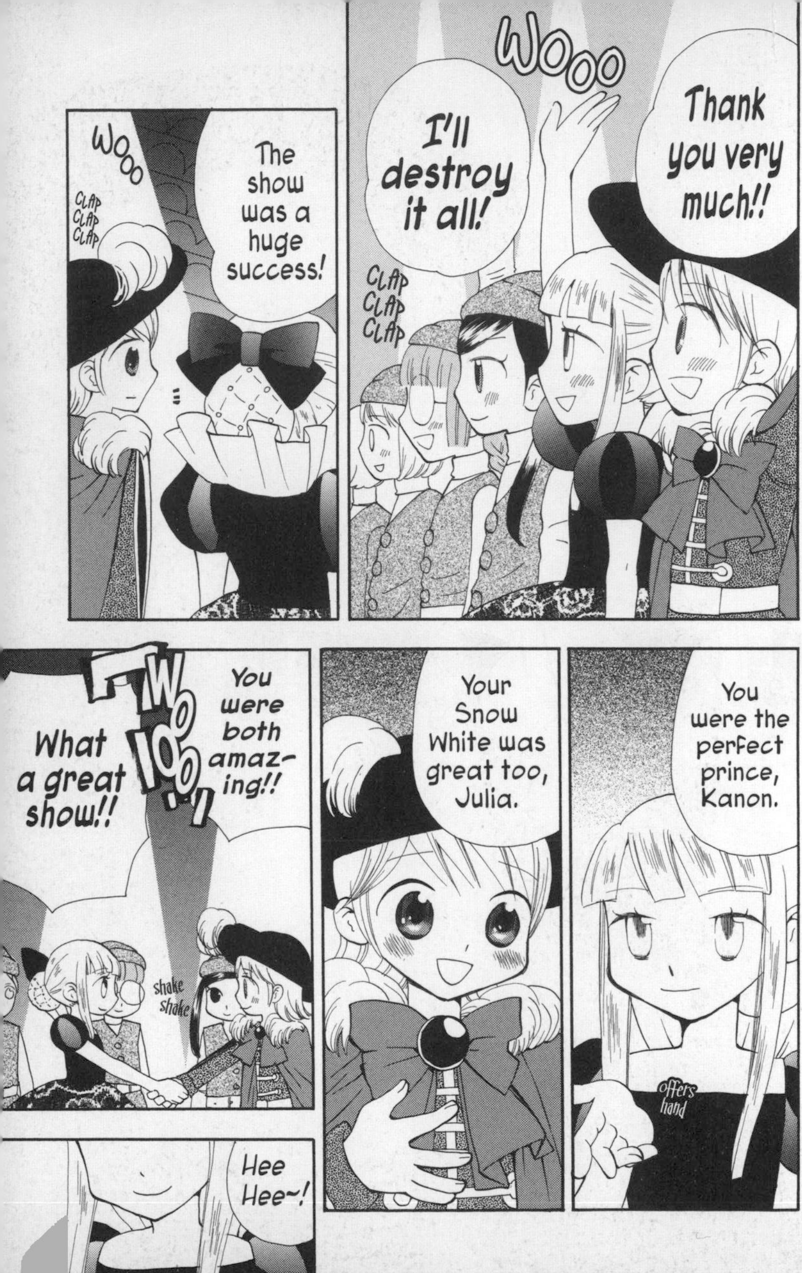
Thank you very much!!
WOOO
I'll destroy it all!
CLAP CLAP CLAP
The show was a huge success!
WOOO
CLAP CLAP CLAP
You were the perfect prince, Kanon.
offers hand
Your Snow White was great too, Julia.
You were both amaz-ing!!
WOOO!
What a great show!!
shake shake
Hee Hee~!

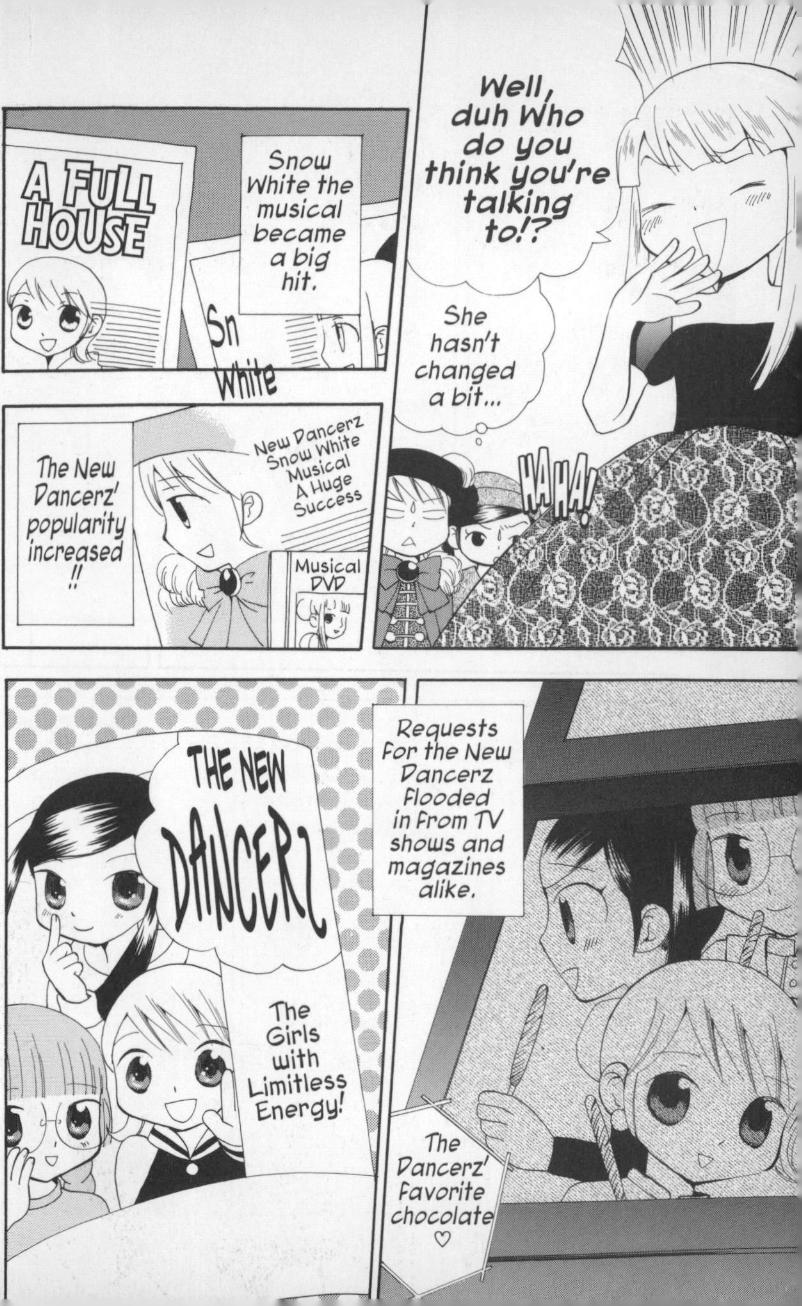

Well, duh Who do you think you're talking to!?
She hasn't changed a bit...
HAHA!
Snow White the musical became a big hit.
A FULL HOUSE
Sn White
New Dancerz Snow White Musical A Huge Success
The New Dancerz' popularity increased !!
Musical DVD
Requests for the New Dancerz flooded in from TV shows and magazines alike.
The Dancerz' favorite chocolate ♡
THE NEW DANCERZ
The Girls with Limitless Energy!

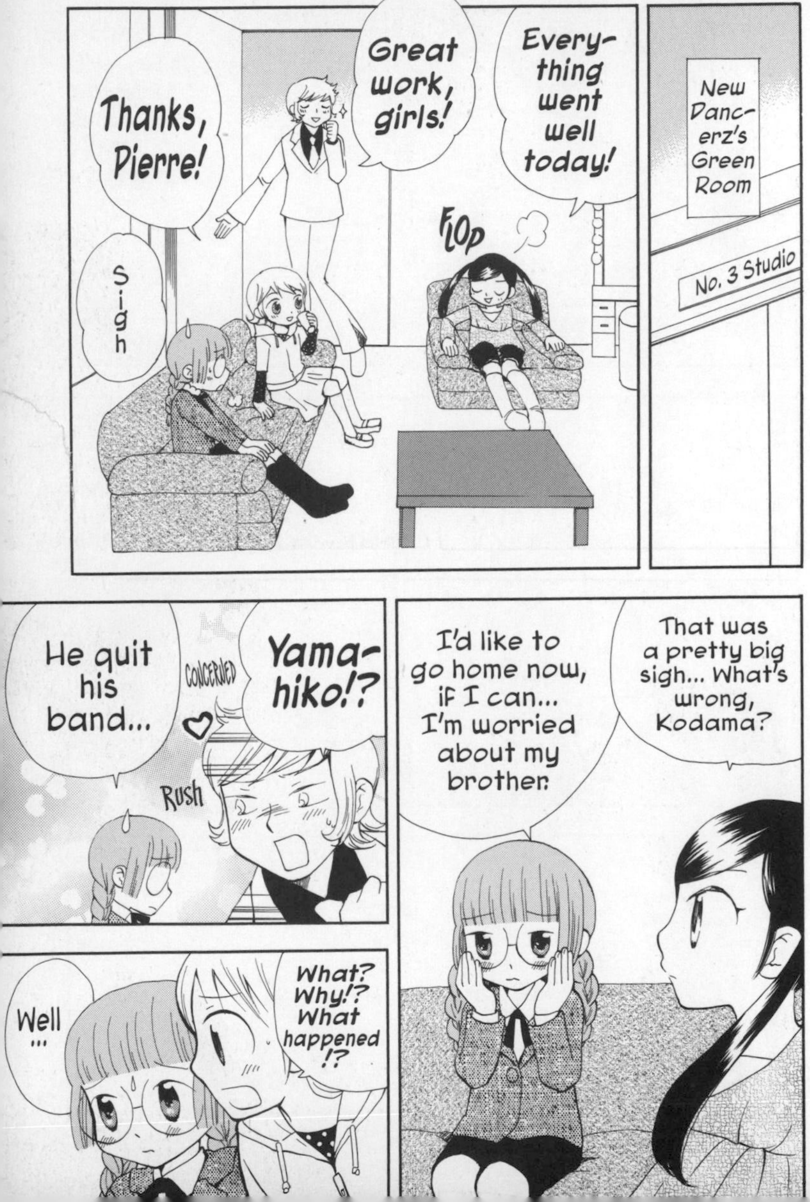
New Dancerz's Green Room
No. 3 Studio
Every-thing went well today!
Great work, girls!
Thanks, Pierre!
FLOP
Sigh
That was a pretty big sigh... What's wrong, Kodama?
I'd like to go home now, if I can... I'm worried about my brother.
Yama-hiko!?
CONCERNED
He quit his band...
RUSH
What? Why!? What happened!?
Well ...

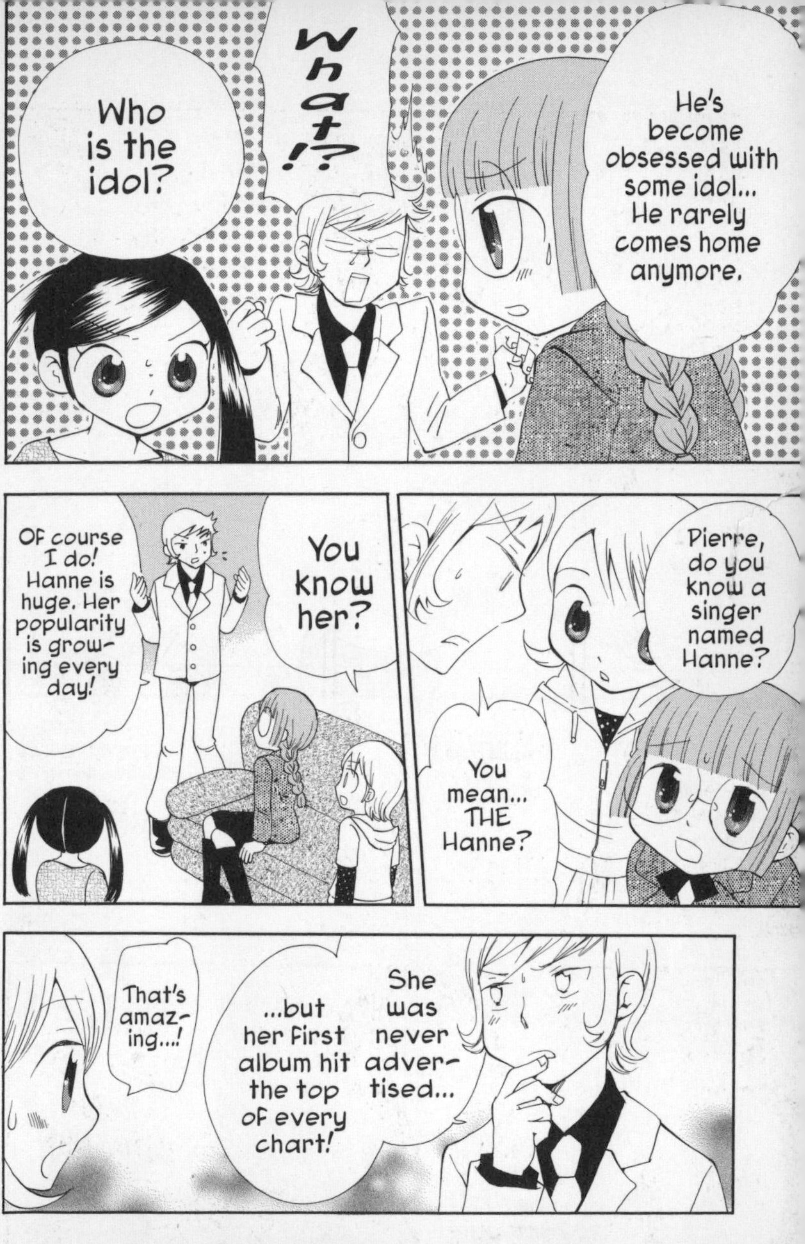
He's become obsessed with some idol... He rarely comes home anymore.
What!?
Who is the idol?
Pierre, do you know a singer named Hanne?
You mean... THE Hanne?
You know her?
Of course I do! Hanne is huge. Her popularity is grow-ing every day!
She was never adver-tised...
...but her first album hit the top of every chart!
That's amaz-ing...!

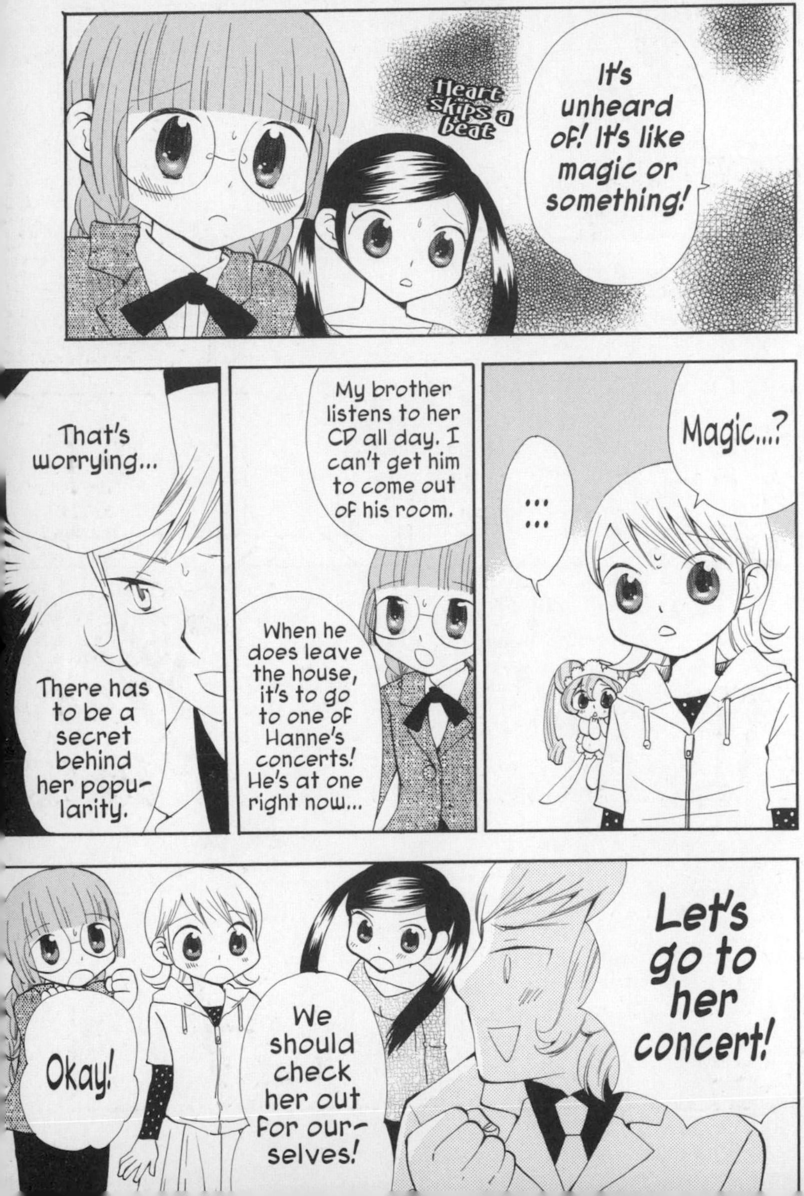
It's unheard of! It's like magic or something!
Heart skips a beat
Magic...?
... ...
My brother listens to her CD all day. I can't get him to come out of his room.
When he does leave the house, it's to go to one of Hanne's concerts! He's at one right now...
That's worrying...
There has to be a secret behind her popu-larity.
Let's go to her concert!
We should check her out for our-selves!
Okay!

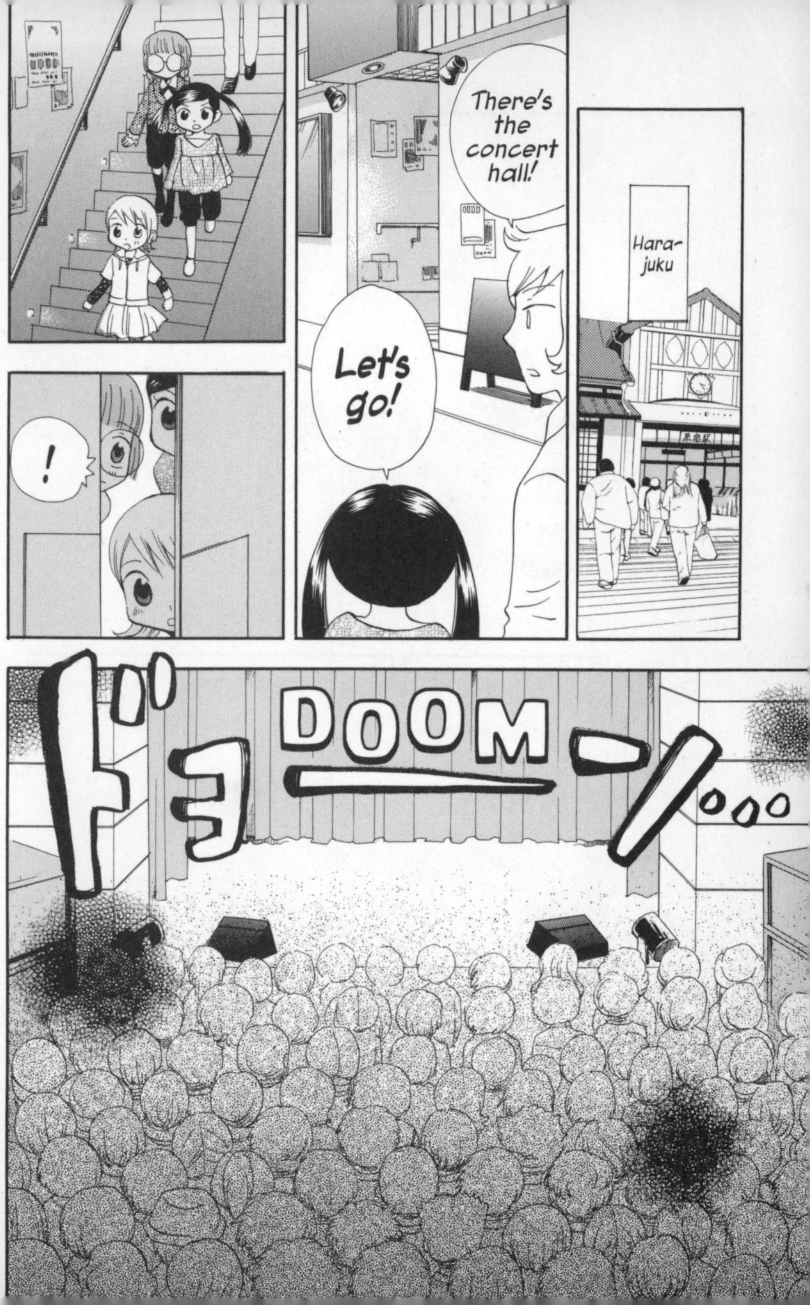
Hara-
juku
There's the concert hall!
Let's go!
!
ドヨーン
DOOM

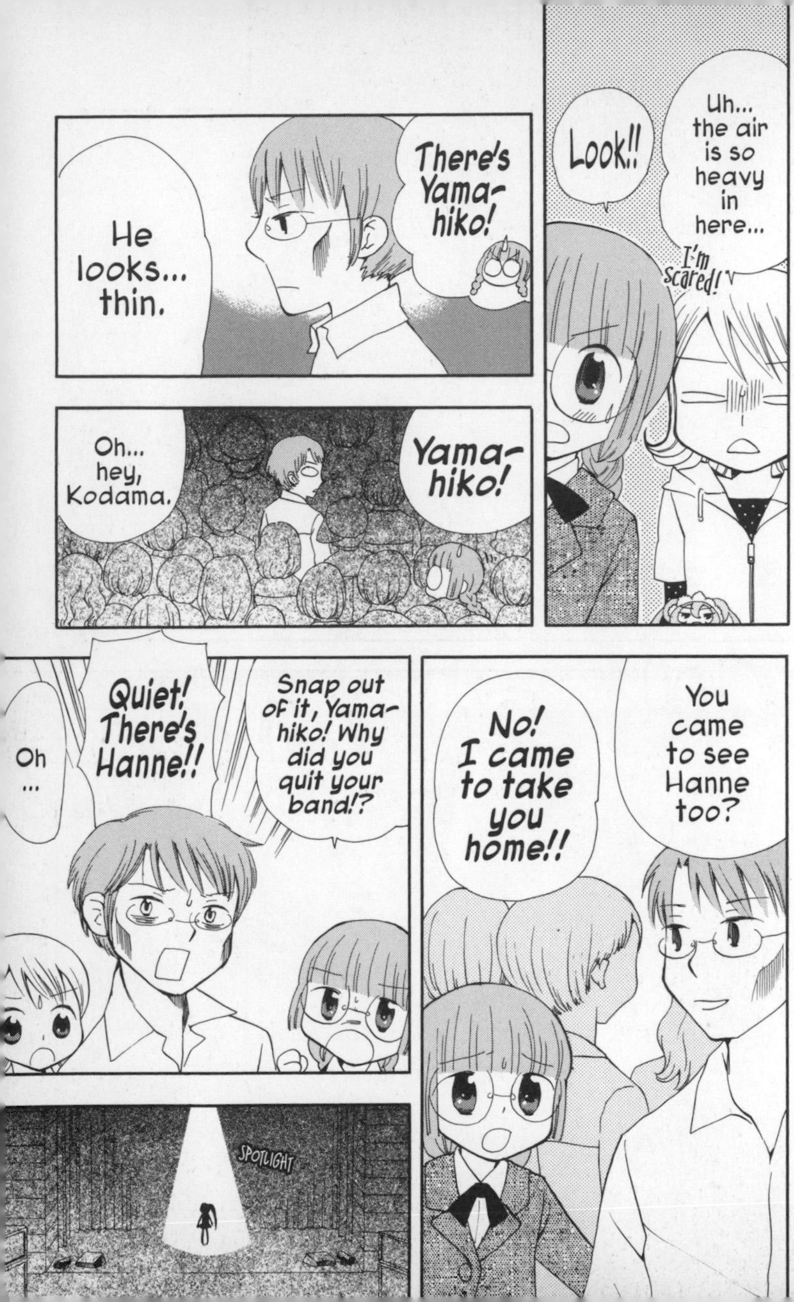
Uh... the air is so heavy in here...
Look!!
I'm scared!
There's Yama-hiko!
He looks... thin.
Yama-hiko!
Oh... hey, Kodama.
You came to see Hanne too?
No! I came to take you home!!
Snap out of it, Yama-hiko! Why did you quit your band!?
Quiet! There's Hanne!!
Oh ...
SPOTLIGHT

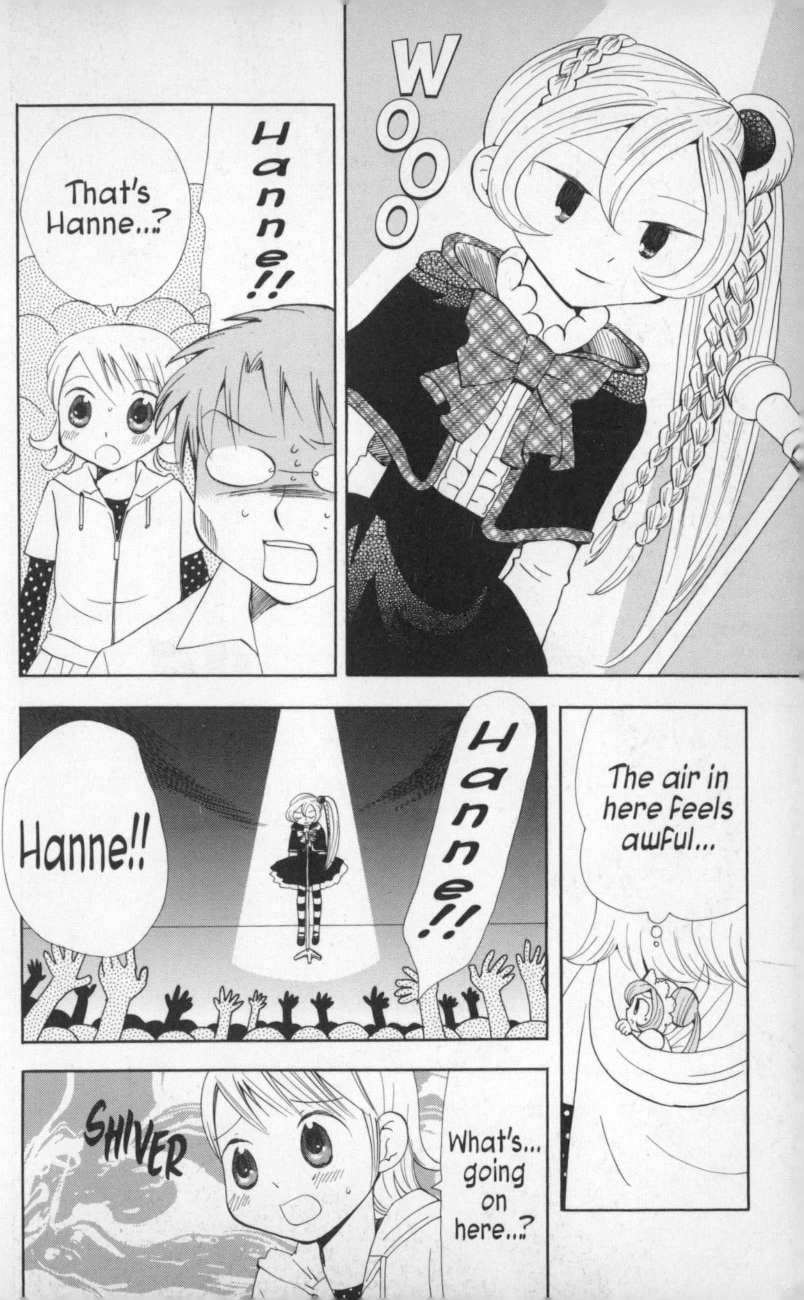
WOOOO
Hanne!!
That's Hanne...?
The air in here feels awful...
Hanne!!
Hanne!!
What's... going on here...?
SHIVER

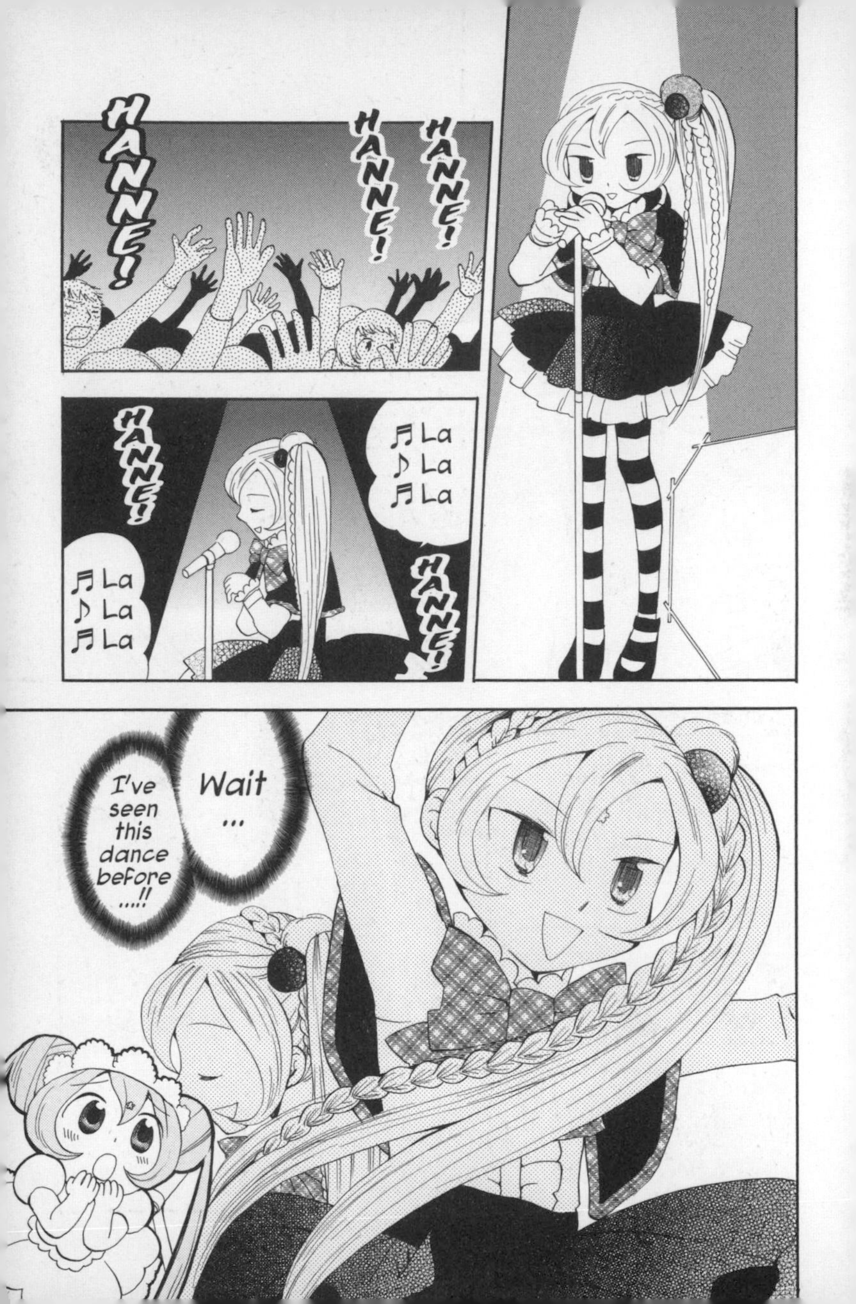
HANNE!
HANNE!
HANNE!
♬ La ♪ La ♬ La
HANNE!
HANNE!
♬ La ♪ La ♬ La
Wait ...
I've seen this dance before .....!!

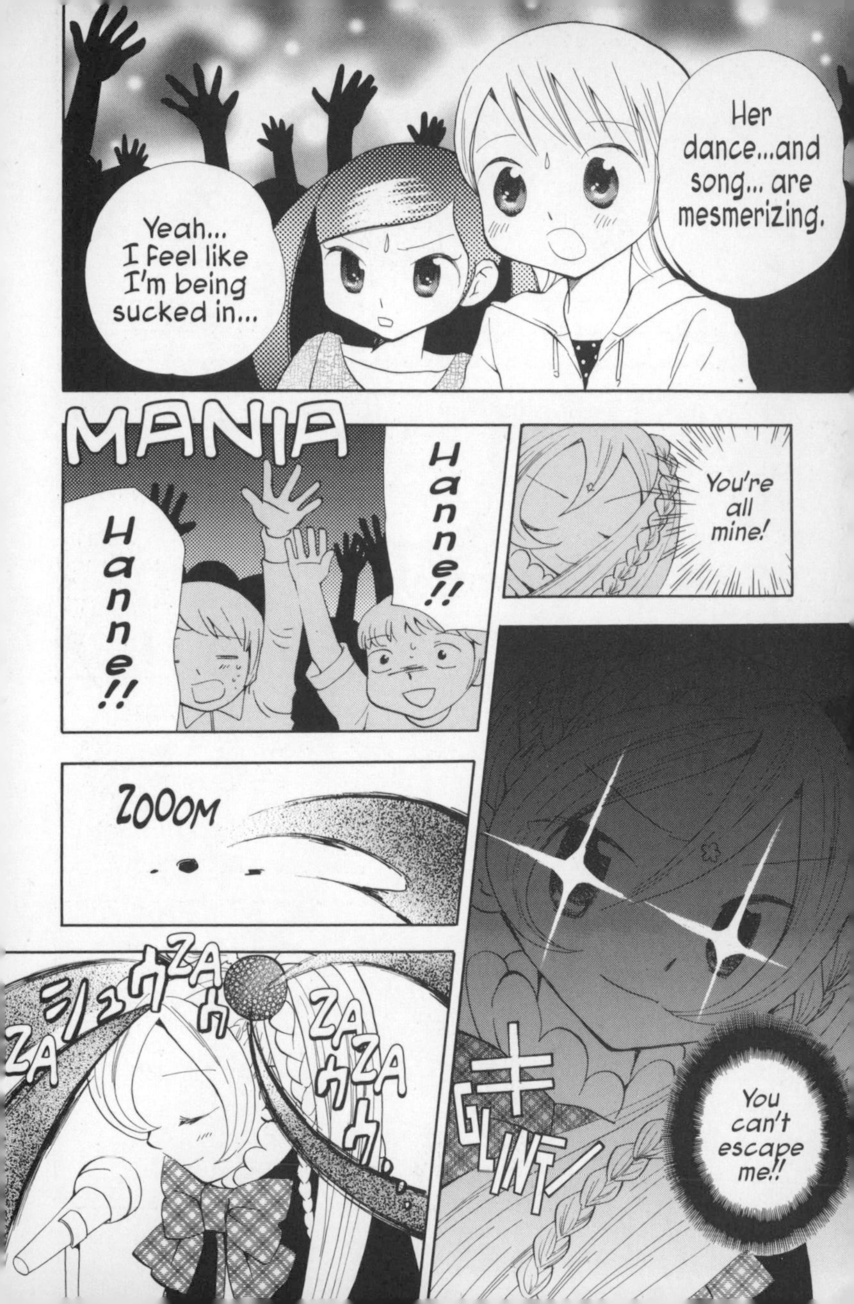
Her dance...and song... are mesmerizing.
Yeah... I feel like I'm being sucked in...
You're all mine!
Hanne!!
MANIA
Hanne!!
GLINT
You can't escape me!!
ZOOOM
ZA ZA
ZA ZA

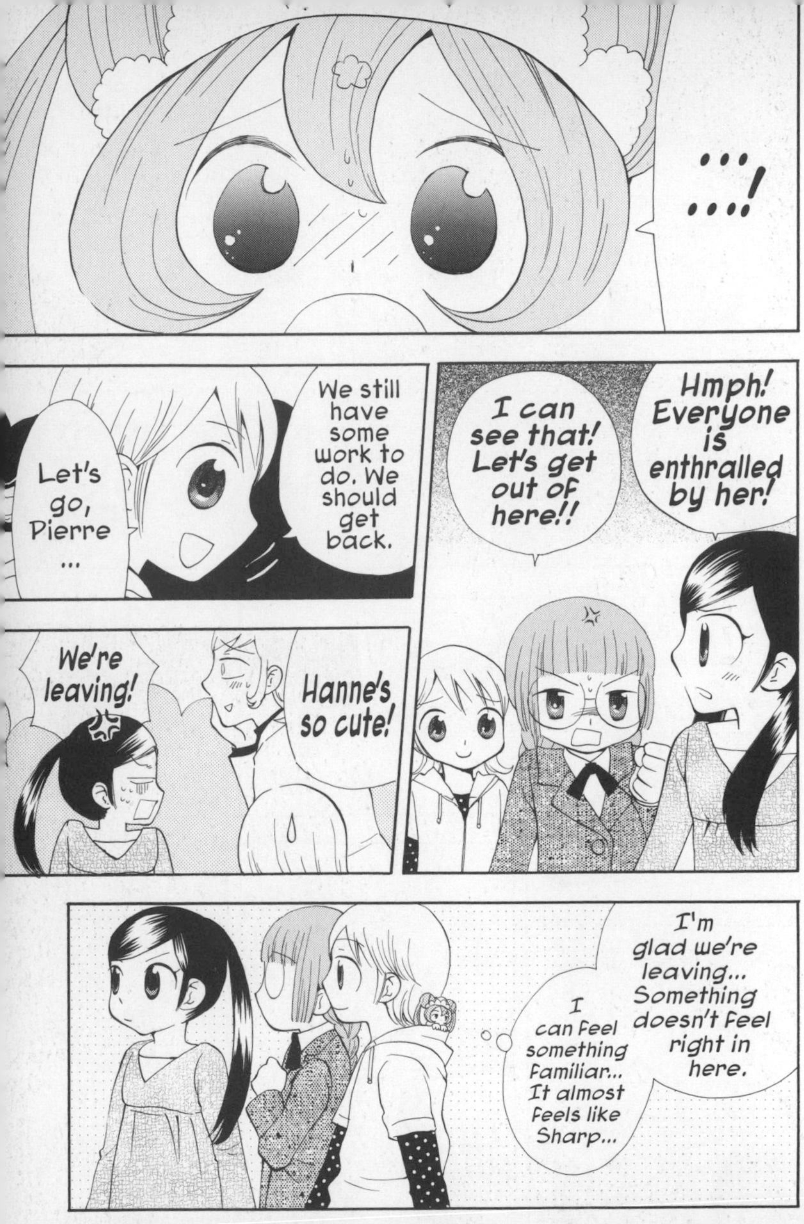

..., ...!
Hmph! Everyone is enthralled by her!
I can see that! Let's get out of here!!
We still have some work to do. We should get back.
Let's go, Pierre ...
Hanne's so cute!
We're leaving!
I'm glad we're leaving... Something doesn't feel right in here.
I can feel something familiar... It almost feels like Sharp...

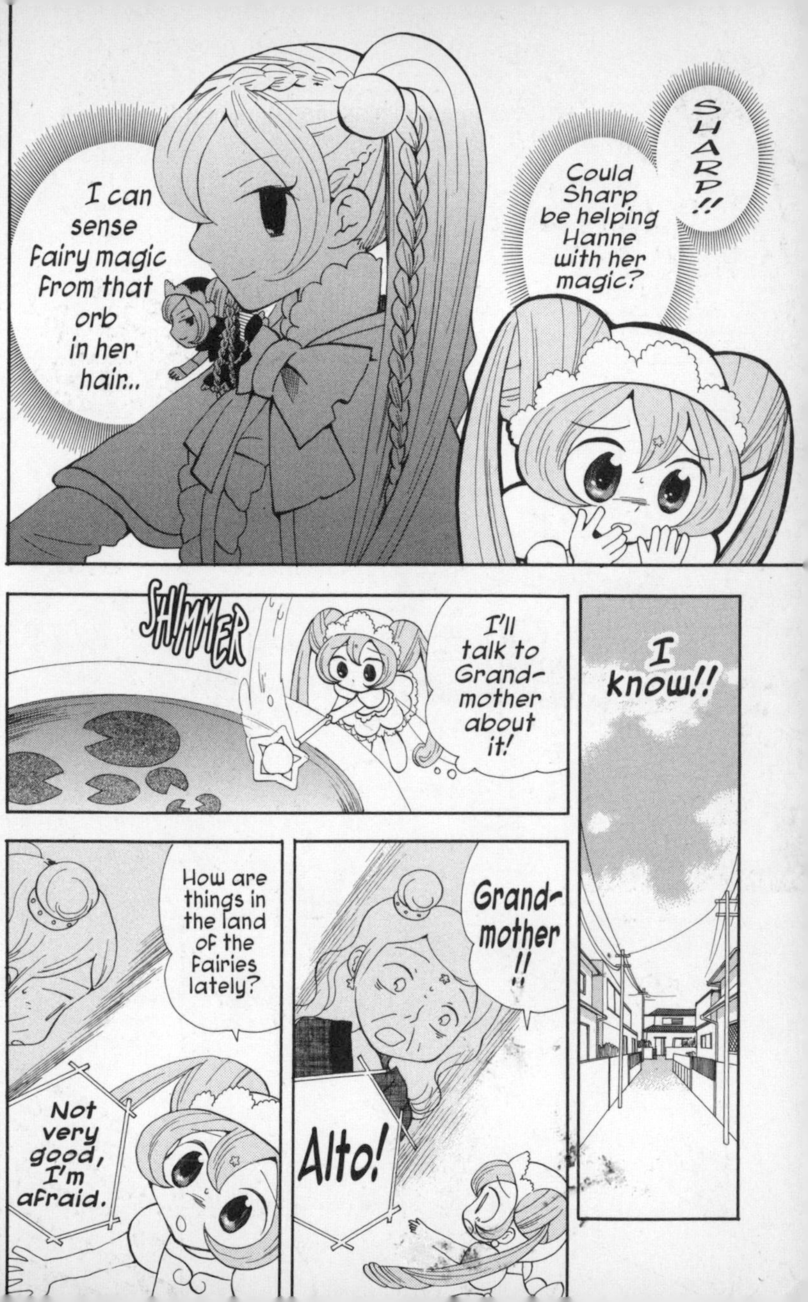
SHARP!!
Could Sharp be helping Hanne with her magic?
I can sense fairy magic from that orb in her hair...
I know!!
I'll talk to Grandmother about it!
SHIMMER
Grandmother!!
Alto!
How are things in the land of the fairies lately?
Not very good, I'm afraid.

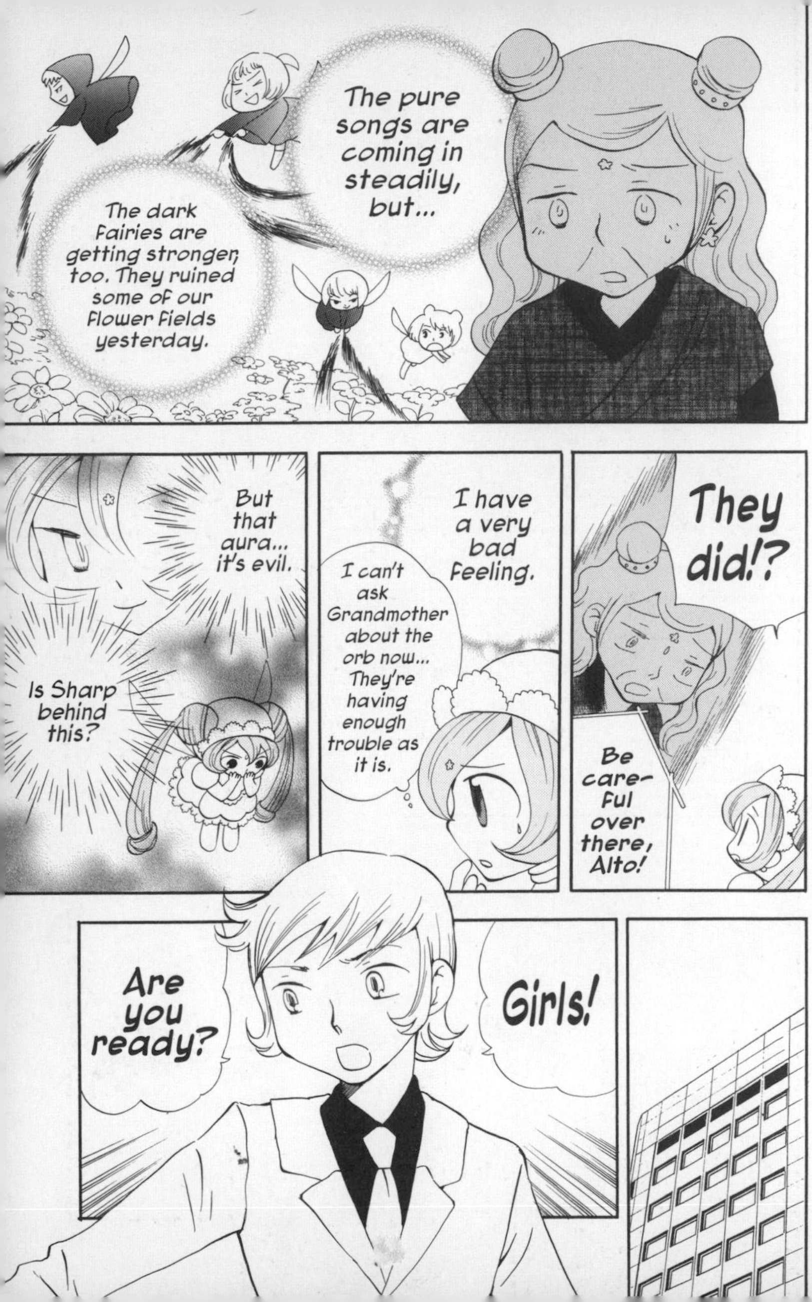
The pure songs are coming in steadily, but...
The dark fairies are getting stronger, too. They ruined some of our flower fields yesterday.
They did!?
Be care-ful over there, Alto!
I have a very bad feeling.
I can't ask Grandmother about the orb now... They're having enough trouble as it is.
But that aura... it's evil.
Is Sharp behind this?
Girls!
Are you ready?

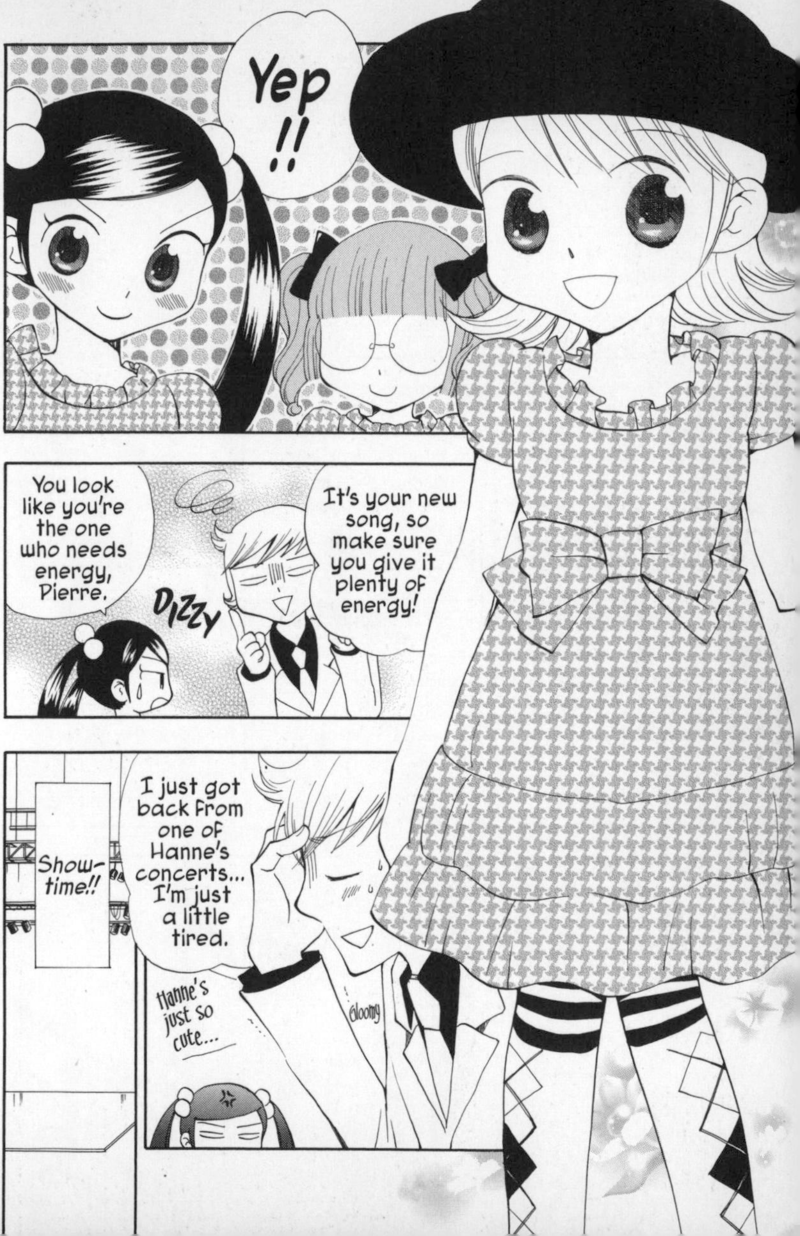
Yep!!
It's your new song, so make sure you give it plenty of energy!
DIZZY
You look like you're the one who needs energy, Pierre.
I just got back from one of Hanne's concerts... I'm just a little tired.
Gloomy
Hanne's just so cute....
Show-time!!

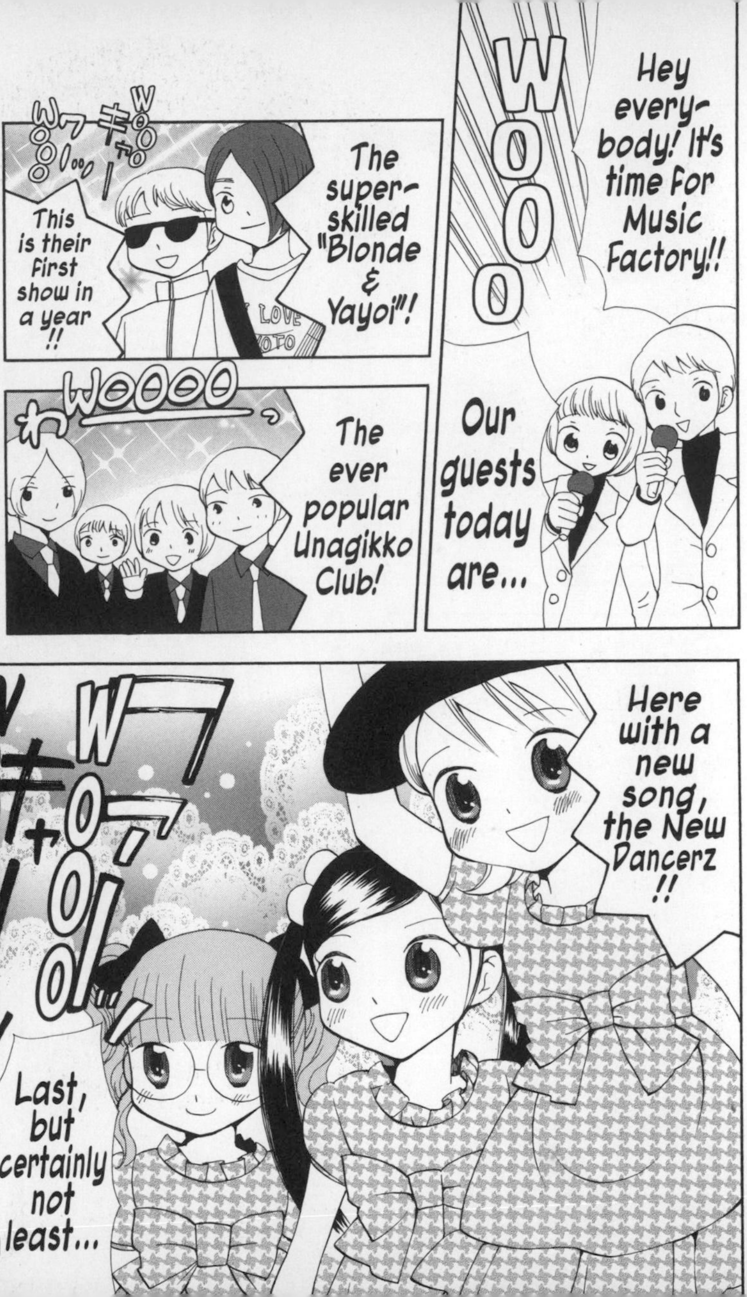
WOOO
Hey every-body! It's time for Music Factory!!
Our guests today are...
The super-skilled "Blonde & Yayoi"!
This is their first show in a year!!
WOOOO
The ever popular Unagikko Club!
Here with a new song, the New Dancerz!!
Last, but certainly not least...

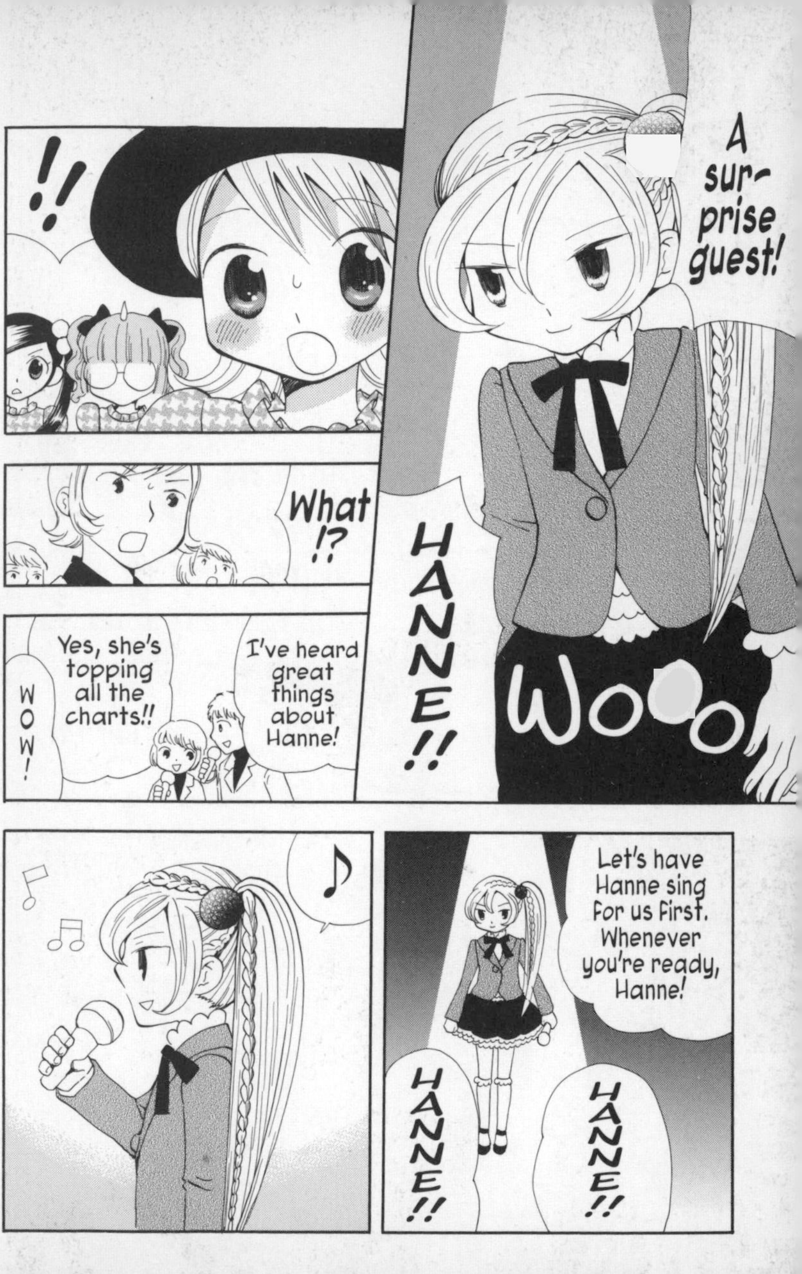
A surprise guest!
HANNE!!
WOOO
!!
What!?
I've heard great things about Hanne!
Yes, she's topping all the charts!!
WOW!
Let's have Hanne sing for us first. Whenever you're ready, Hanne!
HANNE!!
HANNE!!
♪

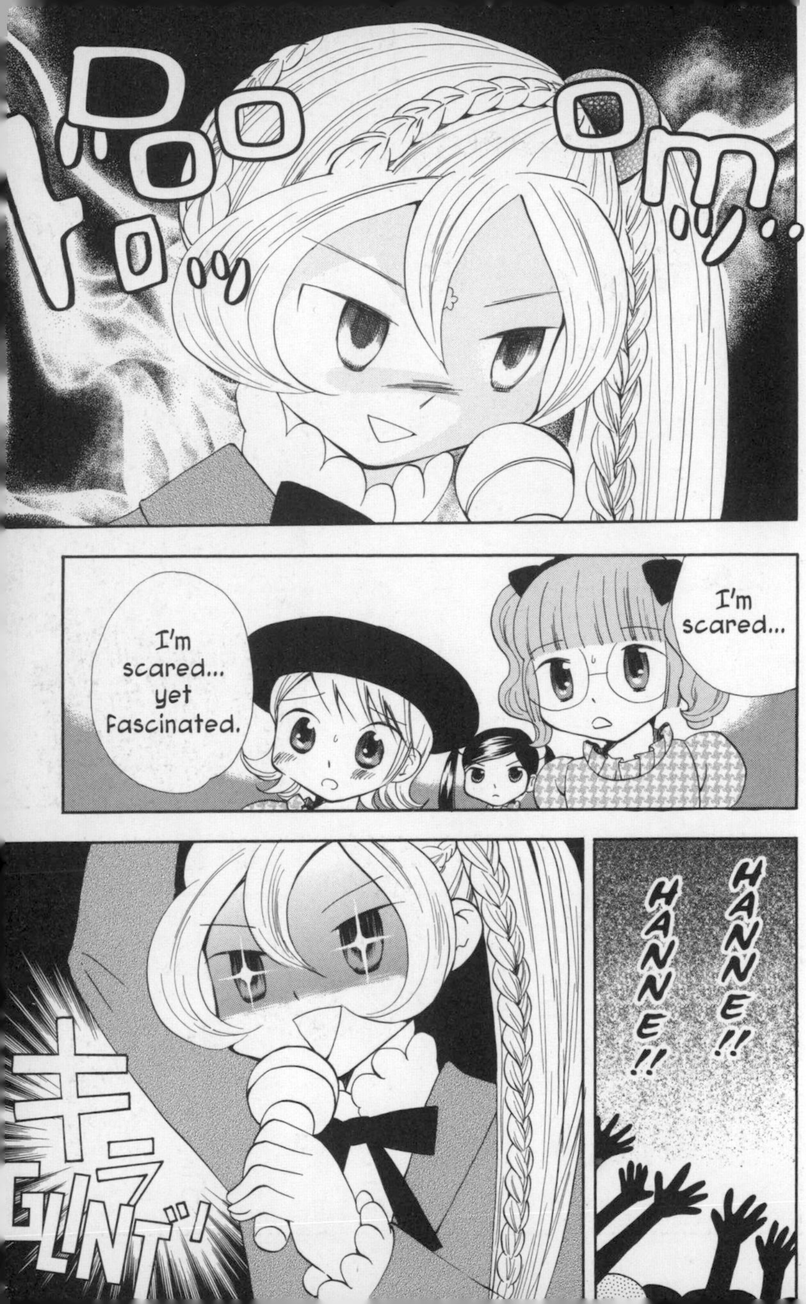

Doooom...
I'm scared...
I'm scared... yet fascinated.
HANNE!!
HANNE!!
キラ
GLINT

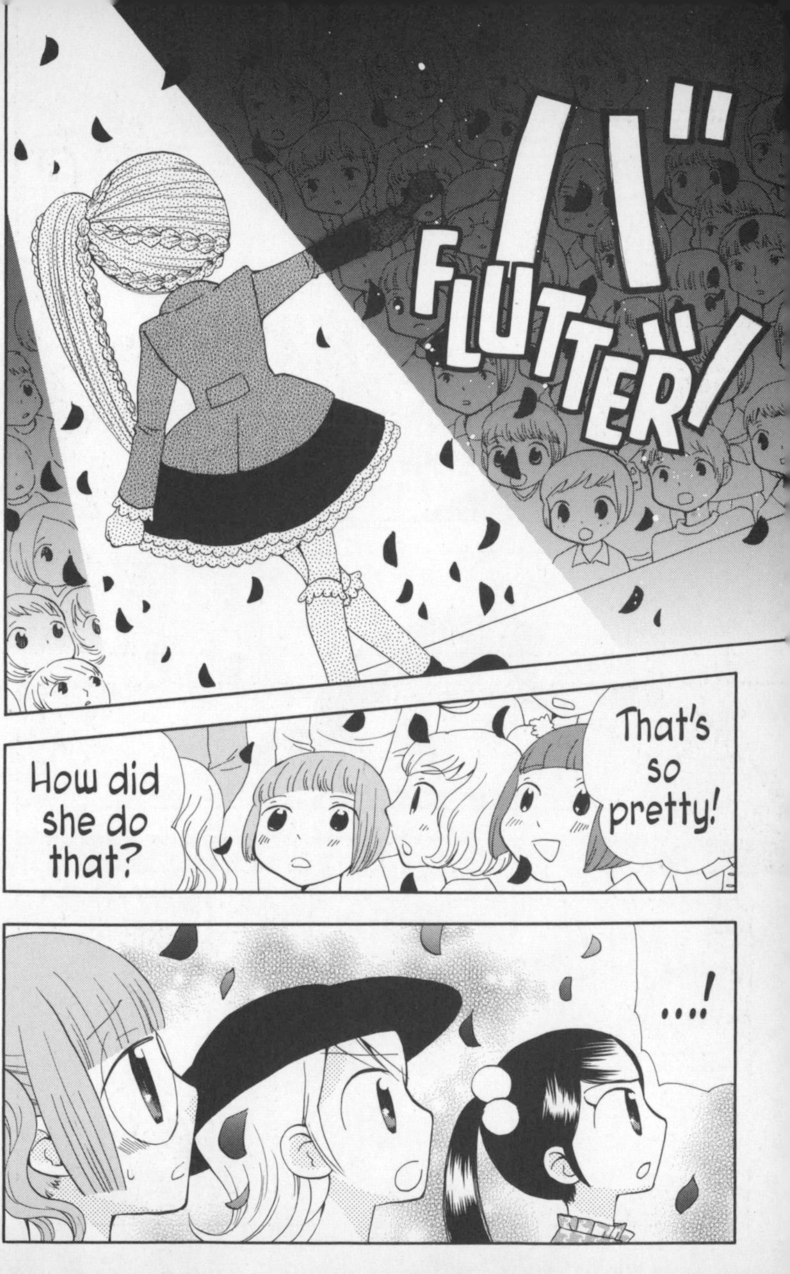
FLUTTER!
That's so pretty!
How did she do that?
...!

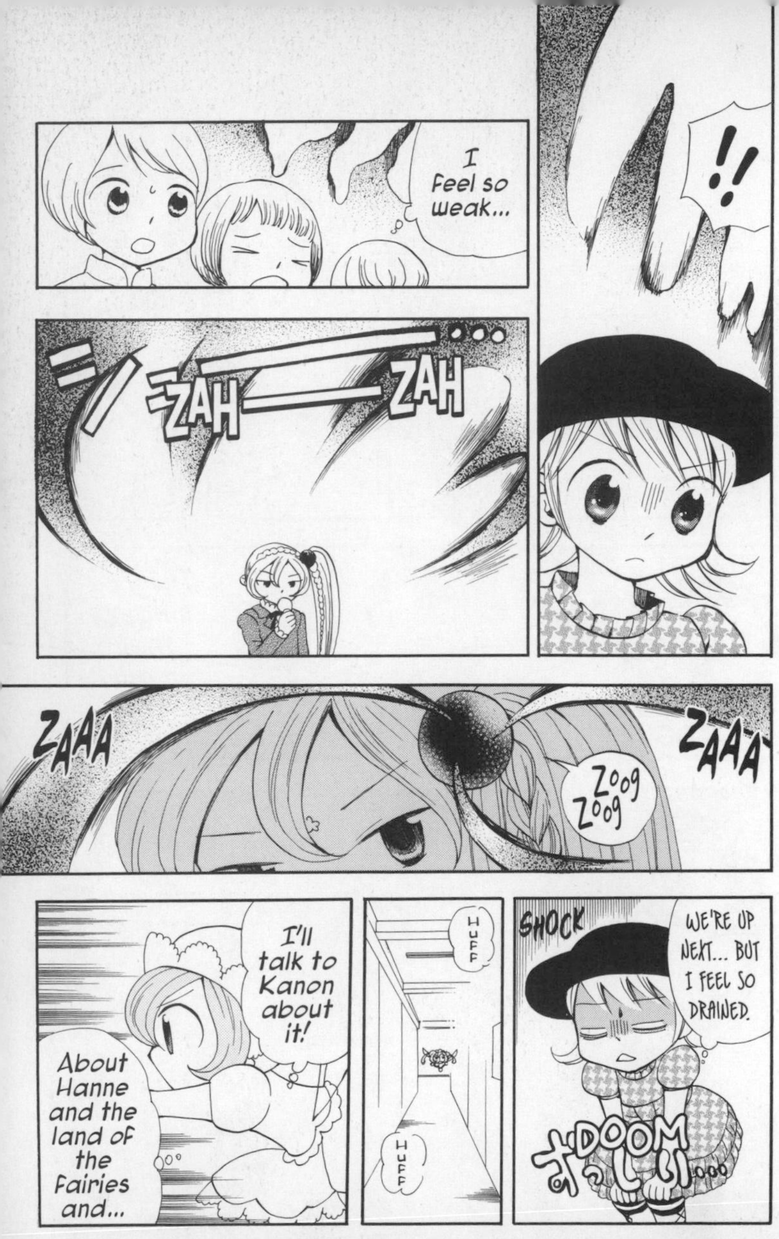
!!
I feel so weak...
ZAH
ZAH
ZAAA
Zoog Zoog
ZAAA
SHOCK
WE'RE UP NEXT... BUT I FEEL SO DRAINED.
DOOM
HUFF
HUFF
I'll talk to Kanon about it!
About Hanne and the land of the Fairies and...

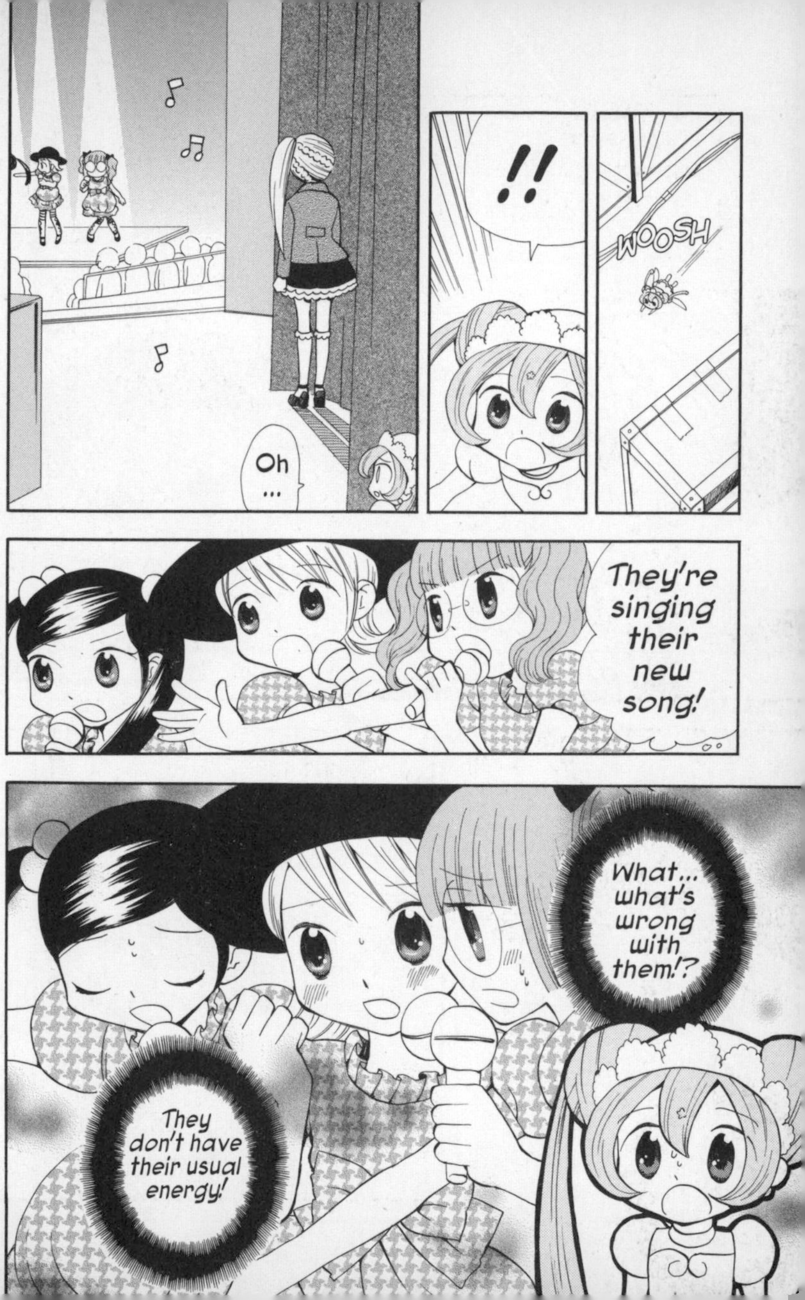
WOOSH
!!
Oh ...
They're singing their new song!
What... what's wrong with them!?
They don't have their usual energy!

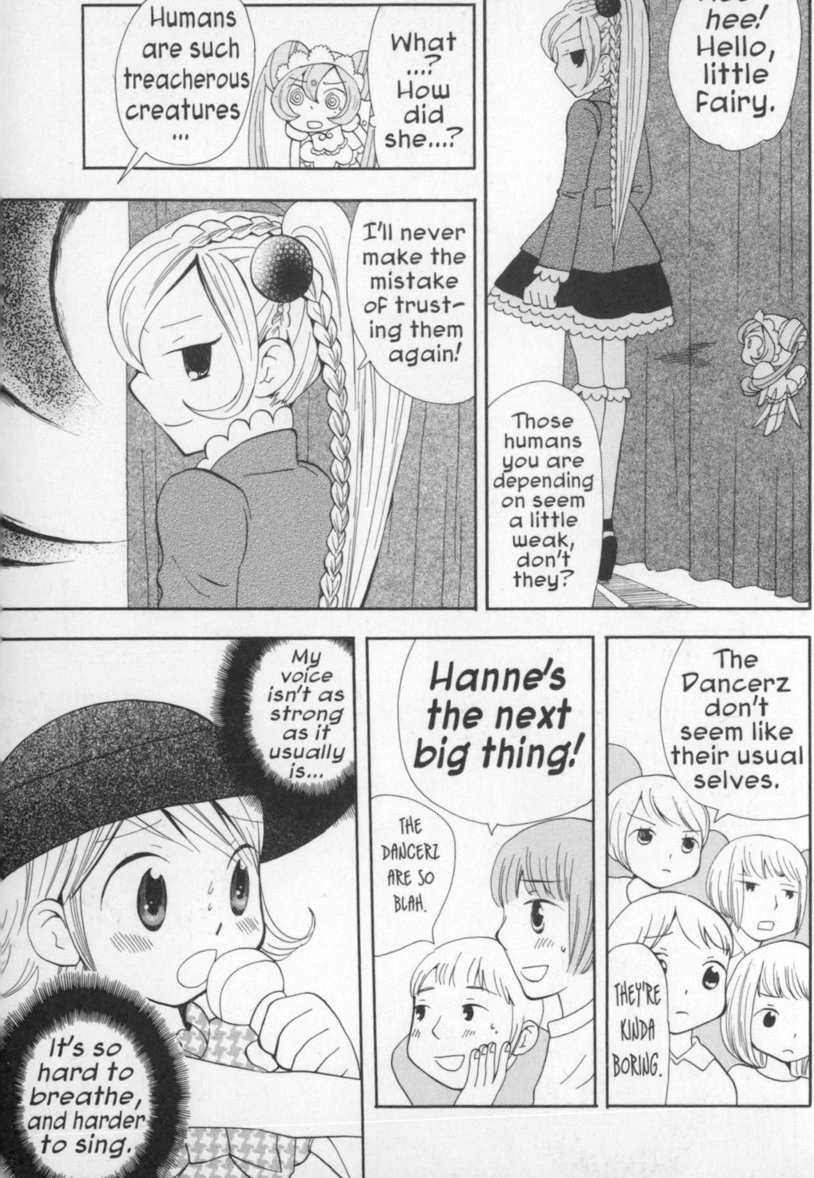
Hee-hee! Hello, little Fairy.
Those humans you are depending on seem a little weak, don't they?
What ....? How did she...?
Humans are such treacherous creatures ...
I'll never make the mistake of trusting them again!
The Dancerz don't seem like their usual selves.
THEY'RE KINDA BORING.
Hanne's the next big thing!
THE DANCERZ ARE SO BLAH.
My voice isn't as strong as it usually is...
It's so hard to breathe, and harder to sing.

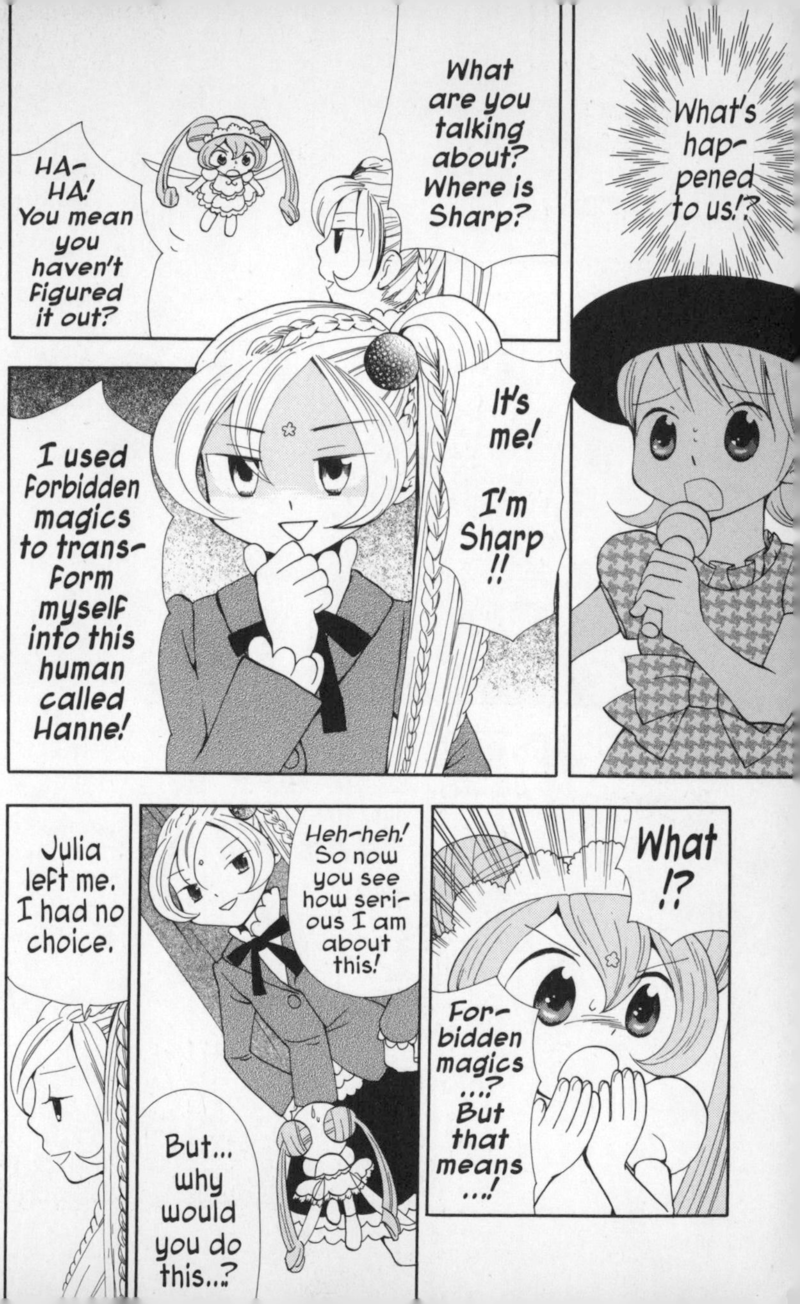
What's hap-pened to us!?
What are you talking about? Where is Sharp?
HA-HA! You mean you haven't figured it out?
It's me!
I'm Sharp!!
I used forbidden magics to trans-form myself into this human called Hanne!
What!?
For-bidden magics...? But that means...!
Heh-heh! So now you see how seri-ous I am about this!
But... why would you do this...?
Julia left me. I had no choice.

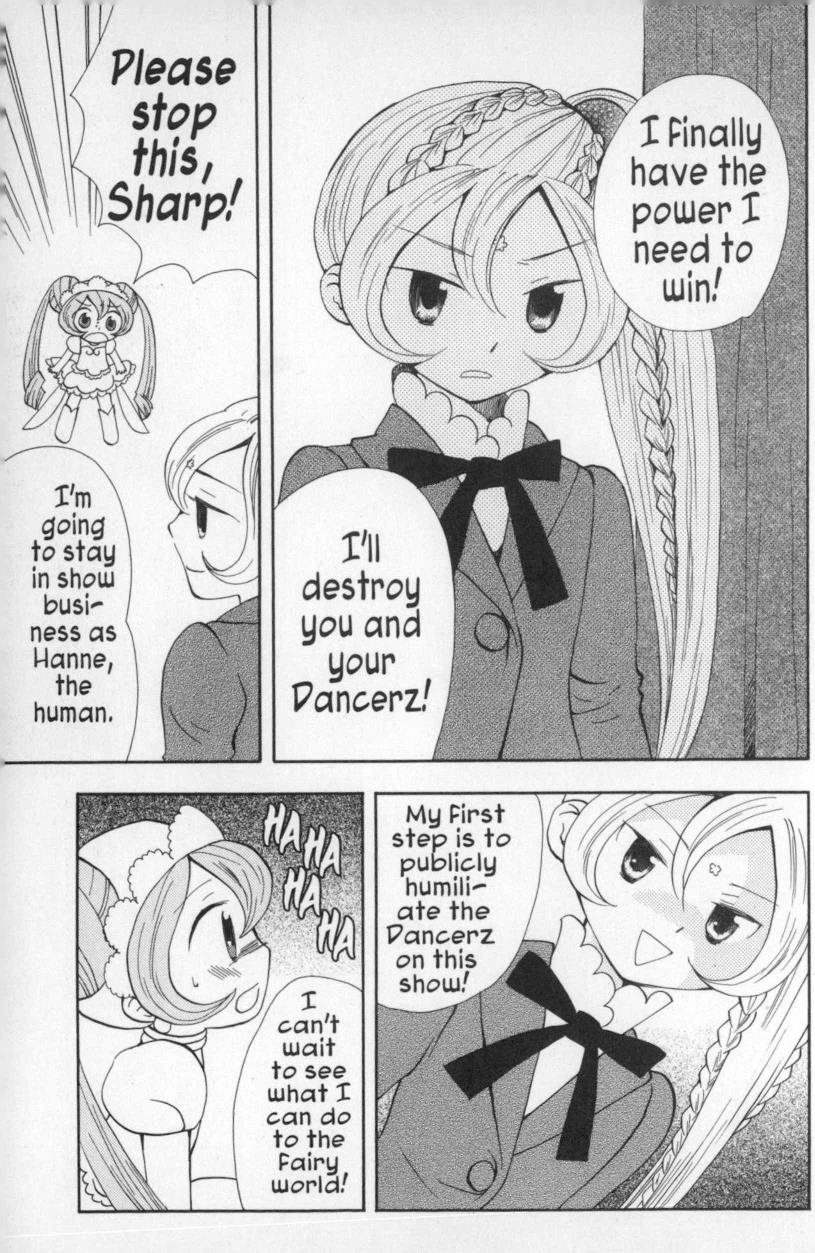
I finally have the power I need to win!
I'll destroy you and your Dancerz!
Please stop this, Sharp!
I'm going to stay in show business as Hanne, the human.
My first step is to publicly humiliate the Dancerz on this show!
HA HA HA HA HA
I can't wait to see what I can do to the fairy world!

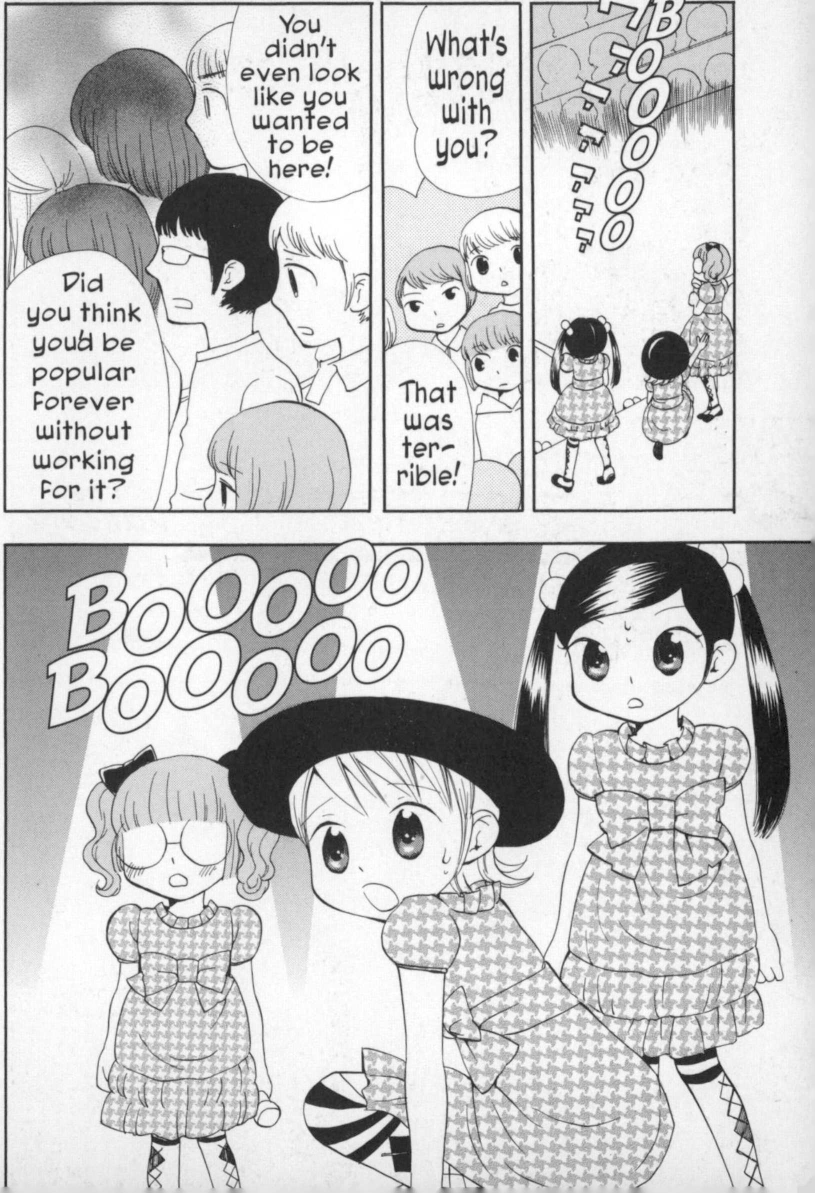
BOOOOOO
What's wrong with you?
That was terrible!
You didn't even look like you wanted to be here!
Did you think you'd be popular forever without working for it?
BOOOOO
BOOOOO

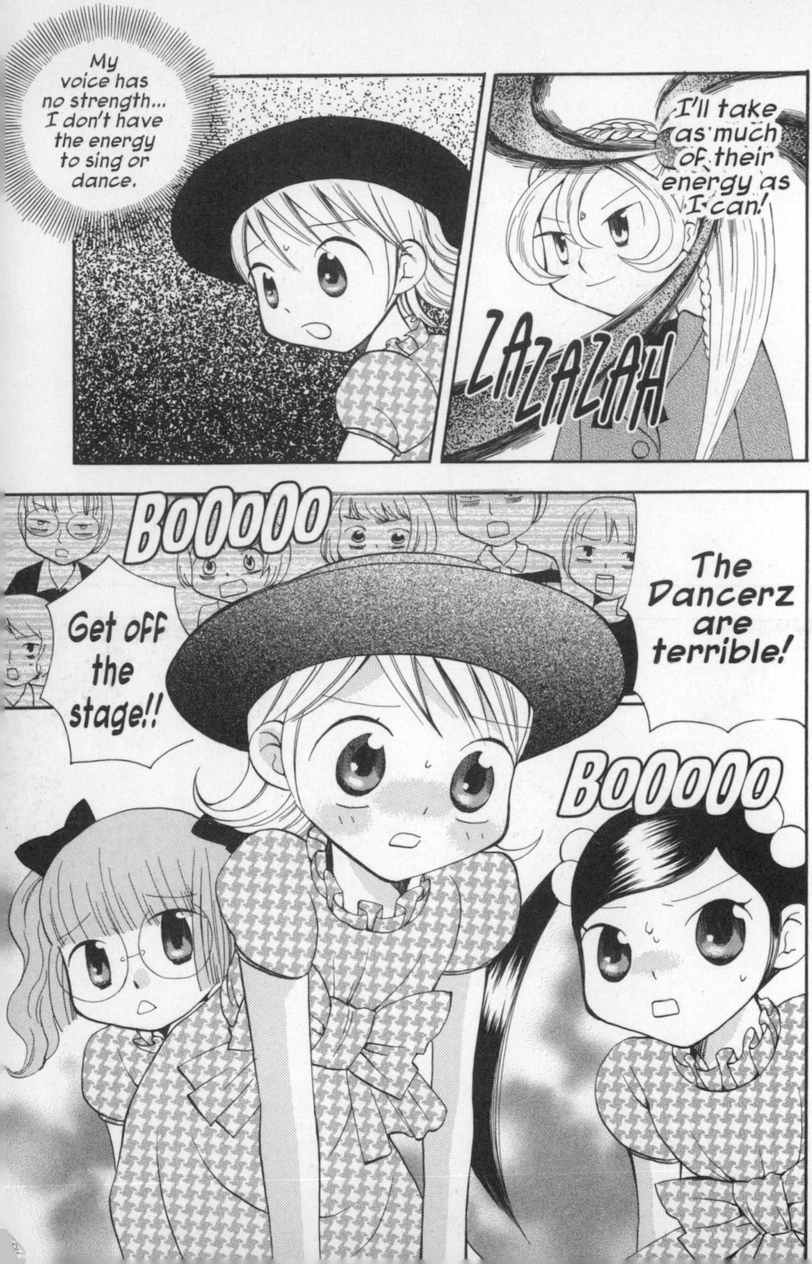
I'll take as much of their energy as I can!
LAZAZAH
My voice has no strength... I don't have the energy to sing or dance.
The Dancerz are terrible!
BOOOOO
BOOOOO
Get off the stage!!

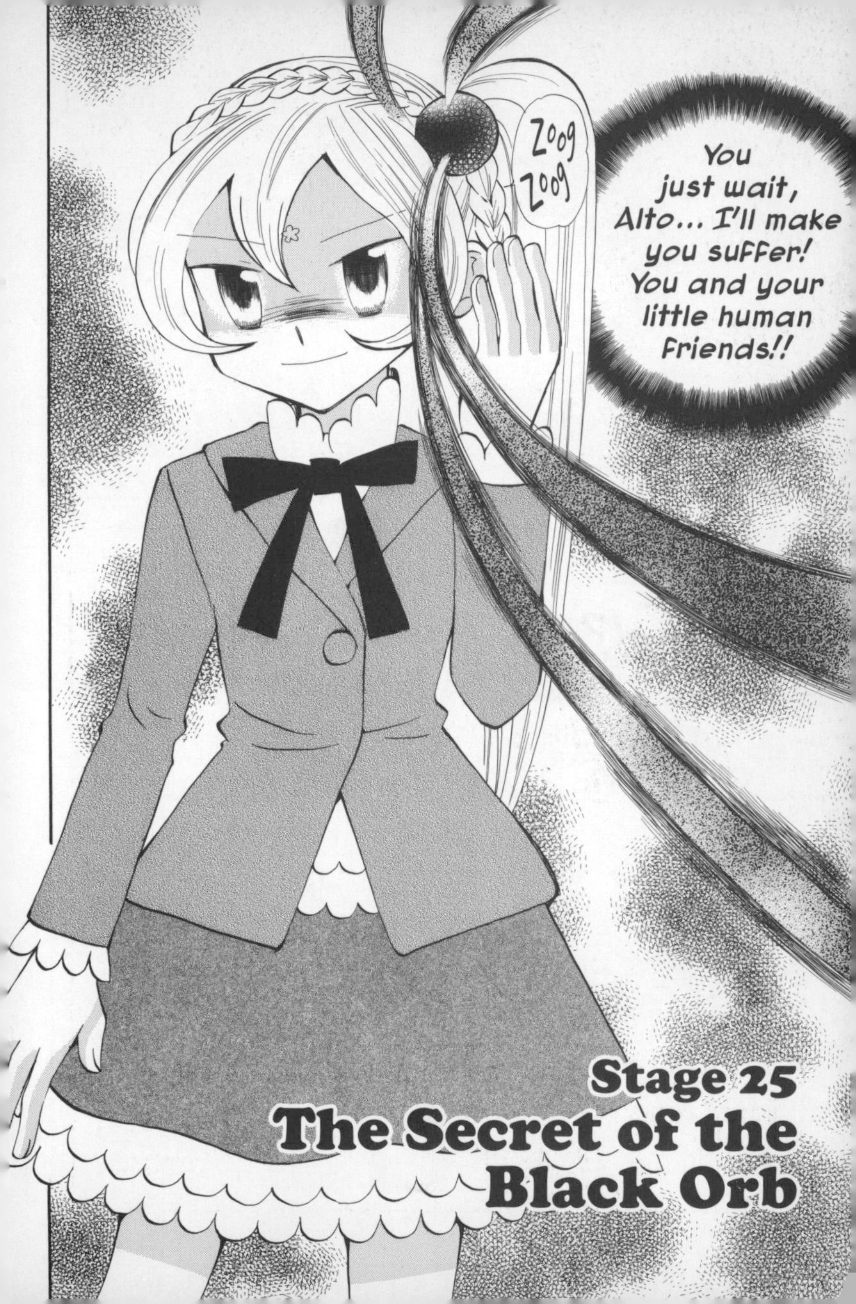
You just wait, Alto... I'll make you suffer! You and your little human friends!!
ZOOG ZOOG

Stage 25
The Secret of the Black Orb

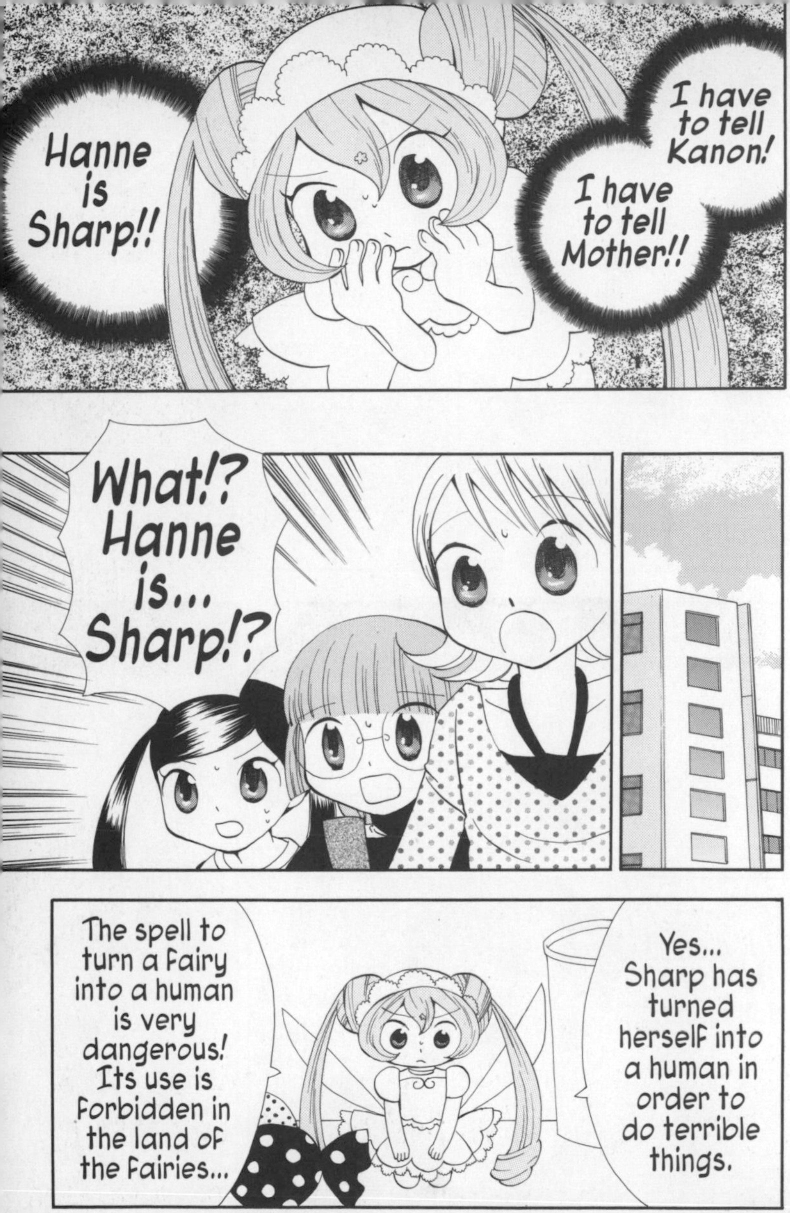
I have to tell Kanon!
I have to tell Mother!!
Hanne is Sharp!!
What!? Hanne is... Sharp!?
Yes... Sharp has turned herself into a human in order to do terrible things.
The spell to turn a fairy into a human is very dangerous! Its use is forbidden in the land of the fairies...

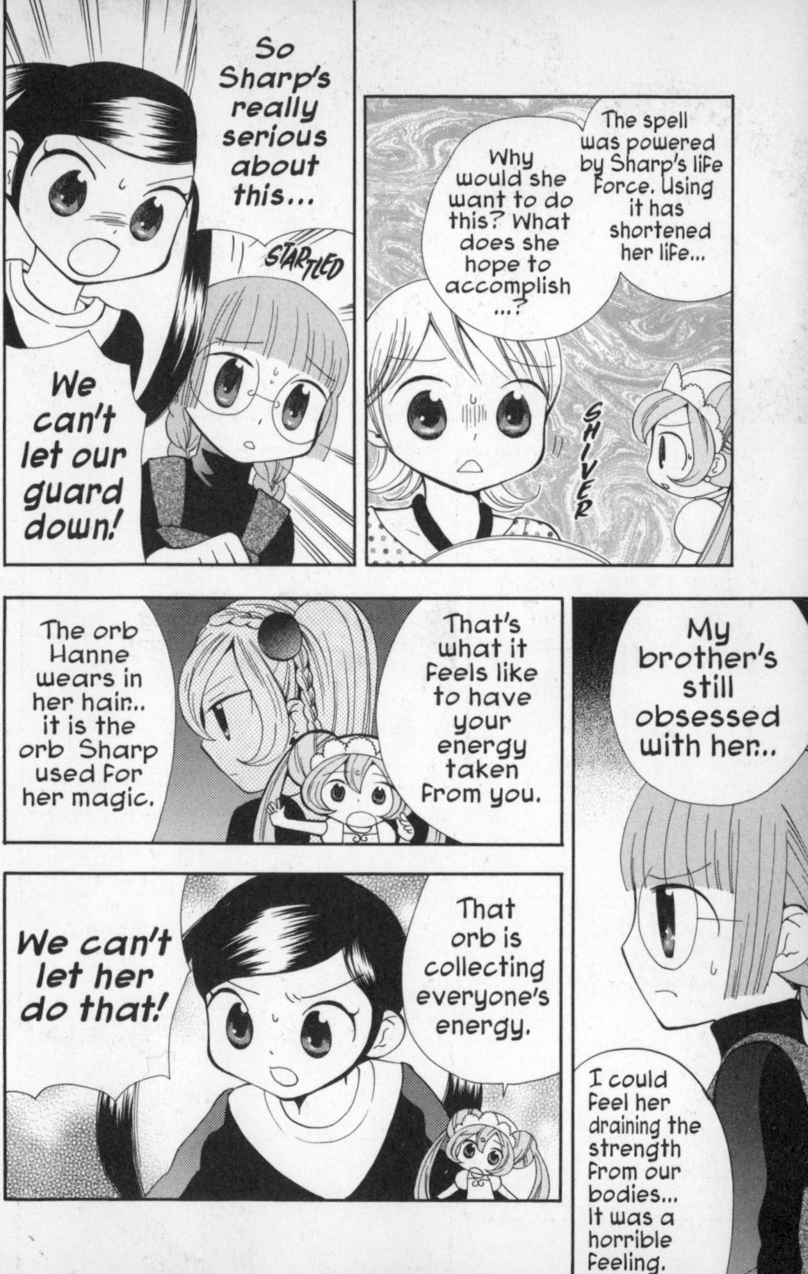
The spell was powered by Sharp's life force. Using it has shortened her life...
Why would she want to do this? What does she hope to accomplish ...?
SHIVER
So Sharp's really serious about this...
STARTLED
We can't let our guard down!
My brother's still obsessed with her..
I could feel her draining the strength from our bodies... It was a horrible feeling.
That's what it feels like to have your energy taken from you.
The orb Hanne wears in her hair.. it is the orb Sharp used for her magic.
That orb is collecting everyone's energy.
We can't let her do that!

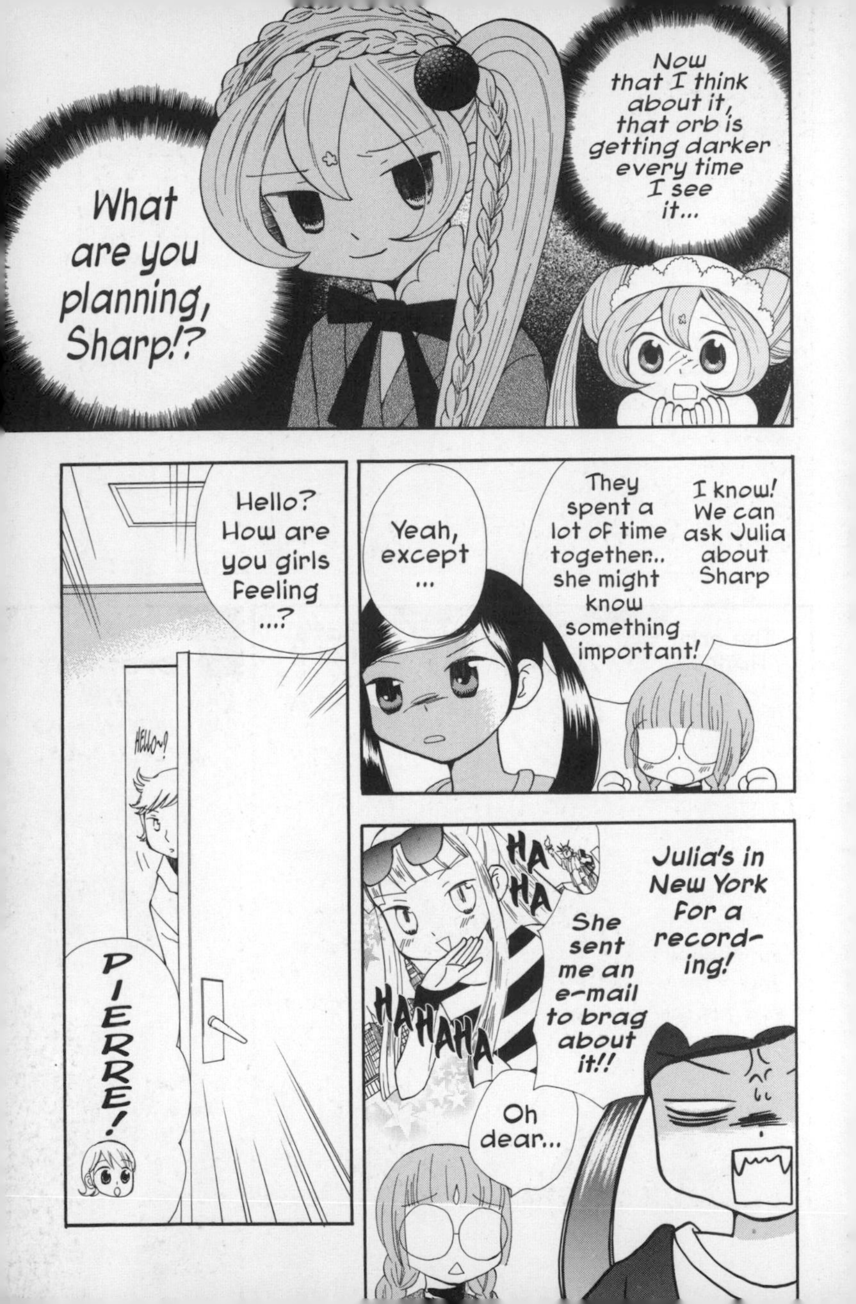
Now that I think about it, that orb is getting darker every time I see it...
What are you planning, Sharp!?
I know! We can ask Julia about Sharp
They spent a lot of time together... she might know something important!
Yeah, except ...
Julia's in New York for a recording!
She sent me an e-mail to brag about it!!
HA HA
HAHAHA
Oh dear...
Hello? How are you girls feeling ...?
HELLO~?
PIERRE!

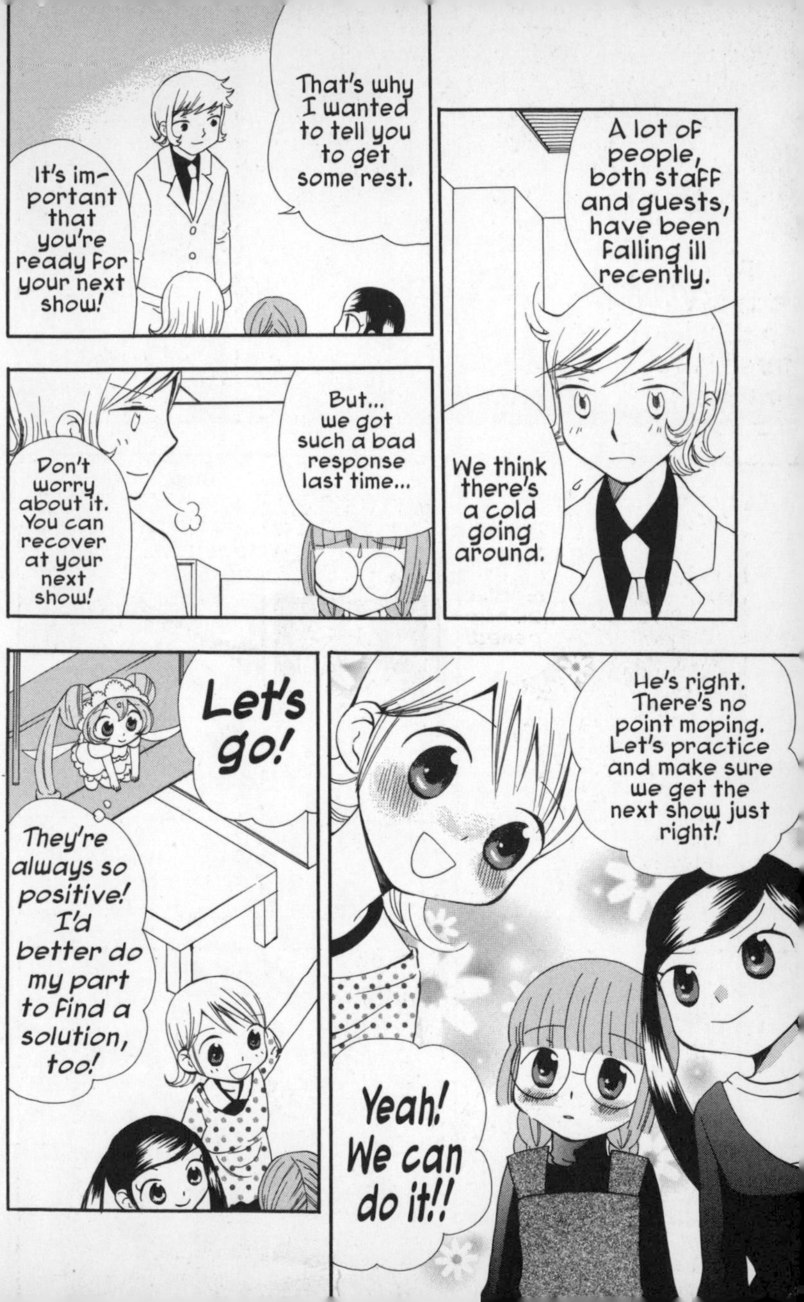

A lot of people, both staff and guests, have been falling ill recently.
We think there's a cold going around.
That's why I wanted to tell you to get some rest.
It's important that you're ready for your next show!
But... we got such a bad response last time...
Don't worry about it. You can recover at your next show!
He's right. There's no point moping. Let's practice and make sure we get the next show just right!
Yeah! We can do it!!
Let's go!
They're always so positive! I'd better do my part to find a solution, too!

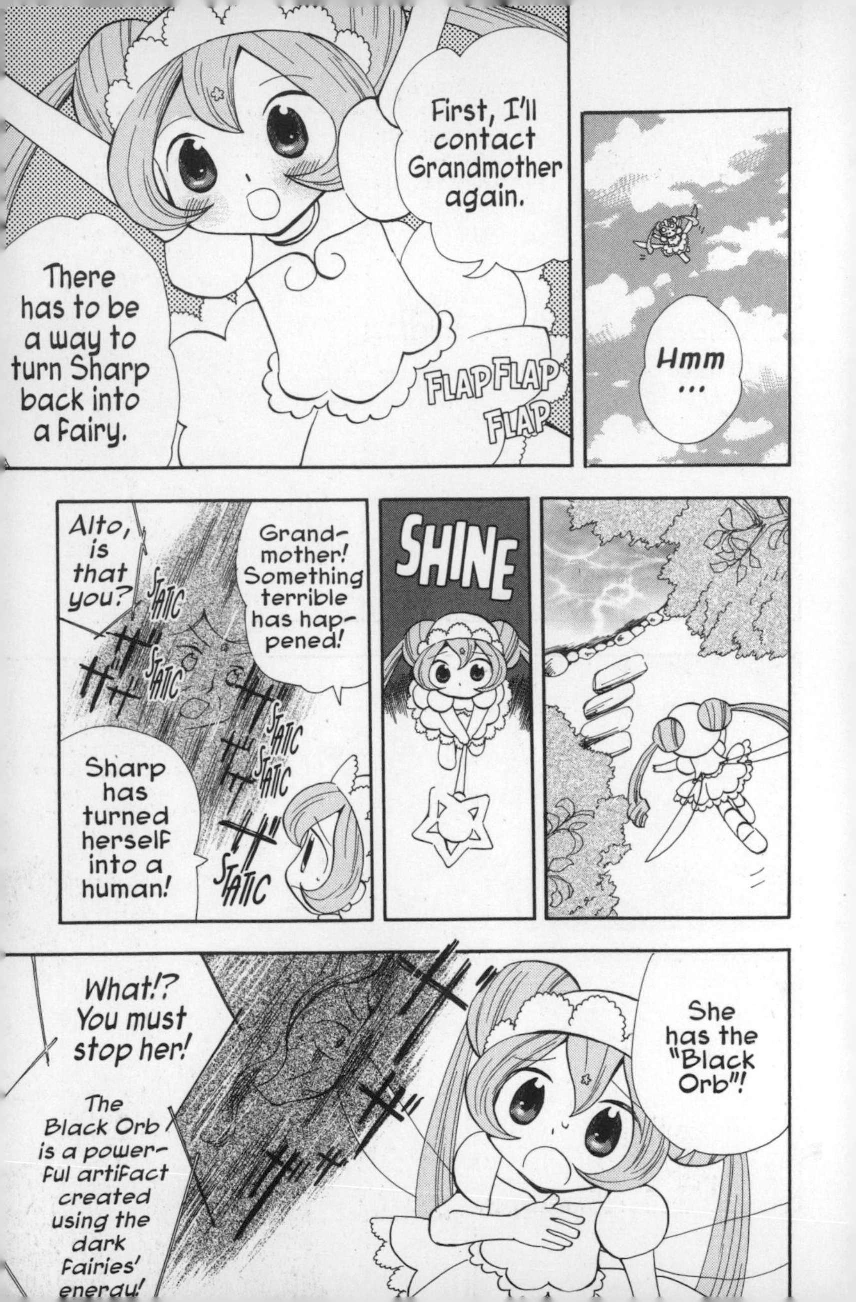
Hmm ...
First, I'll contact Grandmother again.
There has to be a way to turn Sharp back into a fairy.
FLAPFLAP FLAP
SHINE
Grand-mother! Something terrible has hap-pened!
Alto, is that you?
STATIC STATIC
STATIC STATIC
Sharp has turned herself into a human!
STATIC
She has the "Black Orb"!
What!? You must stop her!
The Black Orb is a power-ful artifact created using the dark fairies' energy!

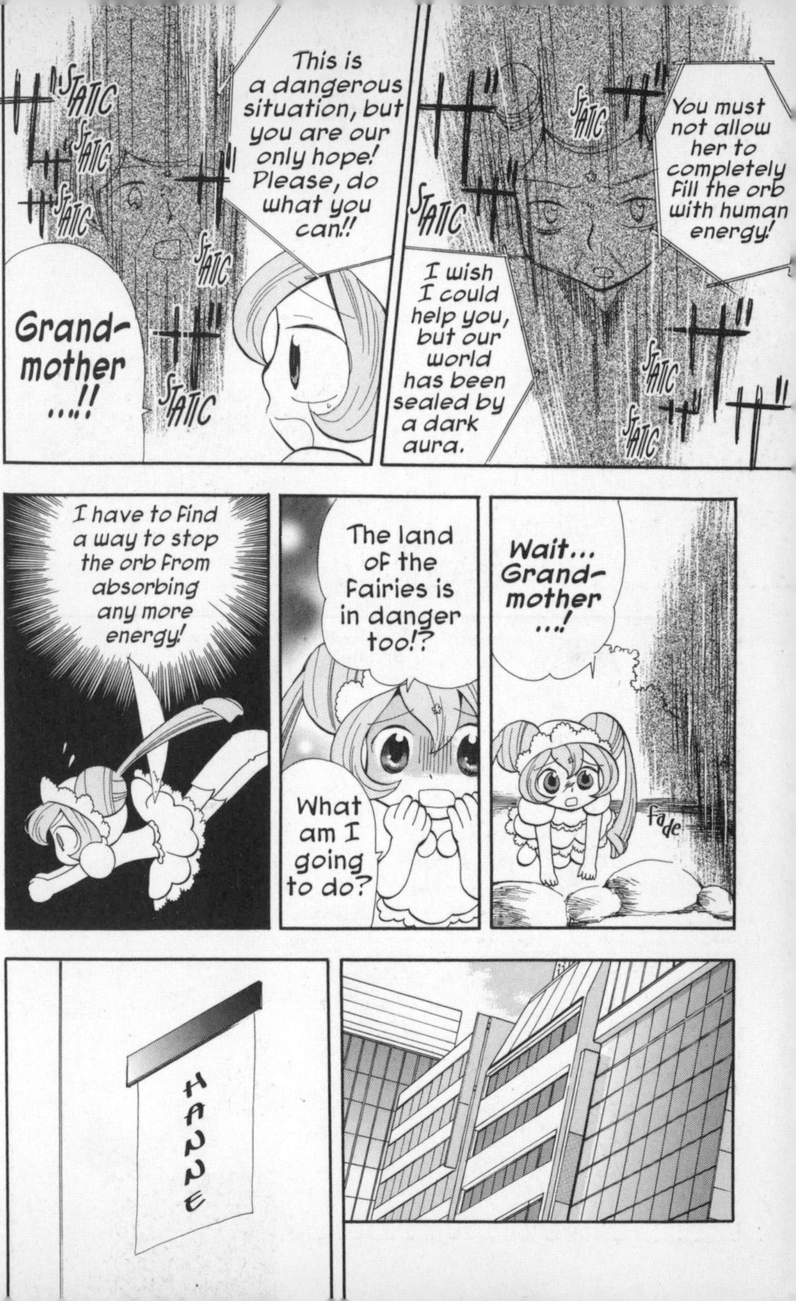
STATIC
You must not allow her to completely fill the orb with human energy!
STATIC
STATIC
STATIC
I wish I could help you, but our world has been sealed by a dark aura.
This is a dangerous situation, but you are our only hope! Please, do what you can!!
STATIC
STATIC
STATIC
STATIC
STATIC
Grand-mother ...!!
Wait... Grand-mother ...!
fade
The land of the fairies is in danger too!?
What am I going to do?
I have to find a way to stop the orb from absorbing any more energy!
HANNE

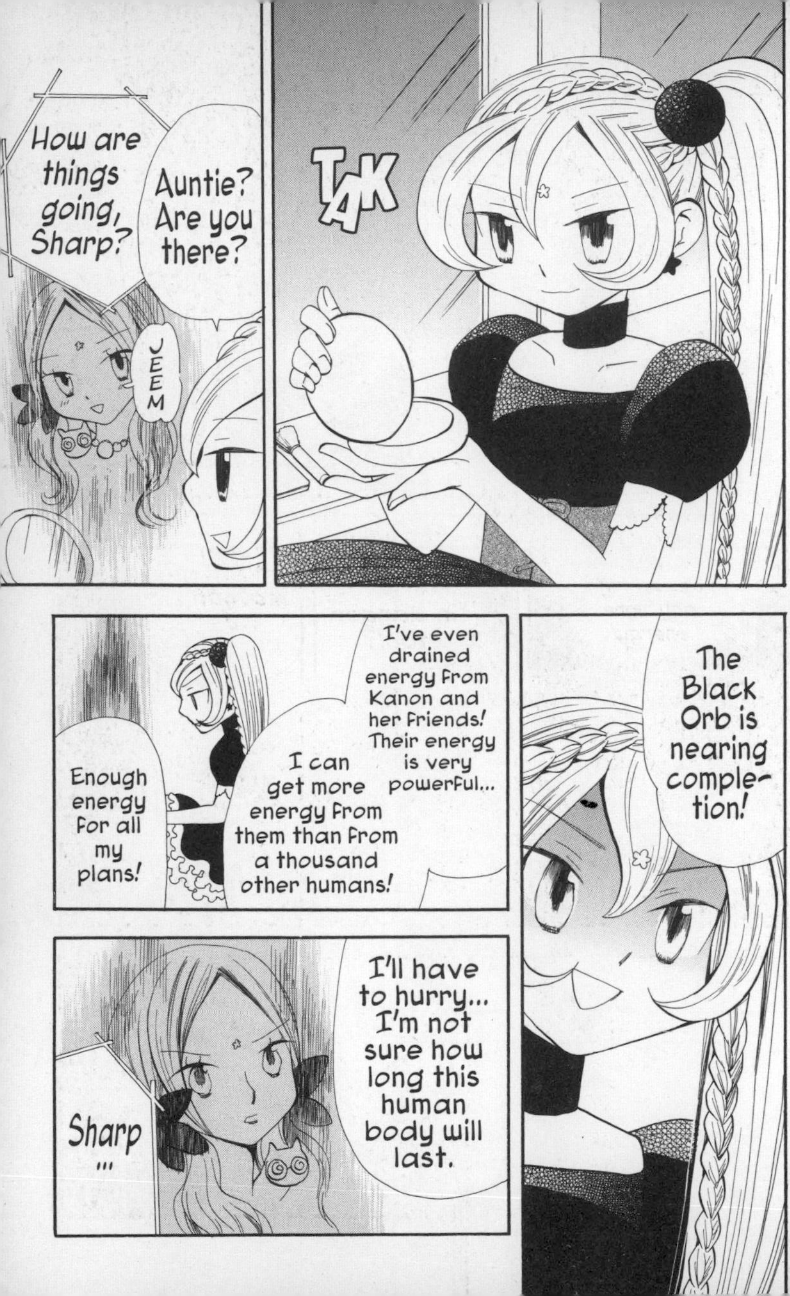
TAK
Auntie? Are you there?
JEEM
How are things going, Sharp?
The Black Orb is nearing comple-tion!
I've even drained energy from Kanon and her friends! Their energy is very powerful...
I can get more energy from them than from a thousand other humans!
Enough energy for all my plans!
I'll have to hurry... I'm not sure how long this human body will last.
Sharp ...

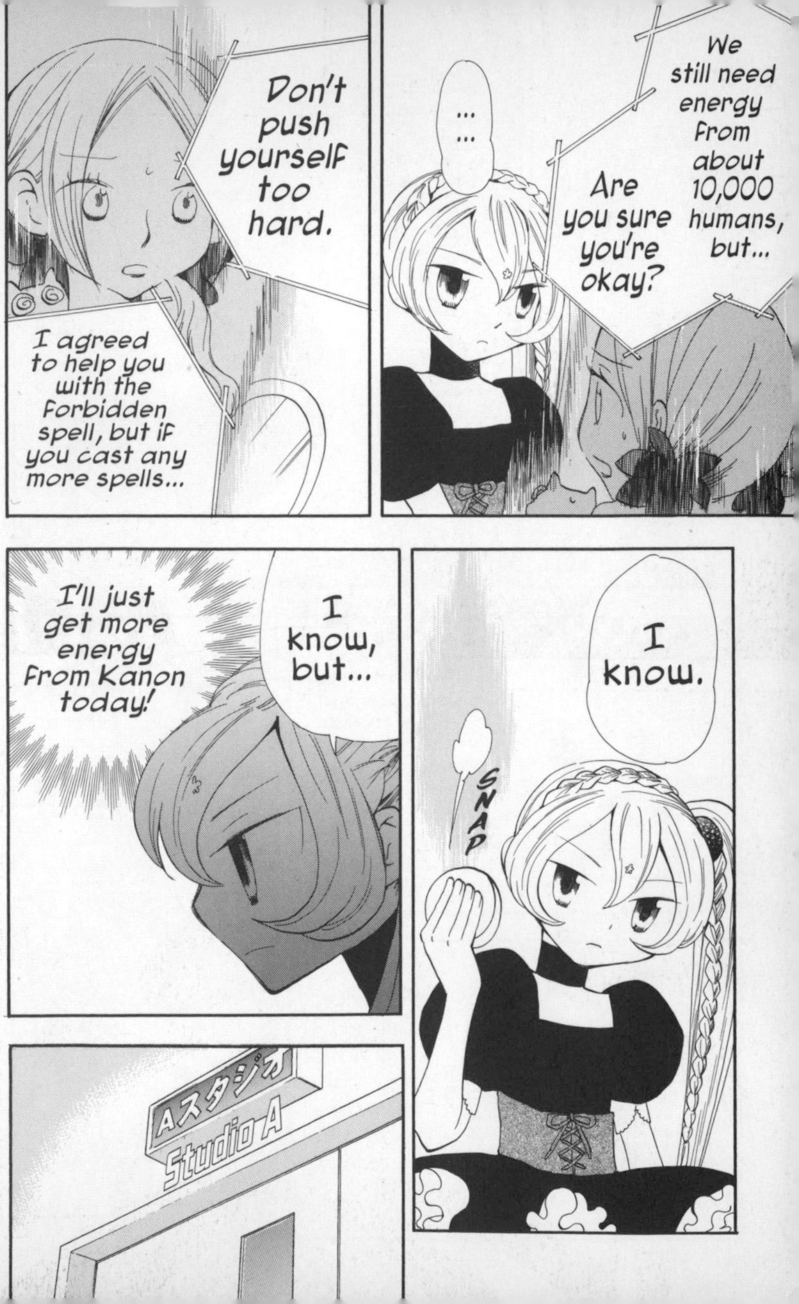
We still need energy from about 10,000 humans, but...
Are you sure you're okay?
... ...
Don't push yourself too hard.
I agreed to help you with the forbidden spell, but if you cast any more spells...
I know.
SNAP
I know, but...
I'll just get more energy from Kanon today!
Aスタジオ
Studio A

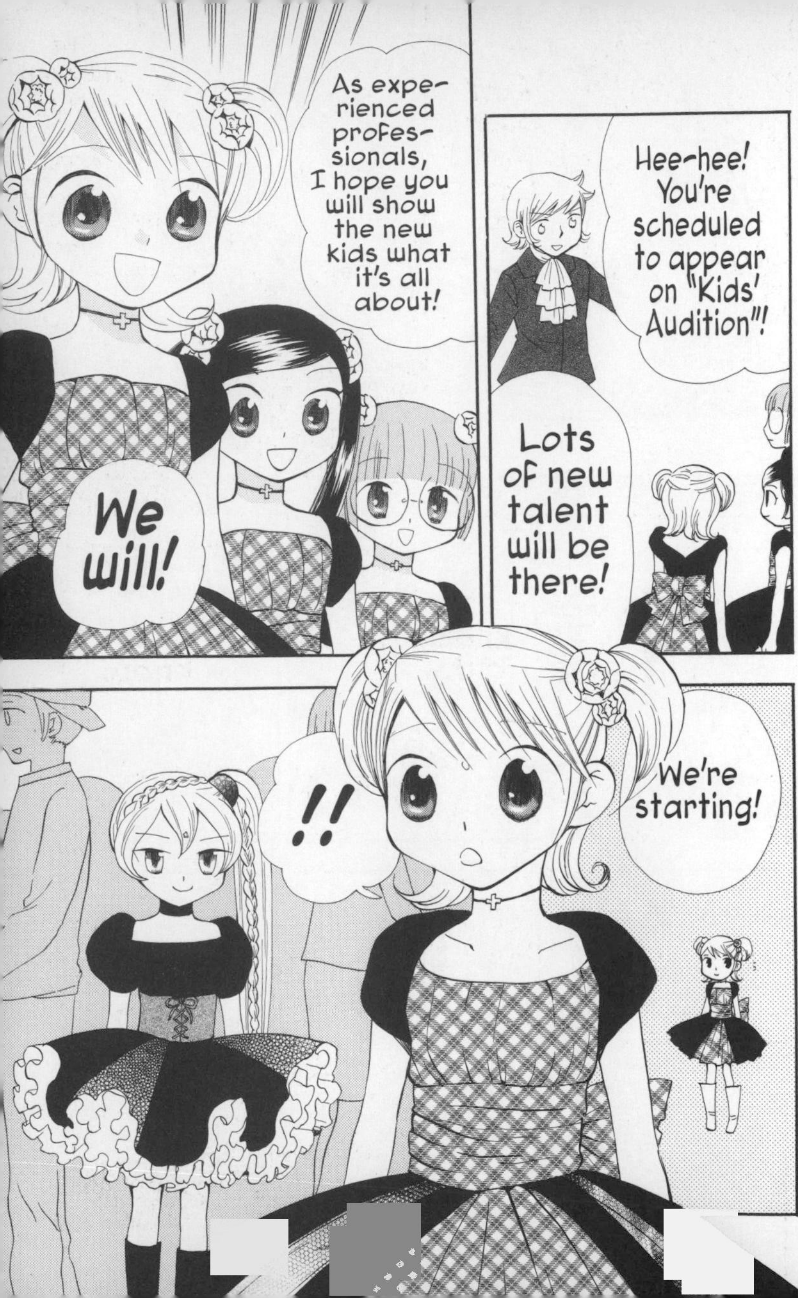
Hee-hee! You're scheduled to appear on "Kids' Audition"!
Lots of new talent will be there!
As experienced professionals, I hope you will show the new kids what it's all about!
We will!
We're starting!
!!

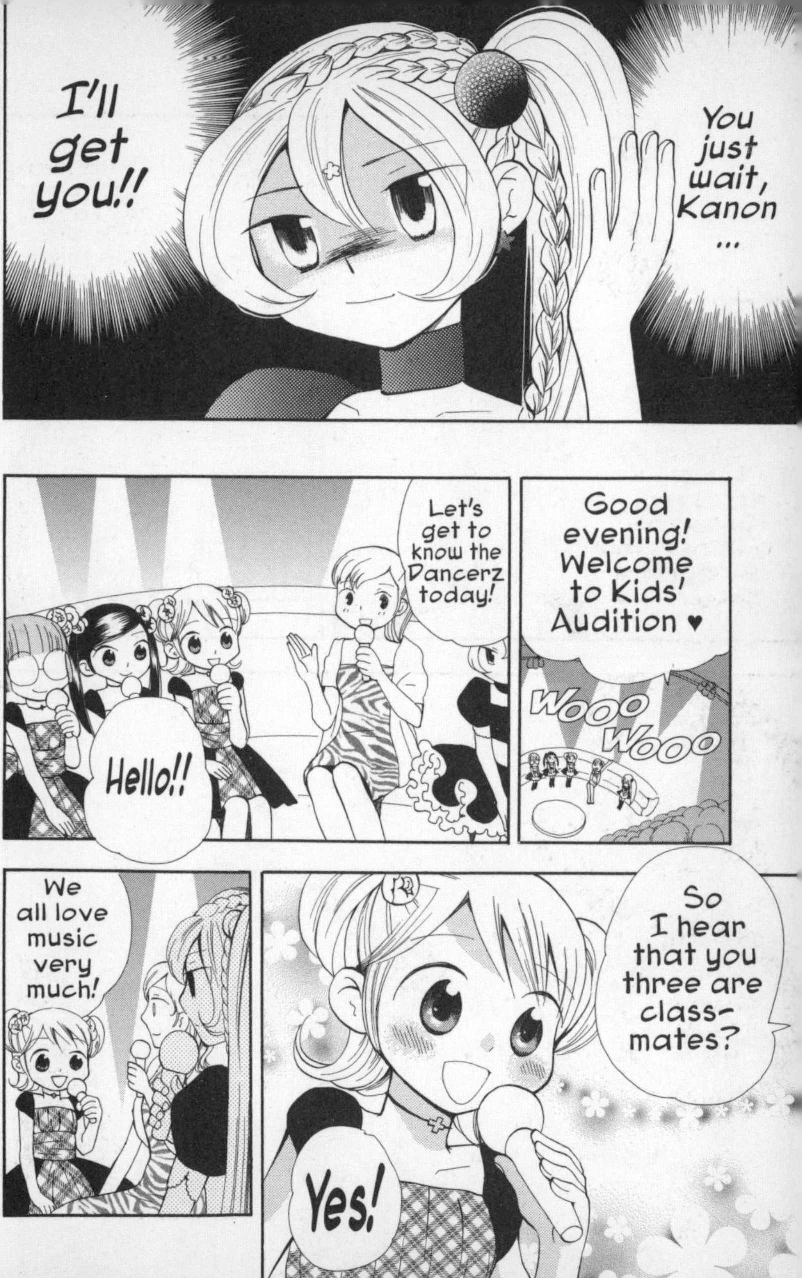
You just wait, Kanon ...
I'll get you!!
Good evening! Welcome to Kids' Audition ♥
WOOO WOOO
Let's get to know the Dancerz today!
Hello!!
So I hear that you three are class-mates?
Yes!
We all love music very much!

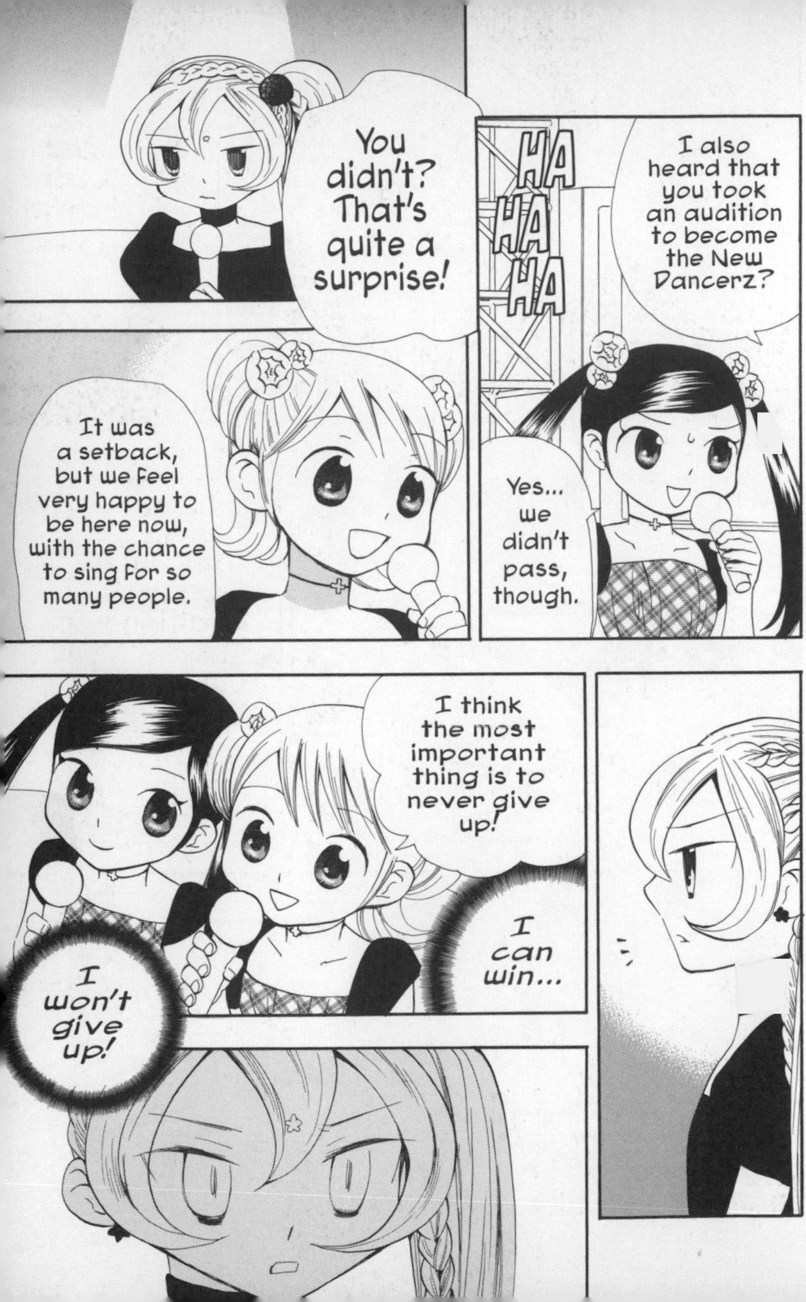

I also heard that you took an audition to become the New Dancerz?
HA HA HA
Yes... we didn't pass, though.
You didn't? That's quite a surprise!
It was a setback, but we feel very happy to be here now, with the chance to sing for so many people.
I think the most important thing is to never give up!
I can win...
I won't give up!

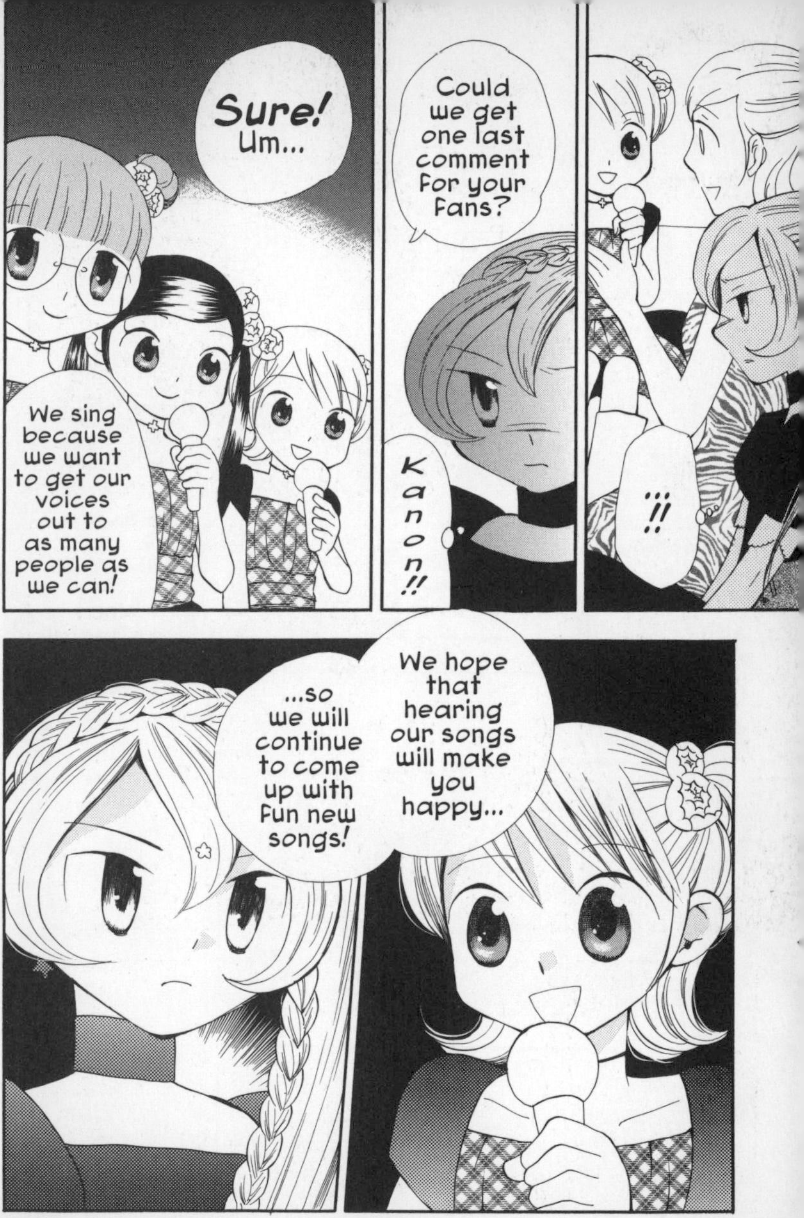
...!!
Could we get one last comment for your fans?
Kanon!!
Sure! Um...
We sing because we want to get our voices out to as many people as we can!
We hope that hearing our songs will make you happy...
...so we will continue to come up with fun new songs!

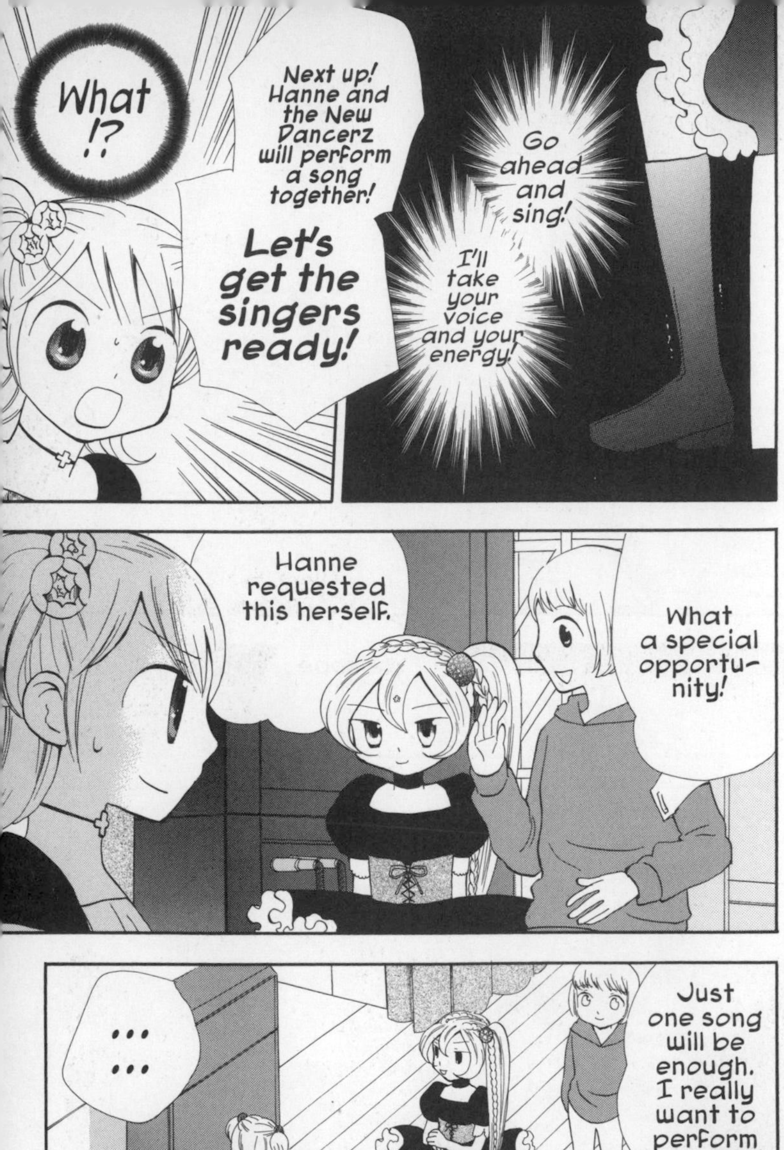
Go ahead and sing!
I'll take your voice and your energy!
Next up! Hanne and the New Dancerz will perform a song together!
Let's get the singers ready!
What !?
What a special opportu-nity!
Hanne requested this herself.
Just one song will be enough. I really want to perform with you!
... ...

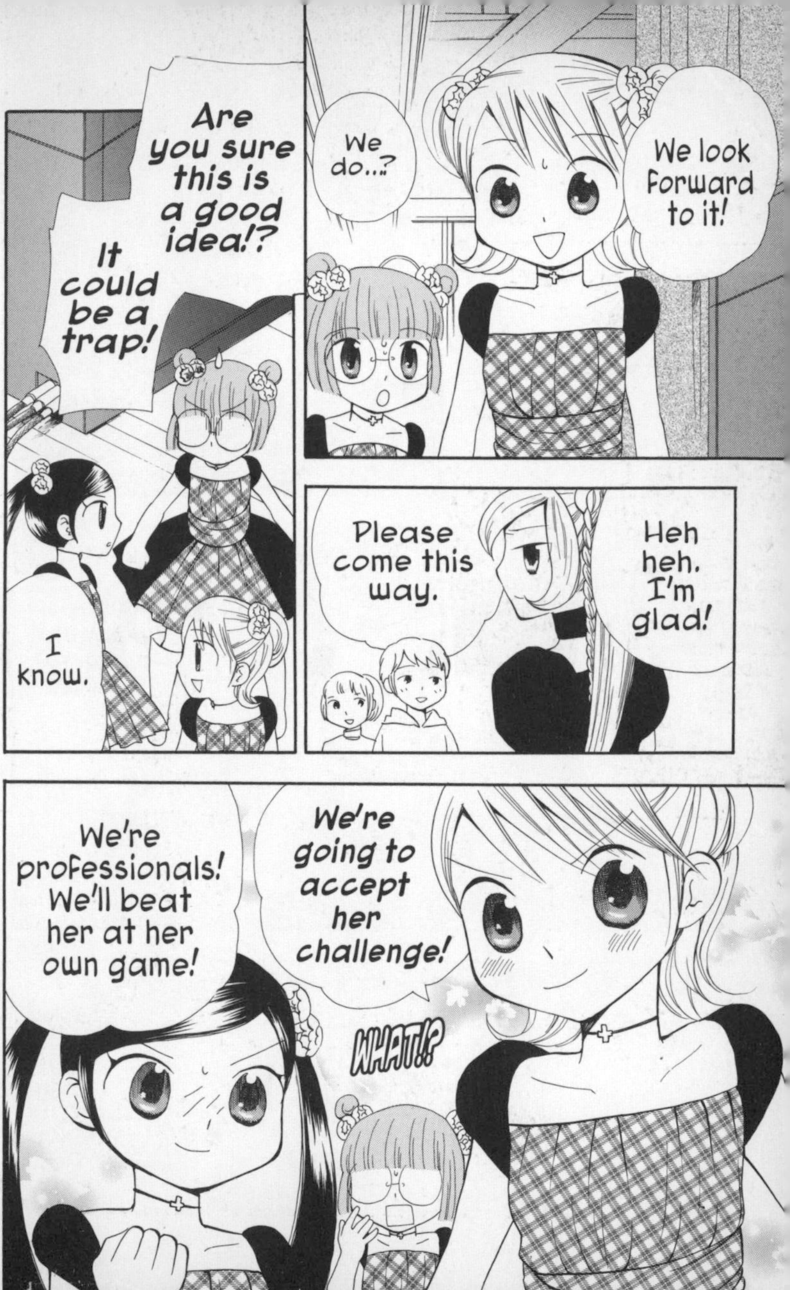
We look forward to it!
We do...?
Heh heh. I'm glad!
Please come this way.
Are you sure this is a good idea!?
It could be a trap!
I know.
We're going to accept her challenge!
We're professionals! We'll beat her at her own game!
WHAT!?

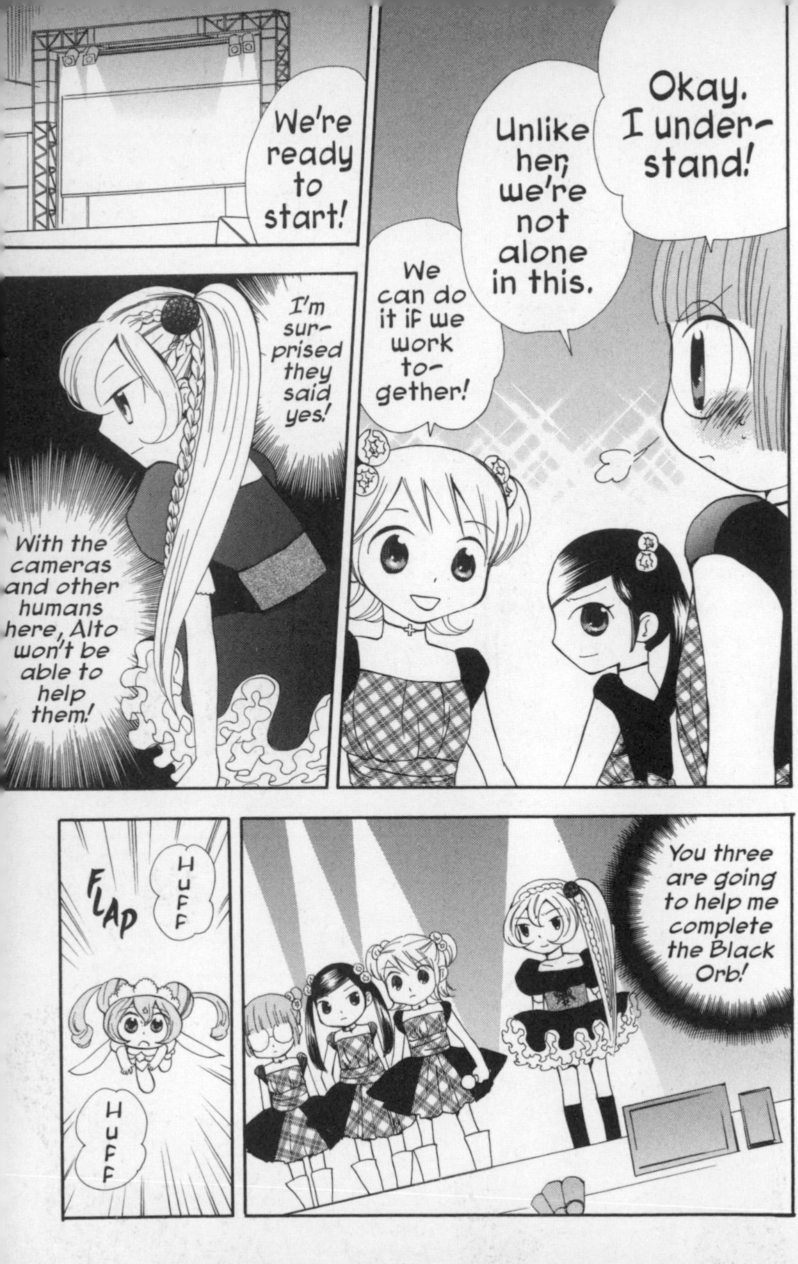
Okay. I understand!
Unlike her, we're not alone in this.
We can do it if we work together!
We're ready to start!
I'm surprised they said yes!
With the cameras and other humans here, Alto won't be able to help them!
You three are going to help me complete the Black Orb!
HUFF
FLAP
HUFF

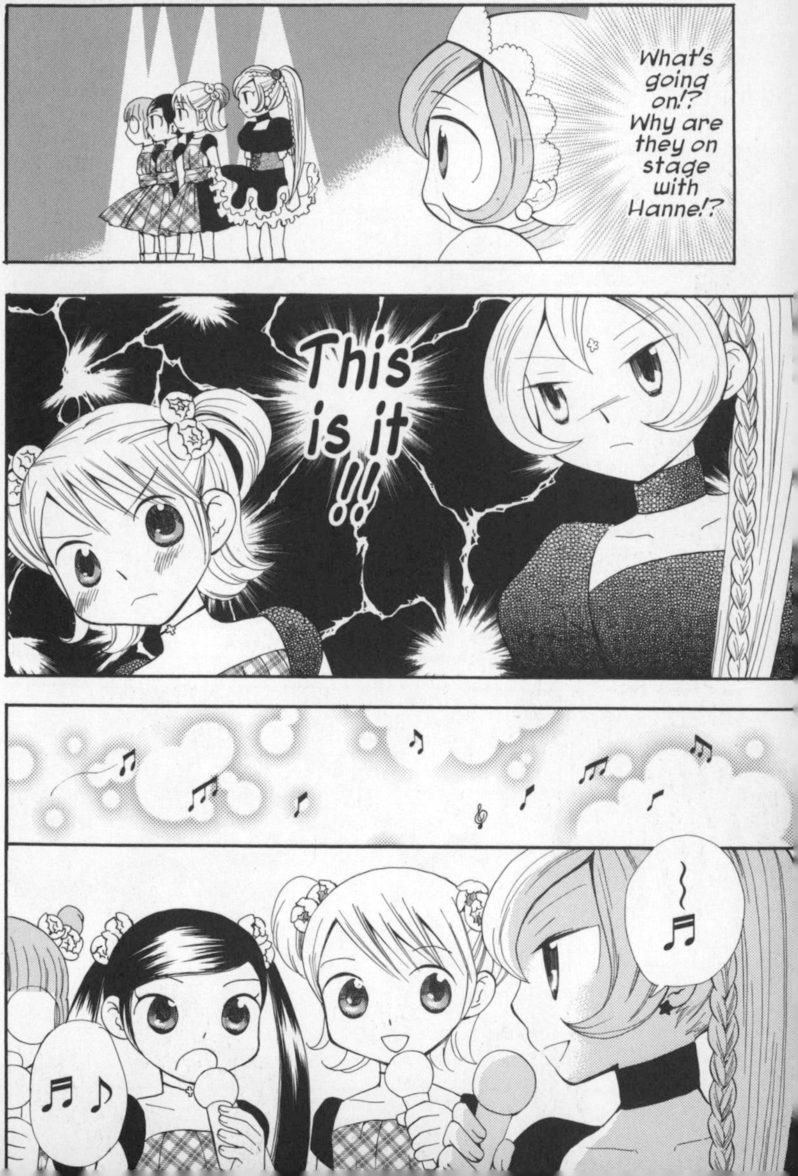
What's going on!? Why are they on stage with Hanne!?
This is it!!

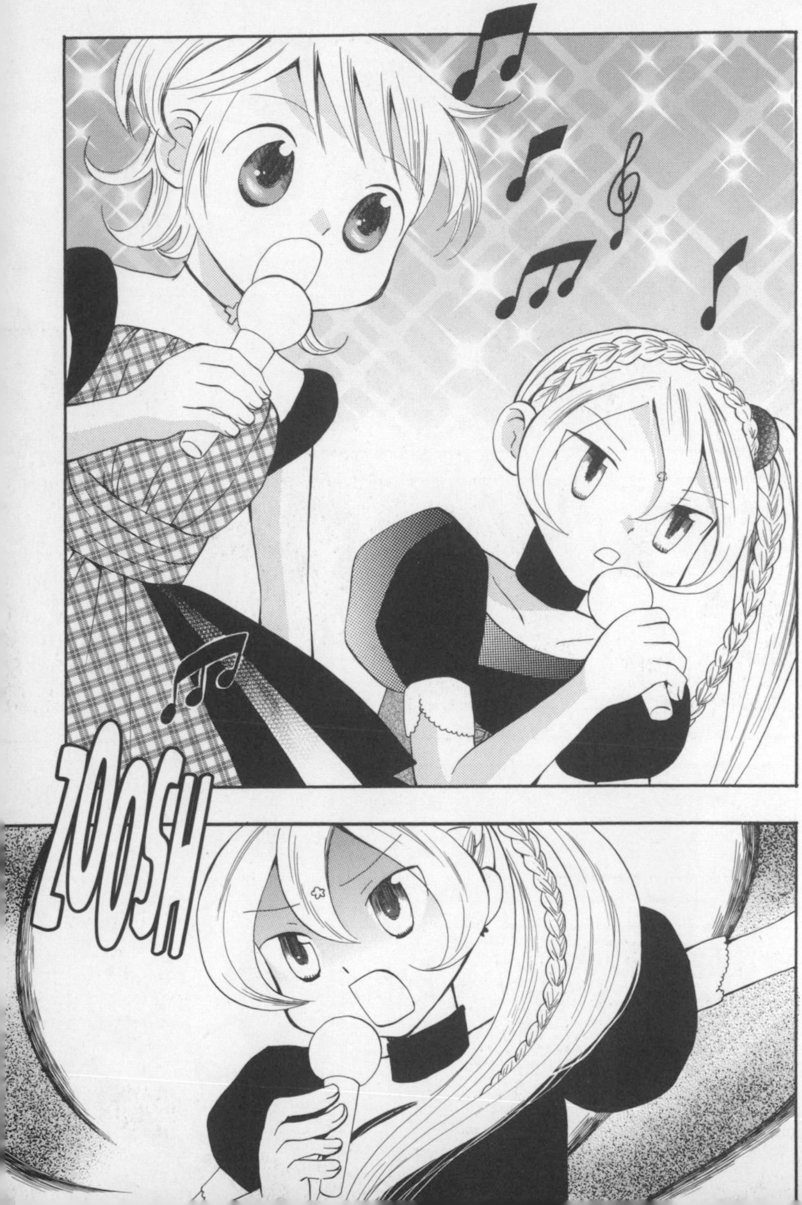
ZOOSH

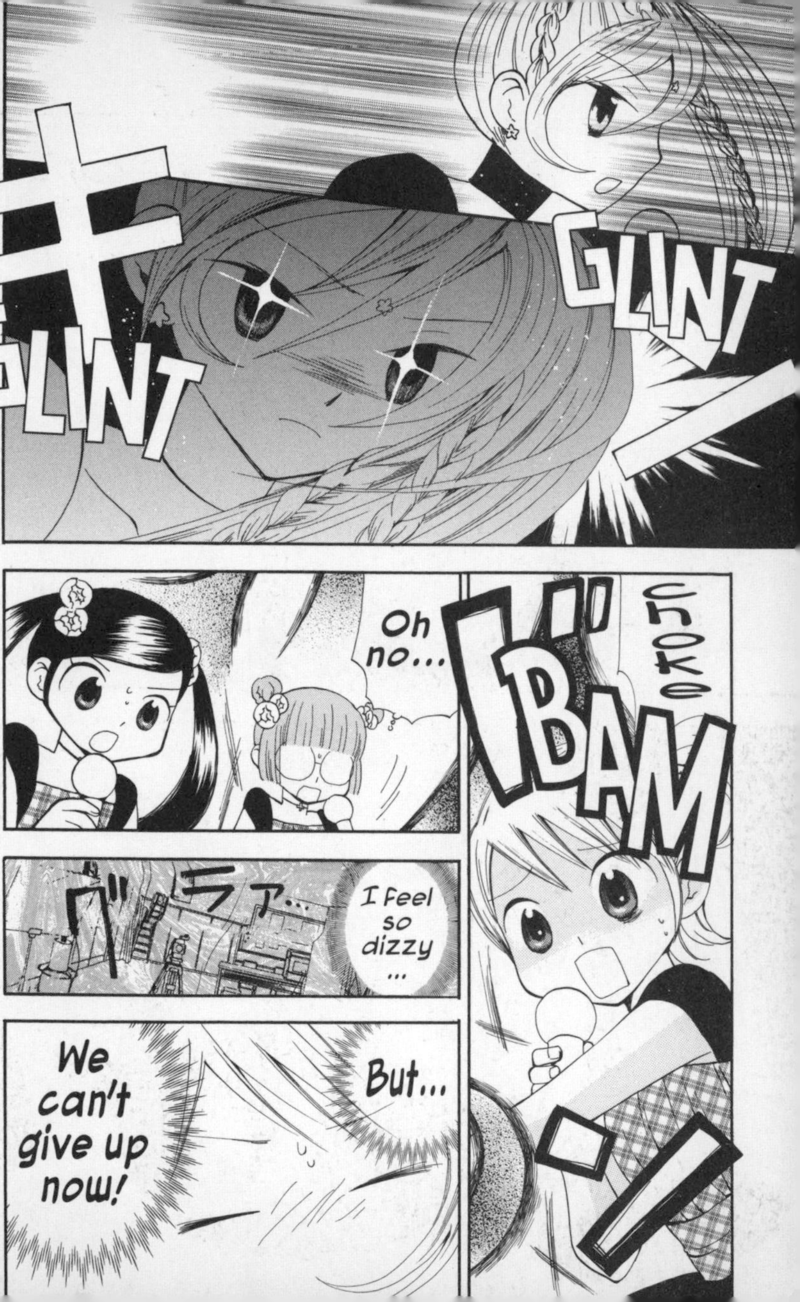
GLINT
GLINT
choke
BAM
!
Oh no...
I feel so dizzy ...
But...
We can't give up now!

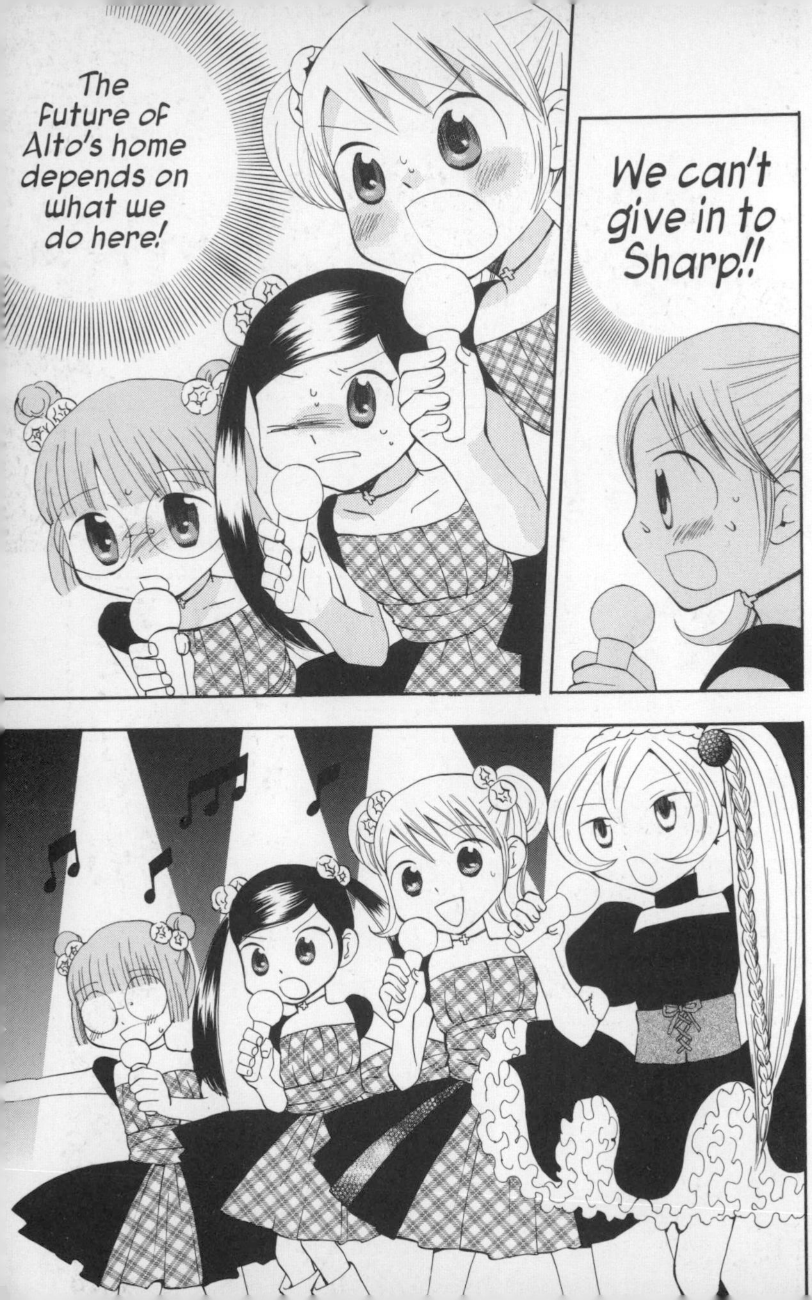
We can't give in to Sharp!!
The future of Alto's home depends on what we do here!

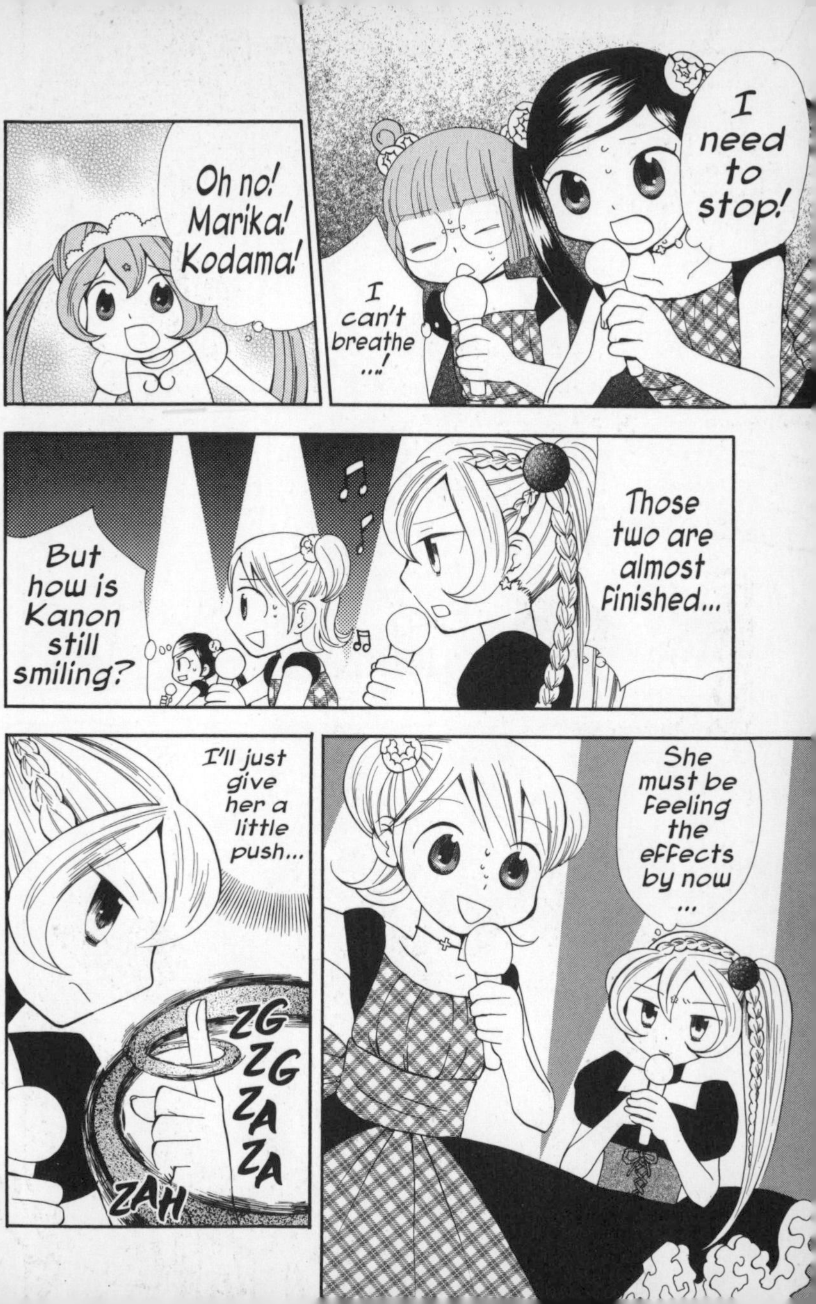
I need to stop!
I can't breathe...!
Oh no! Marika! Kodama!
Those two are almost finished...
But how is Kanon still smiling?
She must be feeling the effects by now ...
I'll just give her a little push...
ZG ZG ZA ZA
ZAH

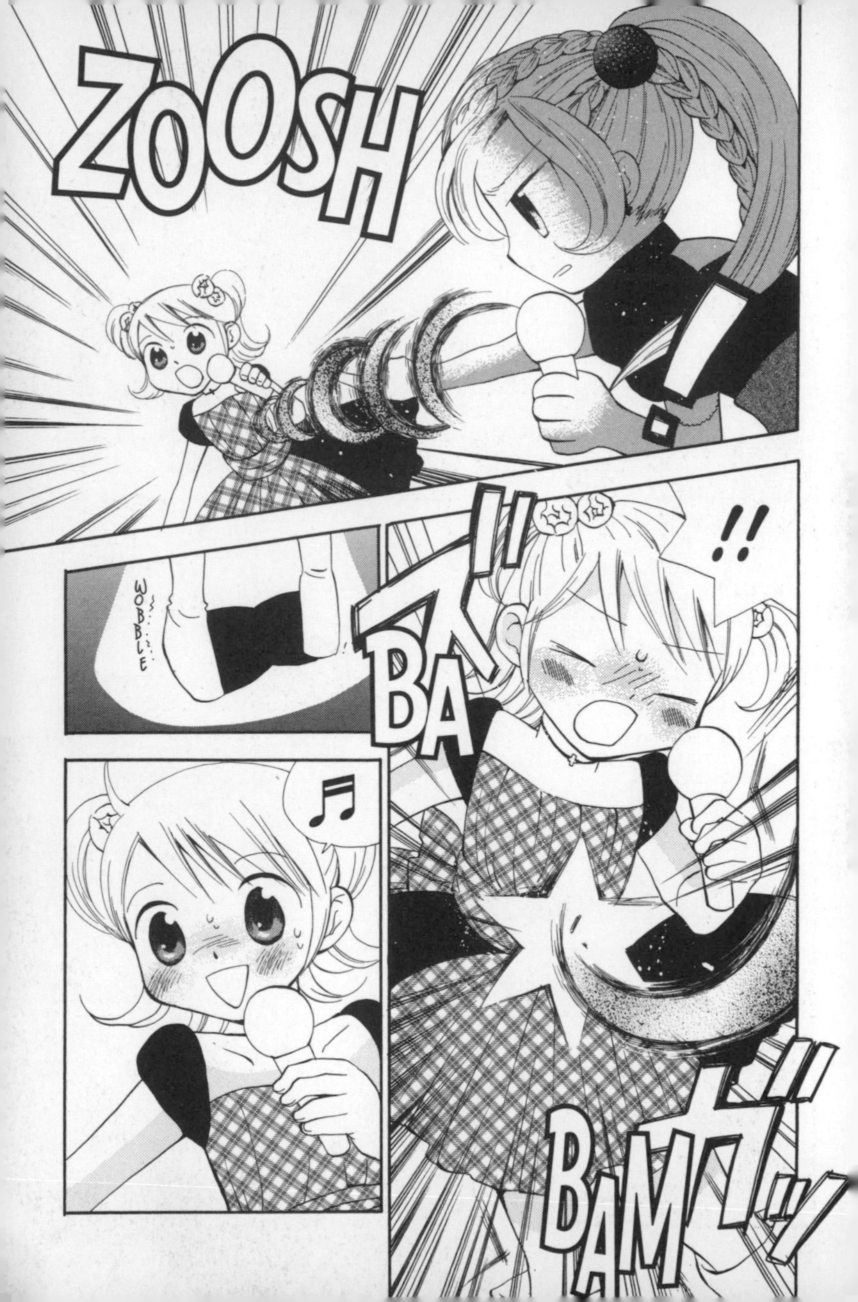
ZOOSH
!!
BA
BAM
WOBBLE

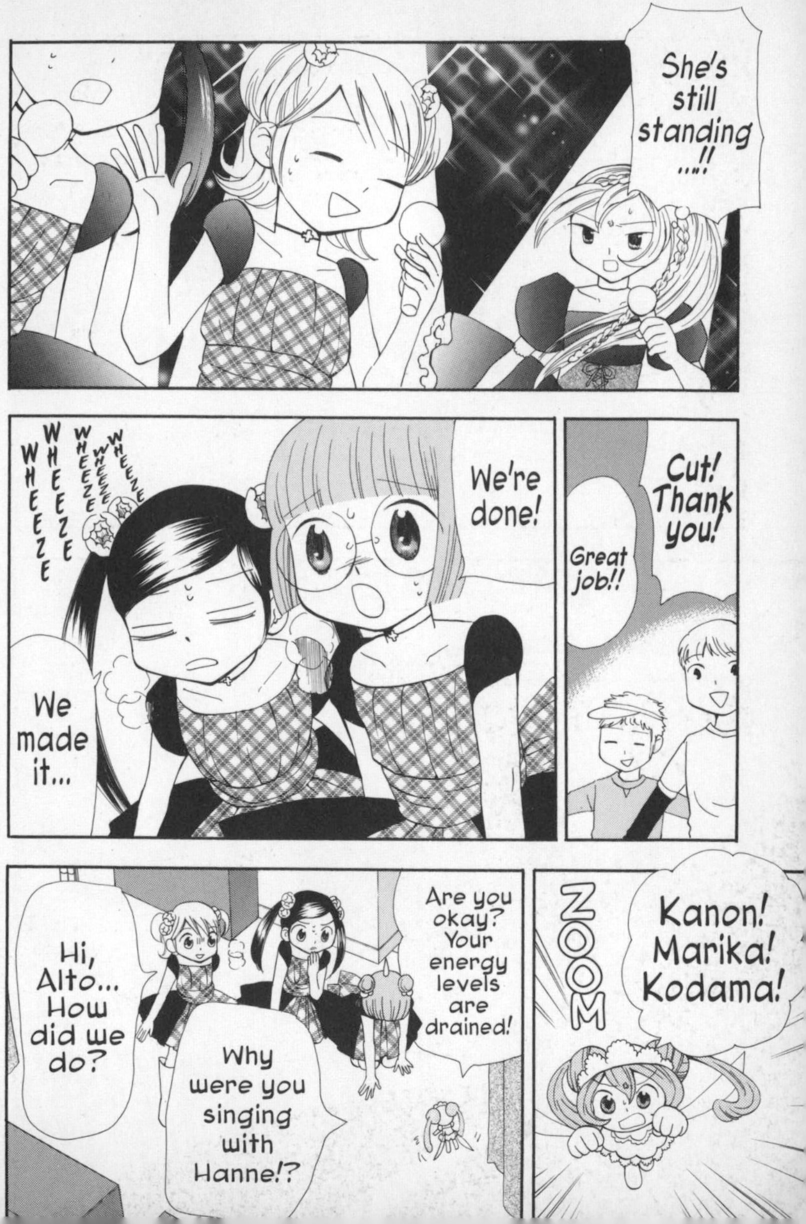
She's still standing ...!!
Cut! Thank you!
Great job!!
We're done!
WHEEZE
WHEEZE
WHEEZE
WHEEZE
WHEEZE
We made it...
Kanon! Marika! Kodama!
ZOOM
Are you okay? Your energy levels are drained!
Hi, Alto... How did we do?
Why were you singing with Hanne!?

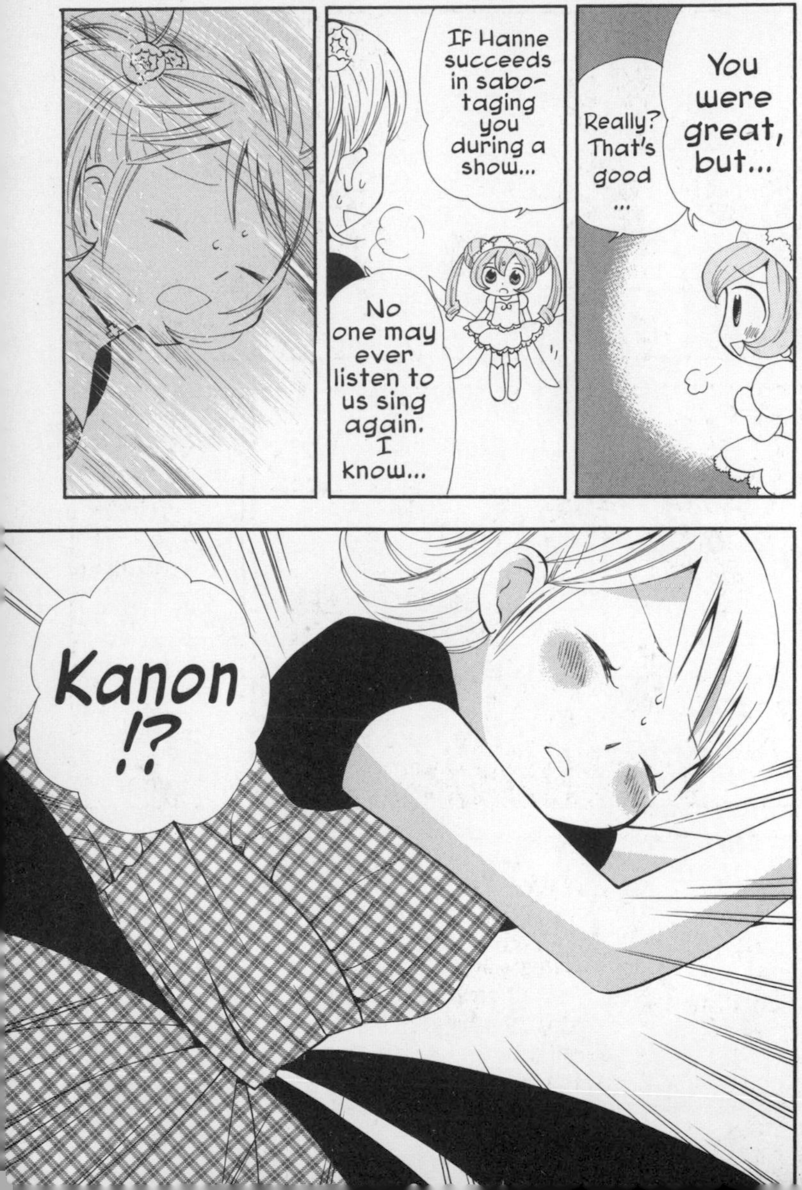
You were great, but...
Really? That's good...
If Hanne succeeds in sabo-taging you during a show...
No one may ever listen to us sing again. I know...
Kanon!?

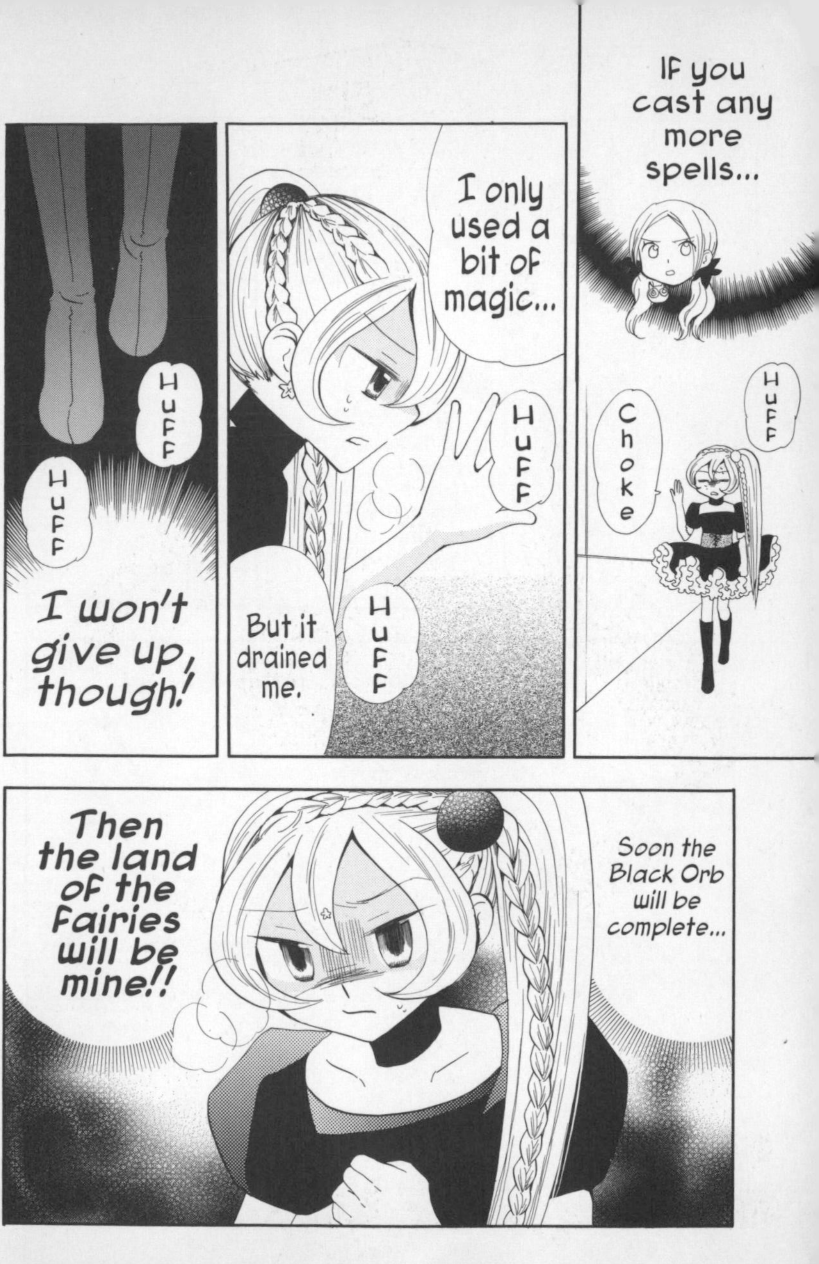
If you cast any more spells...
Huff
Choke
I only used a bit of magic...
Huff
Huff
But it drained me.
Huff
Huff
I won't give up, though!
Soon the Black Orb will be complete...
Then the land of the fairies will be mine!!

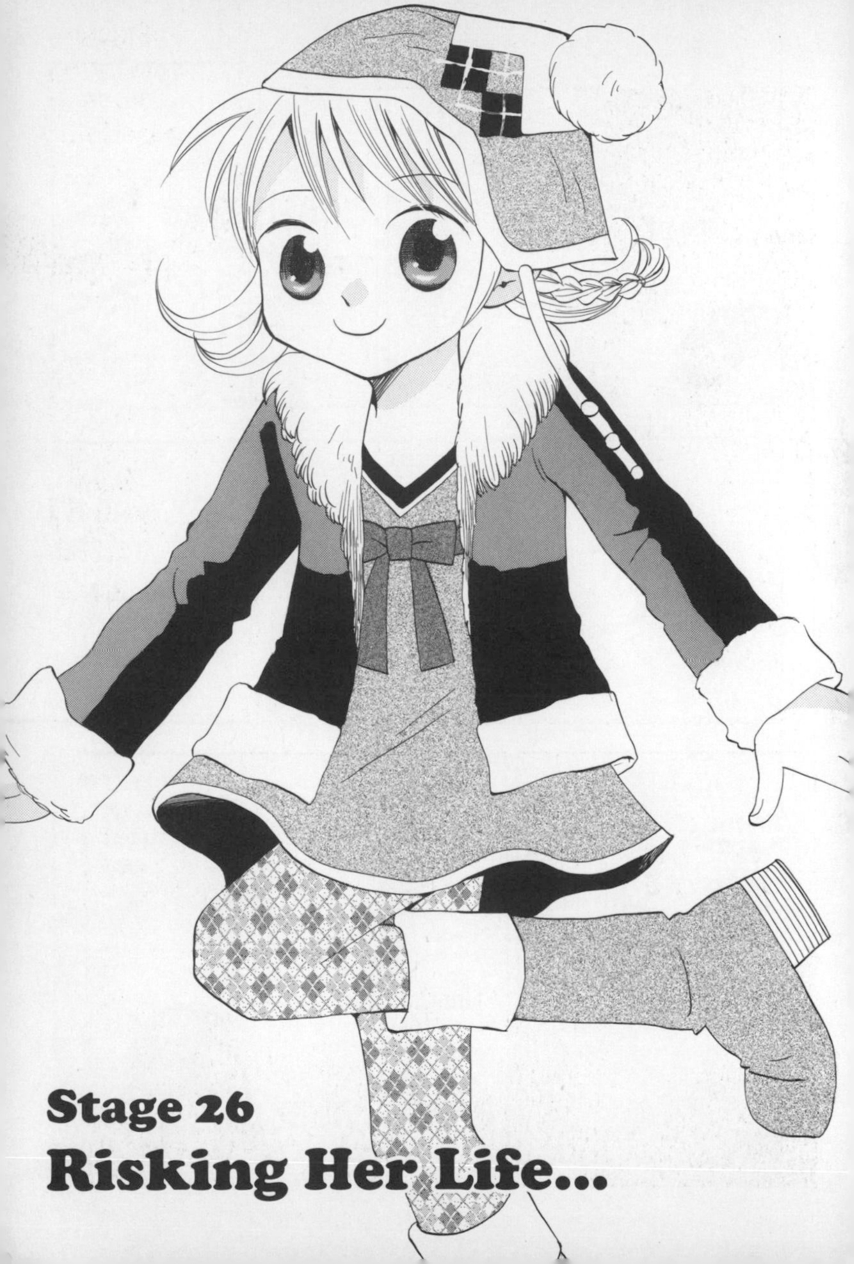

Stage 26
Risking Her Life...

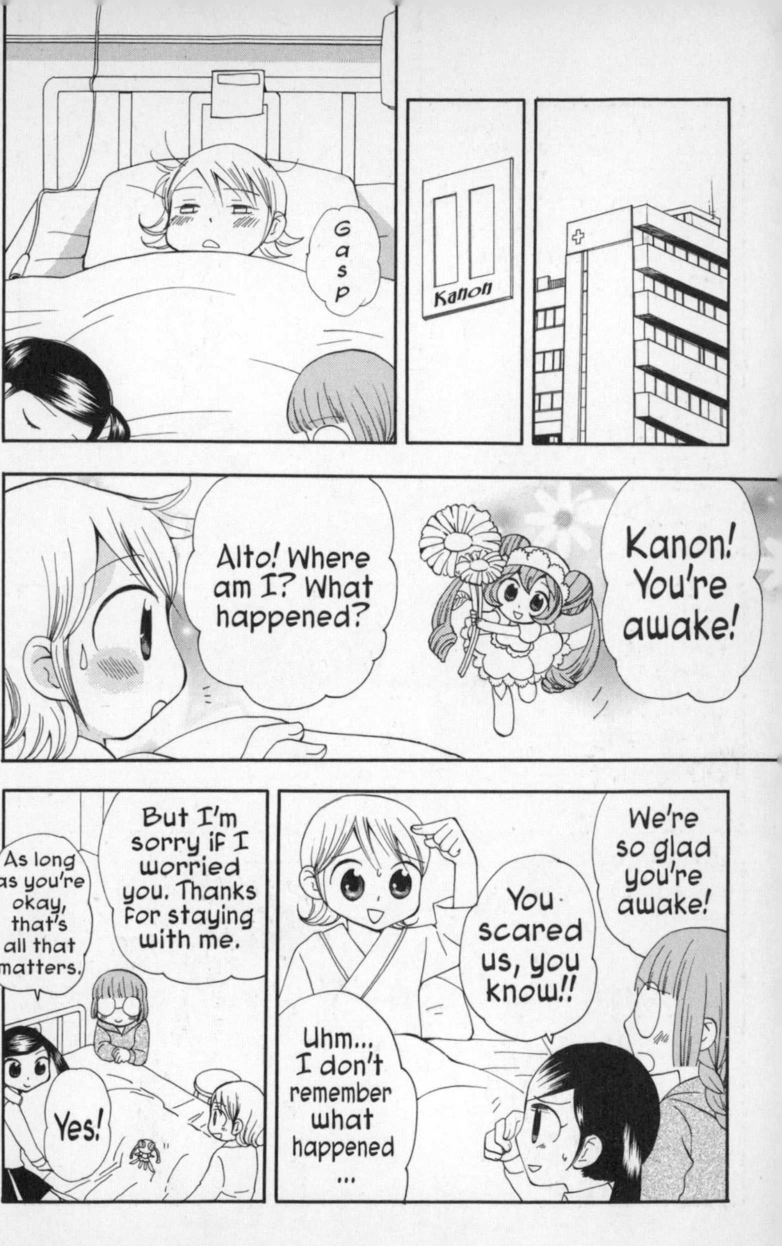
Kanon
Gasp
Kanon! You're awake!
Alto! Where am I? What happened?
We're so glad you're awake!
You scared us, you know!!
Uhm... I don't remember what happened ...
But I'm sorry if I worried you. Thanks for staying with me.
As long as you're okay, that's all that matters.
Yes!

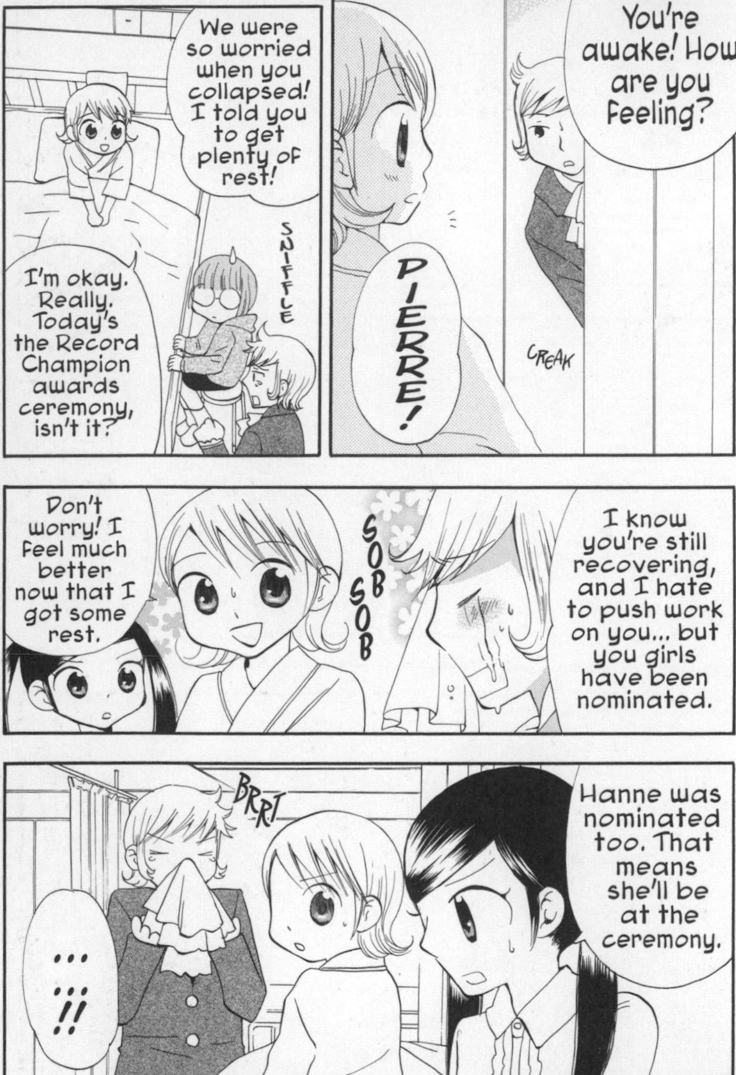
Kanon! You're awake! How are you feeling?
CREAK
PIERRE!
We were so worried when you collapsed! I told you to get plenty of rest!
SNIFFLE
I'm okay. Really. Today's the Record Champion awards ceremony, isn't it?
I know you're still recovering, and I hate to push work on you... but you girls have been nominated.
SOB SOB
Don't worry! I feel much better now that I got some rest.
Hanne was nominated too. That means she'll be at the ceremony.
BRRT
......
!!

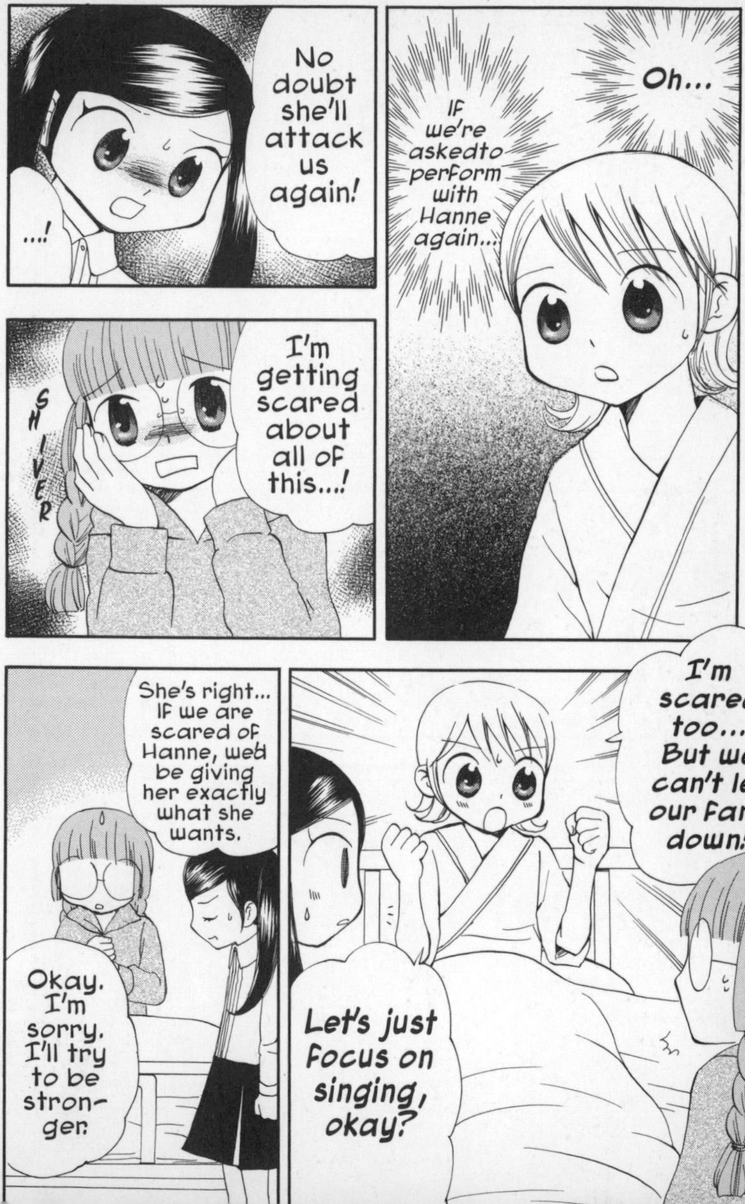
Oh...
If we're askedto perform with Hanne again...
No doubt she'll attack us again!
...!
I'm getting scared about all of this...!
SHIVER
I'm scared too... But we can't let our fans down!
Let's just focus on singing, okay?
She's right... If we are scared of Hanne, we'd be giving her exactly what she wants.
Okay. I'm sorry. I'll try to be stron-ger.

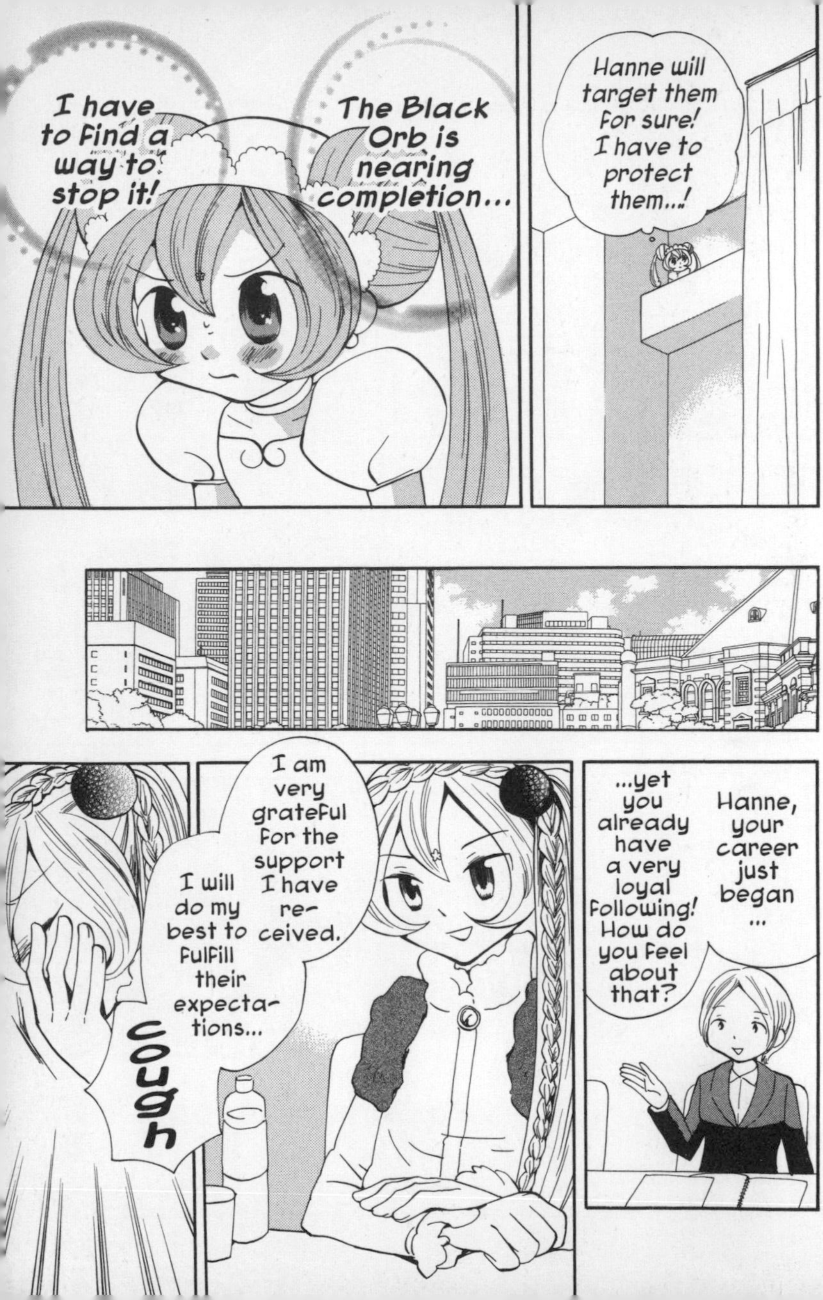
Hanne will target them for sure! I have to protect them...!
The Black Orb is nearing completion...
I have to find a way to stop it!
Hanne, your career just began...
...yet you already have a very loyal following! How do you feel about that?
I am very grateful for the support I have re-ceived.
I will do my best to fulfill their expecta-tions...
Cough

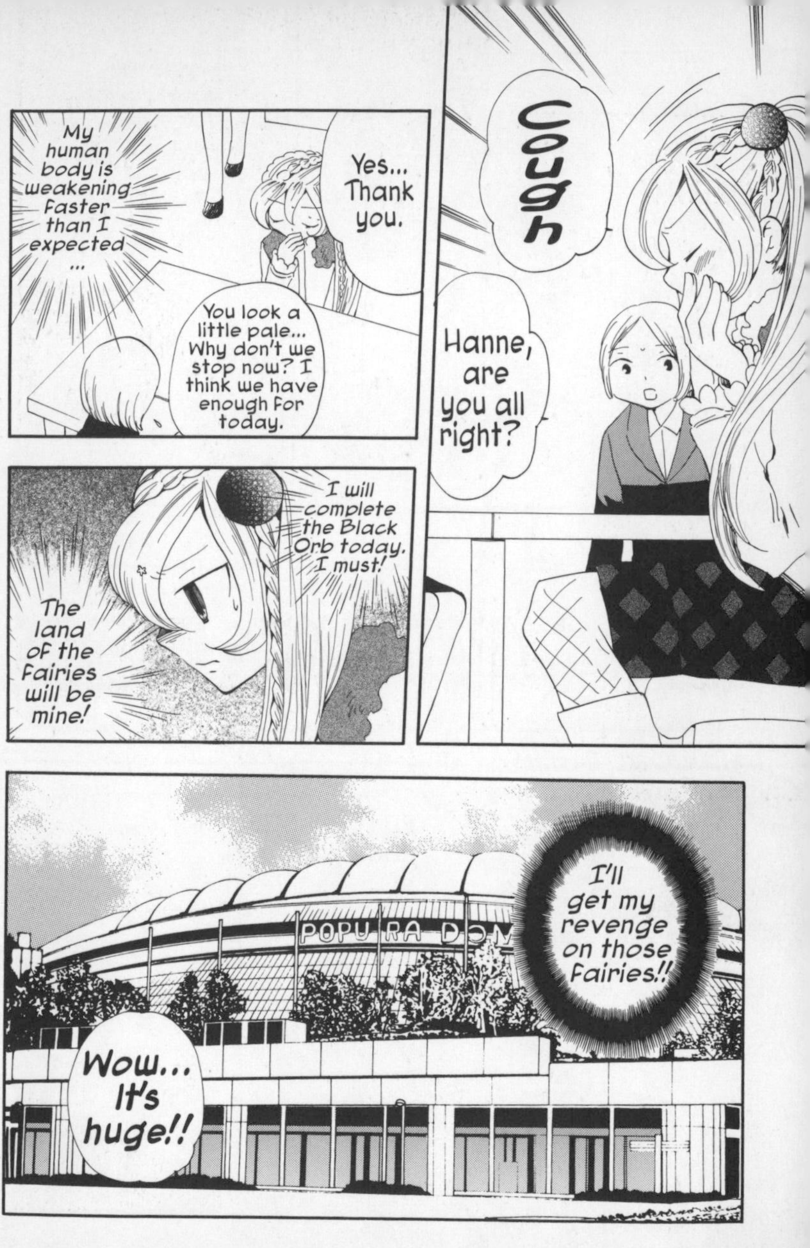
Cough
Hanne, are you all right?
Yes... Thank you.
You look a little pale... Why don't we stop now? I think we have enough for today.
My human body is weakening faster than I expected ...
I will complete the Black Orb today. I must!
The land of the fairies will be mine!
I'll get my revenge on those fairies!!
POPU RA DOM
Wow... It's huge!!

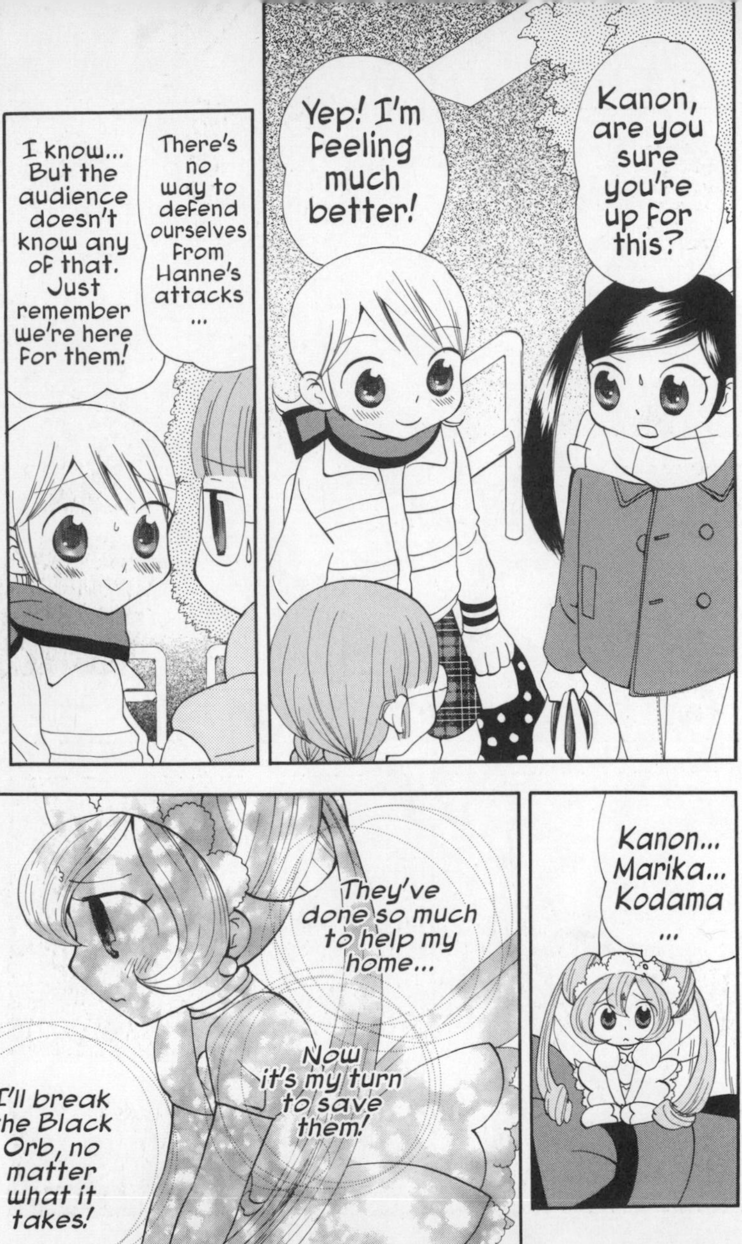
Kanon, are you sure you're up for this?
Yep! I'm feeling much better!
There's no way to defend ourselves from Hanne's attacks ...
I know... But the audience doesn't know any of that. Just remember we're here for them!
Kanon... Marika... Kodama ...
They've done so much to help my home...
Now it's my turn to save them!
I'll break the Black Orb, no matter what it takes!

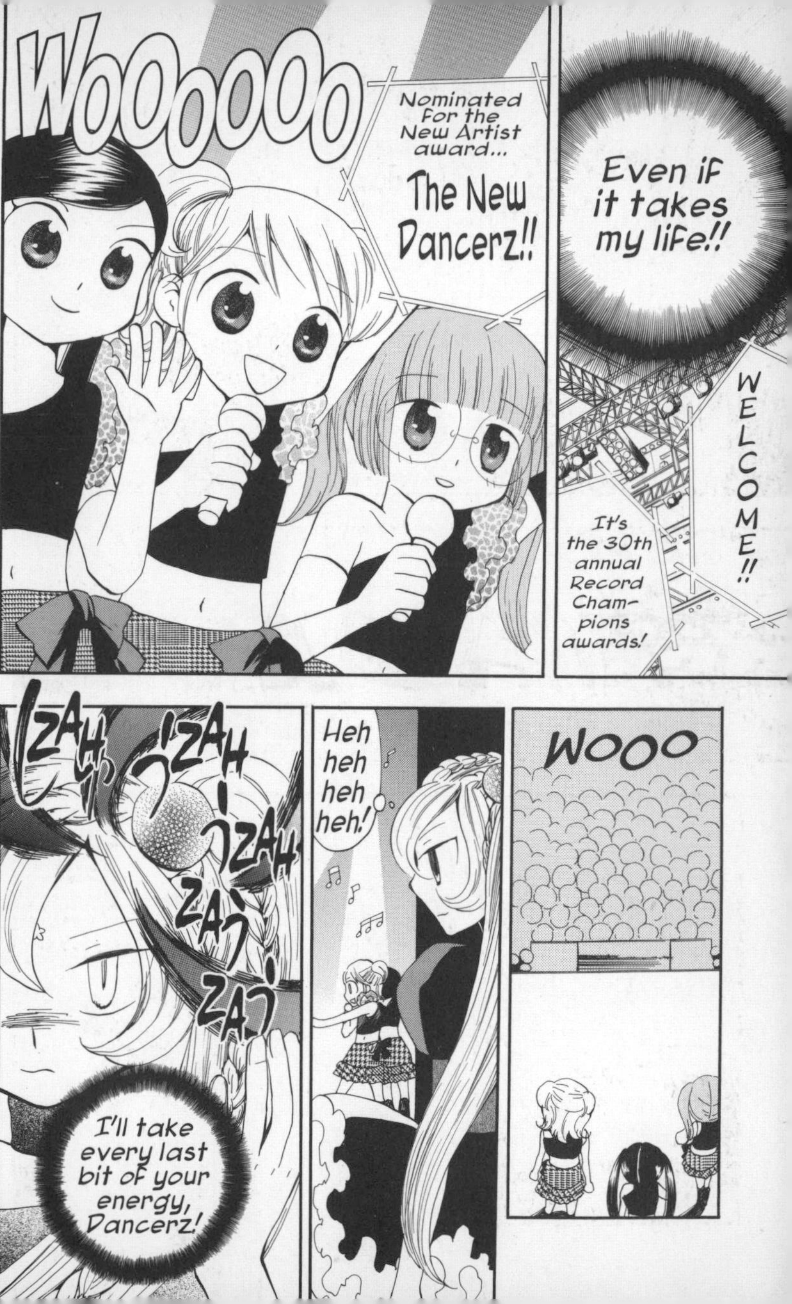

Even if it takes my life!!
WELCOME!!
It's the 30th annual Record Champions awards!
Nominated for the New Artist award...
The New Dancerz!!
WOOOOOO
WOOO
Heh heh heh heh!
ZAH ZAH ZAH ZA ZA
I'll take every last bit of your energy, Dancerz!

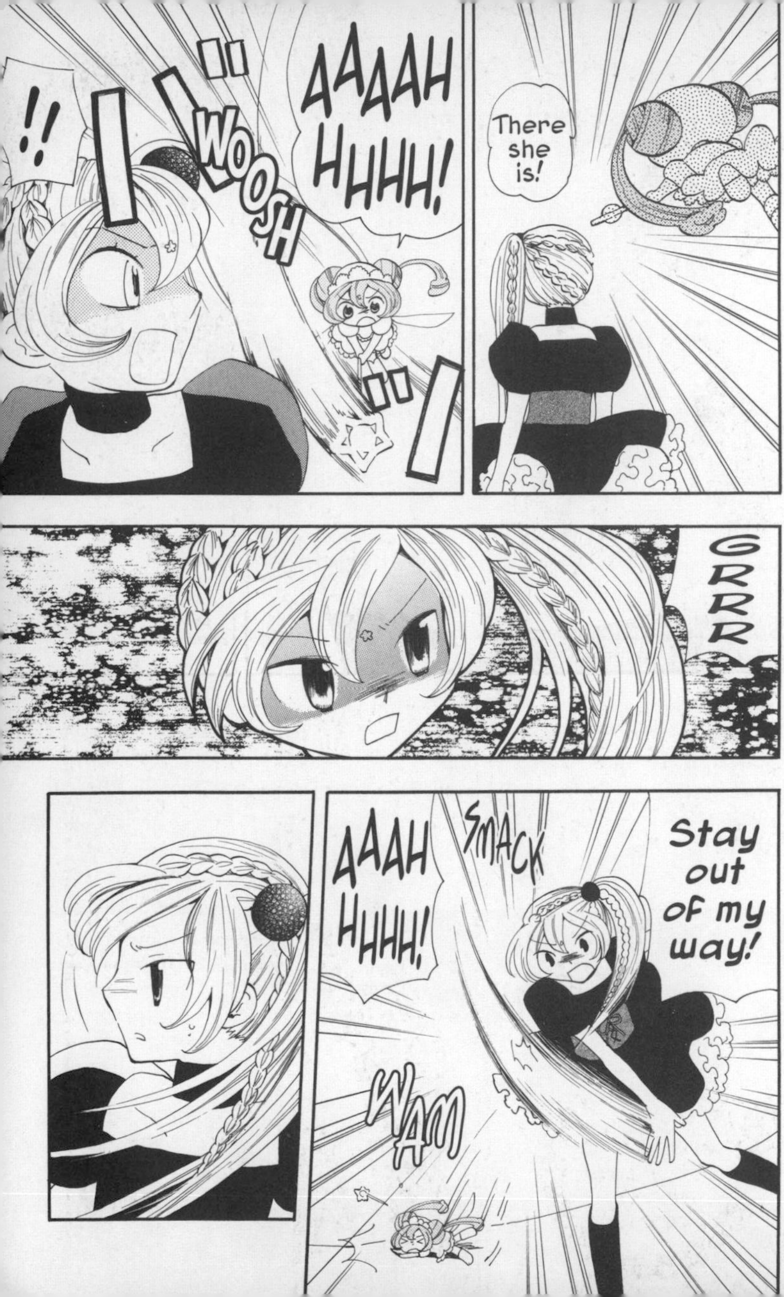
There she is!
AAAAH HHHH!
WOOSH
!!
GRRR
Stay out of my way!
SMACK
AAAH HHHH!
WAM

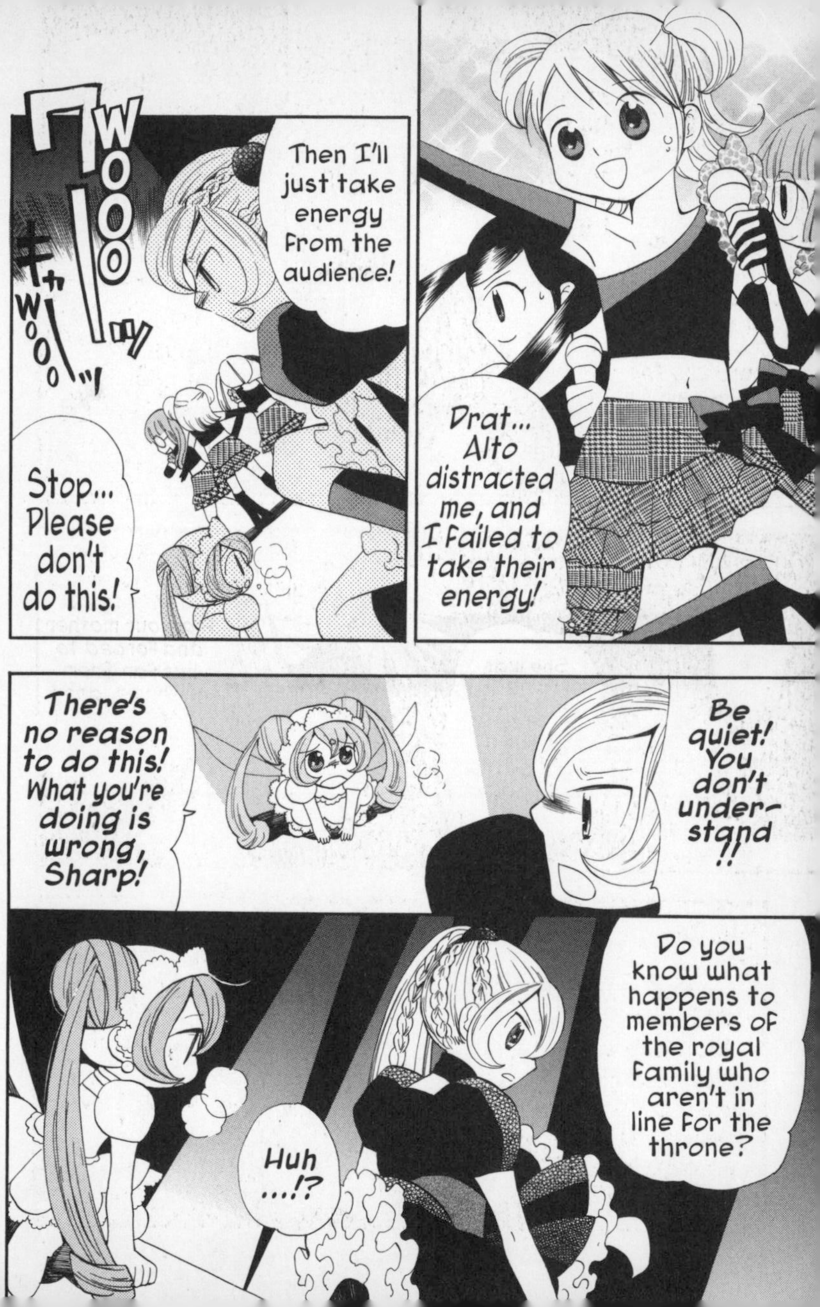
Drat... Alto distracted me, and I failed to take their energy!
Then I'll just take energy from the audience!
WOOOO
WOOOO
Stop... Please don't do this!
Be quiet! You don't under-stand!!
There's no reason to do this! What you're doing is wrong, Sharp!
Do you know what happens to members of the royal family who aren't in line for the throne?
Huh ...!?

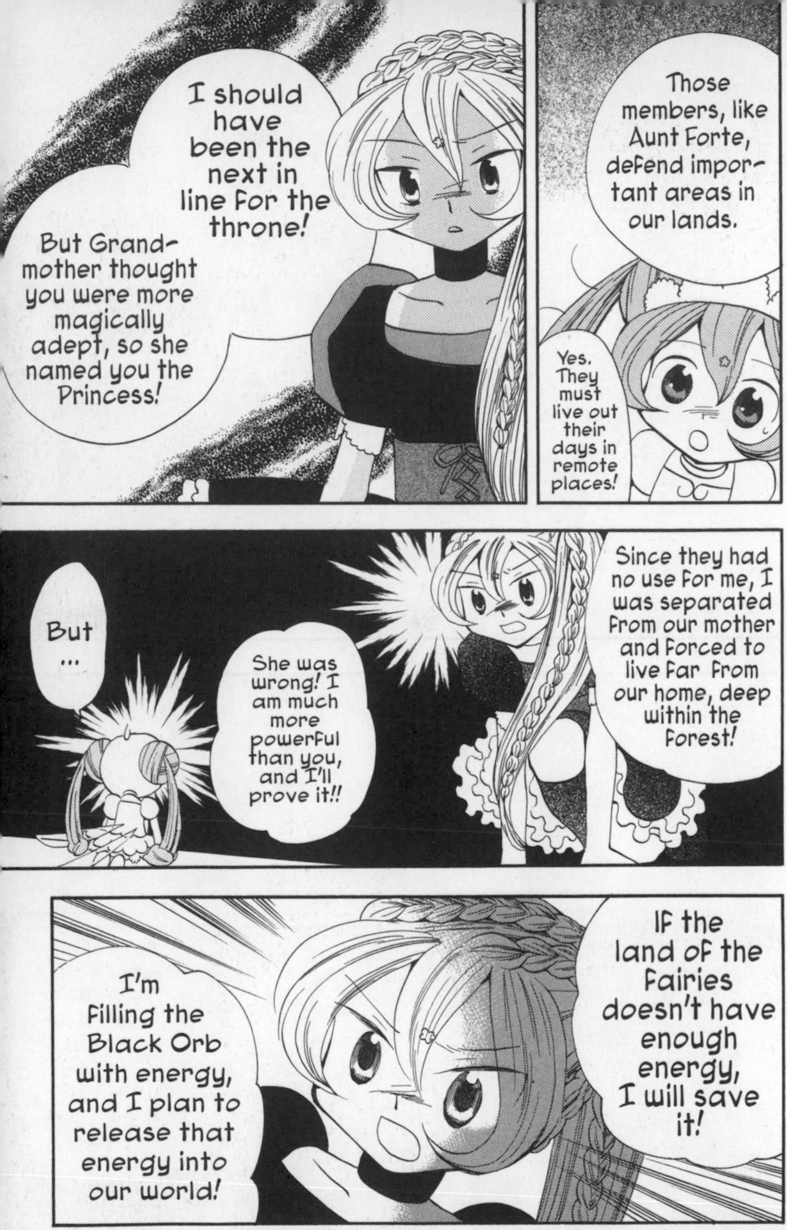
Those members, like Aunt Forte, defend important areas in our lands.
Yes. They must live out their days in remote places!
I should have been the next in line for the throne!
But Grandmother thought you were more magically adept, so she named you the Princess!
Since they had no use for me, I was separated from our mother and forced to live far from our home, deep within the forest!
She was wrong! I am much more powerful than you, and I'll prove it!!
But ...
If the land of the fairies doesn't have enough energy, I will save it!
I'm filling the Black Orb with energy, and I plan to release that energy into our world!

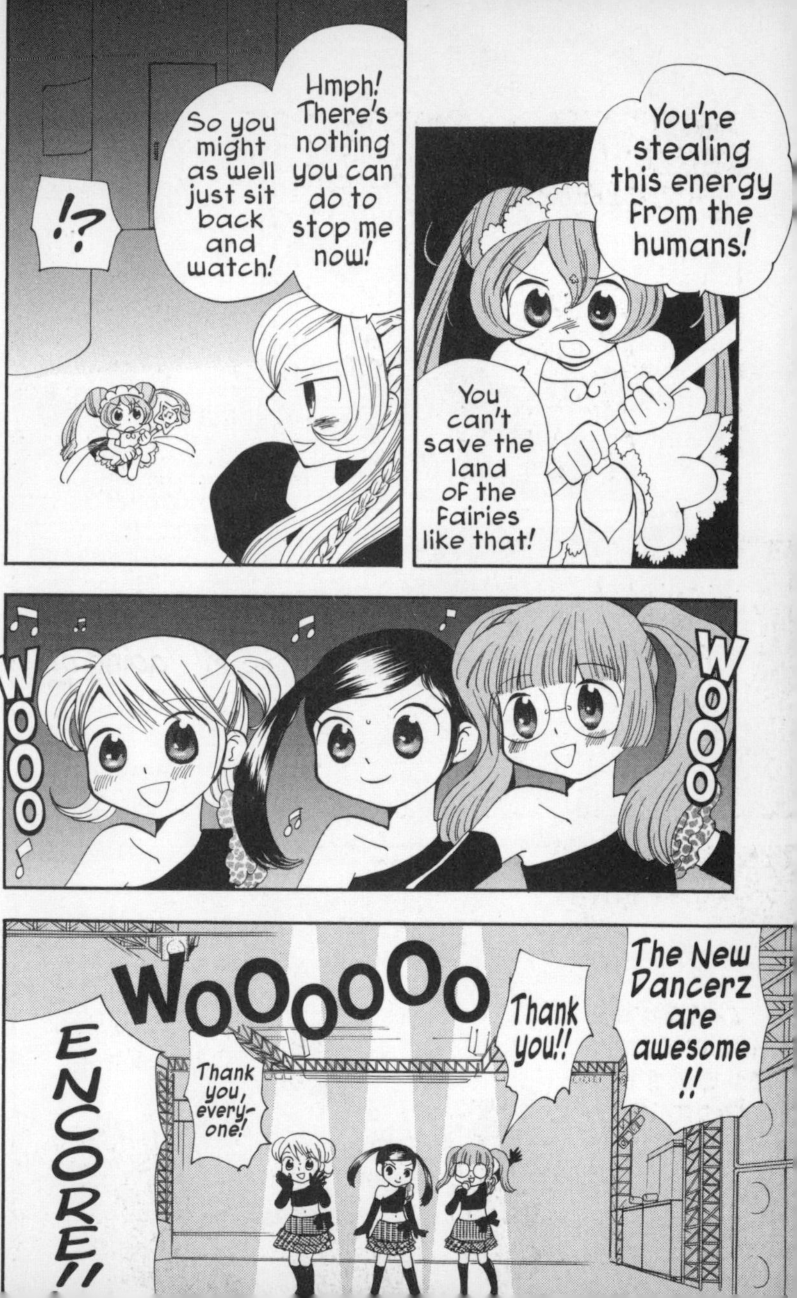
You're stealing this energy from the humans!
You can't save the land of the fairies like that!
Hmph! There's nothing you can do to stop me now!
So you might as well just sit back and watch!
!?
WOOO
WOOO
The New Dancerz are awesome!!
Thank you!!
WOOOOOO
Thank you, every-one!
ENCORE!!

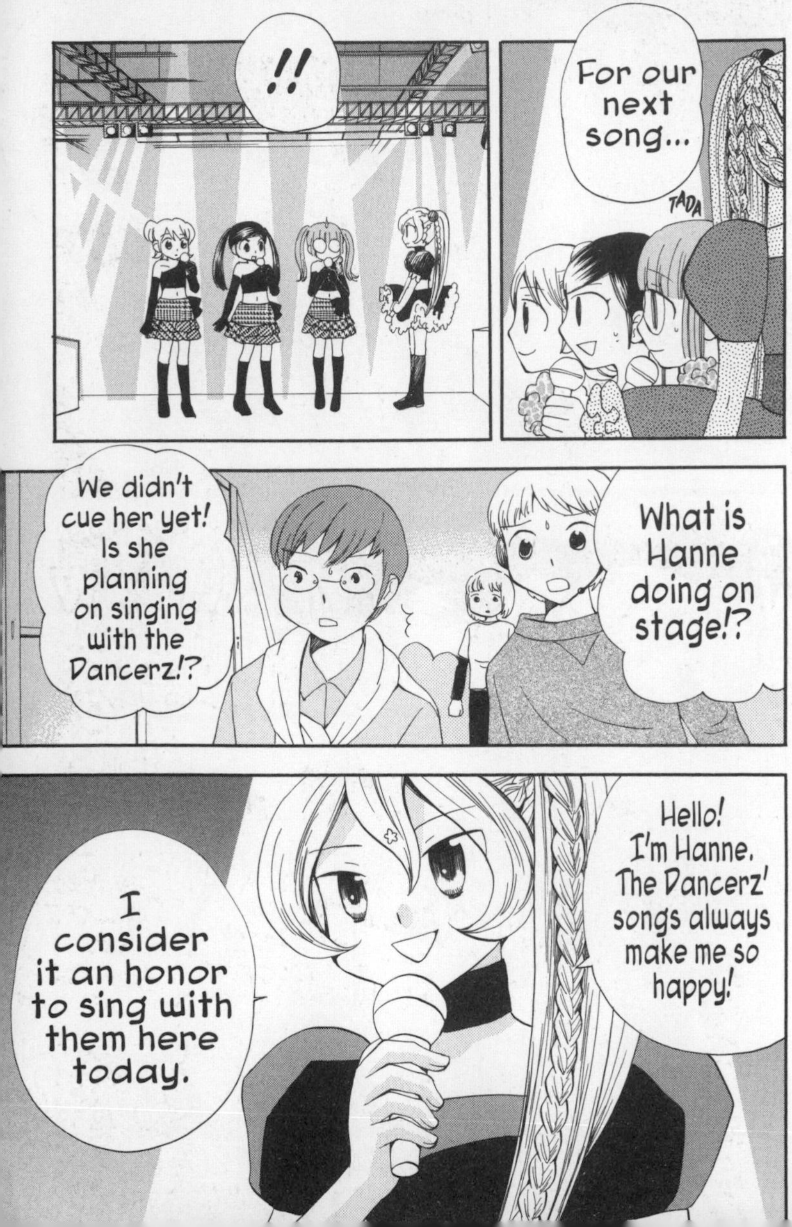
For our next song...
TADA
!!
What is Hanne doing on stage!?
We didn't cue her yet! Is she planning on singing with the Dancerz!?
Hello! I'm Hanne. The Dancerz' songs always make me so happy!
I consider it an honor to sing with them here today.

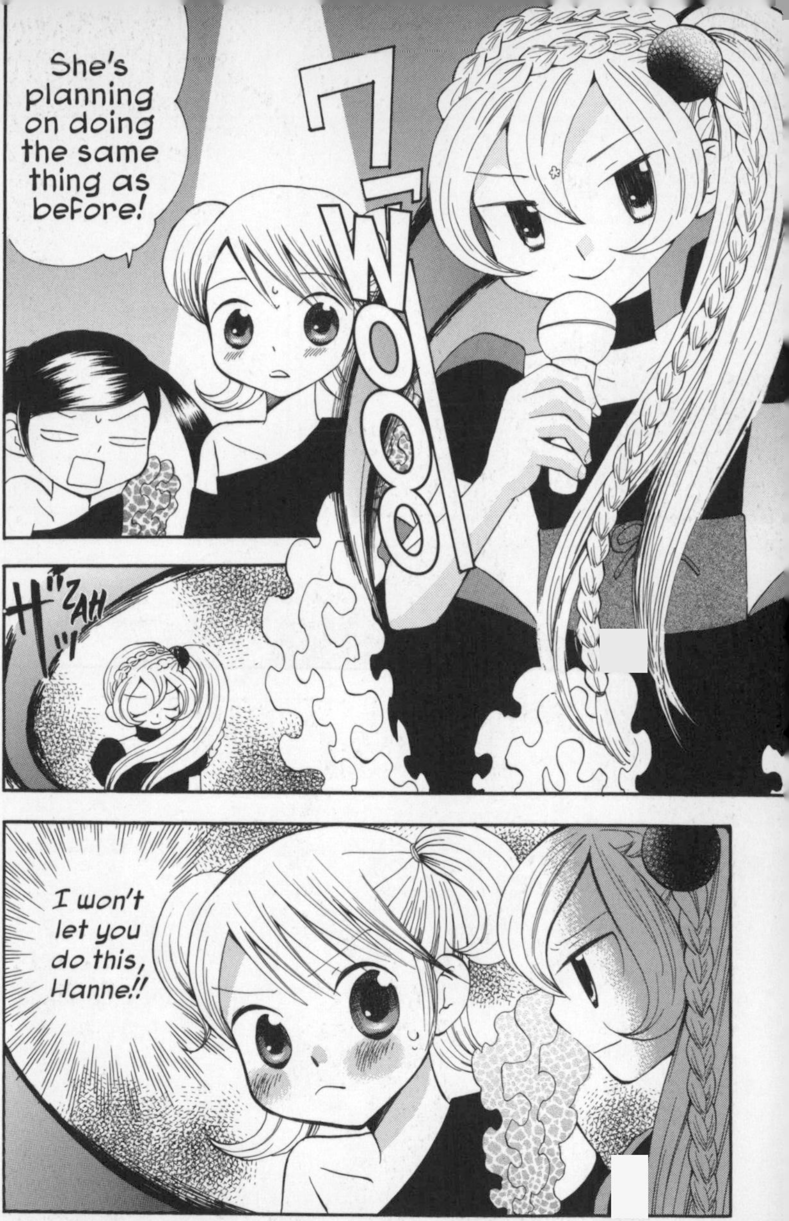
She's planning on doing the same thing as before!
WOOO
ZAH
I won't let you do this, Hanne!!

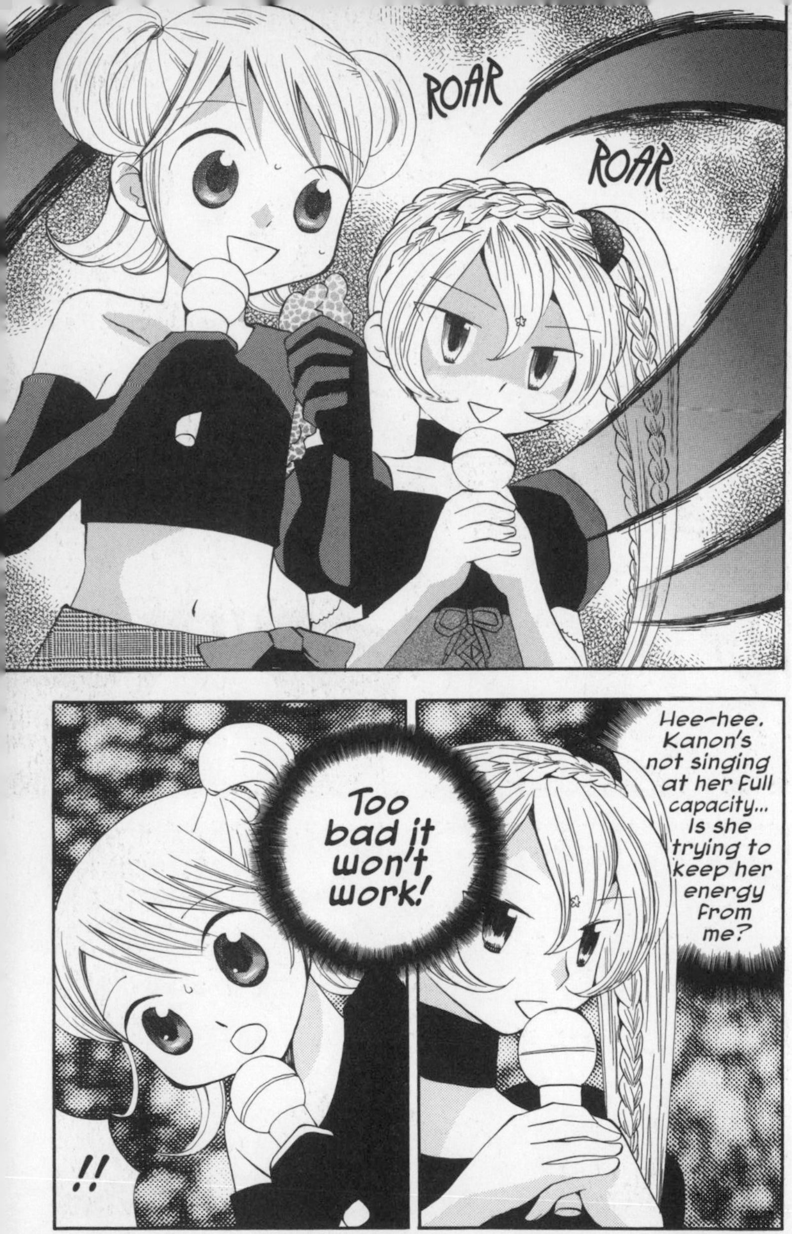
ROAR
ROAR
Hee-hee. Kanon's not singing at her full capacity... Is she trying to keep her energy from me?
Too bad it won't work!
!!

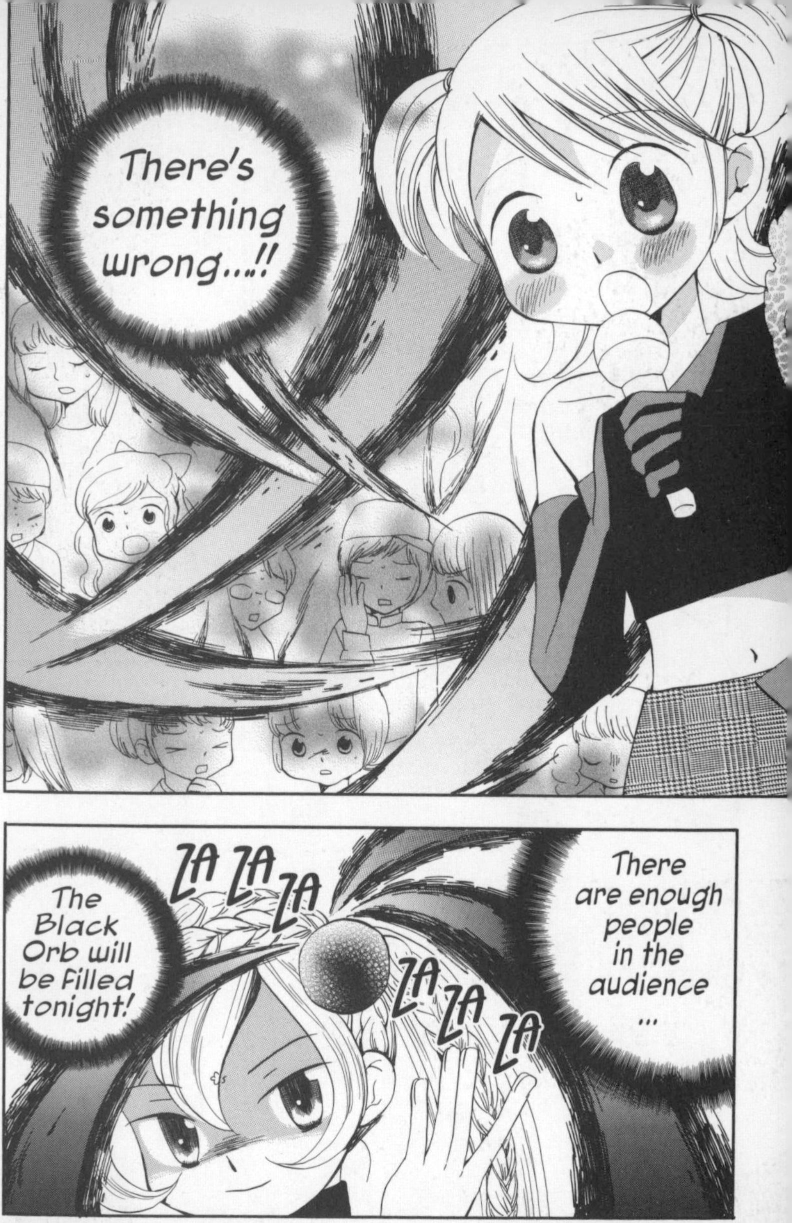
There's something wrong...!!
There are enough people in the audience ...
ZA ZA ZA
ZA ZA ZA
The Black Orb will be filled tonight!

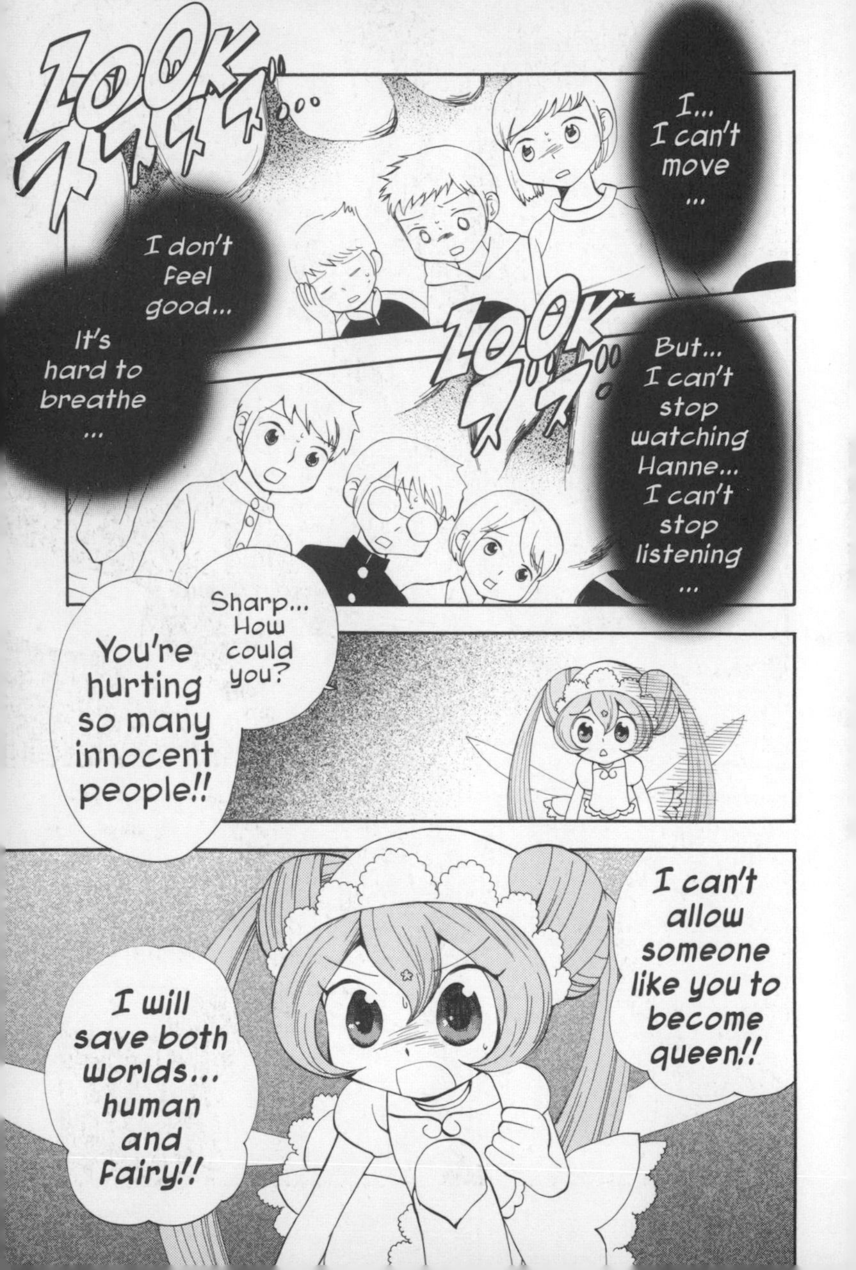
I... I can't move ...
ZOOK
I don't feel good...
But... I can't stop watching Hanne... I can't stop listening ...
ZOOK
It's hard to breathe ...
Sharp... How could you?
You're hurting so many innocent people!!
I can't allow someone like you to become queen!!
I will save both worlds... human and fairy!!

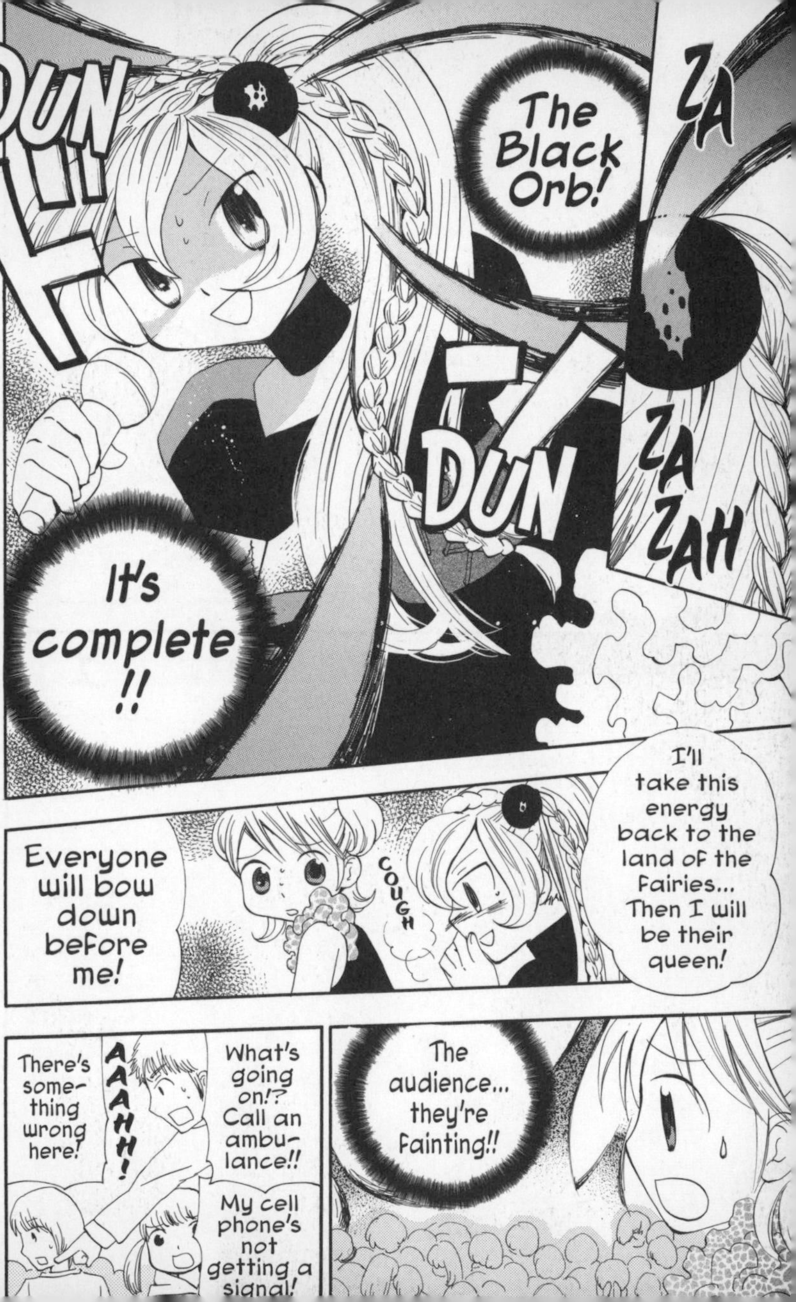
ZA
ZA ZA ZAH
The Black Orb!
DUN
DUN
It's complete!!
I'll take this energy back to the land of the fairies... Then I will be their queen!
COUGH
Everyone will bow down before me!
The audience... they're fainting!!
What's going on!? Call an ambulance!!
AAAHH!
There's something wrong here!
My cell phone's not getting a signal!

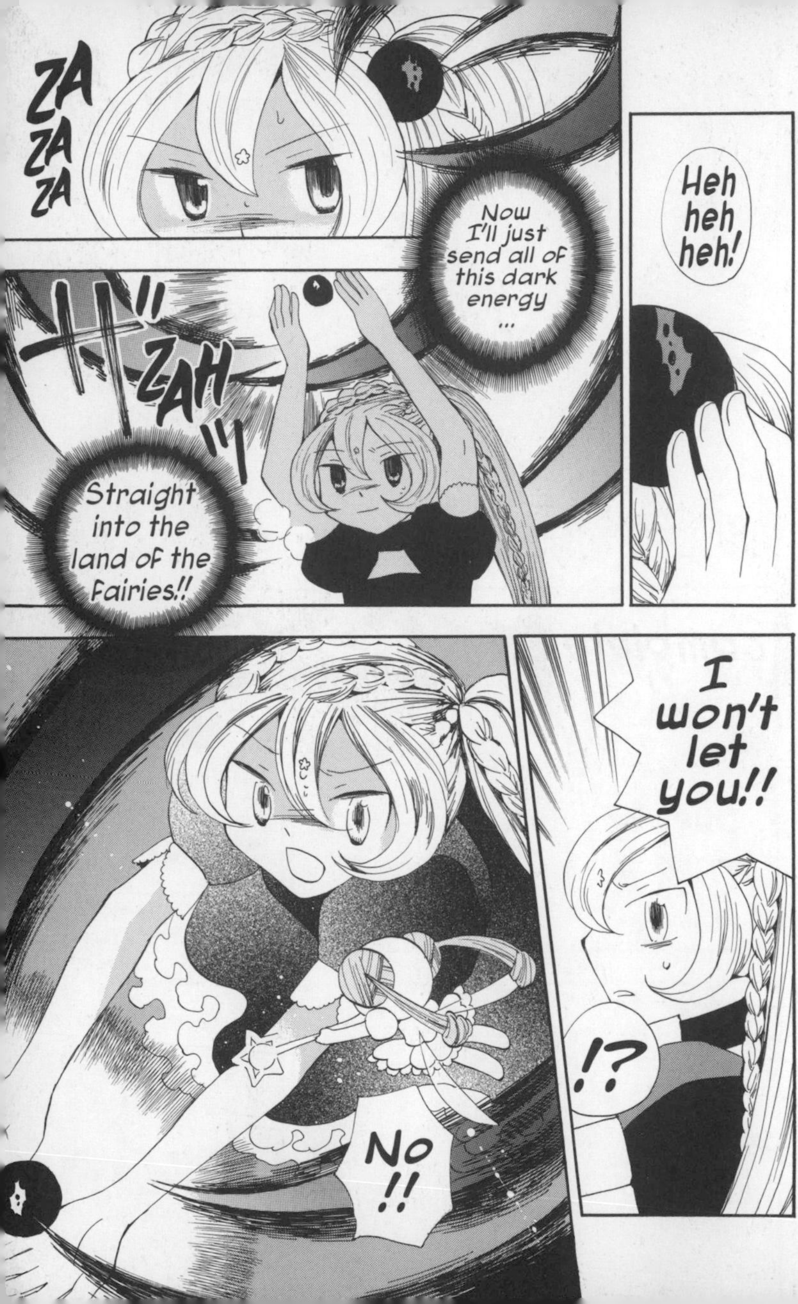

Heh heh heh!
ZA ZA ZA ZA
Now I'll just send all of this dark energy ...
ZAH
Straight into the land of the fairies!!
I won't let you!!
!?
No !!

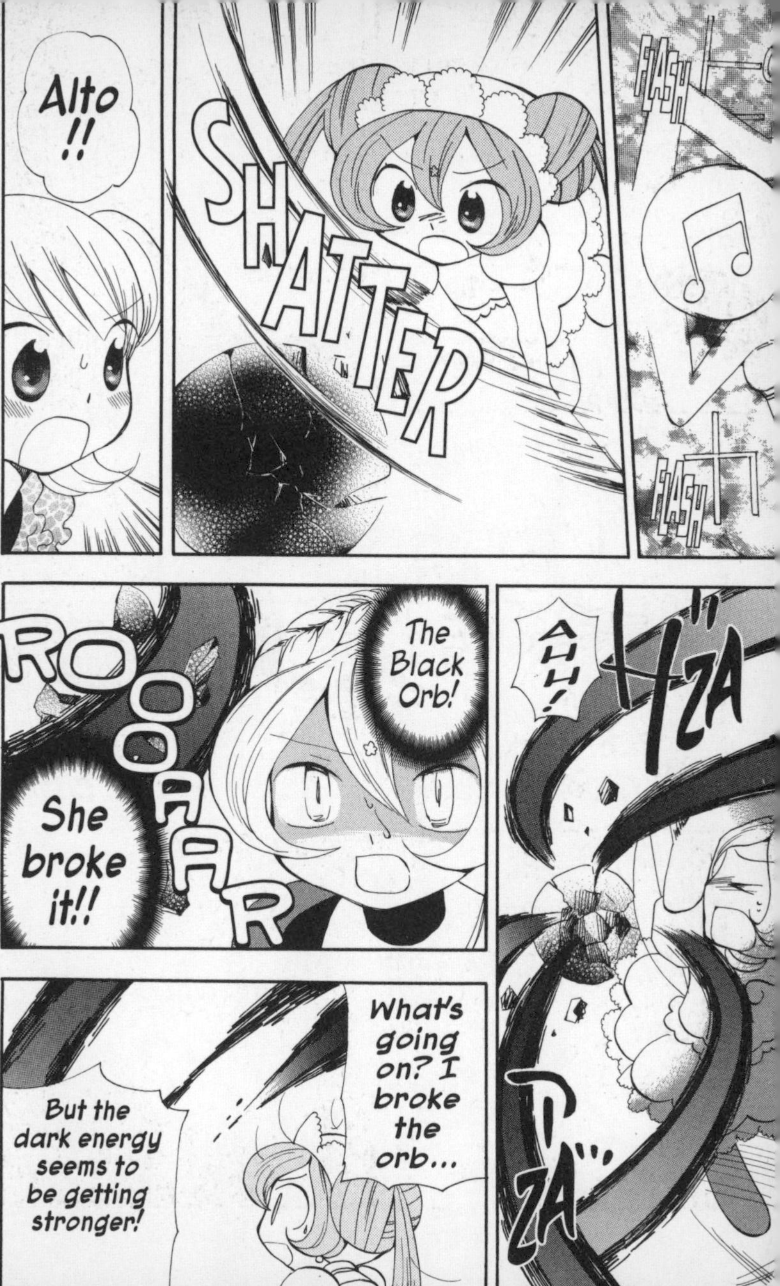
FLASH
FLASH
SHATTER
Alto!!
AHH!
ZA
ZA...
The Black Orb!
She broke it!!
ROOOAAR
What's going on? I broke the orb...
But the dark energy seems to be getting stronger!

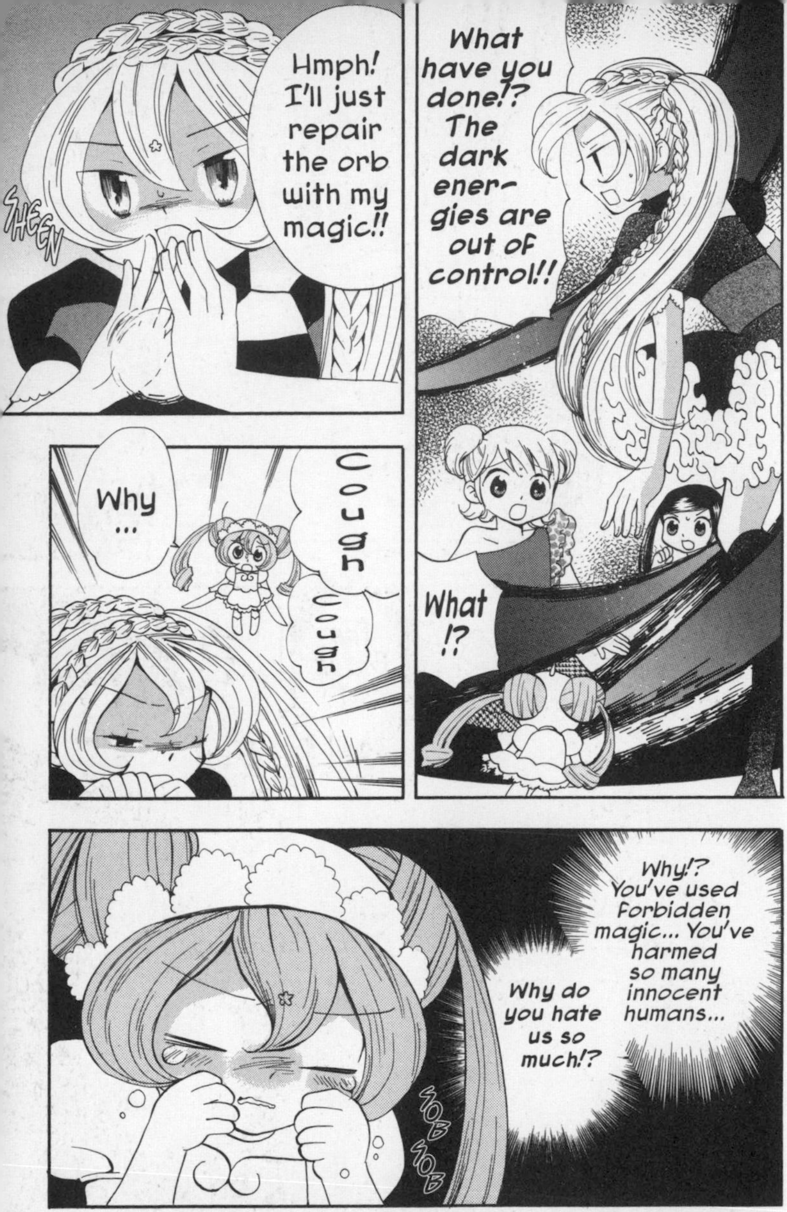
What have you done!? The dark ener-gies are out of control!!
What !?
Hmph! I'll just repair the orb with my magic!!
SHEEN
Cough Cough
Why ...
Why!? You've used forbidden magic... You've harmed so many innocent humans...
Why do you hate us so much!?
SOB SOB

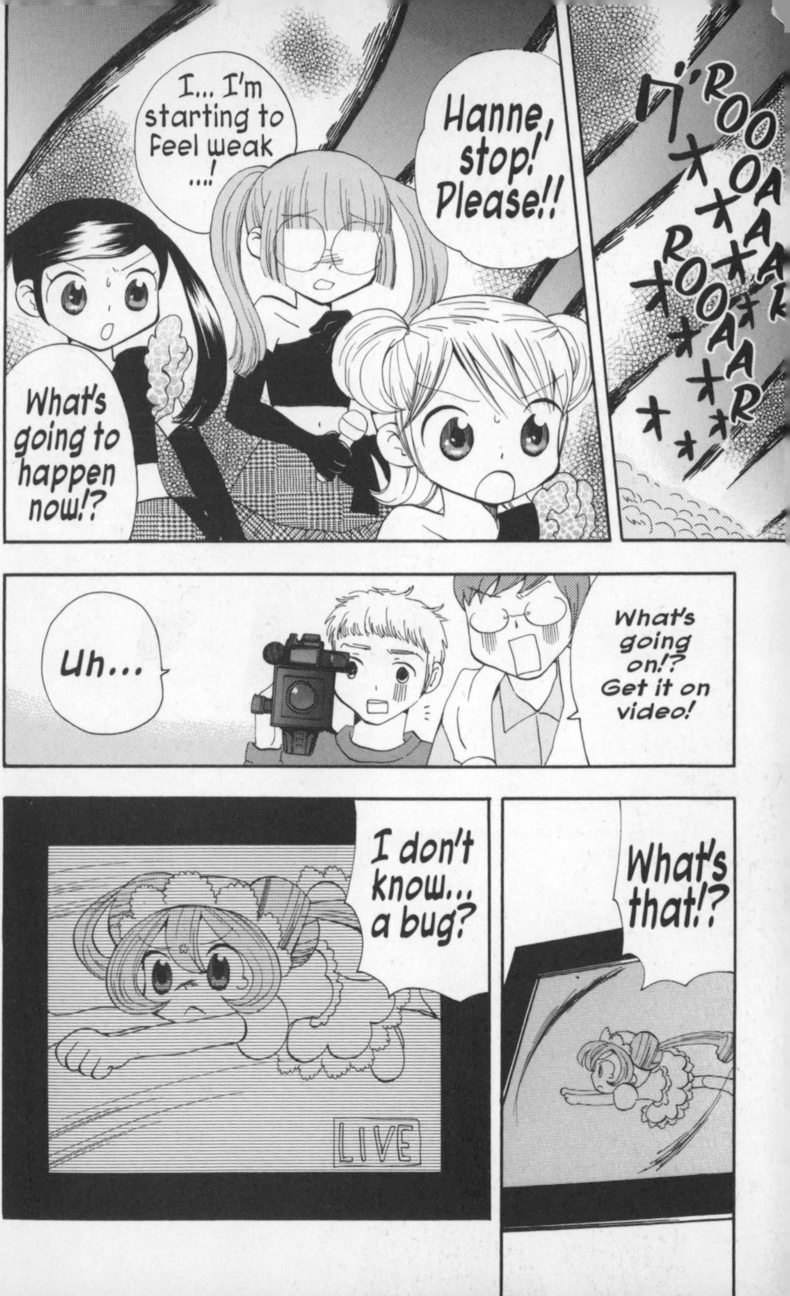
グ'ROOOAAAK
ROOAAR
Hanne, stop! Please!!
I... I'm starting to feel weak ...!
What's going to happen now!?
What's going on!? Get it on video!
Uh...
What's that!?
I don't know... a bug?
LIVE

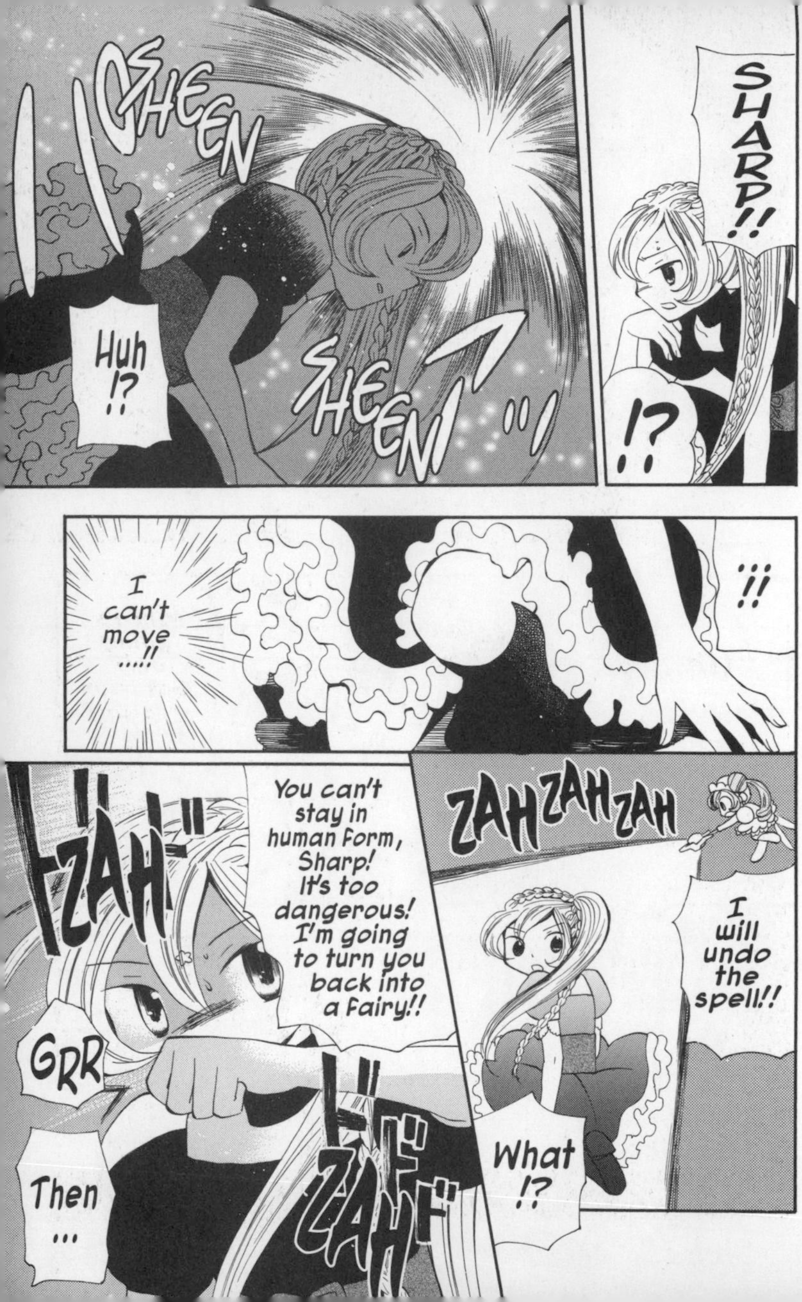
SHARP!!
!?
SHEEN
SHEEN
Huh!?
!!
I can't move ....!!
ZAH ZAH ZAH
I will undo the spell!!
What!?
You can't stay in human form, Sharp! It's too dangerous! I'm going to turn you back into a fairy!!
ZAH
GRR
ZAH
Then ...

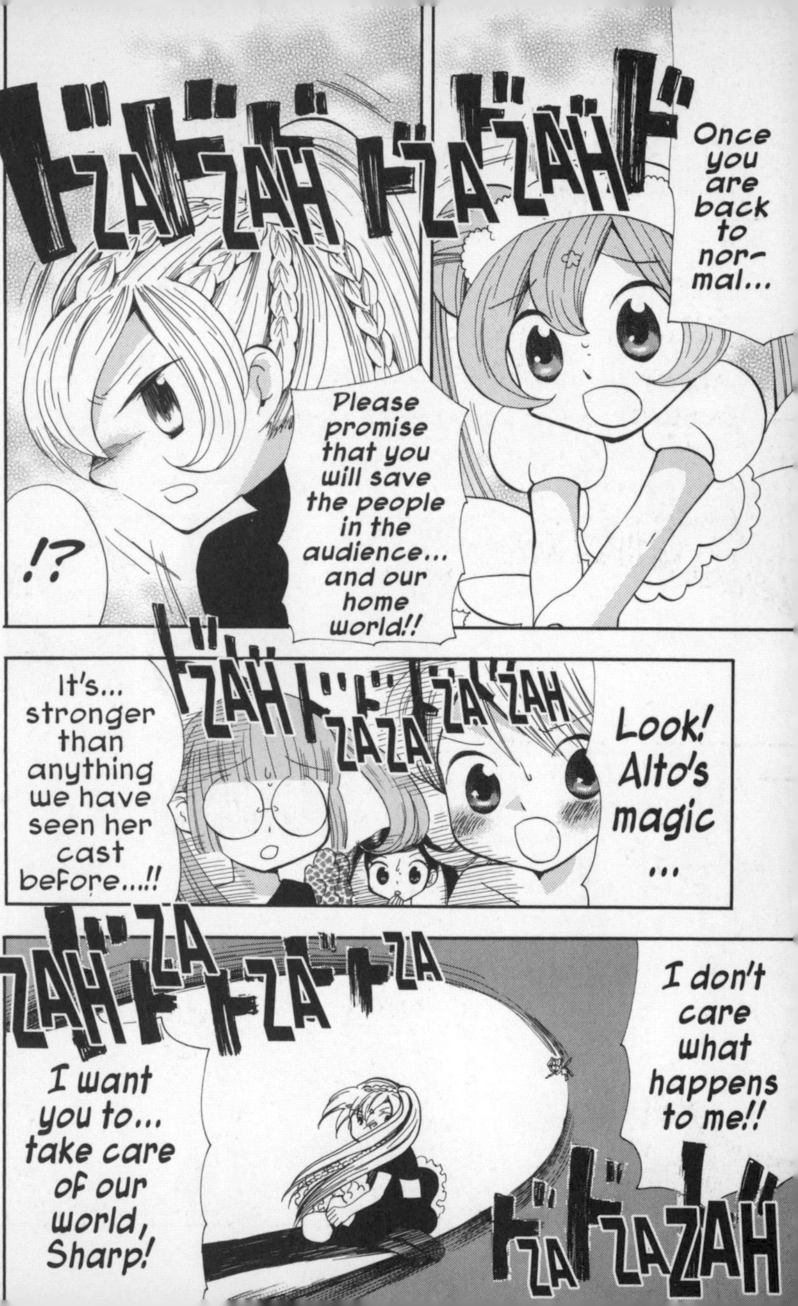
ZA ZAH ZAH
ZA ZAH
Once you are back to normal...
Please promise that you will save the people in the audience... and our home world!!
!?
ZAH ZAZA ZA ZAH
Look! Alto's magic ...
It's... stronger than anything we have seen her cast before...!!
ZAH ZA ZA ZA
I don't care what happens to me!!
ZA ZA ZAH
I want you to... take care of our world, Sharp!

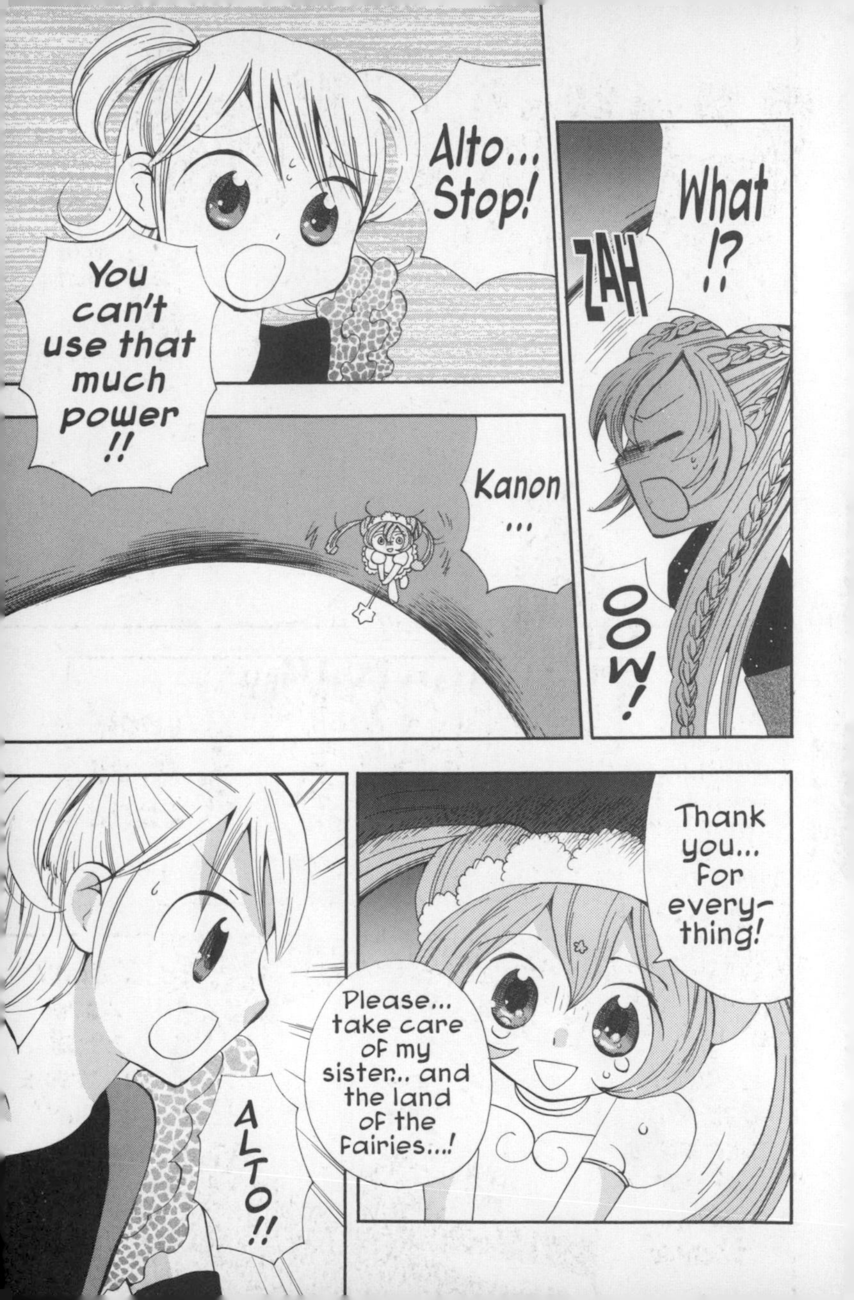
Alto... Stop!
You can't use that much power !!
What !? !!
ZAH
OOW!
Kanon ...
Thank you... for every-thing!
Please... take care of my sister... and the land of the fairies...!
ALTO!!

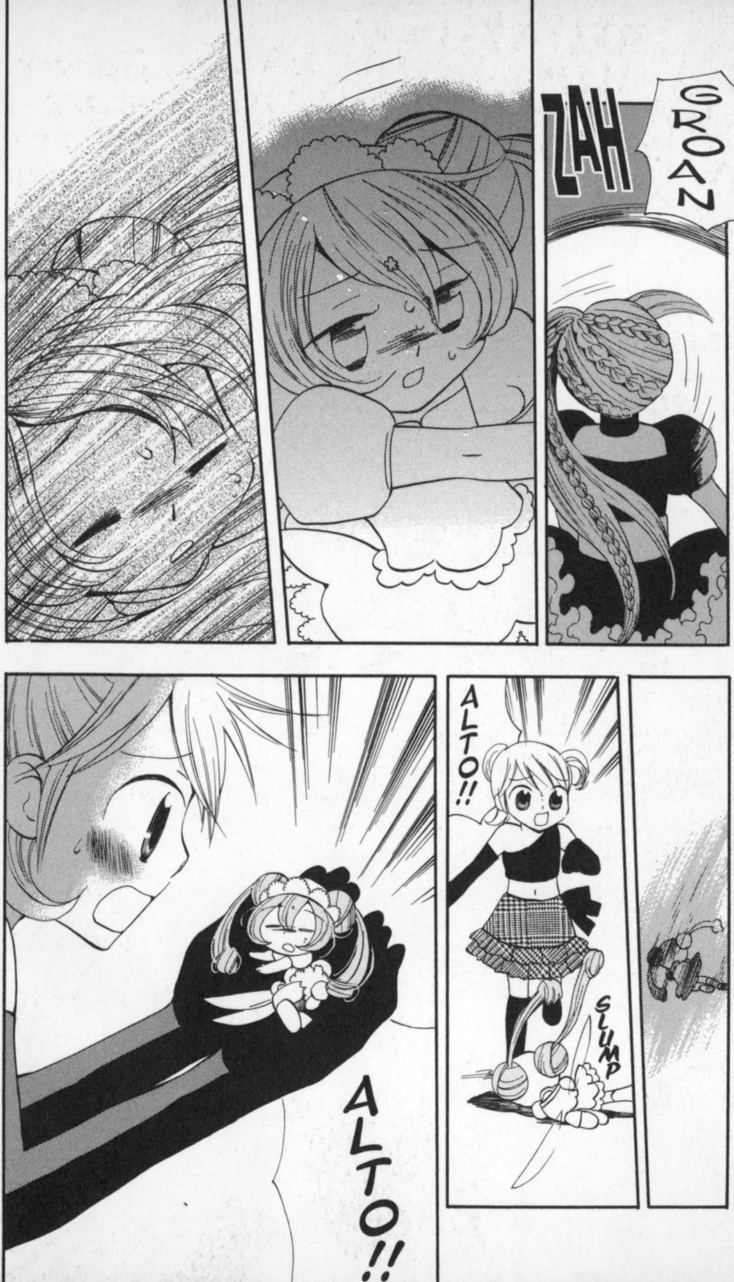
GROAN
ZAH
ALTO!!
SLUMP
ALTO!!

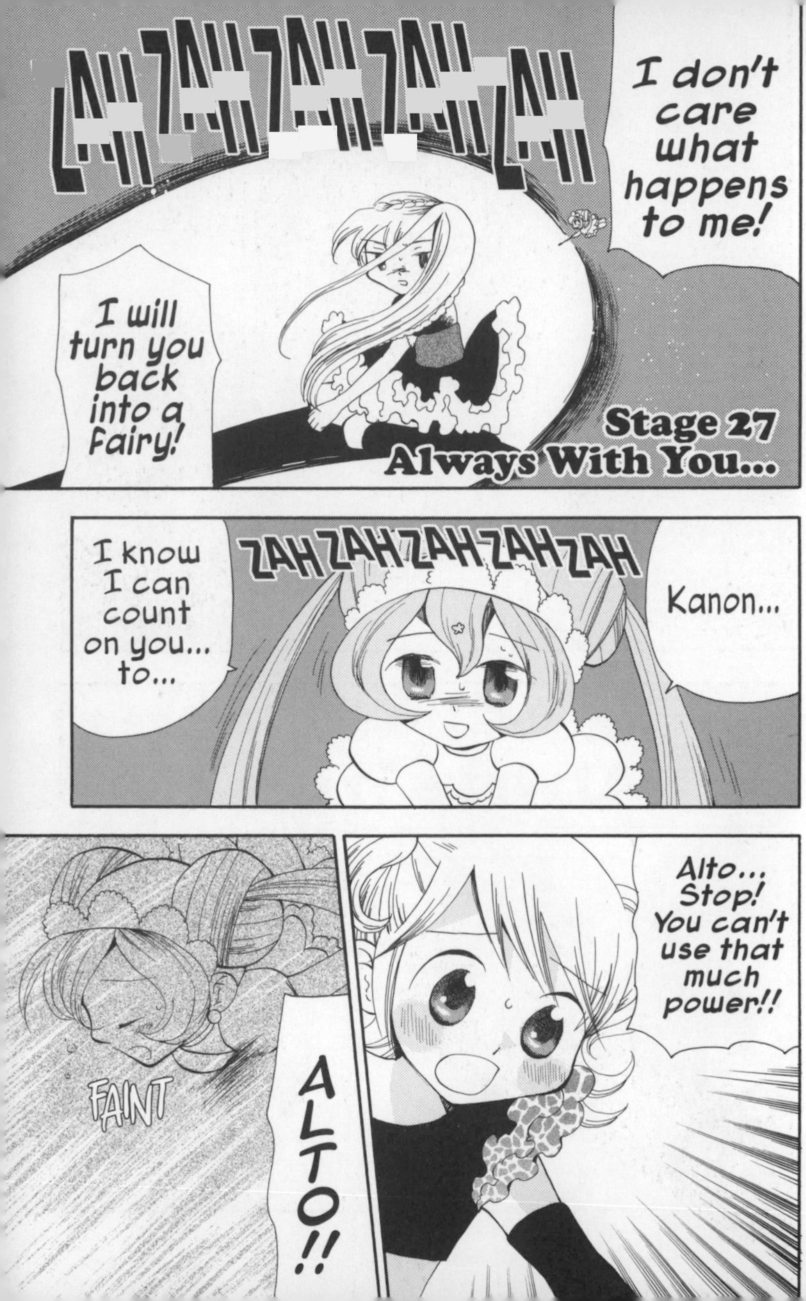
I don't care what happens to me!
I will turn you back into a fairy!
Stage 27
Always With You...
Kanon...
ZAH ZAH ZAH ZAH ZAH
I know I can count on you... to...
Alto... Stop! You can't use that much power!!
ALTO!!
FAINT

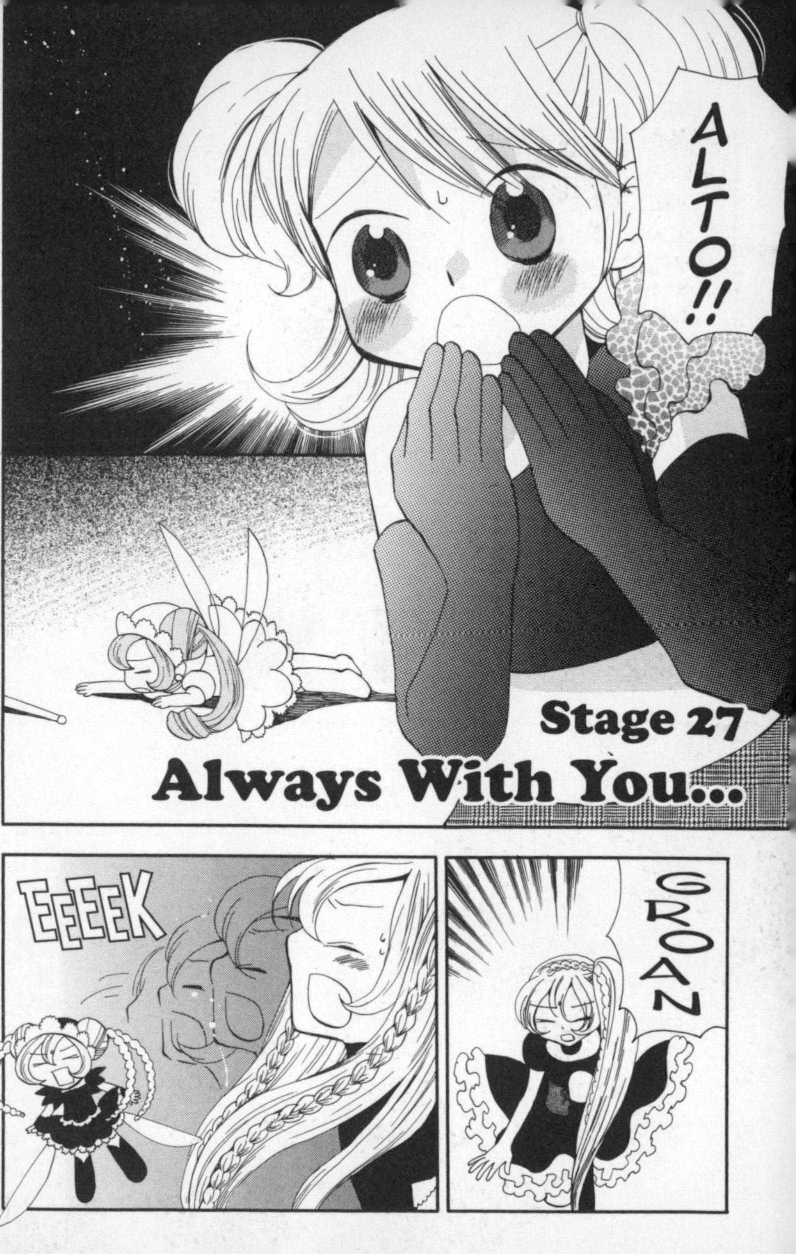
ALTO!!
Stage 27
Always With You...
GROAN
EEEEK

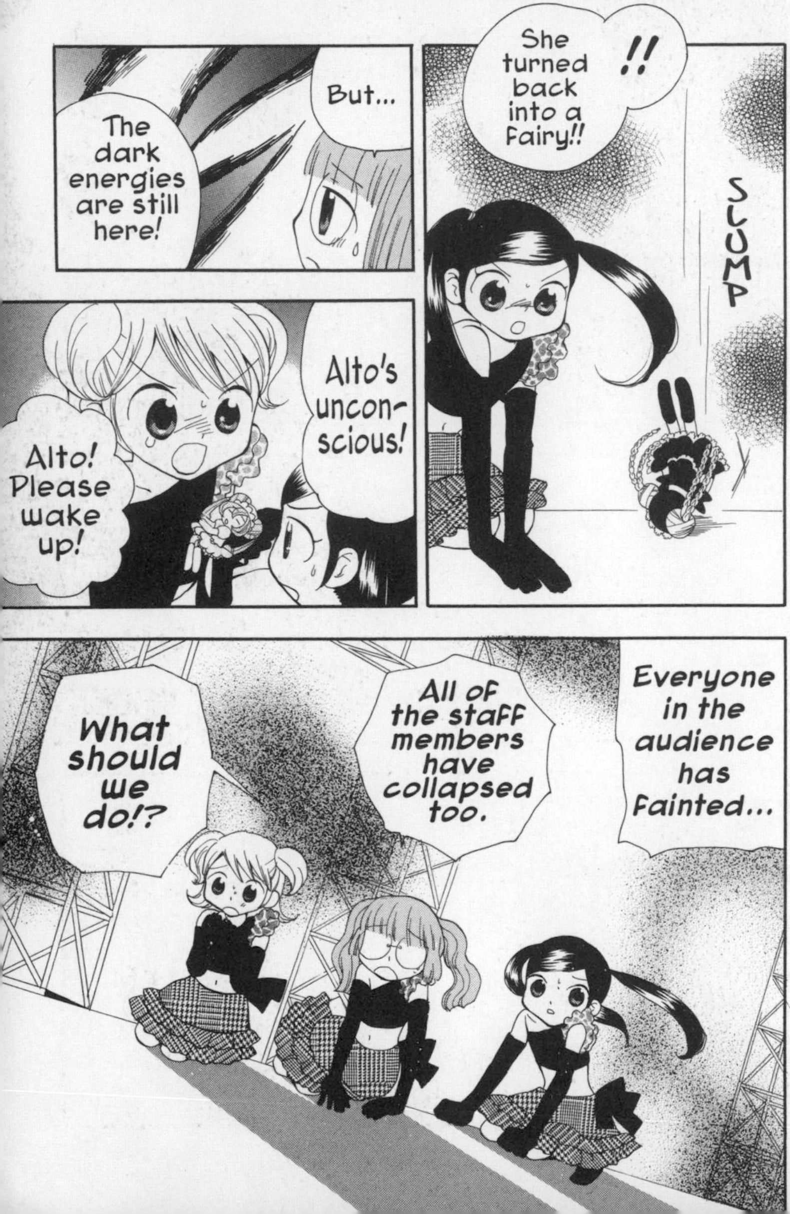
She turned back into a fairy!! !!
SLUMP
But...
The dark energies are still here!
Alto's uncon-scious!
Alto! Please wake up!
Everyone in the audience has fainted...
All of the staff members have collapsed too.
What should we do!?

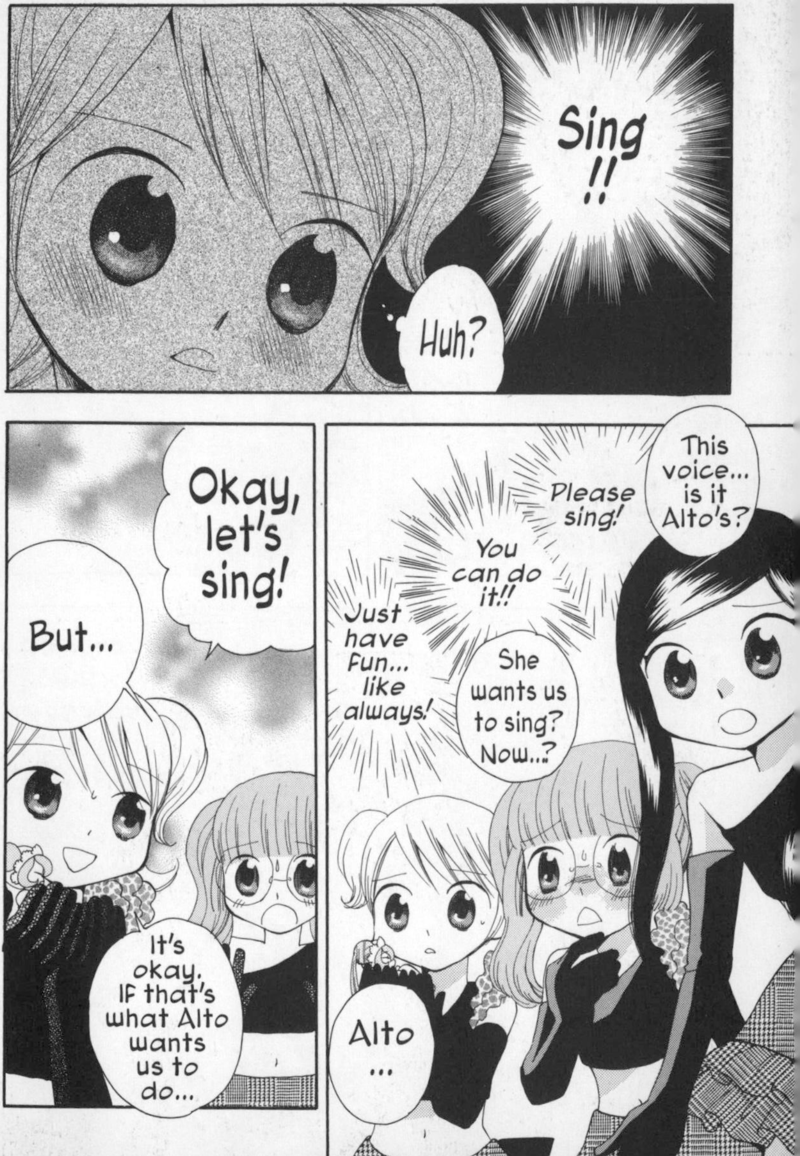
Sing !!
Huh?
This voice... is it Alto's?
Please sing!
You can do it!!
Just have fun... like always!
She wants us to sing? Now...?
Alto ...
Okay, let's sing!
But...
It's okay. If that's what Alto wants us to do...

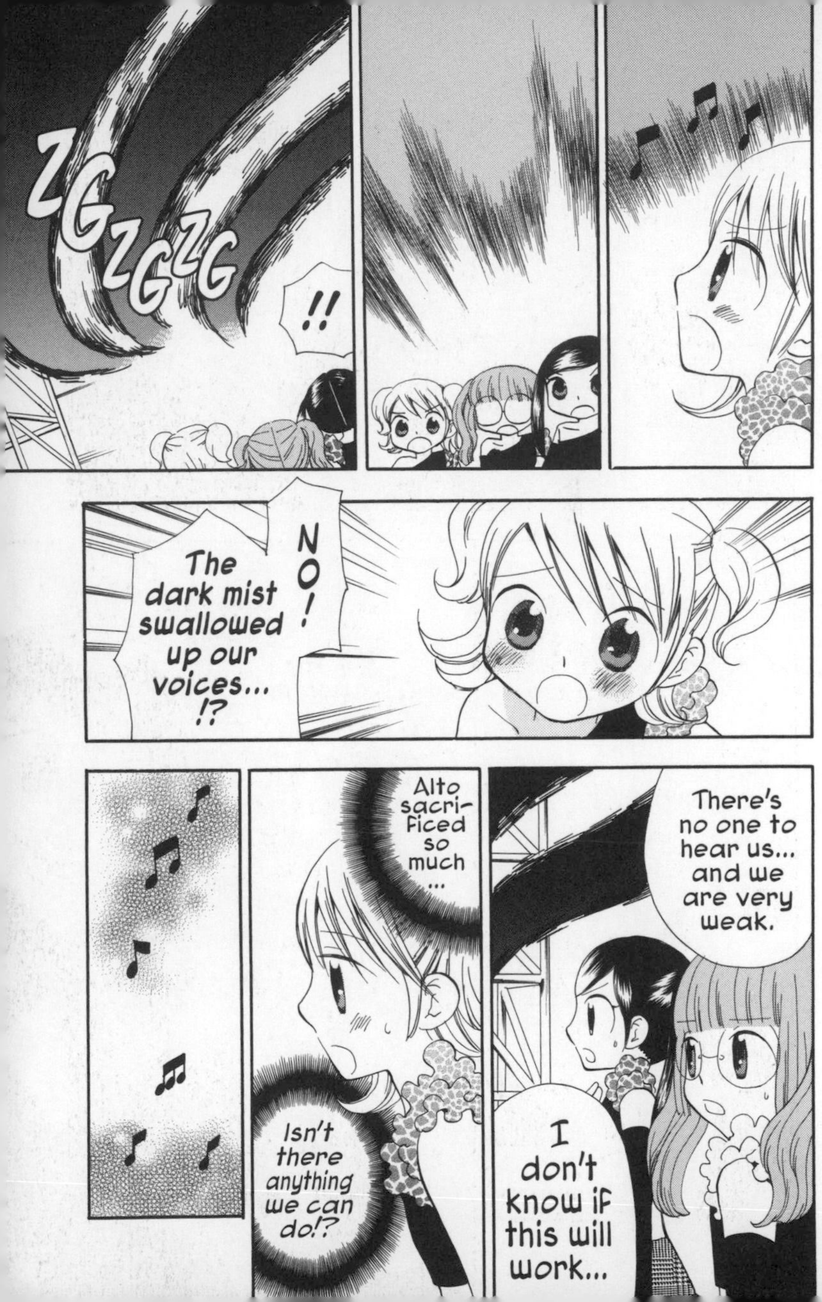
ZGZGZG
!!
NO!
The dark mist swallowed up our voices...!?
There's no one to hear us... and we are very weak.
I don't know if this will work...
Alto sacrificed so much...
Isn't there anything we can do!?

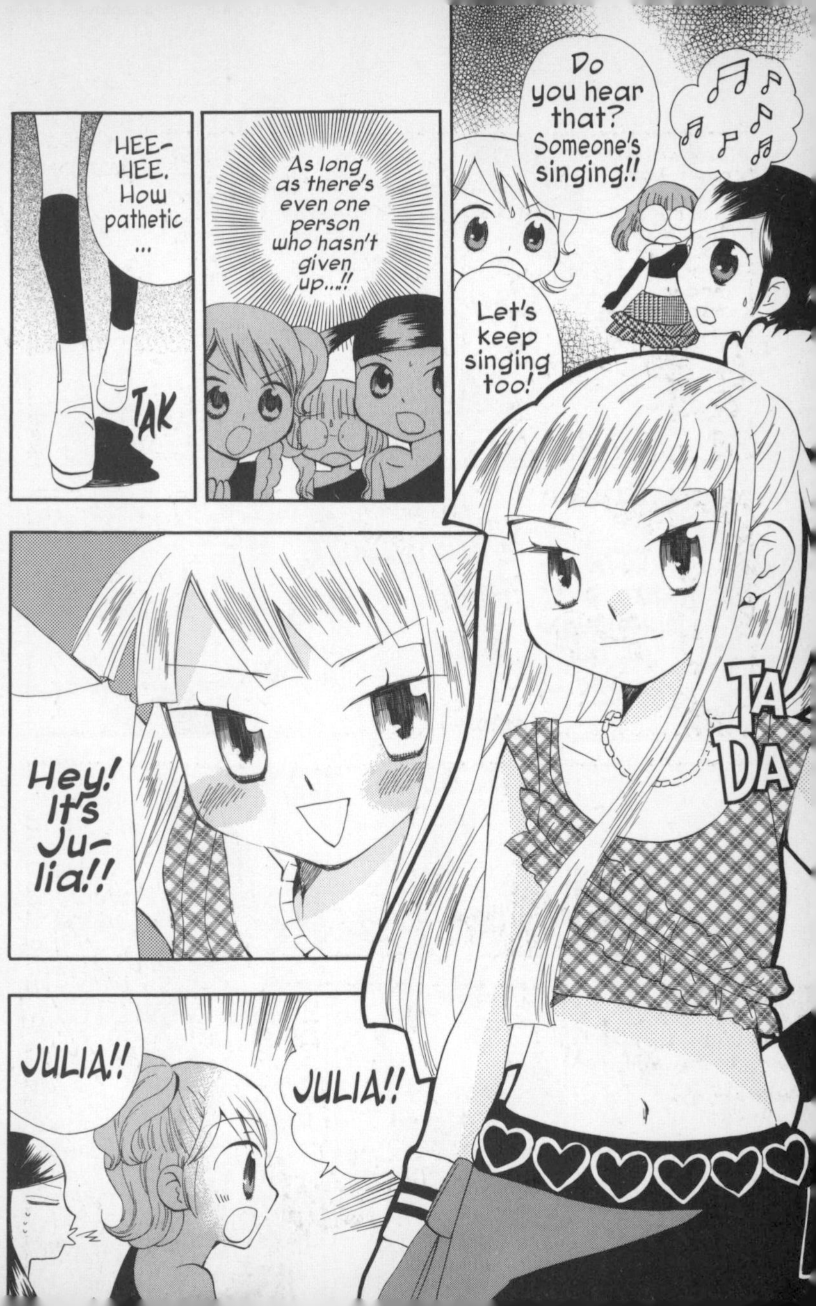

Do you hear that? Someone's singing!!
Let's keep singing too!
TA DA
As long as there's even one person who hasn't given up...!!
HEE-HEE. How pathetic...
TAK
Hey! It's Ju-lia!!
JULIA!!
JULIA!!

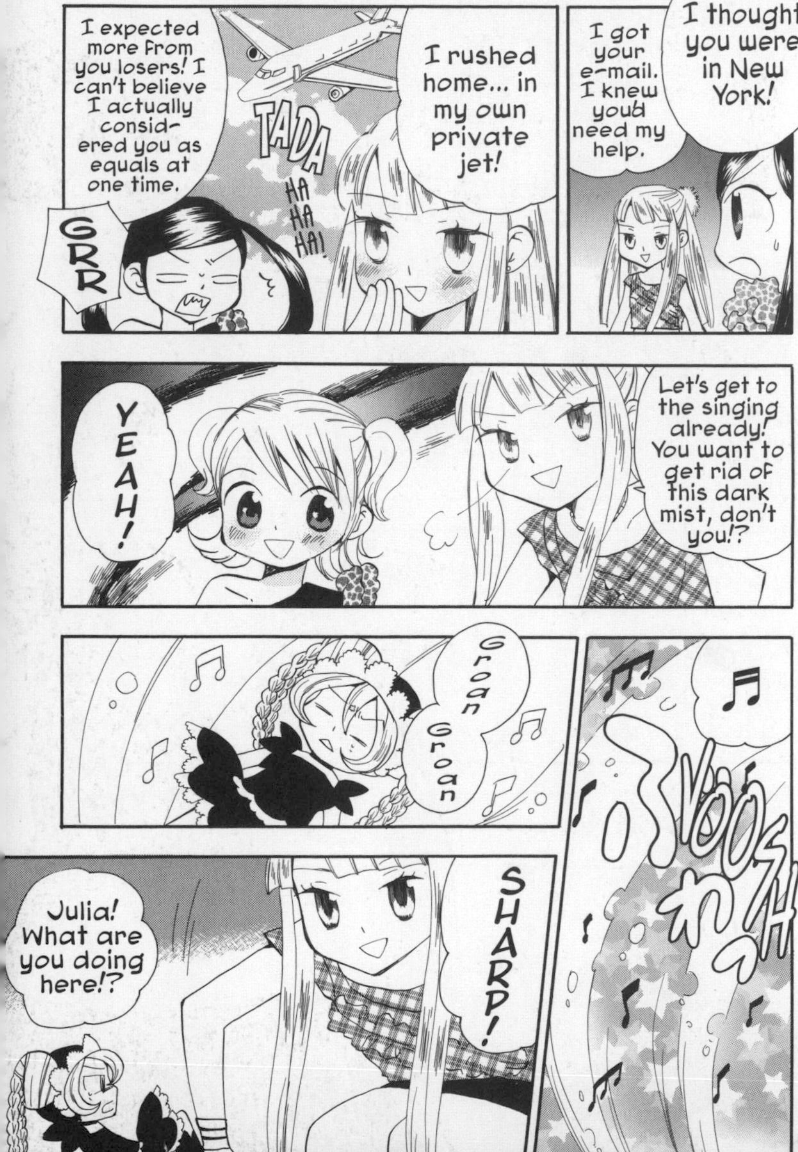

I thought you were in New York!
I got your e-mail. I knew you'd need my help.
I rushed home... in my own private jet!
TADA
HA HA HA!
I expected more from you losers! I can't believe I actually consid-ered you as equals at one time.
GRR
Let's get to the singing already! You want to get rid of this dark mist, don't you!?
YEAH!
VOOSH
Groan Groan
SHARP!
Julia! What are you doing here!?

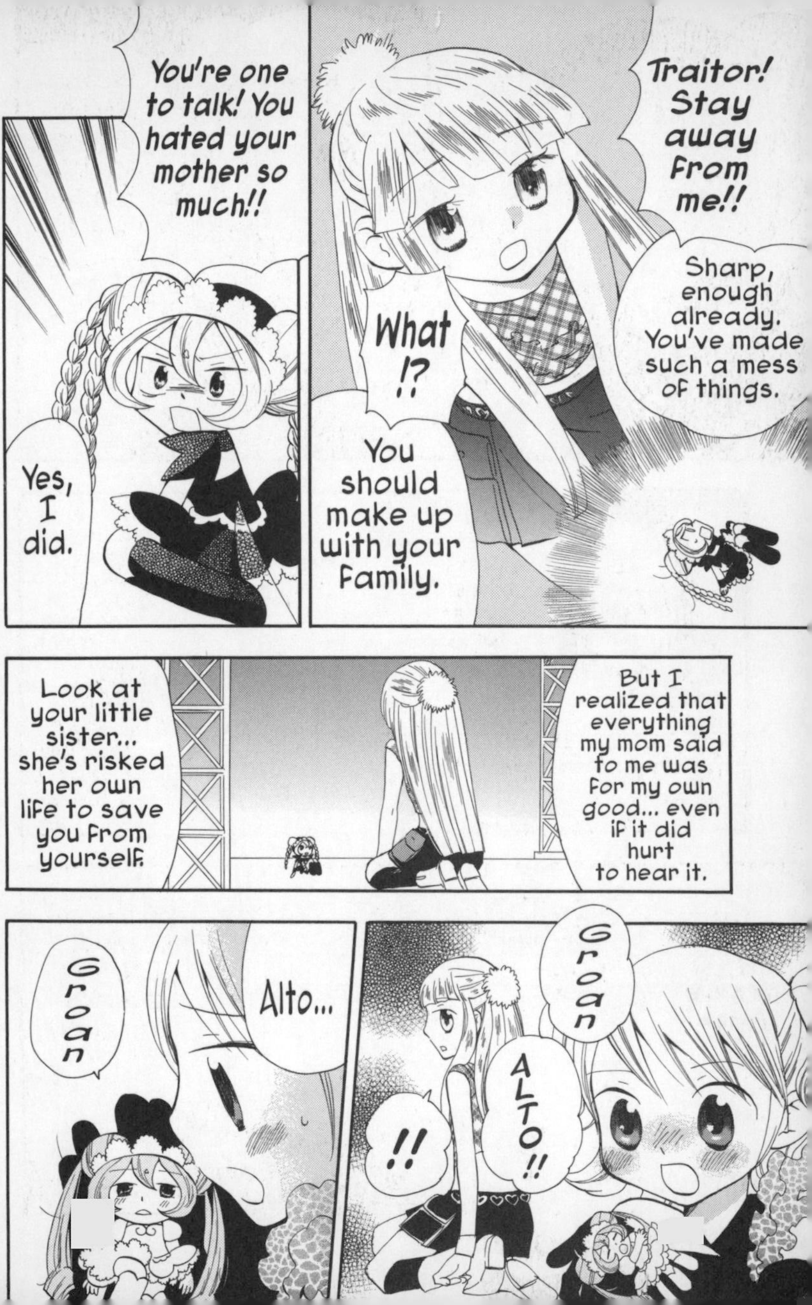

Traitor! Stay away from me!!
Sharp, enough already. You've made such a mess of things.
What!?
You should make up with your family.
You're one to talk! You hated your mother so much!!
Yes, I did.
But I realized that everything my mom said to me was for my own good... even if it did hurt to hear it.
Look at your little sister... she's risked her own life to save you from yourself.
Groan
ALTO!!
!!
Alto...
Groan

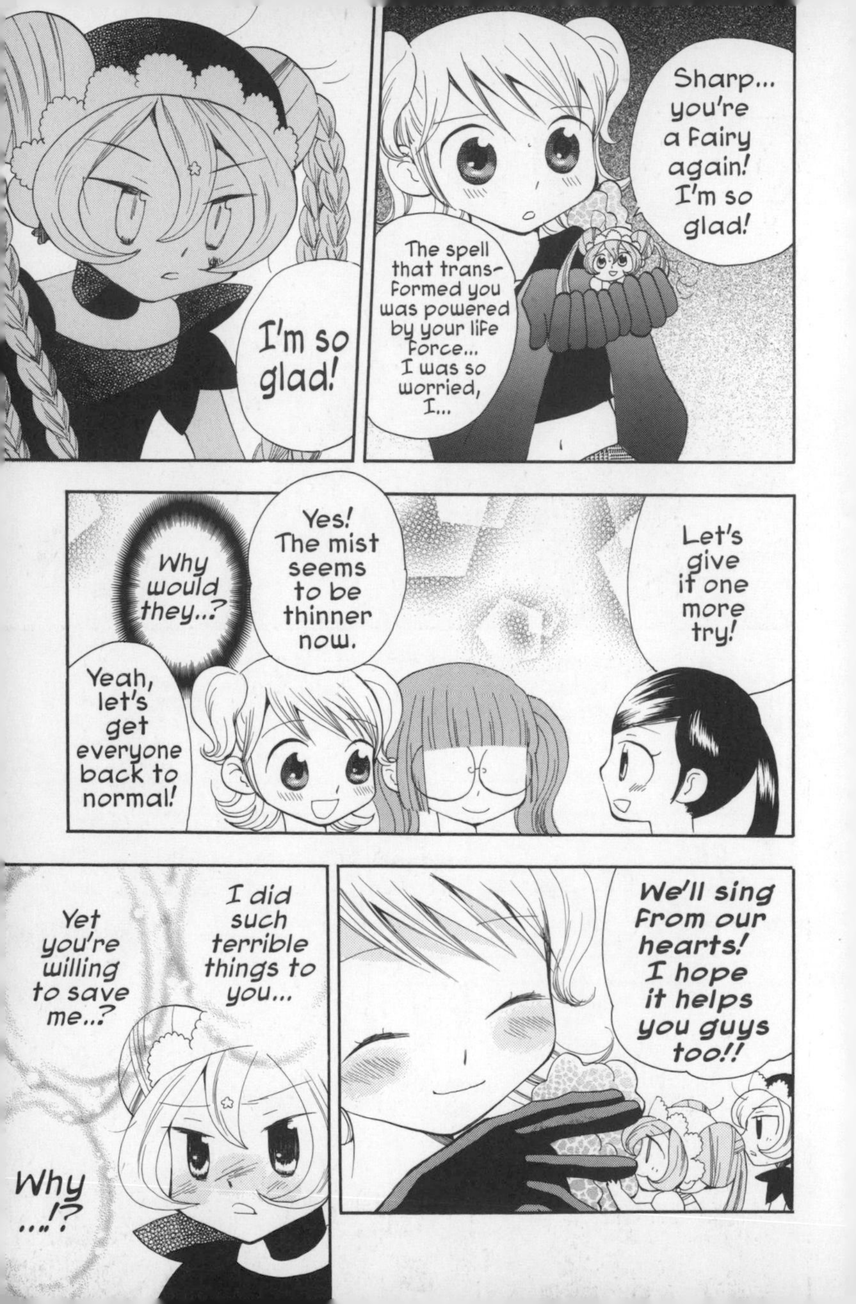
Sharp... you're a fairy again! I'm so glad!
The spell that trans-formed you was powered by your life force... I was so worried, I...
I'm so glad!
Let's give it one more try!
Yes! The mist seems to be thinner now.
Why would they...?
Yeah, let's get everyone back to normal!
We'll sing from our hearts! I hope it helps you guys too!!
I did such terrible things to you...
Yet you're willing to save me..?
Why ...!?

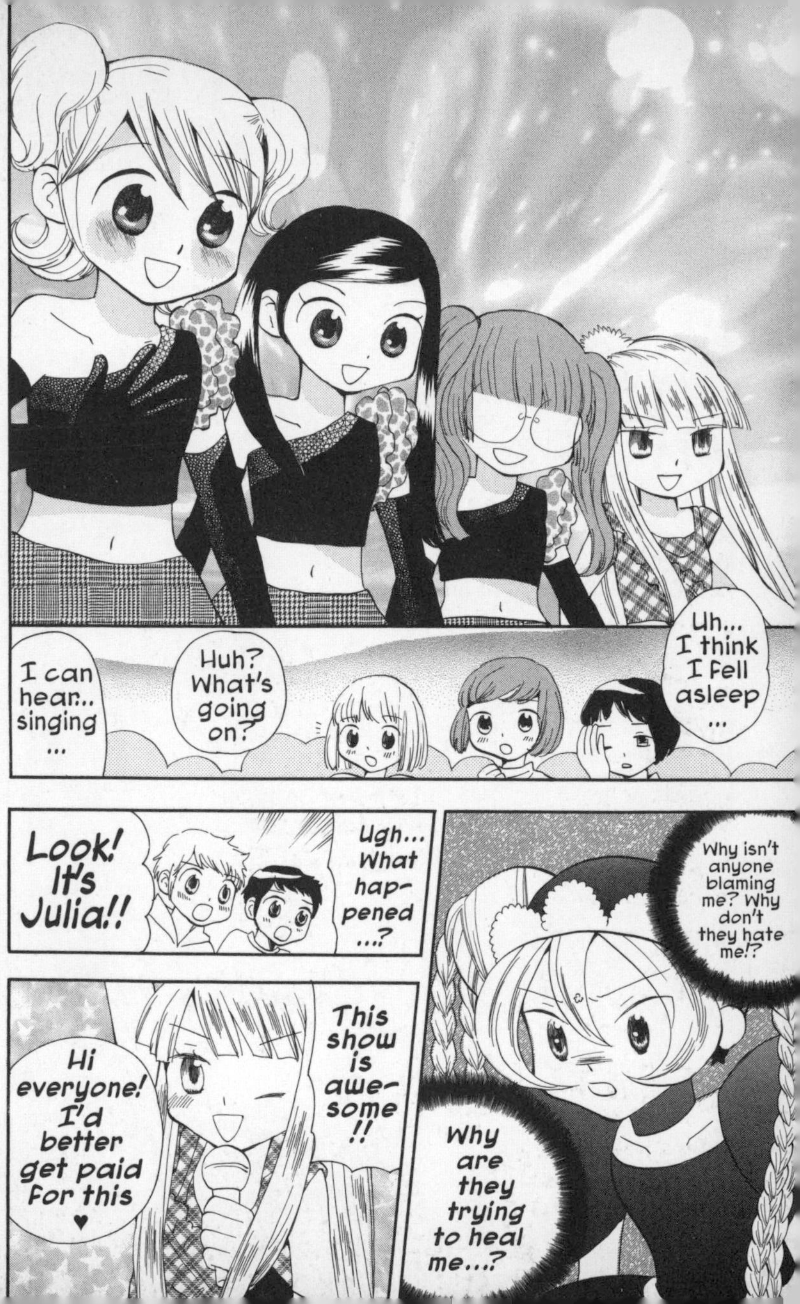
Uh... I think I fell asleep ...
Huh? What's going on?
I can hear.. singing ...
Why isn't anyone blaming me? Why don't they hate me!?
Why are they trying to heal me...?
Ugh... What hap-pened ...?
Look! It's Julia!!
This show is awe-some!!
Hi everyone! I'd better get paid for this ♥

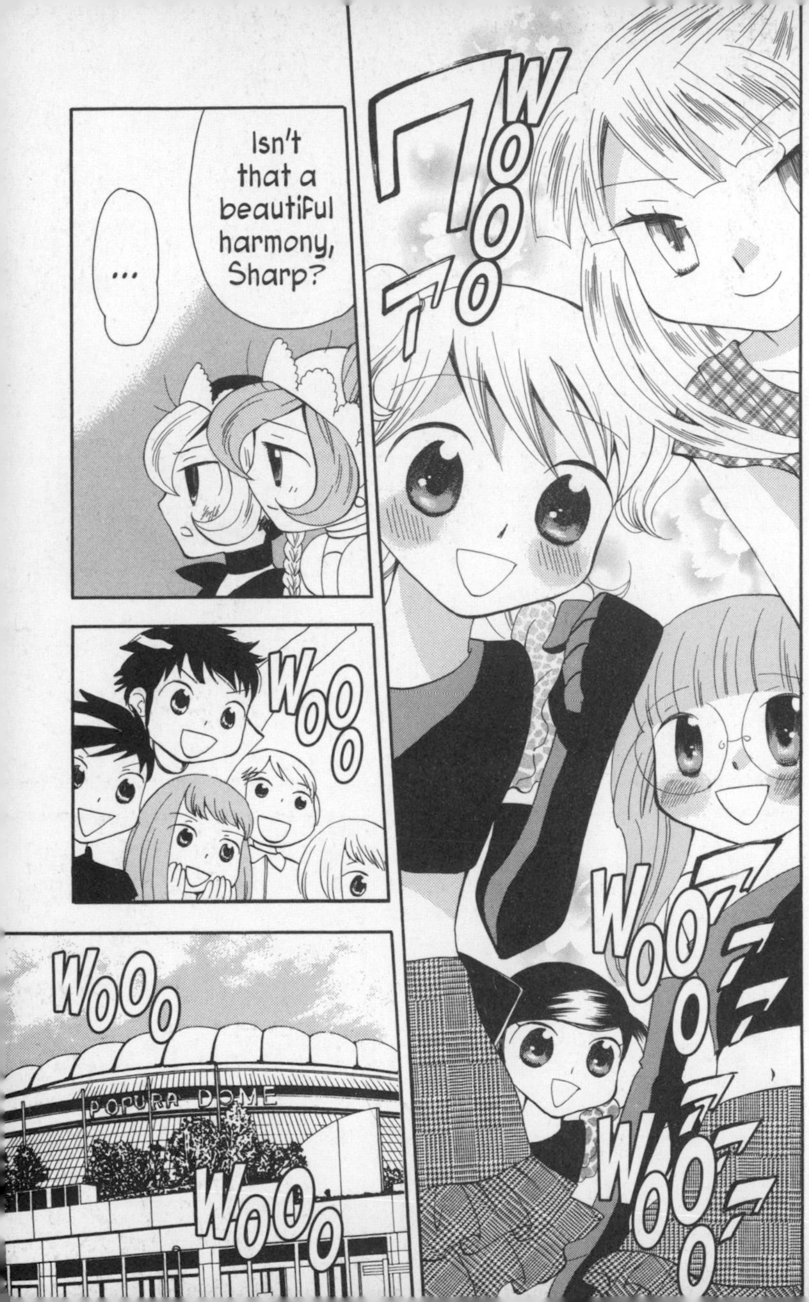
WOOOO
WOOO
WOOO
Isn't that a beautiful harmony, Sharp?
...
WOOO
WOOO
POPURA DOME
WOOO

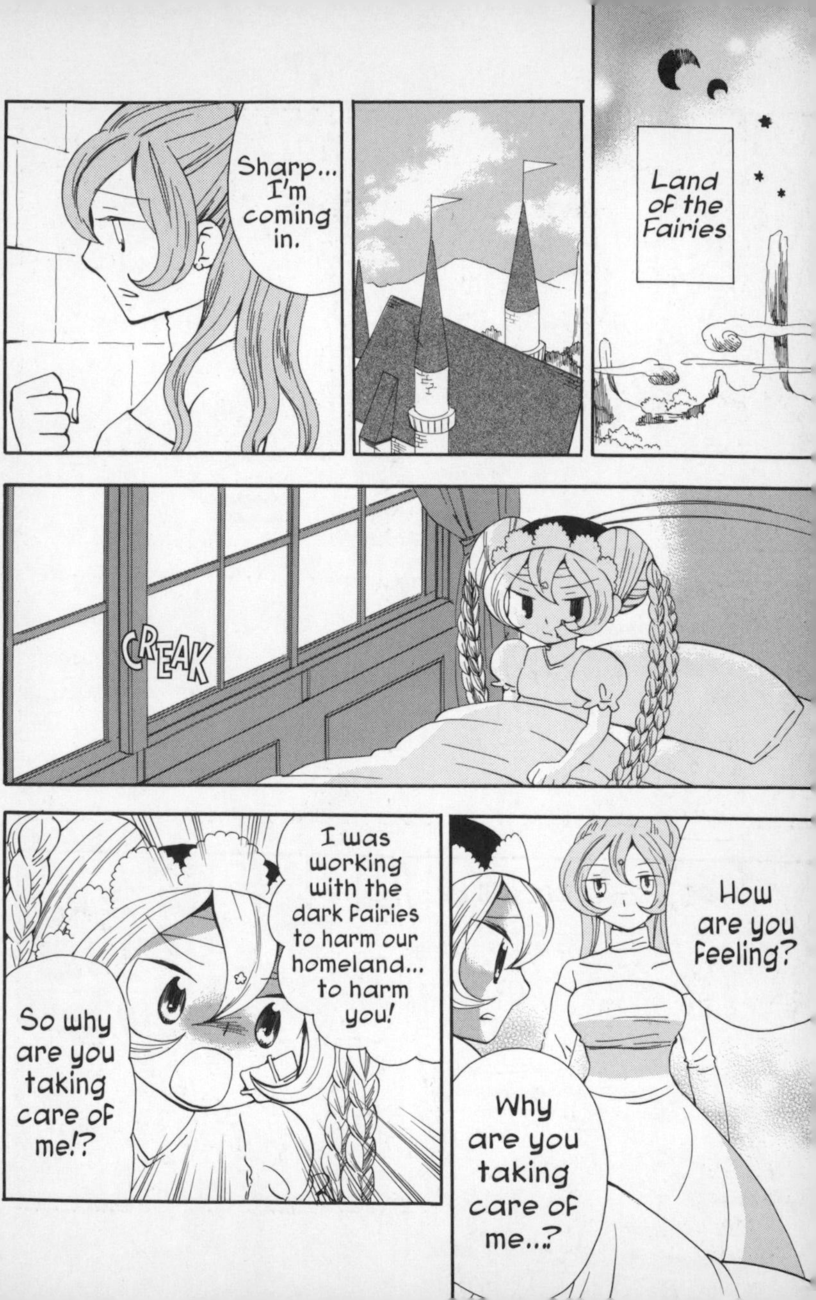
Land of the Fairies
Sharp... I'm coming in.
CREAK
How are you feeling?
Why are you taking care of me...?
I was working with the dark fairies to harm our homeland... to harm you!
So why are you taking care of me!?

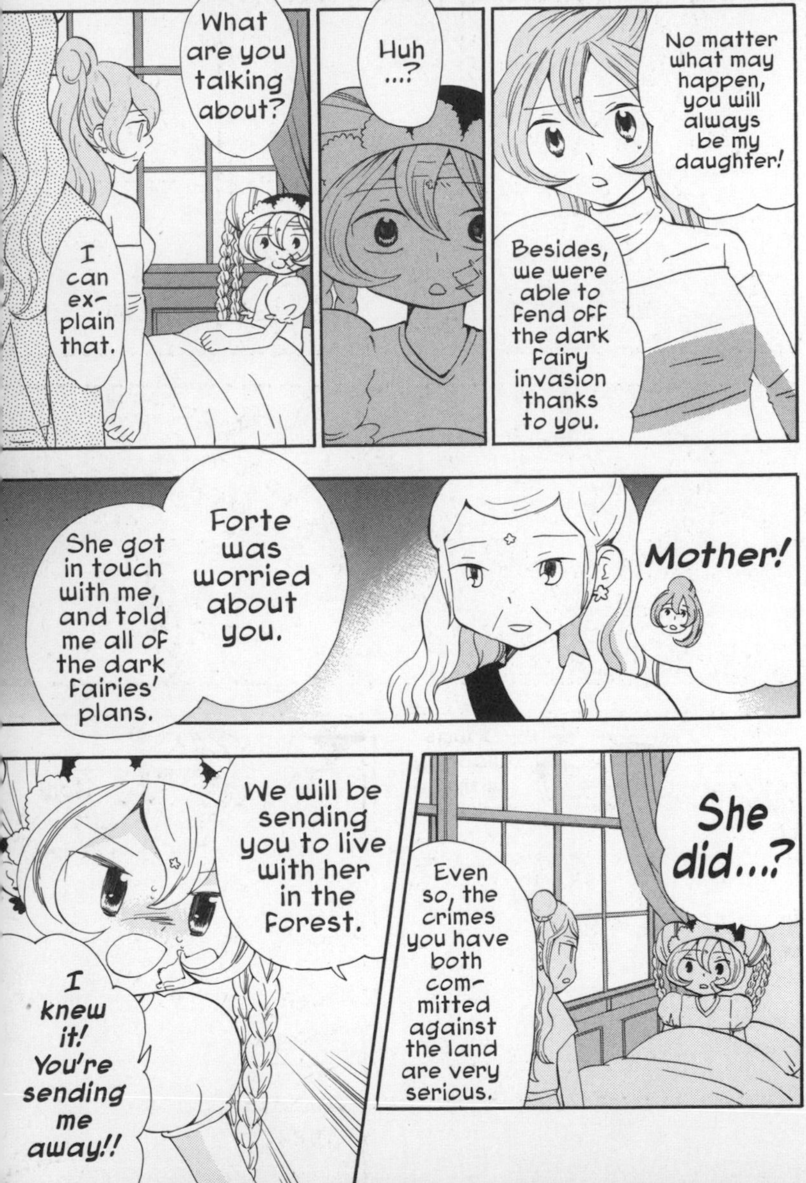
No matter what may happen, you will always be my daughter!
Besides, we were able to fend off the dark fairy invasion thanks to you.
Huh ...?
What are you talking about?
I can ex-plain that.
Mother!
Forte was worried about you.
She got in touch with me, and told me all of the dark fairies' plans.
She did...?
Even so, the crimes you have both com-mitted against the land are very serious.
We will be sending you to live with her in the forest.
I knew it! You're sending me away!!

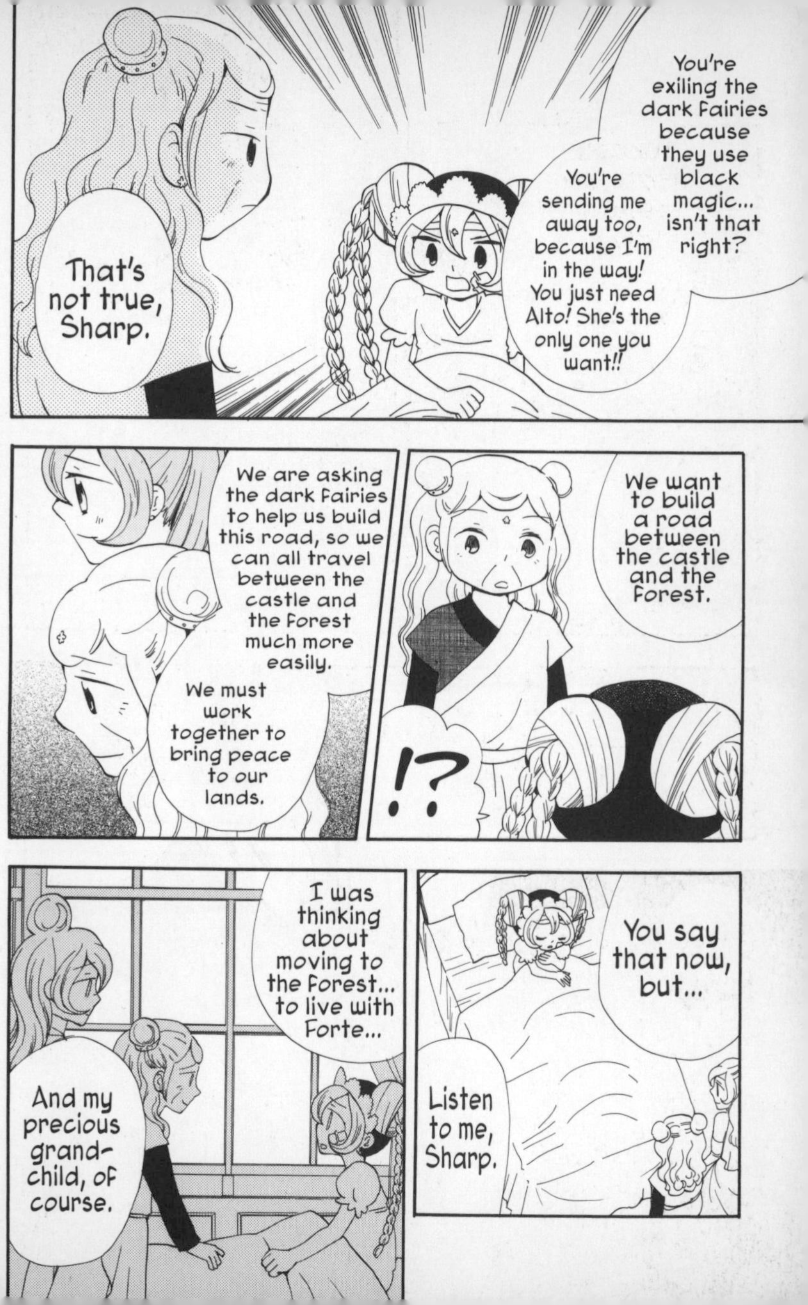
You're exiling the dark fairies because they use black magic... isn't that right?
You're sending me away too, because I'm in the way! You just need Alto! She's the only one you want!!
That's not true, Sharp.
We want to build a road between the castle and the forest.
!?
We are asking the dark fairies to help us build this road, so we can all travel between the castle and the forest much more easily.
We must work together to bring peace to our lands.
You say that now, but...
Listen to me, Sharp.
I was thinking about moving to the forest... to live with Forte...
And my precious grand-child, of course.

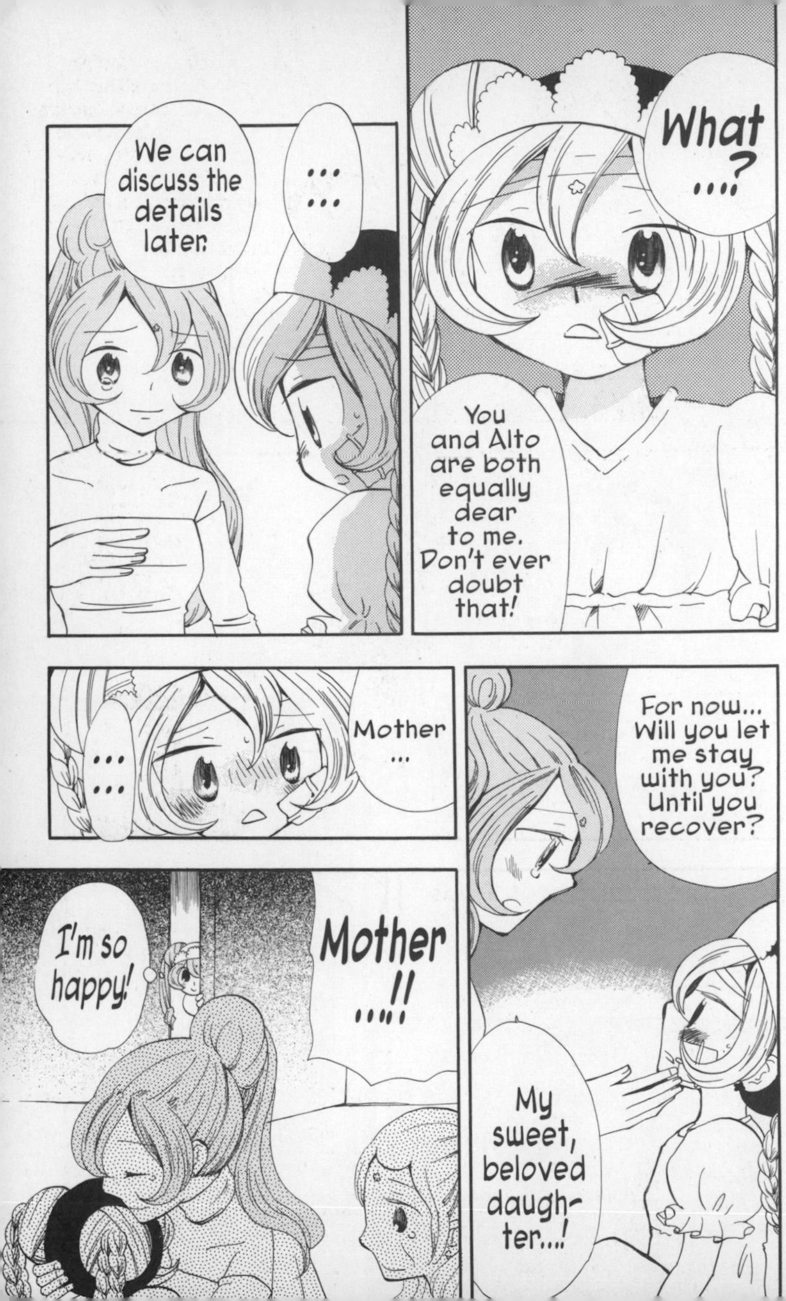

What ...?
You and Alto are both equally dear to me. Don't ever doubt that!
......
We can discuss the details later.
For now... Will you let me stay with you? Until you recover?
My sweet, beloved daughter...!
Mother ...
......
Mother ...!!
I'm so happy!

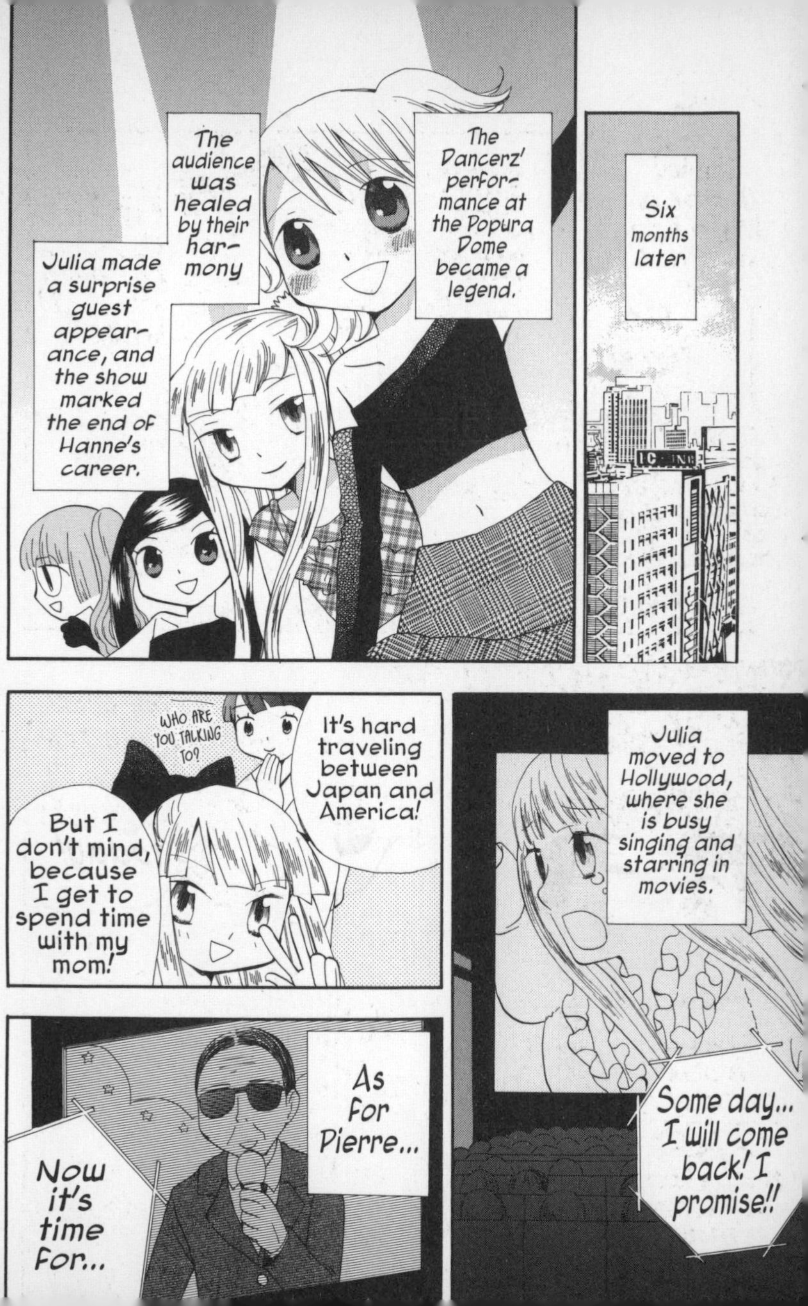
Six months later
The Dancerz' performance at the Popura Dome became a legend.
The audience was healed by their harmony
Julia made a surprise guest appearance, and the show marked the end of Hanne's career.
Julia moved to Hollywood, where she is busy singing and starring in movies.
Some day... I will come back! I promise!!
It's hard traveling between Japan and America!
WHO ARE YOU TALKING TO?
But I don't mind, because I get to spend time with my mom!
As for Pierre...
Now it's time for...

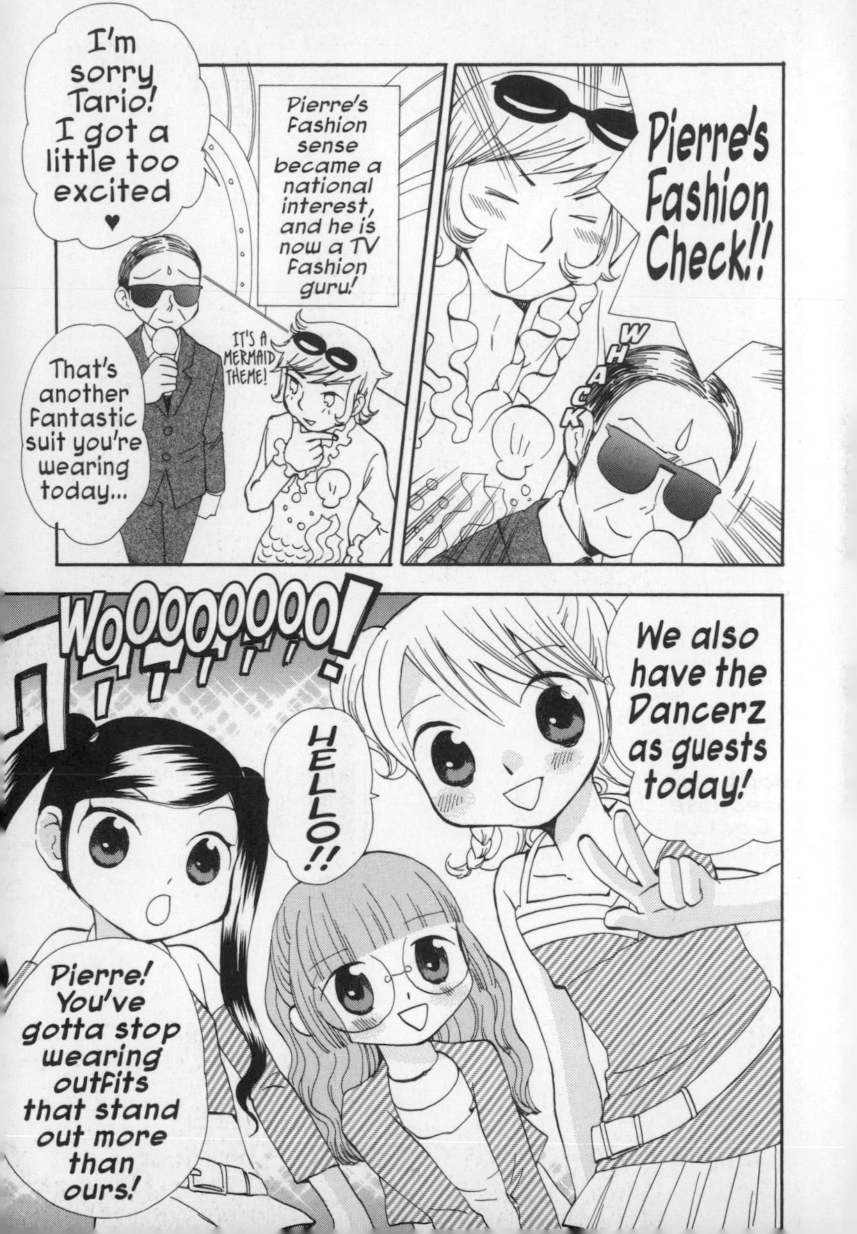
Pierre's Fashion Check!!
WHACK
Pierre's Fashion sense became a national interest, and he is now a TV Fashion guru!
I'm sorry Tario! I got a little too excited ♥
IT'S A MERMAID THEME!
That's another Fantastic suit you're wearing today...
WOOOOOOOO!
We also have the Dancerz as guests today!
HELLO!!
Pierre! You've gotta stop wearing outfits that stand out more than ours!

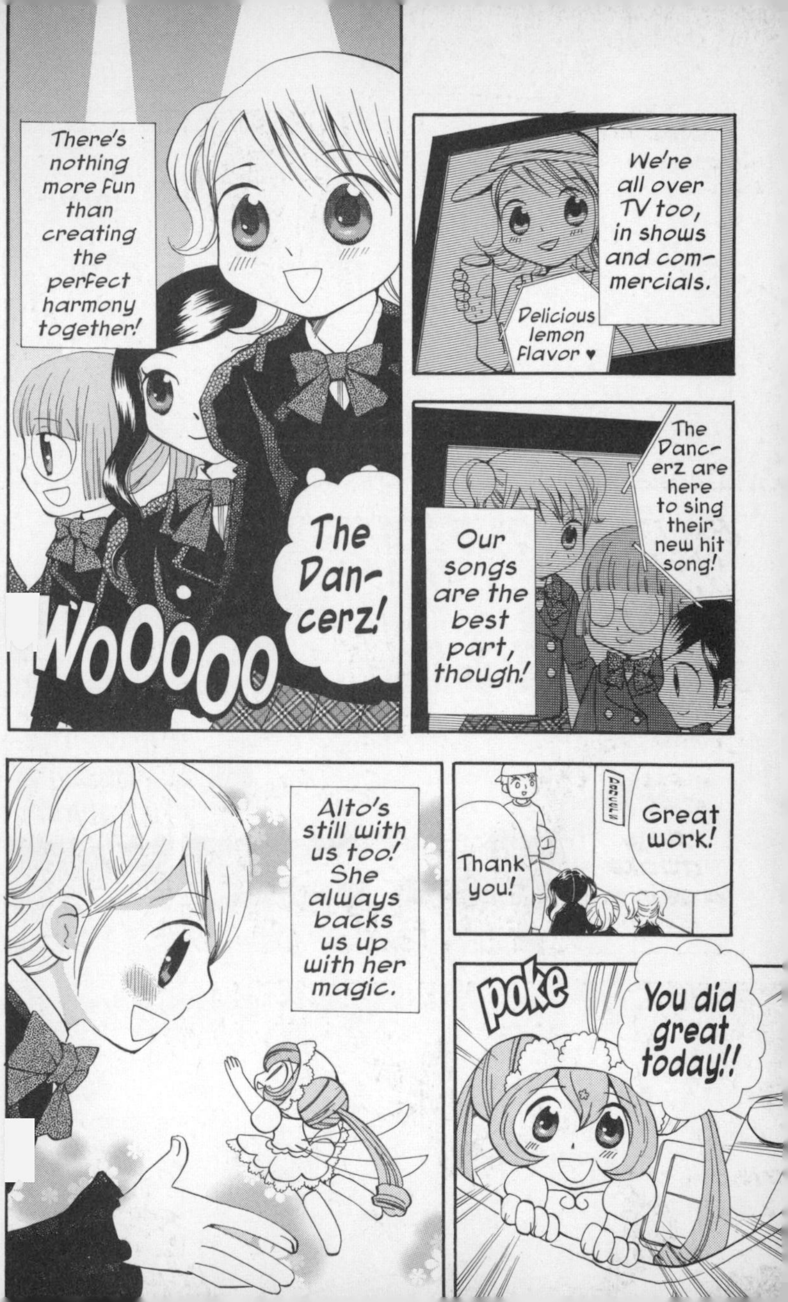
We're all over TV too, in shows and commercials.
Delicious lemon flavor ♥
The Dancerz are here to sing their new hit song!
Our songs are the best part, though!
There's nothing more fun than creating the perfect harmony together!
The Dan-cerz!
WOOOOO
Great work!
Thank you!
poke
You did great today!!
Alto's still with us too! She always backs us up with her magic.

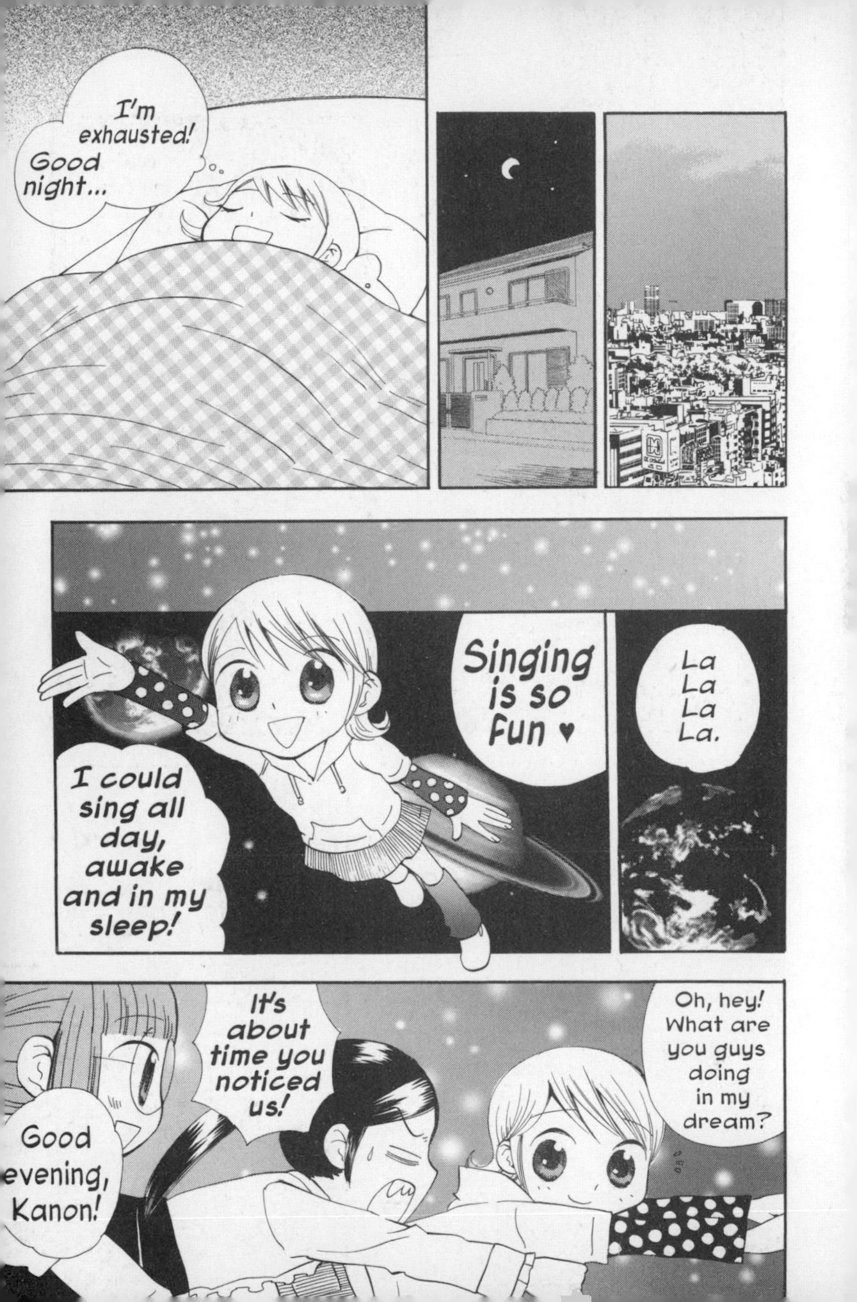
I'm exhausted! Good night...
La La La La.
Singing is so fun ♥
I could sing all day, awake and in my sleep!
Oh, hey! What are you guys doing in my dream?
It's about time you noticed us!
Good evening, Kanon!

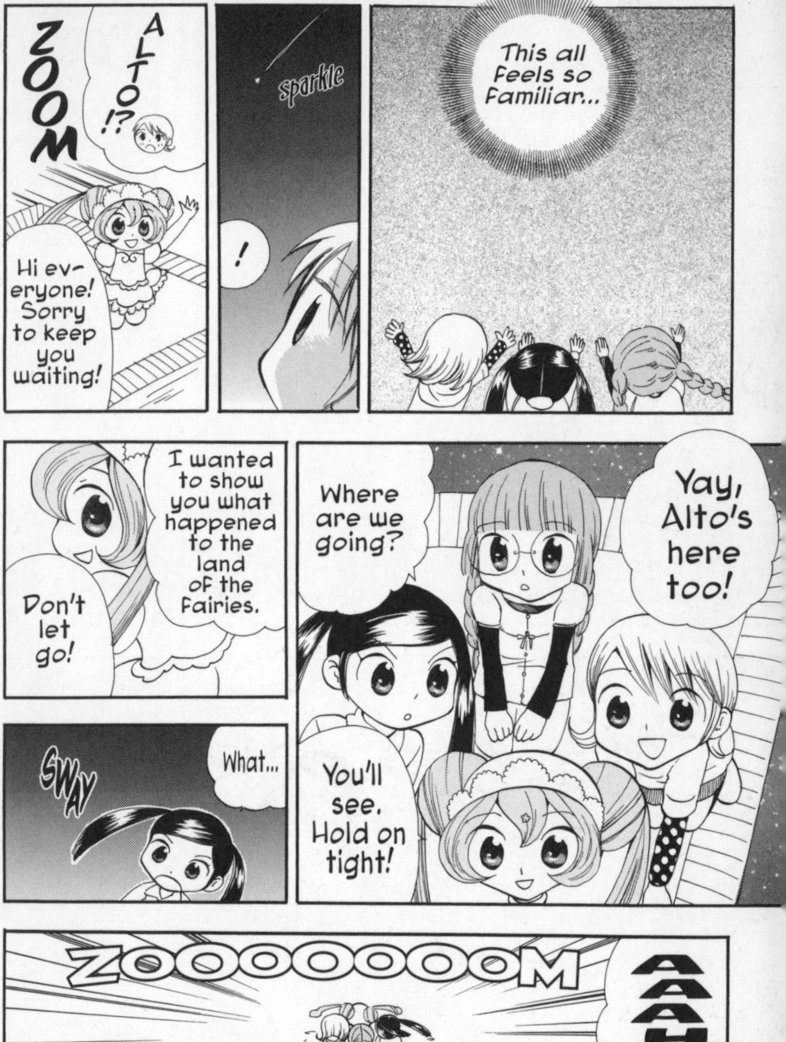
This all feels so familiar...
sparkle
!
ALTO!?
ZOOM
Hi ev-eryone! Sorry to keep you waiting!
Yay, Alto's here too!
Where are we going?
You'll see. Hold on tight!
I wanted to show you what happened to the land of the fairies.
Don't let go!
What...
SWAY
AAAHH!
ZOOOOOOOM

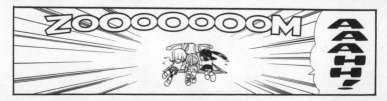

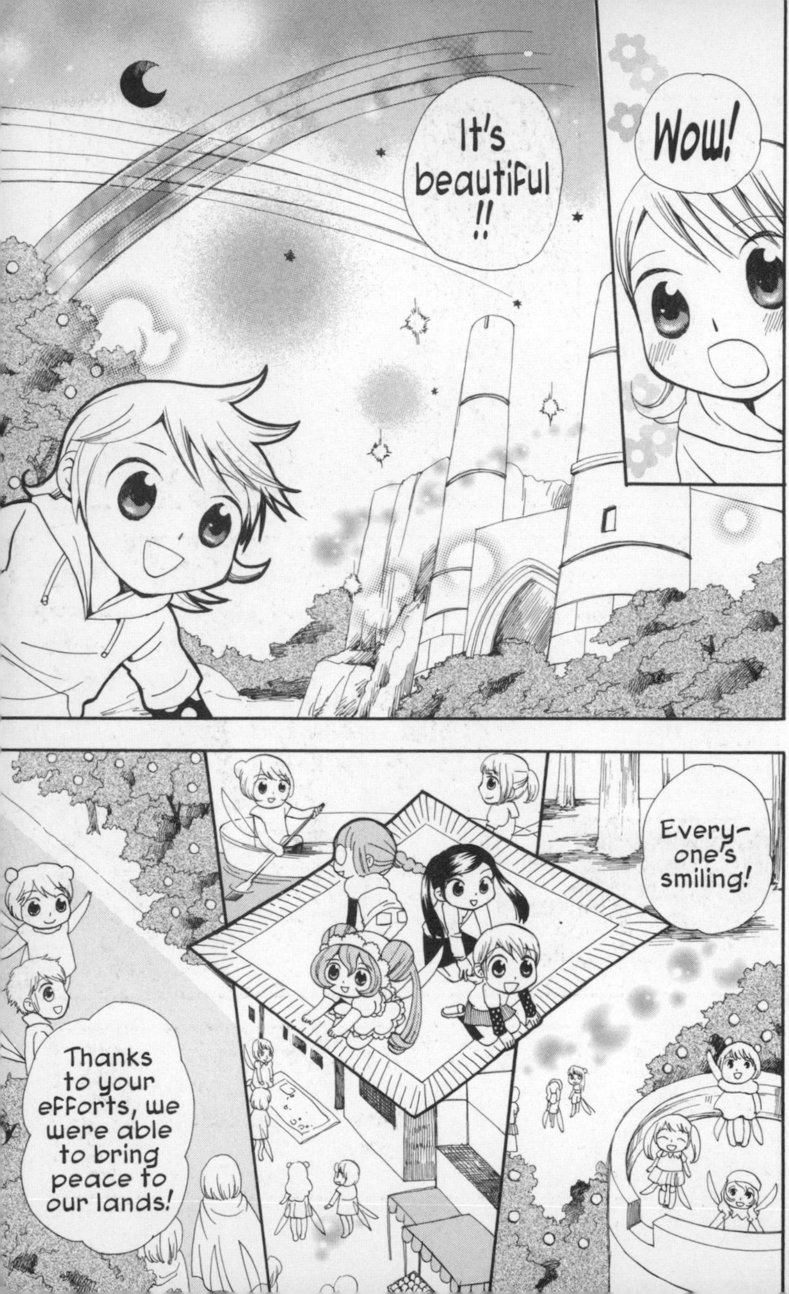
Wow!
It's beautiful!!
Every-one's smiling!
Thanks to your efforts, we were able to bring peace to our lands!

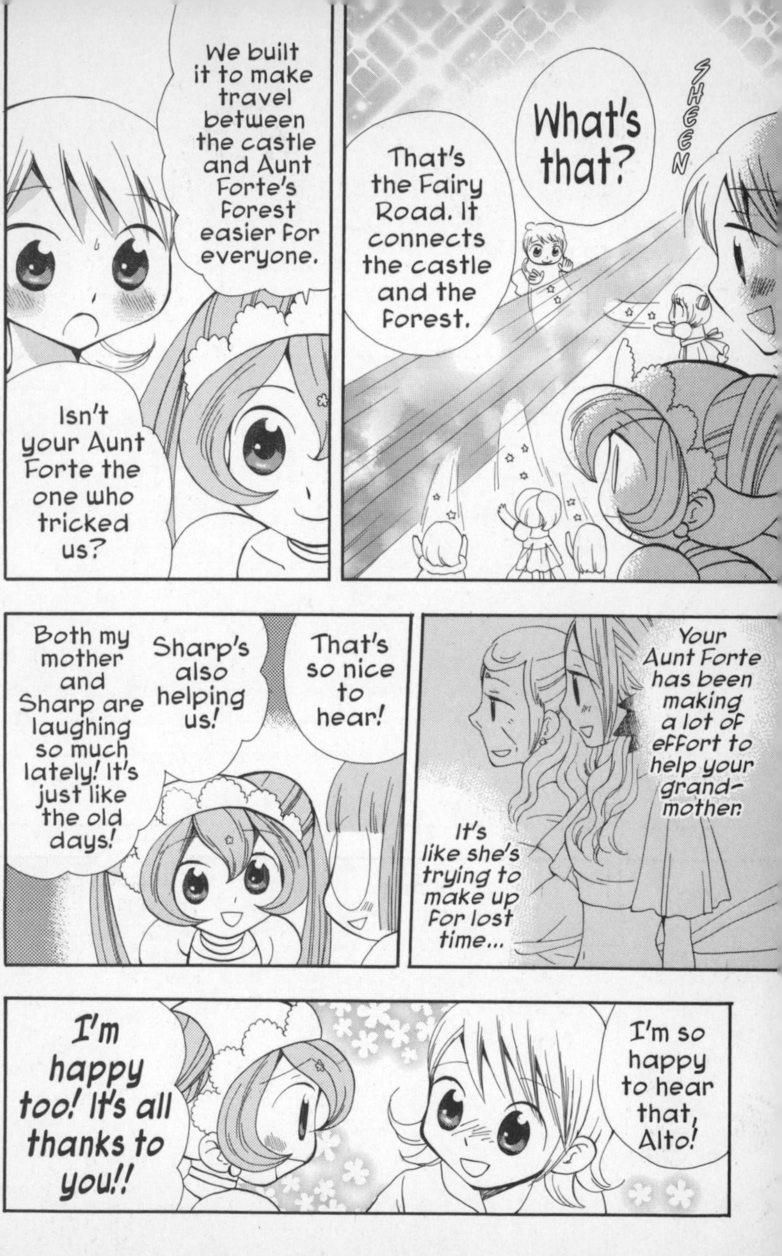
What's that?
SHEEN
That's the Fairy Road. It connects the castle and the forest.
We built it to make travel between the castle and Aunt Forte's forest easier for everyone.
Isn't your Aunt Forte the one who tricked us?
Your Aunt Forte has been making a lot of effort to help your grandmother.
It's like she's trying to make up for lost time...
That's so nice to hear!
Sharp's also helping us!
Both my mother and Sharp are laughing so much lately! It's just like the old days!
I'm so happy to hear that, Alto!
I'm happy too! It's all thanks to you!!

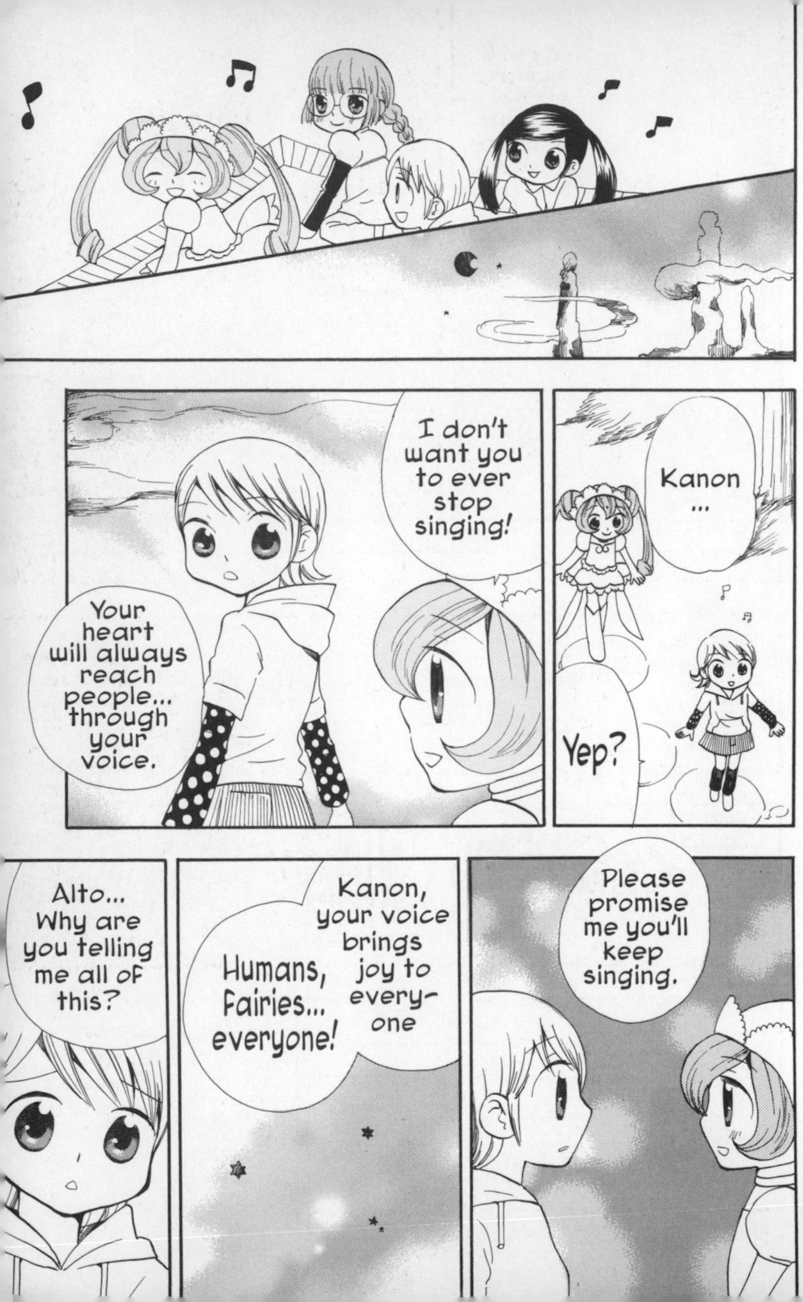
Kanon ...
Yep?
I don't want you to ever stop singing!
Your heart will always reach people... through your voice.
Please promise me you'll keep singing.
Kanon, your voice brings joy to every-one
Humans, Fairies... everyone!
Alto... Why are you telling me all of this?

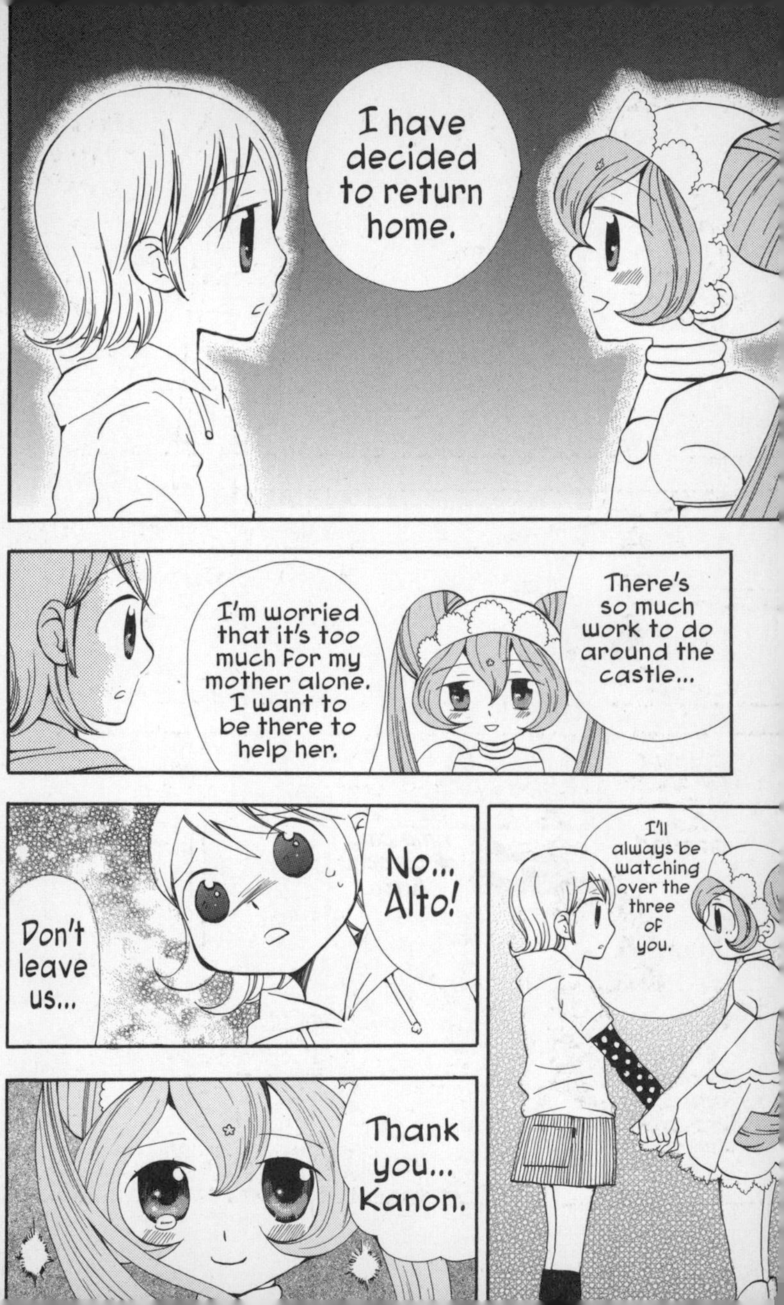
I have decided to return home.
There's so much work to do around the castle...
I'm worried that it's too much for my mother alone. I want to be there to help her.
I'll always be watching over the three of you.
No... Alto!
Don't leave us...
Thank you... Kanon.

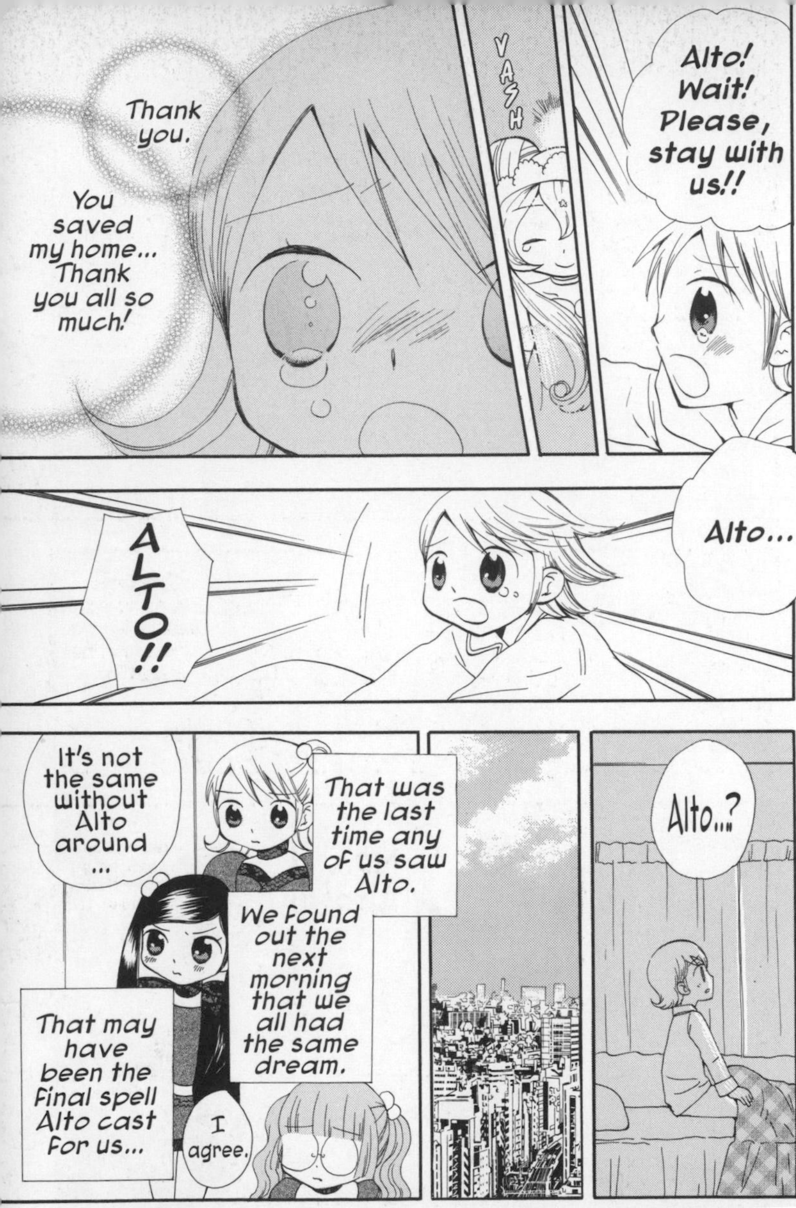
Alto! Wait! Please, stay with us!!
VASH
Thank you.
You saved my home... Thank you all so much!
Alto...
ALTO!!
Alto...?
That was the last time any of us saw Alto.
It's not the same without Alto around ...
We found out the next morning that we all had the same dream.
That may have been the final spell Alto cast for us...
I agree.

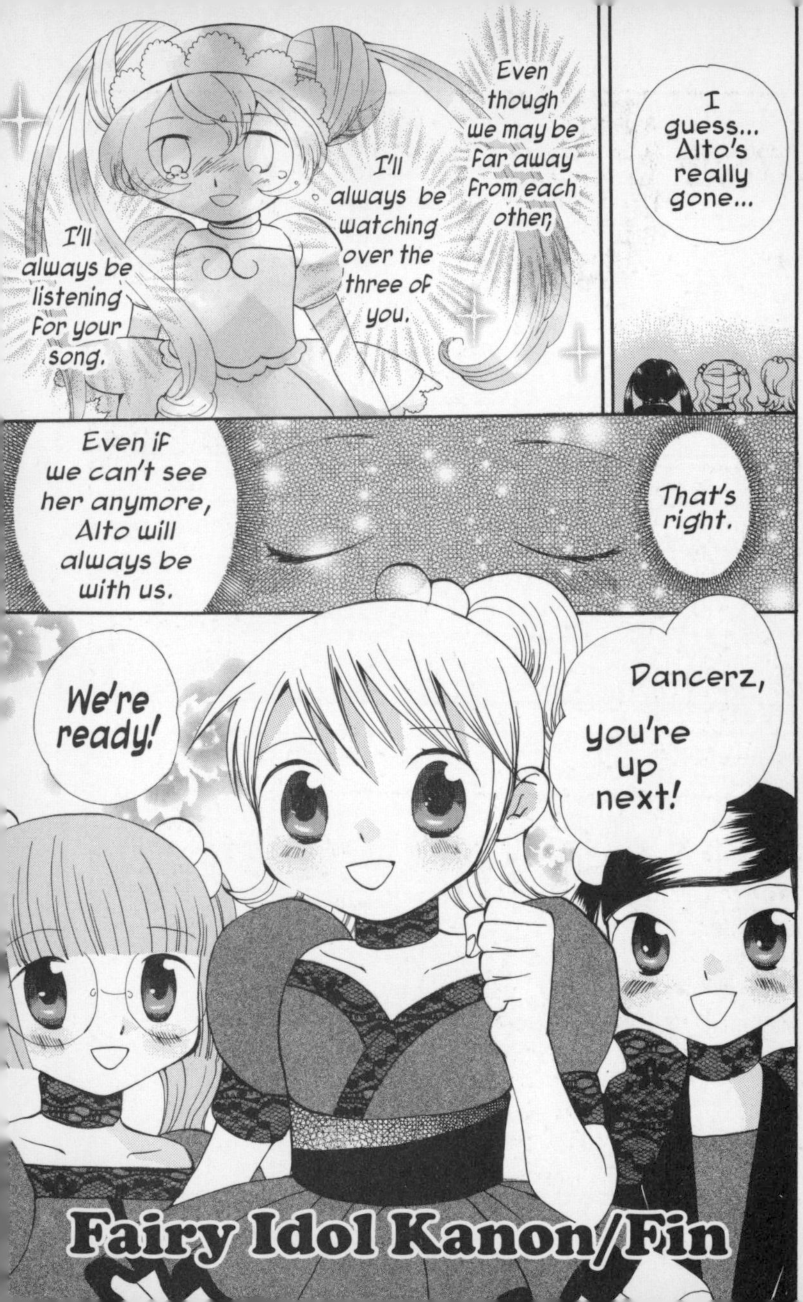
I guess... Alto's really gone...
Even though we may be far away from each other,
I'll always be watching over the three of you.
I'll always be listening for your song.
That's right.
Even if we can't see her anymore, Alto will always be with us.
Dancerz, you're up next!
We're ready!
Fairy Idol Kanon/Fin

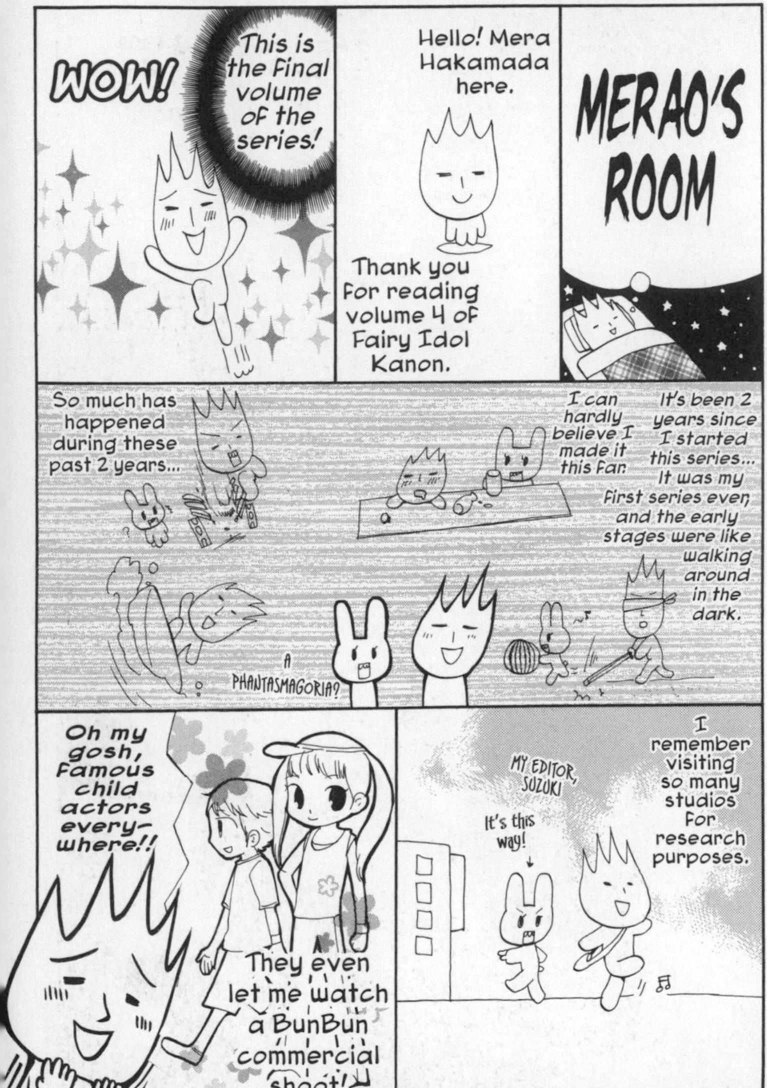
MERAO'S ROOM
Hello! Mera Hakamada here.
Thank you for reading volume 4 of Fairy Idol Kanon.
WOW!
This is the final volume of the series!
It's been 2 years since I started this series... It was my first series ever, and the early stages were like walking around in the dark.
I can hardly believe I made it this far.
A PHANTASMAGORIA?
So much has happened during these past 2 years...
I remember visiting so many studios for research purposes.
MY EDITOR, SUZUKI
It's this way!
Oh my gosh, famous child actors every-where!!
They even let me watch a BunBun commercial shoot!

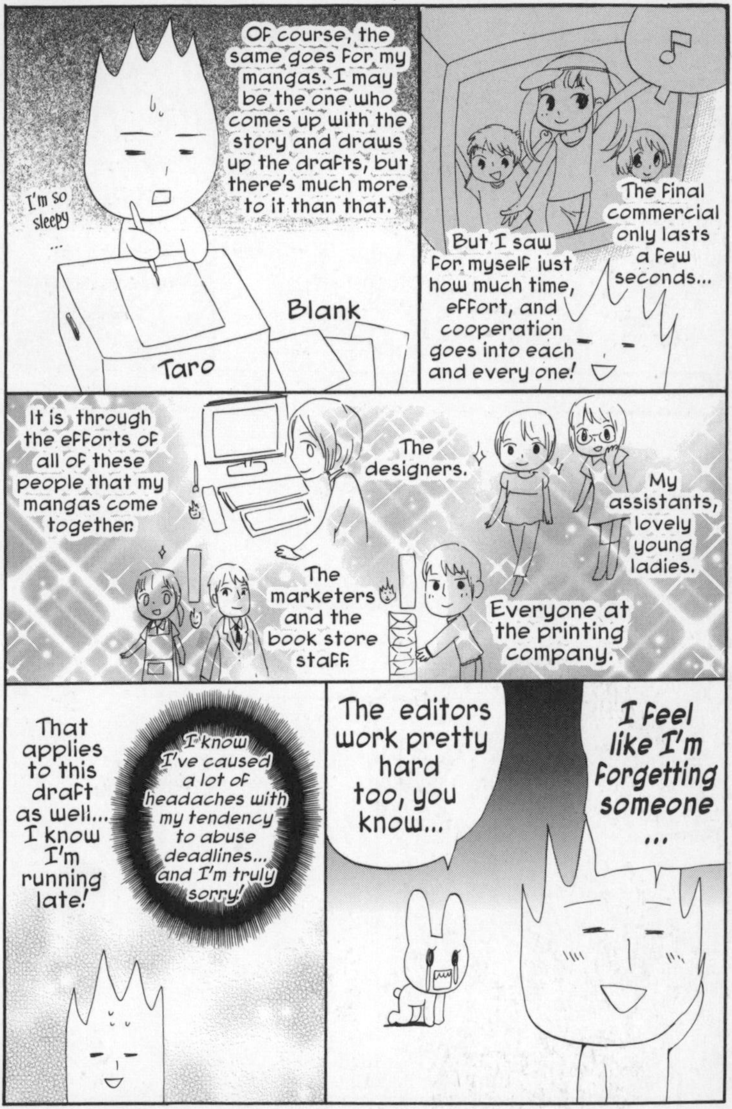
The final commercial only lasts a few seconds...
But I saw for myself just how much time, effort, and cooperation goes into each and every one!
Of course, the same goes for my mangas. I may be the one who comes up with the story and draws up the drafts, but there's much more to it than that.
I'm so sleepy ...
Blank
Taro
My assistants, lovely young ladies.
The designers.
It is through the efforts of all of these people that my mangas come together.
Everyone at the printing company.
The marketers and the book store staff.
I feel like I'm forgetting someone ...
The editors work pretty hard too, you know...
That applies to this draft as well... I know I'm running late!
I know I've caused a lot of headaches with my tendency to abuse deadlines... and I'm truly sorry!

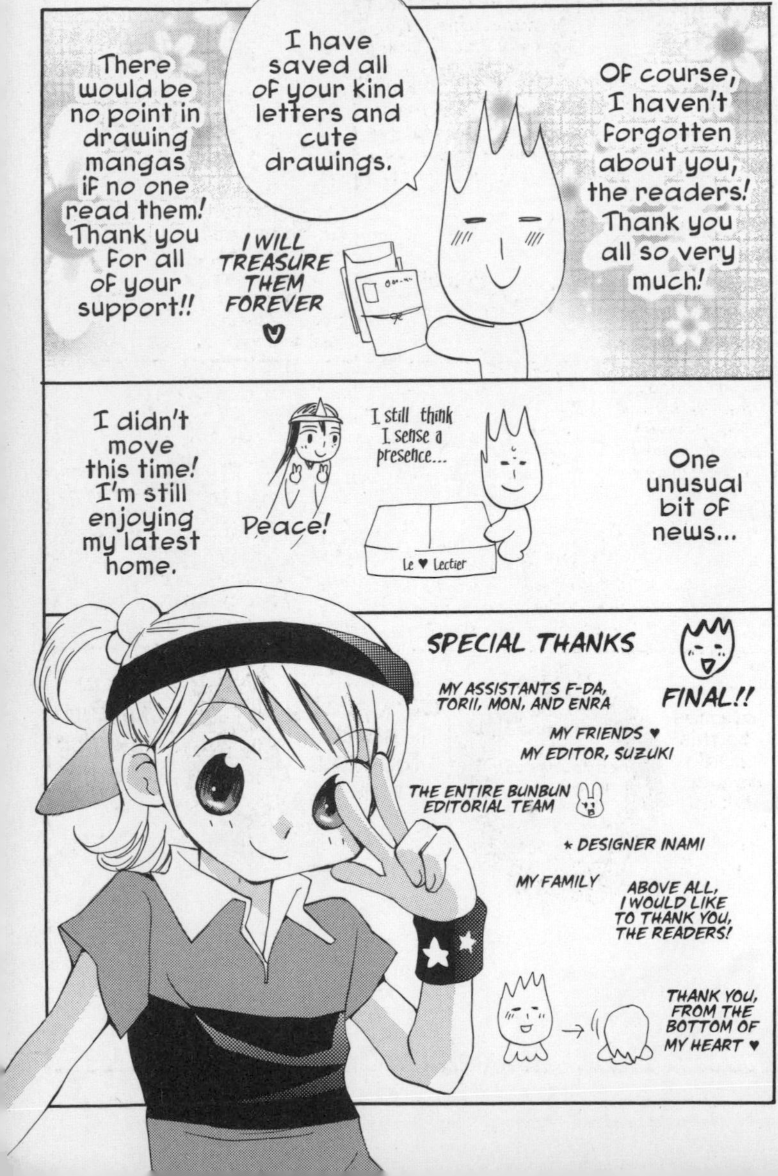
Of course, I haven't forgotten about you, the readers! Thank you all so very much!
I have saved all of your kind letters and cute drawings.
There would be no point in drawing mangas if no one read them! Thank you for all of your support!!
I WILL TREASURE THEM FOREVER ♥
One unusual bit of news...
I still think I sense a presence...
Le ♥ Lectier
Peace!
I didn't move this time! I'm still enjoying my latest home.
SPECIAL THANKS
FINAL!!
MY ASSISTANTS F-DA, TORII, MON, AND ENRA
MY FRIENDS ♥
MY EDITOR, SUZUKI
THE ENTIRE BUNBUN EDITORIAL TEAM
⋆ DESIGNER INAMI
MY FAMILY
ABOVE ALL, I WOULD LIKE TO THANK YOU, THE READERS!
THANK YOU, FROM THE BOTTOM OF MY HEART ♥

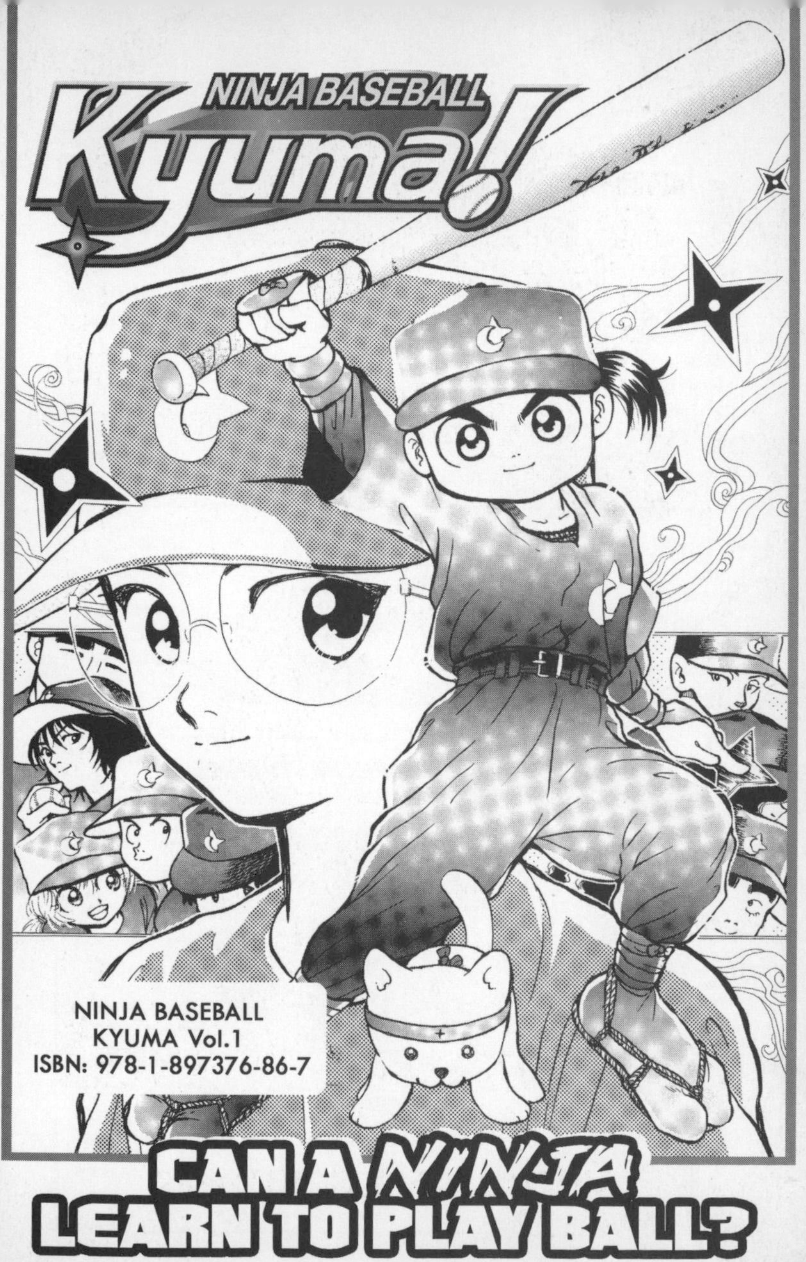
NINJA BASEBALL
Kyuma!
NINJA BASEBALL
KYUMA Vol.1
ISBN: 978-1-897376-86-7

CAN A NINJA LEARN TO PLAY BALL?

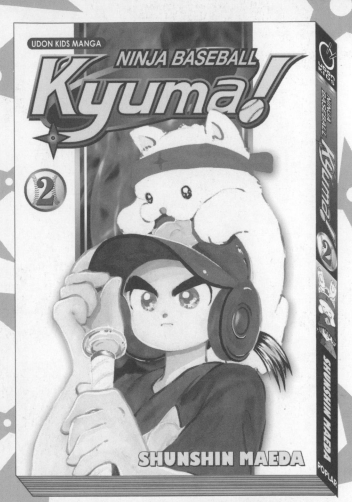

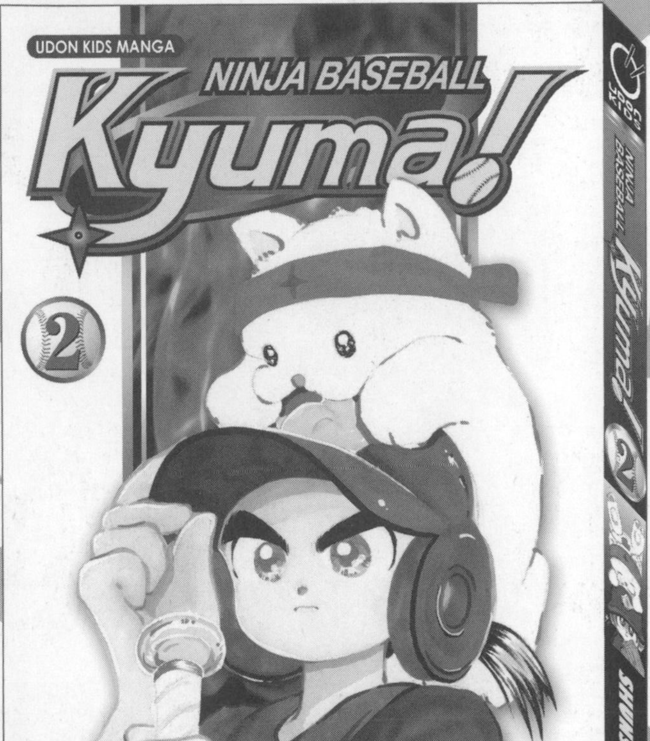
UDON KIDS MANGA
NINJA BASEBALL
Kyuma!
2
SHUNSHIN MAEDA
UDON KIDS
NINJA BASEBALL Kyuma! 2
SHUNSHIN MAEDA
POPLAR

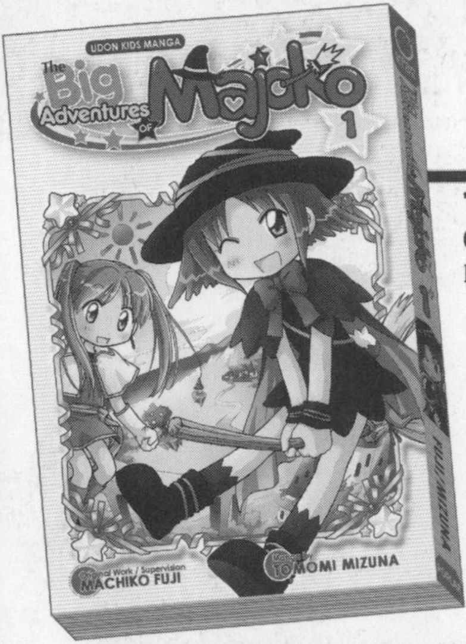
UDON KIDS MANGA
The Big Adventures of Majoko
1
MACHIKO FUJI
TOMOMI MIZUNA

THE BIG ADVENTURES OF MAJOKO Vol.1

ISBN: 978-1-897376-81-2

THE BIG ADVENTURES OF MAJOKO Vol.2

ISBN: 978-1-897376-82-9

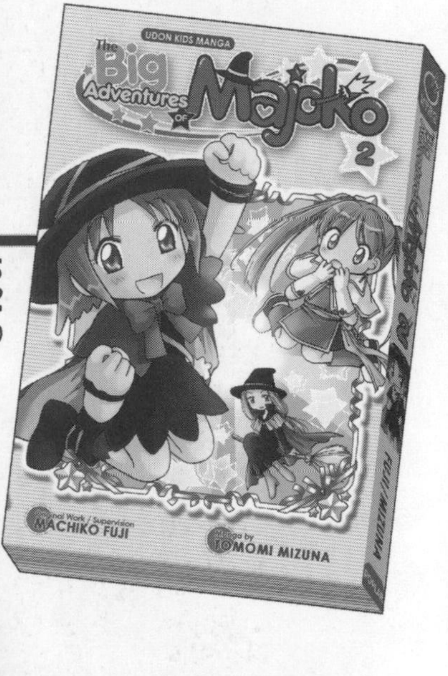
UDON KIDS MANGA
The Big Adventures of Majoko
2
MACHIKO FUJI
TOMOMI MIZUNA

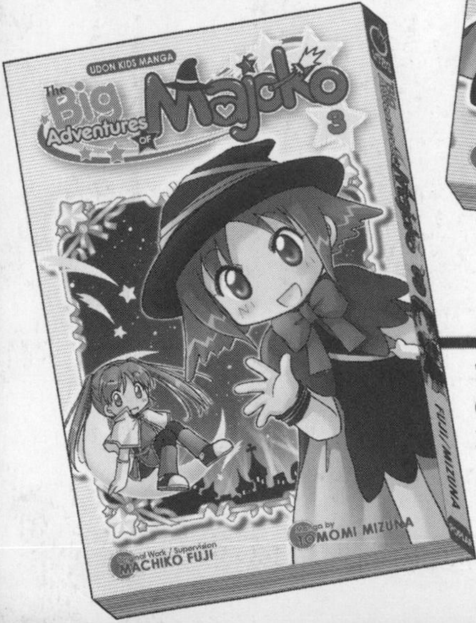
UDON KIDS MANGA
The Big Adventures of Majoko
3
MACHIKO FUJI
TOMOMI MIZUNA

THE BIG ADVENTURES OF MAJOKO Vol.3

ISBN: 978-1-897376-83-6

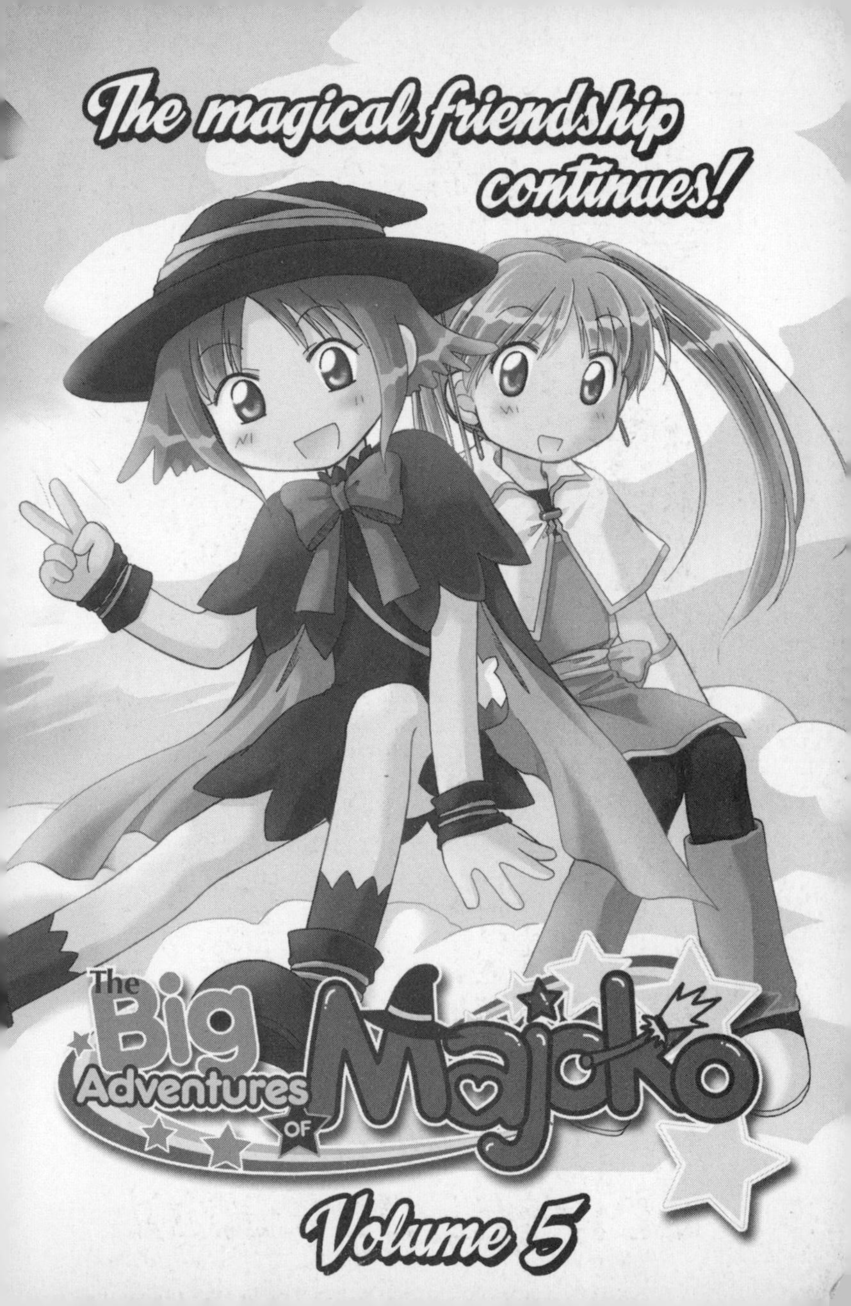
The magical friendship continues!
The Big Adventures of Majoko
Volume 5

THE BIG ADVENTURES
OF MAJOKO Vol.5
ISBN: 978-1-897376-85-0

COMING OCT 2010!

THE GALAXY HAS SOME NEW BEST FRIENDS!

SWANS in SPACE

SCI-FI ADVENTURES FOR GIRLS!

SWANS IN SPACE Vol. 1
ISBN: 978-1-897376-93-5

SWANS in SPACE
VOLUME 2

© Lunlun Yamamoto

AVAILABLE NOW!

SWANS IN SPACE Vol.2
ISBN: 978-1-897376-94-2

UDON KIDS MANGA
SWANS in SPACE
LUN LUN YAMAMOTO
1
SPACE PATROL
FULL COLOR MANGA!

UDON KIDS MANGA
FAIRY IDOL
Kanon
1
MERA HAKAMADA

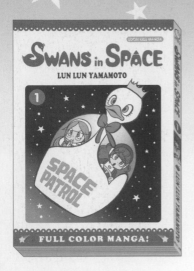

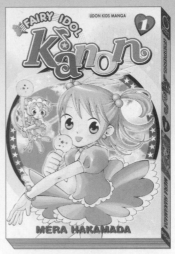

SWANS IN SPACE

Vol.1
ISBN: 978-1-897376-93-5

Vol.2
ISBN: 978-1-897376-94-2

Vol.3 *(Oct 2010)*
ISBN: 978-1-897376-95-9

FAIRY IDOL KANON

Vol.1
ISBN: 978-1-897376-89-8

Vol.2
ISBN: 978-1-897376-90-4

Vol.3
ISBN: 978-1-897376-91-1

Vol.4
ISBN: 978-1-897376-92-8

MangaforKids.com

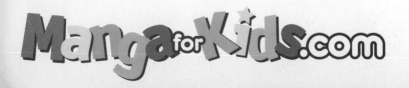

FAIRY IDOL

Kanon

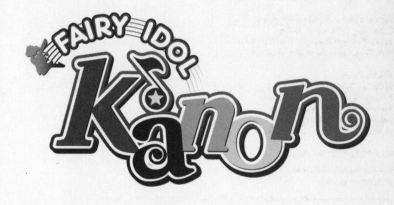

VOLUME 4

Story & Art: Mera Hakamada

Translation: M. Kirie Hayashi
Lettering: Marshall Dillon
English Logo Design: Hanna Chan
Art Cleanups: Jennifer Skarupa

UDON STAFF
Chief of Operations: Erik Ko
Project Manager: Jim Zubkavich
Managing Editor: Matt Moylan
Editor, Japanese Publications: M. Kirie Hayashi
Marketing Manager: Stacy King

FAIRY IDOL KANON Vol.4

©Mera Hakamada 2004
All rights reserved.

Original Japanese edition published by POPLAR Publishing Co., Ltd. Tokyo
English translation rights arranged directly with POPLAR Publishing Co., Ltd.

English edition of FAIRY IDOL KANON Vol. 4
©2010 UDON Entertainment Corp.

Any similarities to persons living or dead is purely coincidental.

English language version produced and published by UDON Entertainment Corp.
P.O. Box 5002, RPO MAJOR MACKENZIE
Richmond Hill, Ontario, L4S 0B7, Canada

www.udonentertainment.com

First Printing: October 2010
ISBN-13: 978-1-897376-92-8   ISBN-10 : 1-897376-92-8
Printed in Canada

S!

This is the BACK of the book!

Fairy Idol Kanon is a comic book created in Japan, where comics are called **manga.** Manga is read from right-to-left, which is backwards from the normal books you know. This means that you will find the first page where you expect to find the last page! It also means that each page begins in the top right corner.

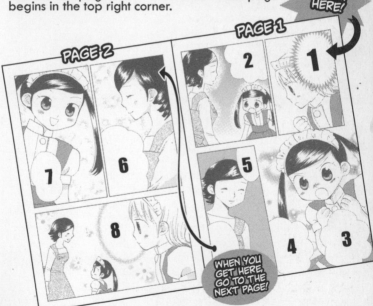

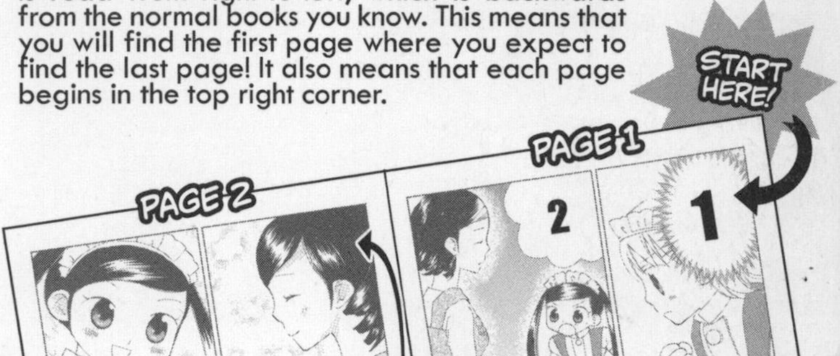
START HERE!
PAGE 1
1
2
3
4
5
WHEN YOU GET HERE, GO TO THE NEXT PAGE!
PAGE 2
6
7
8

Now head to the other end of the book and enjoy **Fairy Idol Kanon!**